"Kauffman's trademark humor captures the reader from the first page and keeps them engrossed with each twist and turn of the plot. For a story that will touch your heart, tickle your funny bone and leave you begging for more, I highly recommend *The Big Bad Wolf Tells All*." —*Romance Reviews Today*

"Deftly spun . . . with a zippy style." —*Kirkus Reviews*

"Entertaining . . . sure to find an audience with the beach-reading crowd." —*Booklist*

"Humor and suspense . . . Fans of Laura Zigman will enjoy this book." —*Library Journal*

"This is one sheepish tale that stands out from the flock of chick-lit patter with a unique zest and fire all its own."
—*BookPage*

The Charm Stone

"Give me more!"—Linda Howard

The Royal Hunter

"Kauffman . . . anchors her readers with sensuality, humor and compassion." —*Publishers Weekly*

"Action-packed adventure, steamy sensuality, and a bewitching plot all come together in a surprising and dramatic ending."
—*Rendezvous*

Your Wish Is My Command

"Whimsical and sexy!"—Jennifer Crusie

Legend of the Sorcerer

"Donna Kauffman has written a spellbinding romance that is so hot, it near sizzles when the pages are turned. . . . This is a really superb book to curl up with and get lost in."
—*New Age Bookshelf*

"Donna Kauffman always knows how to set our hearts afire with passion and romance." —*Rendezvous*

"Ms. Kauffman is an amazing talent." —*Affaire du Coeur*

The Legend MacKinnon

"Intricately woven together . . . This one kept me spellbound. A terrific read." —*Rendezvous*

"*The Legend MacKinnon* is a uniquely exciting, captivating and sensational read. . . . A marvelous new novel."
—*Romantic Times* (4 1/2 stars, Top Pick)

"Sensuous love stories that will heat up the atmosphere wherever you are and some laughs to tickle your fancy. Excellent writing by an author who has mastered the craft of creating characters to die for." —*Belles and Beaux of Romance*

Dear Prince Charming

Donna Kauffman

Bantam Books

DEAR PRINCE CHARMING
A Bantam Book/August 2004

Published by Bantam Dell
A Division of Random House, Inc.
New York, New York

Book design by Virginia Norey

Library of Congress Cataloging-in-Publication Data
Kauffman, Donna.
Dear Prince Charming / Donna Kauffman.
p. cm.
ISBN 0-553-38235-7
1. Women public relations personnel—Fiction. 2. Periodicals—
Publishing—Fiction. 3. Impostors and imposture—Fiction.
4. Advice columnists—Fiction. 5. Sportswriters—Fiction. I. Title.

PS3561.A816D43 2004
813'.6—dc22   2003069651

Manufactured in the United States of America
Published simultaneously in Canada

RRH 10 9 8 7 6 5 4 3 2

I am a woman in the enviable position of living a life surrounded by men. And while not always charming, they each have their own princely qualities. This book is dedicated to them. Mitch, Spence, Brandon &, as always, Mark.

Dear
Prince
Charming

Truth

A key element in successful relationships is honesty. Namely, being able to detect when your significant other isn't practicing it.

—Eric Jermaine,
aka Dear Prince Charming

Chapter 1

At age thirty, Valerie Wagner had begun to fear that the fashion career she'd dreamed of since opening her first *Vogue* at age nine was actually a grand and cruel delusion, and that perhaps medical intervention might be required in getting her over it.

Maybe her fourth-grade teacher, Ms. Spagney, had been right all along. She'd sent *Vogue*-enhanced Valerie home from school the following day with strict instructions to never scare the other students like that again. Privately, Valerie had thought Ms. Spagney could use some heavy kohl eyeliner and spiky bangs herself. It would have done much to hide the deep grooves that came from too many years of frowning down at young, independent thinkers like herself.

However, she'd been objective enough to realize that maybe makeup and hairstyling weren't her strengths. So she'd stared down at her flat chest and thought . . . hmm. Valerie had been the only girl in her sixth-grade class secretly thrilled not to need a training bra. After all, she'd never walk the runways in Milan if she had boobies.

Unfortunately, she'd forgotten about the height clause. By sixteen, even in wobbly heels, with hair gelled to within an inch of its life, she barely flirted with the five-eight mark. Much shorter than the five ten she knew from her by-then slavish devotion to *W* was the minimum of industry standards.

Cruelly, the now-welcome boobies had never appeared.

Undeterred, she'd resolutely turned to design. If she wasn't made to model fashion, by damn, she'd create it. Which would have worked beautifully except stick figures sporting Magic Marker—colored, triangle-shaped outfits weren't exactly going to win her any scholarships. And yet, she'd hung in there, convinced her calling was still within reach. She'd go for a degree in fashion merchandising and work for an upscale chain as a buyer. She envisioned trips to Paris, London, Milan. So what if she had as much chance of balancing her checkbook as she did of discovering the formula for cold fusion? It wasn't like she was going to be spending her own money, right?

Then had come the Big Breakthrough. In her senior year of high school, the brokerage firm her father worked for had transferred him to Chicago. She'd gotten a summer job with *Madame* magazine—for full-figured gals, not call-girl employers—though as switchboard operator she'd heard every hooker joke and pimp pun on the planet. She hadn't minded.

She'd found her people.

Obviously she'd just misinterpreted the gospel according to *Elle*. It wasn't the people populating those glossy pages that called to her. It was the glossy pages themselves. Fashion magazines, the force that drove the industry, deciding what was hip and what was hopelessly last year . . . that was her true calling, her primary function, her niche.

Ten years later she'd become a serial niche killer. There wasn't a job she hadn't held. Or gone on to abandon, feeling more unfulfilled and depressed with each failure. Fortunately, she'd stumbled upon her last hope before getting a prescription for Paxil.

When she'd heard that the owners of Glass Slipper, Inc., the company renowned for performing *life makeovers*, were looking for a publicist for their new endeavor, the bimonthly glossy *Glass Slipper* magazine, she knew she'd found the career Holy Grail she'd been searching for. And it was do-or-die time.

She'd winged her way through what she privately thought was the best job-pitch performance of her life. And by *performance* she meant *audition*, because it had been the acting job of the century. She had no specific qualifications for the job. But when had that stopped her? She might have been slow finding her own niche, but the upside was that she knew a whole lot about everyone else's. So she talked a good game. In fact, talking people into doing things her way was the one special talent she knew she had. In spades.

So when Mercedes Browning contacted her to tell her she'd gotten the job as the publicist for their new endeavor, she hadn't been completely surprised.

The real shock was that she hadn't realized her true calling sooner.

And now, six months to the day later, she'd topped it all by scoring the biggest coup in magazine history. Not only had she landed Prince Charming, the mysterious and elusive best-selling self-help author, as *Glass Slipper*'s spokesperson and exclusive columnist . . . she'd gotten him to agree to show his face to the world for the very first time, on the cover of their launch issue!

Valerie wove her way through the crowded outdoor tables at Sonsi's, Potomac's newest swank spot, where Washington movers and shakers came to see and be seen. Because, honestly, despite Chef Andre's impeccable and well-advertised qualifications, no one was here because they had an undying craving for venison-stuffed pumpkin or Moulard duck wrapped in foie gras and fig.

At the moment, however, she didn't care about unnatural food combinations. She was too busy savoring her triumph and trying to refrain from conga-ing her way around the tables. So many years of trying, of wondering, of worrying if she'd ever get to this moment. Hell, wondering if this moment actually existed. And now, finally, it was here. And it was even better than she could have hoped for.

"Cinderella, eat your heart out," she whispered beneath her breath.

She had the *Glass Slipper*; she had Prince Charming; she even had her own fairy godmother—three of them, in fact. All she needed now was the Be-Dazzler-encrusted pumpkin carriage and the fairy tale would be complete. Her smile spread to a grin. However, her brand-new, sporty little MINI would definitely do in the meantime. Life was good.

She waved to the Godmother Collective as she spied their table. Mercedes Browning, Aurora Favreaux, and Vivian dePalma—the founders of Glass Slipper, Inc., and now *Glass Slipper* magazine—nodded, fluttered, and lifted a drink, in that order, in her general direction as she navigated the final handful of tables.

Flushed with her success and hoping she didn't look as smug as she felt—oh, what the hell, how often did one reach a career pinnacle?—Valerie took her seat across from the three women. "Everything is set," she announced. "Nigel is on board. We shoot the cover Monday morning."

"We never had a doubt!" Vivian exclaimed, lifting a bottle of Cristal from the ice bucket next to the table. Her trademark flame-red hair had been teased into a spiky pouf around her head, her makeup had been stenciled on with laserlike accuracy, and her outfit was as outrageous as always. Of course, most women couldn't make zebra prints work. Valerie had quickly learned that Vivian wasn't most women. The youngest of the three at sixty-eight, Vivian was also the most outspoken. "Let me pour you a glass or three, honey. Lord knows, you've earned it."

"A proper celebration is definitely in order," Aurora added after a quick frown at Vivian. Swathed in layers of gossamer silk, Aurora had that effortless, delicate Southern charm that quite successfully hid the steel magnolia beneath.

"So, everything is in order, then? You've spoken with Elaine, I assume? No other last-minute emergencies?" Mercedes' expression was serious as always. Valerie privately thought of her as the Eeyore of the group. It had come as no shock to learn that, prior to launching their life-makeover empire, Mercedes had been headmistress of a private New England girls' boarding school.

"For heaven's sake, Mercy, let the girl have some bubbly before you start interrogating her." Vivian handed Valerie her glass, then topped off the other three. "I'm sure everything is just fine." She beamed at Valerie, but her gaze was sharp as ever. "You've all but taken over the reins of this whole endeavor, haven't you?"

Valerie was surprised by the comment, but as Vivian seemed to mean it as a compliment, she continued to smile. "Hardly. Elaine is doing the work of ten people," she said, referring to the managing editor. "I'm in constant awe."

"But you were clever enough to come up with the spokesperson and cover model idea," Vivian commented.

"Yes, but of course we had no idea Mr. Jermaine would refuse to deal with anyone but me. I just did what I had to to ensure he signed with us."

Aurora flipped her scarf at Vivian. "Of course you did, dear. And we're ever so grateful." She lifted her glass a bit higher as she turned her attention to them all. "Here's to our new venture, and the dynamite publicist who single-handedly assured us a smashing debut!"

"Hear, hear," Vivian agreed readily. "Here's to knocking those bitchy industry insiders on their collective jealous ass! And they said our plan to launch a magazine in this *economic climate* was foolhardy. Ha!"

Mercedes' frown only deepened, but she tipped glasses with the rest of them, then spoke before they'd barely finished swallowing. "You've confirmed with Mr. Jermaine the cover shoot for Monday?"

Valerie assured her she had, even as Vivian rolled her eyes.

"We're all looking so forward to finally meeting him in the flesh," Aurora said, leaning forward a bit, the multiple rings on her fingers sparkling as the sun reflected off the champagne glass.

"Flesh you've promised is cover-model worthy," Vivian reminded her.

"Oh, you won't be disappointed, trust me," Valerie said, enjoying the feel of the fizz as it tickled her nose. Did it get better than this?

"If he's as good-looking as you say, I find it surprising he's kept his light under a bushel for so long," Aurora offered.

"I don't think he really thinks about his looks one way or the other." Although privately she agreed with Aurora. Eric was six feet plus of tanned muscle and beachboy godliness. He already had women all over America swooning with his no-bullshit insight into the male mind. He was proof positive that caring, sensitive men did exist. All that and drop-dead gorgeous, to boot. She wouldn't be surprised if the female population took one look at the way his perfectly sun-streaked and tousled blond hair fell in endearingly boyish waves across his broad, tanned forehead, those stunning aqua-blue eyes, and a mouth that Cupid must have had a hand in sculpting . . . and had a spontaneous group orgasm. He'd certainly left her feeling a bit damp. "He's just a very private person."

"That's putting it mildly," Mercedes said. "We've been reduced to negotiating via phone conferences." She settled her napkin in her lap as their salads arrived.

Valerie said a silent thank-you for the timely intrusion. Mercedes had been the only one who hadn't been all that enthusiastic about hiring Eric sight unseen. It was too late now, however, so there was no point in yammering on about it yet again.

"I can only hope that the man is worth the large sum of money we've paid for his services," Mercedes commented after the young waiter left.

Valerie smiled with easy confidence at this. "I don't think anyone is going to be disappointed."

Vivian fanned her throat. "Honey, if that look in your eye is any indication—"

"For heaven's sake, Vivi, eat your salad," Aurora told her, then glanced at Valerie. "So he's a real hunk, huh?"

"On a scale of one to ten? He's a twelve."

Vivian and Aurora both sighed.

"And despite being so private, he's surprisingly outgoing. You're going to be very happy with your investment." She poked at the mandarin orange peeking out from its hiding place behind the arugula and goat cheese. If it was up to her, there would be a law against fruits and vegetables coexisting in the same salad. Probably why she hadn't lasted long as a food designer for *Ladies Home Weekly*. "He said that this whole career of his started from a small, impromptu group of women he chatted with anonymously on the Internet. It snowballed unexpectedly, but he continued to keep his name out of it. I think he was still keeping other career options open at the time and this was sort of a side thing. I know he had no idea it would take off like it did, and by then, the whole mystique thing was part of the Prince Charming persona, so he stuck with it."

"I suppose demystifying the male gender wouldn't exactly make him popular with other men," Aurora commented.

Vivian sighed. "But the women sure have appreciated it."

They certainly had, Valerie thought. In droves. Eric's Dear Prince Charming column was syndicated nationwide and all four of his books—mostly compilations of past columns, with some additional commentary—had hung around on the best-seller lists for months at a time. "I think we just got lucky. When I saw that piece in the trades about his syndication deal coming up for renewal the same time as his next publishing contract, and that he wasn't rushing to sign on again for either, I thought, why not approach him? Maybe he was burning out, or maybe he was just tired of hiding out. I thought we might be able to offer him just the right deal."

Vivian lifted her glass again. "And that we did!"

"Hear, hear," Aurora agreed, finishing off her glass, then covering her mouth when she hiccupped. "Best five hundred grand we've ever spent."

Mercedes just took a deep breath and downed the rest of her champagne.

Valerie knew that come Monday, even Mercedes would be won over. Her greatest fear when she'd first met Eric was that he'd be a paunchy, balding guy who looked like he had a better shot at demystifying her taxes than her love life. She couldn't have been proven more spectacularly wrong. Cinderella rules! "Well, you'll all get the chance to see just how well your money has been spent at the photo shoot."

Just then her cell phone buzzed. "Excuse me," she said, and slipped it from her bag to check the readout. It was Eric. "Speak of the devil," she said with a smile, and flipped the phone open. "Hello, handsome, we were just—"

"Valerie?"

With just that one word, Valerie knew something was wrong. She just managed to keep the concern out of her voice, and hopefully off her face. "It sure is. What's up?"

"We need to talk. Right away. It's—it's important."

She glanced up to find the three older women staring at her expectantly. She smiled and nodded, the picture of confidence. Once an actress, always an actress. "Certainly. I'm just having lunch with Mercedes, Aurora, and Vivian. We're celebrating. Why don't you—"

"I don't know if it can wait," he said, cutting her off, sounding even more anxious.

Tamping down any hint of alarm, she said, "Just a moment," then covered the phone. "Why don't I just take this inside; it won't take a minute."

Mercedes frowned. Vivian appeared curious and Aurora concerned. "Is there a problem, dear?" she asked quietly.

Valerie shook her head. "Just last-minute production details."

"Is that *him*?" Vivian asked.

"*Him*?" Valerie asked, feigning confusion, thinking fast. She'd answered the phone with "Hello, handsome," hadn't she? Dammit. "Oh, *him*! No, no, this is, uh, one of Nigel's people." She leaned forward. "It's the accent, gets me every time."

Vivian and Aurora smiled in complete comprehension. Mercedes' frown lifted a fraction. Valerie took the small opening and pushed her chair back. "I'll only be a minute."

Her mind racing ahead, she tried to fathom what Eric's problem could possibly be, but nothing sprang to mind. Maybe he had a conflicting engagement with the shoot on Monday. Well, he was going to have to reschedule. Getting Nigel had been her second miracle and no way was she going to risk losing him on this project. They were so close.

As soon as she got a table or two away, she uncovered the phone. "Hi, Eric. I have some privacy now. I'm sure whatever it is, we can handle it. Is this about the shoot on Monday?"

"In a manner of speaking, yes."

She frowned. "I've spoken with Nigel's people and we're confirmed. This is really going to be a wonderful opportunity for us all, Eric. You couldn't be in better hands."

"I know."

He sounded quiet, almost . . . remorseful. She was just inside the doorway and waiters were bustling past her with heavily laden trays. She shifted her back to the noise and cupped her hand over her ear, praying it was just the surroundings and that she'd misinterpreted the tone in his voice. "So, what is the problem?"

"I've—I need to talk with you. Before—before we go any further with this."

No personal pep talk in the world would have prevented the alarm from creeping into her mind. "But we're all set, aren't we?" She wanted to add, "You signed a contract. With a lot of zeroes attached. We sent you a check," but managed not to. Just barely. However, she couldn't keep from glancing over her shoulder, back to the table. All three women were staring in her direction. She managed a brief smile and motioned that she was almost done. She turned her back to them and edged farther into the waitstaff passageway. "Can't you just tell me now? I'm sure we can resolve whatever it is—"

"Valerie, I'm gay."

He'd just blurted it out in a rush. So fast, she couldn't really absorb it. In fact, after she managed to close her mouth and put the phone back to her ear, she was certain she'd misheard him. "I'm sorry," she said, forcing a light laugh. "It sounded like you just said you're—"

"Gay. I did. And I am. Dammit, I didn't want to tell you this way!" There was a pause, which she had no earthly way of filling. She was as frozen as one of Andre's ice sculptures.

"I—can we please see each other?" he went on. "Now? Can you get out of this lunch? I'll meet you anywhere. I—I know I should have told you sooner. I thought I could go through with this, but—"

That snapped her out of it in a way nothing else could. "Excuse me? *Go through with it?* Of course you're going to go through with it. You signed a contract." She knew she sounded a little agitated. Okay, a lot agitated. But her whole brand-spanking-new career was flashing before her eyes. It didn't take nearly long enough.

"I know this comes as a shock."

"A *shock*? I'd say this is more than a shock. This is a freaking disaster!" She took a deep breath, tried desperately to recapture an ounce of inner calm. "Where are you? We obviously need to talk. I'll meet you."

He sighed heavily. "Thank you."

Reality began to sink in. Prince Charming. The man who'd proved that a guy existed who saw women as human beings first, and sex objects second . . . was gay. She shook her head. *Like we shouldn't have seen that coming.*

"I just want you to know, I didn't mean to hurt you," he was saying. "Or anyone, really."

"For a guy who dispenses advice to women about men, you just spouted one of the all-time lamest excuses on the face of the planet." She knew she shouldn't lose her temper, but apparently her acting skills had limits after all.

"I know, and you have every right to be upset. But truly, don't worry. I'll make it up to you. Somehow."

"Second lamest statement," she hissed, making a passing waiter step around her a bit more gingerly. "Are you sure you're the real Prince Charming?"

There was a long pause, then he said, "I can barely hear you, too much noise. Call me when you leave the restaurant."

And then the line clicked off. She stared at the phone, thinking that if she just stood there long enough, she could will that entire conversation into some hallucinatory void, a stress-induced daydream. Except who in their right mind would dream up a nightmare like that?

So many thoughts crowded her mind, she didn't know where to begin. She started to move automatically toward the restaurant's exit when she remembered her lunch companions. *Shit, shit, and more shit.* She couldn't just walk out without giving an explanation, but what in the hell was she going to tell them? Oh, by the way—Prince Charming, the guy you just gave a half million bucks to, ensuring magazine launch history? The gorgeous hunk known to women all over the planet as proof positive that understanding, nurturing men did, indeed, exist? Well, as it happens, he's more than just a guy deeply in touch with his feminine side.

She grabbed a glass of something alcoholic off a passing tray and downed it before the waiter even knew it was missing. She looked down, half-expecting to see her blue Ann Taylor suit had turned into rags. And her red and white MINI out in the lot had probably turned into a pumpkin.

She hadn't even made it to midnight, dammit.

👑

Revelations

In all relationships, secrets are kept and disclosures are made. The key to survival is how you handle things when the former becomes the latter.

Chapter 2

Jack Lambert was no Prince Charming. Just ask his ex-wife. Or, for that matter, any number of women dotting the globe. *Charming,* they might go for. *Hell of a good time?* Probably. But *princely?* That particular adjective wouldn't make anyone's list.

"You sure you haven't been self-medicating? I don't know shit about giving advice to women." Jack elbowed Eric in the gut and went in for the layup.

Eric swung around, jumped up, and smacked the ball away before it could float over the rim. "I don't want you to give advice," he said, barely breathing hard as he chased the ball down, despite the summer sun beating down on them both. He dribbled the ball, moving slowly around the perimeter of the key as Jack shadowed his every move. "But trust me, this is going to be mutually beneficial. It's a solution to both of our problems."

Jack's current problem was unemployment. He was a sportswriter for an international news wire service, or had been until three days ago, when the service had been sold to the Reverend Yun Yun Yi, a right-wing religious zealot who made Reverend Moon come off looking like Mister Rogers. Jack had been stuck in Dubai at the time, writing about women's tennis. It had taken him two days and four flights to get back to his small apartment in Alexandria. Virginia, not Egypt. Although since his divorce, it could have easily been either.

Jack read Eric's feint perfectly—not a surprise, considering they'd been shooting hoops one-on-one since they were both eleven—and blocked his shot, taking the ball out of the key, then dribbling, taking his time. Sweat had long since soaked through his T-shirt. He paused long enough to peel it off, mop his face, then tie it around his head, do-rag style, hoping to keep the sweat from stinging his eyes. "How did you even know I was back?" Jack asked, not really wanting to focus on the unemployment issue.

Eric tossed his shirt to the side of the fenced-in court, removing any doubt that he'd let himself go in the nine months since they'd last seen each other. Bastard probably didn't even have to work at it, Jack thought in disgust. Eric had always been such a natural jock, he still wondered how his best friend had ended up writing advice columns, of all things, instead of, say, playing in the NBA or the MLB. But then, God knew, he'd had enough women that if any guy could explain them, it would be Eric. Jack would just stick with writing about bocce ball and cliff-diving, thanks. Something he had a chance in hell of understanding.

He bounce-passed the ball to Eric, who bounced it back and said, "I saw in the *Times* last week that StatsComm was being bought out by the venerable Triple Y. I gave you four days max to be back in D.C. job-hunting."

Well, he'd nailed that one. No point in letting the man gloat, though. "So, what makes you think I don't already have another gig lined up?" He slapped the ball, then drove up the middle, taking a hard shoulder and an elbow in the ribs for the effort.

"Maybe you do," Eric said, laughing as he rebounded the rim shot, then slam-dunked it. "But really, Lambert"—he was grinning now—"how many wire services are looking for a guy to cover Ping-Pong?"

"Hey." Jack smacked the ball away, then went right up in his face, bodies colliding as he hit one off the backboard. "I've said it before, but it bears repeating. Anybody can cover basketball. It takes a real man to observe events like Paris to Dakaar, Australian-rules football, or the wild action of the Women's World Ping-Pong Championships, and turn it into a no-holds-barred must-read." Eric rebounded the ball and Jack followed him out of the key, covering him with his hands up. "Which leads me back to the obvious question: What, exactly, does my sports-god background bring to the advice-for-the-lovelorn table?"

"My readers aren't *lovelorn*," Eric retorted, turning and backing them both up as he looked for his opening. "They're intelligent, capable, caring women who are tired of being dicked around by the assholes of the world." Despite the fact that Jack was all but lying on Eric's sweaty back, he missed the feint and Eric beat him for a three-pointer that was nothing but net. Grinning, he wiped the sweat off his forehead as Jack retrieved the ball. "That would be you, in case you were wondering."

Smiling despite the heckling—they'd long since turned that into an art form—he shot the ball hard at Eric's chest. "Hey, now. I never claimed to understand what women want. In fact, I willingly admit I have no idea. Hence my current marital status. And more to the point, I don't want to know. Frankly, the way women's minds work scares me."

Eric slapped his palm on the ball, shot it back just as hard. "No, the way Shelby's mind worked scared you. Not every woman's a psycho."

"She wasn't a *psycho*. And so much for *intelligent, capable,* and *caring*," Jack said with a laugh.

Eric rolled his eyes as he came in, covering Jack's moves. "As I re-call, she wasn't much interested in anyone's advice, either. To this day, I can't understand why it took you almost two years to figure out her game."

"Temporary dementia and the lack of a good prenuptial agree-ment?" he shot back. It had been three years since he'd signed the di-vorce papers, and he tried not to think about his eighteen-month union to the former Shelby Lane . . . well, pretty much ever. "Word to the wise, man, never *ever* mix alcohol, South Pacific sunsets, and a woman wearing a bikini made out of dental floss." He made his move, went in hard, and muscle slapped against muscle as they both grunted, scuffled, then jumped at the same time. Jack hooted as the ball swooshed past the rim.

"Yeah, well, maybe you should have been reading my columns in-stead of the sports stats," Eric shot back, finally breathing a bit more heavily. "Might have saved yourself some major heartache."

Jack stopped and bent over, propping his hands on his thighs as he took a moment to catch his breath. "Not to mention a substantial chunk of my now nonexistent income."

"Which brings me back to my offer." But instead of getting right into it, Eric looked away, then down at the ball he was bouncing on automatic pilot, as his thoughts had definitely gone elsewhere.

Jack straightened, squinting as clouds shifted and the sun caught him square in the face. "You in some kind of trouble or something?"

"In a manner of speaking. But first . . . there's something I have to tell you. Specifically about those women in bikinis—American Dental Association—approved or otherwise—and why they will never be a threat to yours truly."

Now it was Jack's turn to pause. Eric was being his wry, amusing self, but if Jack didn't know better, he'd swear that beneath the acer-bic commentary, his friend sounded sort of . . . scared shitless. Then it hit him and he groaned. "Oh, no. Shit, no. Tell me you didn't. Despite the fact that this will finally give me years of verbal payback possibilities, you mean too much to me to wish this on you. Tell me you did *not* finally let some woman talk her way into your wallet. Because you might think it's your heart she's got her claws into, buddy—and no disrespect to the future Mrs. Jermaine—but I'd get started on that prenup right now. Consider this friendly advice from the still-indebted."

Eric shot the ball at him, a little harder than necessary. "Jack, it's not like that."

He caught it against his chest, then propped it under his arm. This was a momentous occasion. He couldn't shoot hoops and enjoy every second of watching his friend finally admit to falling in love. "Damn, it sure took you long enough." He laughed and shook his head. "Another icon shattered. You were my proof that single men *can* live happily ever after . . . and stay single."

Eric didn't laugh. In fact, Jack had never seen him look so damn serious. "Did you ever stop to wonder *why* I'm still single? Why there's never been a steady woman—any woman, really—in my life?"

"Don't pull that lonely shit on me. You write touchy-feely advice about understanding women's needs, and you and I both know they've always been crawling out of the woodwork, wanting nothing more than to spend some time with Mr. I Understand Your Needs. Even if they don't know who you really are. Hell, your motto in high school was *Why Settle for One?* It's the greatest gig going; you're a fucking genius."

Eric smiled briefly. "You're still sore because I got Most Likely to Be a Calvin Klein Model in the senior yearbook."

Jack snorted, started dribbling the ball again. "Hardly. I'm above parading around like some kind of beauty-pageant contestant."

"Unless parading around meant scoring with Andrea Ralston."

Jack sighed in immediate and fond remembrance. "Andrea." He pronounced it as she had, Ahn-DRAY-ah. "To this day I get a hard-on when I hear a woman with an Aussie accent."

"Must make covering Australian football a real interesting experience."

"True, true. Yet somehow I manage." He took a shot, rebounded the ball. Eric didn't join him. In fact, when he turned, he saw that Eric was still standing where he'd left him, looking all serious and upset. He shot him the ball, but Eric just caught it against his chest and held it. "What the hell's up, man?"

Eric surprised him by quietly asking, "Have you ever wondered, you know, about why I'm good at what I do?"

"I think we've already covered the *fucking genius* factor, Calvin."

Eric didn't laugh. "This is even harder than I thought it was going to be." He swore under his breath. "Okay, you know what? I can't find an easy way to tell you this. I've wanted to for years, but I was afraid it would, I don't know, ruin everything between us. But I'm in a jam, a really serious one, and so—well, maybe things happen the way they do for a reason." He looked up and held Jack's gaze squarely. "I'm just going to say it straight out and trust you not to freak."

"Great, then we'll both know what the hell you're talking about."

Eric sighed. "There are no women, Jack. There won't *be* any women. Ever. I'm gay."

Jack's jaw dropped. "I'm sorry, did you just say you were—"

"GAY!" Eric all but shouted. "Queer as the day is long. A raving homosexual." He shot the ball hard at him. "Jesus, why does everyone have to make this so goddamn hard?"

Jack caught it reflexively, but it might as well have been a foreign object. Hell, suddenly everything was foreign. He was staring at Eric, who was clearly not kidding around. His sweaty, macho, ripped, jock of a best friend, Eric. Gay. The guy he'd snapped towels at in the boys' locker room. The guy who smacked him on the butt in football and pounded his ass routinely into the ground on the racquetball court. Gay. The guy he'd known since he was nine and was closer to than anyone walking this planet. Had talked trash with this guy, talked women with him. Talked life.

Gay.

Nope. It wasn't computing.

"Say something, man," Eric said quietly.

Jack took a deep breath, blew it out. Despite the riot of emotions and thoughts swirling through his mind, he did recognize the absolute importance of this moment, knew he had to handle it right. That despite his confusion . . . and whatever the hell he was feeling, first and foremost, he was Eric's friend. Hell, they were all but family to each other. He couldn't blow this.

But he had no idea where to start. He bounced the ball back to Eric, like everything would make more sense if they just kept shooting hoops, kept things normal. Normal. He wanted to laugh. What the hell did that mean anymore? "What do you mean, *everyone*," he said finally, latching on to the one piece of information he could process rationally. "Who have you told?"

"You and Valerie." Eric bounced an easy layup off the backboard, shot the ball back to Jack, apparently willing to let him steer the conversation. For now, anyway.

Jack took a shot. Missed. "Who the hell is Valerie?"

"The publicist for *Glass Slipper* magazine. I just signed a contract to be the spokesperson for their launch issue. I don't know if you've heard of it, but it's the new arm of their company, Glass Slipper, Incorporated, based out in Potomac. They specialize in makeovers—extreme, whole-life makeovers—mostly for women, but occasionally they handle other—"

"Yeah, okay, got it." Jack took another shot, missed, then gave up the pretense that he was even remotely handling this smoothly, and let the ball drop. He pulled his shirt off his head, wiped his face.

"So . . ." He had nothing. His brain had locked up. He just kept seeing the past, their past, like a movie reel playing inside his head. Jack and Eric. Playing peewee football together at age eleven. Eric Jermaine. Star high-school quarterback. Six two, two hundred twenty pounds. Jock of the Year and total chick magnet from birth.

A guy whose roof he'd lived under throughout high school. A guy he'd seen buck naked any number of times and vice versa. The only person he trusted one hundred percent. Would trust with his very life. And all this time he'd been keeping a huge secret?

Stone-cold serious now, Jack said, "How long have you—you know? Known?"

Eric sighed quietly. "I did the denial thing through school, but I've probably known most of my life." He smiled faintly, tried for a laugh. "And if you're thinking about . . . you know, well, don't. You're not my type."

Jack plainly saw the strained tension beneath the attempt at humor. Guilt immediately replaced disbelief. For Eric to carry such a huge burden for so many years and not feel he could trust Jack enough to tell him? Yes, that hurt. A lot, as it turned out. But, more important, it made him feel like he'd failed the one person who meant more to him than anyone. Who had done more for him than anyone. "So," he said at length, struggling desperately not to let Eric down now. "I guess those summers we spent up in your tree house reading *Playboy*, you really were reading the articles?"

Eric laughed, the tension lifted a little. "Pretty much."

Jack shook his head, willed the shock to subside . . . and all the myriad attendant questions that went with it. "Why didn't you tell me sooner? And none of that bullshit about not trusting me. You know me better than anyone."

"Hell, Jack, I could barely admit it to myself."

He thought about that for a moment. "Did your mom know?"

Eric nodded.

"When?"

He huffed out a breath. "Hell, I don't know, probably a lot longer than I thought. She brought it up to me right after we graduated college."

Jack knew Eric had sacrificed a lot for his mother. His father had died when he was a kid and his mom had never been in very good health. In fact, he'd given up a good job as an engineer in California to come back here and take care of her until she died. That train of thought broke off as certain things began to fall into place. "So that's why you took the job offer in San Francisco instead of following up with the guys who'd been scouting you for four years? That whole song and dance you fed me about being burned out on football, what was that? A crock of shit?"

"Not entirely. You have to understand the struggle I was fighting, man. High school? I just figured maybe I wasn't meeting the right girls, or I was a late bloomer."

Jack snorted. "I'm sure the entire varsity cheerleading squad would be laughing themselves sick if they could hear you right now."

"You'd be surprised what you can talk yourself into. And out of. If you need to badly enough."

Jack fell silent. He wanted to understand, but he honestly had no idea what life had been like for Eric. "I can't believe you kept it quiet."

"Trust me. Me, either. I figured it would be all over when I got to college. Things would be so different. Then the academic scholarship fell through and—"

"Maryland offered you a full ride to play football," Jack said, starting to realize just how screwed his best friend had been.

"Exactly. With Mom's health the way it was, it was too good an opportunity to pass up. But I knew it meant four more years of locker-room shit and everything else that goes along with being a team player. So when that firm in San Francisco made me the offer halfway through my senior year, it was like a life preserver thrown to a drowning man."

Jack swore under his breath. He knew the next part of the story. Eric hadn't been out West six months when his mother fell seriously ill. The kind of ill she wasn't going to recover from. He'd come back East, worked a string of dead-end jobs to make ends meet while taking care of her. Jack had just started to get decent work at that point, so he traveled wherever they sent him. At the time, it had been a stepping-stone to his bigger dream, that of being a staff sports reporter for a big newspaper.

Only he'd quickly realized he'd already found his niche. Other than Eric, he had no close friends, and frankly, he'd never wanted any. Too much damn work. Life on the road suited him perfectly. More important, he enjoyed writing the stories that no one else wanted to cover, about sports most people had never heard of. He'd sent money back as much as he'd been able, knowing things were rough. But he'd never had any idea of just how rough.

"So why not come out then?" he asked. "If she already knew, I mean, why not? Was she weird about it?"

"No, no, not at all. In fact, she was the one who pushed me to take the Bay Area job in the first place. She wasn't happy when I gave it up to come back, but there was no way I was putting her in some facility, and it wouldn't have been right to drag her across the country and away from everything she knew, her friends."

"Yeah, I remember." It had been a very tough time for Eric. "I just wish you'd told me. Maybe I could have helped somehow. I don't know, done something for you. Both of you." He shook his head, guilt creeping back in.

Eric picked up the ball and they both walked back over to the fence. He snagged his shirt, tugged it on. "You were there for me. You were the only one I could unload on, about the stress, the worry, the loss, all of it."

"Yeah, I know, but—"

"You were also just starting out, and it was obvious to anyone with two eyes how much you loved what you were doing. I wasn't going to drag you into any more of my crap. Hell, I didn't even know what end was up at that point in my life. Then the on-line chat thing started and it filled the void, at least temporarily. It was very . . . I don't know, freeing. Just being anonymous and talking with people."

They left the courts that were part of the amenities provided by the Alexandria apartment complex Jack lived in and headed upstairs to his place on the fourth floor.

Jack was feeling worse by the moment. Eric was a great one for making everything seem fine and dandy on the surface, but Jack, of all people, should have known better. He always thought he'd done his best to be there for Eric. But it was now clear his best hadn't even come close. "You should have told me."

Eric shook his head. "The whole advice thing was a fun game that blossomed into something real. I had no idea it would become serious, much less a career."

A college girlfriend of Eric's had dragged him into an on-line chat with a bunch of her friends, joking that he was the prince she'd let get away. Being funny, he'd signed on as Prince Charming, and had ended up being the guy they'd all turned to with their man troubles. Jack remembered ribbing Eric mercilessly about trolling for anonymous sex by being Mr. Sensitive. Eric had ended up with the last laugh, though, when one of the women had jokingly said he should start his own advice column, demystifying men for all the frustrated women out there. And the Dear Prince Charming empire had been born.

Jack let them into his apartment and headed straight for the fridge. If there was ever a Miller Time, this was it. He grabbed two bottles, popped off the caps, and handed one to Eric. They wandered out onto the terrace balcony and dropped into the pair of green plastic lawn chairs Jack had put out there. So he wasn't much on interior design. Or exterior, for that matter. But plastic didn't get moldy from neglect while he traveled. Martha Stewart he was not. Hell, Jackie Stewart probably had more style than he did.

"Besides," Eric was saying, "I figured the whole Mr. Mystery Author thing would work for me." His mouth kicked up in a wry grin. "You know, hetero advice columnist by day, happening homo by night."

"Ha, ha. So what happened? Or . . ." Jack trailed off for a moment as the rest of the story fell into place. "So I wasn't that far off, then? I mean, have you been leading a secret life? Is there someone, uh, you know, special? Is that what this is all about?" He wasn't sure how he felt about that. Hell, he still wasn't sure how he felt about it.

Eric shook his head. "There have been men I've wanted to get to know better. But I haven't dared let things progress beyond a casual fling. The Mystery Author thing sort of backfired. Who knew the Prince Charming thing would take off and every media hack with a camera would be hunting me down? I had this recurring nightmare of the front page of *The Globe* sporting horribly lit photos of me taken at some leather bar in Dupont Circle." He shook his head, sipped his beer. "You don't know how badly I wanted to tell you. A million times over. But . . ." He paused, looked away. "You are, for all intents and purposes, my brother. My only family. Bullshit aside, I care what you think. I—I didn't want you to think less of me. I didn't think I could take that."

"Jesus." Jack swore under his breath. "Do you think that little of me? Never mind. I'm pretty sure you're going to piss me off if we go any further there, so just shut up, okay? I know now, that's what matters. And for the record, I'm not going anywhere."

Eric looked at him then, the relief and gratitude on his face making Jack feel even worse for yelling at him in the first place. God only knew what he'd have done, or how he'd have handled it, if things were reversed.

"I know it might make things weird," Eric said. "But trust me. I'm still me. I'm the same guy, nothing has really changed. It's just that I happen to prefer—"

"Let's not go there, either," Jack said, not ashamed to admit it was going to take him a bit longer to deal with the visuals that were going to accompany this news flash. He finished off his beer. "But if there is no, uh, significant other, then why now? Does it have something to do with this gig you took at the new magazine?"

"Yeah. I decided it was time to end the anonymous author thing. My contract for the column was up for renewal and I hadn't proposed anything on my option for my book publisher. I kept stalling because I just couldn't keep going on with the whole thing. I didn't know what to do. Then Valerie came along."

"*Valerie?* Oh, right, the publicist chick."

Eric just shot him a look. "She's not a *chick*. She's a professional who takes her job very seriously. I—I like her. A lot. And the offer she made me seemed like the perfect solution. At the time, anyway."

"What's your deal with them? What did you sign on for?"

"I agreed to do a little PR for them, and write an exclusive monthly column for their first year. Six issues total."

"Okay. How does all this affect the agreement?"

"It doesn't. If I was willing to keep my sexual preference a secret. Only I'm not. I can't go on like this. But exposing my face to the world is one thing. If I were to come *all* the way out, I'd be ruining Valerie's career, and turning *Glass Slipper* into a national joke."

"And I fit into this grand scheme where?"

"Well . . . I was sort of hoping I could get you to stand in for me. Be a body double, basically."

"Excuse me?" Jack's feet fell to the floor with a *thump* from their propped position on the balcony railing.

"It's just one day of work. Contractually, someone has to show up at the cover shoot. It can't be me. Not the real me, anyway."

There were so many things wrong with this whole conversation, Jack didn't know where to begin. "When is this thing?" he asked, hoping he at least had some time to find some other solution to Eric's problem. *Any* other solution.

"Uh . . . Monday."

Jack rubbed the back of his neck, not sure whether to laugh or curse a blue streak. He did a little of both. "You're not a fucking genius; you're fucking insane. Even if I was willing—which I'm not—we'd never pull off a stunt like this. You have to know that. I mean, I don't know what the answer is here. I understand where you're coming from and all, but can't you just, you know, wait a while longer? Until your contract is up? It's not that much longer."

"No," Eric stated flatly, and it was clear he wasn't going to be swayed.

Not being able to comprehend just what pressures and stresses his friend had been under for all these years, Jack could hardly call him on the decision.

"Besides," Eric went on, "no matter when I do it, *Glass Slipper* will take a hit. And my career will be over. The genius of this plan is that everybody gets what they want, and nobody gets hurt." He rushed on before Jack could say anything. "It's one cover shoot. I can handle the print interview that appears in the inaugural issue, and do the rest of the promo Valerie has scheduled over the phone. I've done radio around here for years that way."

"Precisely. People might not know your name, or your pretty face, but they do know your voice."

"We both have deep voices. A deep voice is a deep voice. Radio distorts things, especially when you're not in a studio. And you're not going to have to talk to that many people at the shoot. They're keeping this whole thing as hush-hush as they can, so nothing spoils the launch. Trust me, that's the least of your worries."

"Key word here being *worries*."

"I know it's a lot to ask," Eric said directly. "I know that."

"What were you thinking, agreeing to this? Never mind." Jack swore silently. He couldn't get past the fact that he'd somehow let his closest friend down in some fundamental way by not being there for him all those years. Especially given everything Eric had done for him. When he thought about it like that, letting some people take a few pictures of him didn't seem like all that much to ask in return.

"At the time it sounded like a brilliant plan. I'd reveal myself to my readers and come all the way out at the same time. My advice is just as valid, no matter what my gender preference is," Eric said. "But as much as I'd like to believe we live in an enlightened society, you and I both know it won't work that way if I go public. And the closer I got to the cover shoot, and the better I got to know Valerie . . . well, this is a big career break for her, and I realized I just couldn't do it. To any of them, really."

Jack knew for a fact that his friend was one of the most compassionate human beings on the face of the earth. He knew this because all those years ago while Eric had been tending to his sick mother, he'd also been tending to a homeless Jack. "No way were you going to be able to screw those old ladies out of their money. You had to know that from the start."

"I don't know," Eric said. "I was feeling pretty desperate, like I was losing my mind. When Valerie approached me with the deal, it just seemed like my ticket out. Of all of it. So I grabbed it. Anyway, it's too late to second-guess it now. I've signed the contract."

Jack said nothing for several long moments, then blew out a long breath and said a silent prayer. "So . . ." He looked over at Eric. "I don't actually have to dispense advice, or give interviews or anything?"

Eric's eyes lit up, but otherwise he tried not to appear too excited when he responded. "I don't think so. You'll have to meet with Valerie; she's the only other one who will know about the switch."

Jack's gaze narrowed. "What do you mean *will* know? You haven't told her about this little plan of yours yet? I thought you said you'd told her everything?"

"I told her I was gay. And that I couldn't go through with the cover shoot. But I told her not to worry, that I would make it up to her. I met with her earlier today and we talked, but I needed to talk with you before I could say anything else."

"Oh, brilliant. Fucking brilliant. She'll never go for this. You do realize she could just sue your ass—mine, too, probably—from here to the moon and back. It's fraud, Eric. We can't possibly get away with—"

But Eric was already shaking his head. "Her career is on the line here, too. And I've gotten to know her pretty well. She's a good, decent person who works very hard. Too hard, if you ask me. But I know this job means everything to her. A lawsuit would bury the magazine before it ever gets off the ground and kill her career along with it. I don't think we have to worry. She'll get on board. It's her only hope."

Jack really didn't give a flying fuck about the publicist. He didn't wish her ill, but childhood guilt about one pal was enough of a burden at the moment. "You don't *think* so?"

"We can hammer out all the details tomorrow night. We're having dinner at her place."

"Oh, we are, are we?"

"Well, that's my plan. I was going to call her, you know, after we get things straight between us."

"Pretty sure of yourself there, Peter Pan."

Eric leaned back, tried to ease the tension between them with a crooked grin. "Oh, so this is how it's going to be? I come out to my best friend and he starts cracking gay jokes?"

Dear Prince Charming

"You're making me prance around on the cover of a national women's magazine as Prince Charming?" Jack stroked his chin, pretending to ponder. "Pretty much, yeah."

Eric just laughed. "Fine, I can handle that. And you know I do intend to compensate you very well for your—"

"I don't want your money," Jack said flatly. There was no reason he couldn't look for a job while he did this thing for Eric. How long could a photo shoot take, anyway? "We both know how much I owe you."

"Hey, I wasn't playing that card. I'm not—"

"I know. Which is precisely why I'm not taking a red cent from you. You saved my life. The least I can do is give you back yours."

Eric fell silent.

Jack wasn't generally comfortable with emotional moments. Just ask Shelby. "Besides, if it's my face on the magazine, I'll get all the babes, right?"

Eric snorted. "Like you need more. But yes, mercifully, you can have them all. In fact, I'll be sure to forward those bags of mail directly to you from now on."

"Let's not get hasty here."

"And I am going to pay you. I have to, or I just won't feel right about this."

"I swear to God, if you mention money one more time—"

"The contract was for mid-six figures. I can handle it, okay?"

Jack's mouth dropped open. No words came out.

Eric grinned. "I thought that would get you."

"Telling women what they want to hear is worth that many zeroes? Jesus, man. For that kind of smack, *I'll* tell them what they want to hear."

"Which would be great, except you'd have to know what that is. Women actually *want* to hear what I have to say."

"Oh, that's how it's going to be? I pull your ass out of the fire and

{ 33 }

you get to dump on my inability to . . . what would you call it in one of your columns . . . open up? Get in touch with my emotions?"

Eric just grinned and downed the rest of his beer. "Look at it this way, now we're both going to hell."

Jack groaned. "Like I wasn't headed there already."

First dates

When entertaining a man in your home for the first time, try to overlook any Neolithic behavior. Trust me, he's just as nervous as you are. It's just that, in general, men don't handle nerves with the same finesse as women. While a woman will quietly anguish over whether the meal will come together on time . . . the guy is trying hard not to do or say anything that will rule out any chance he might score. Meaning, he's certain to do something wrong. And they say women are the hormonal ones.

Chapter 3

Valerie straightened the silverware, then fiddled with the napkins, folding them this way, then that. Not that it mattered how nice the table looked. It was unlikely Eric would notice. Although, on second thought, maybe he would.

She could schmooze with the best of them if someone else was doing the cooking, and providing the atmosphere to go with it. But she hated entertaining in her own home. Her Northeast row house was nicely furnished, but her people skills didn't extend to hosting gracious dinner parties.

Giving up on her linen origami maneuvers, she sank heavily into one of the four mismatched ladder-back chairs arranged around the small, refurbished antique dining room table. For the umpteenth time she went over her conversation with Eric the day before. She still couldn't believe this was happening to her.

After leaving the restaurant, she'd met him at a park near his home in Adams Morgan. His beautiful, bronzed features had been the picture of abject apology as he'd taken her hand. So strong and comforting, his deep voice all masculine and calm as he explained that he wanted his life back, but he couldn't screw her over to get it. She'd asked him—not entirely calmly—just how he thought backing out of his agreement seventy-two hours before he was to sit for the cover of their launch issue, *wasn't* screwing her over?

Eric had explained everything, from childhood on up. And though she'd felt for him—any woman looking into those piercing blue eyes would have to have a heart made of stone, and panties made of moisture-repellant fabric, not to—she was still pissed at him. No matter that he even blushed gorgeously. She was going to lose her job! What would she do? Where would she go?

She'd tried to talk him—and herself—into believing that it wouldn't be so bad if he came out. She had gay male friends she turned to for advice all the time. In fact, they were the only ones who'd honestly answer two of life's most burning questions: "Does this skirt make my ass look J. Lo curvy or like the rear end of a truck squeezed into spandex tubing?" and "What can I cook for my date that looks fabulous, tastes like heaven, guarantees me at least thirty minutes of foreplay . . . and doesn't actually require, you know, cooking?"

But they also weren't the ones who had signed a six-figure contract. In the end, that argument had lasted a grand total of five minutes. Of course it was going to matter. Eric's legions of devoted readers—who the godmothers were banking on becoming their devoted readers—saw him as the man of their dreams; the man who made them believe that one day *their* prince might, indeed, come; the man they put up as the example to their husbands and boyfriends of what all women want their men to be. And now he was just going to say, oh, by the way, I'm gay? Those same men would laugh themselves sick. Women everywhere would feel betrayed. And *Glass Slipper* magazine would become a national joke.

He swore to her he'd think of some way to salvage things, but with less than forty-eight hours left before the cover shoot, she didn't see how. Then he'd called her last night and said he had it all worked out and would be over for dinner Saturday night to explain everything. A dinner for three.

She looked at the plates and linen napkins and wondered if Eric's attorney cared about coordinated table settings. Because who else could he be bringing with him?

She'd spent a sleepless night trying to come up with her own plan. But she had to face facts. She'd have to come clean with the god-mothers. It would kill the magazine before it even launched, causing the loss of her job and God knew who else's, along with a whole lot more money than what they'd paid to Eric. But what choice did she have? And if Eric paraded in here with his lawyer and thought he could wriggle his way out of his contract, their little dinner party would end before the hors d'oeuvres got cold. She was not going to be bullied around. The godmothers had their own team of legal bea-gles. If that's the way Eric intended to play it, he was going to have a fight on his hands.

Not that she'd be around to witness it. She'd be too busy standing on the unemployment line.

She reached for the glass of wine she'd poured herself the instant it had become socially acceptable to do so. Okay, so it had been shortly after lunch. But it was Saturday, and she'd spent the day wrangling editors and making phone calls, trying to reschedule every-thing. She deserved an early glass of wine. Or three.

"Sue me," she muttered, then choked a little when it occurred to her that if litigation was going to be the outcome of this situation, she was no doubt going to be featured prominently in the courtroom proceedings.

She absently wondered if her retro black Chanel would be considered tastefully penitent . . . or icily aloof. Not that it mattered, of course. Jailhouse orange was still completely unbecoming with her short brown bob and fair skin.

Her phone rang and she dragged herself out of the chair, automatically smoothing her hair, and the two-piece business suit she wore, despite the fact she was entertaining at home. It was best to maintain professionalism in case Eric brought in the big guns.

She hoped it was Eric, telling her that he'd had a change of heart, had decided to go through with the cover shoot and honor his contract. She snagged the phone on the second ring, surprised to hear her father on the other end of the line. "Hi, Dad, is everything okay?"

There was a pause, then, "Yes, of course it is." He cleared his throat and Valerie had the brief impression that he was somewhat miffed with her assumption that he'd only be calling if something was wrong. Except that was exactly the case, so she refused to feel guilty.

"How is Mom?" she said, mentally kicking herself for rushing in to smooth over the awkward moment. Her relationship with both her parents was basically one long string of awkward moments.

"She's fine. Busy as usual. In New York at a conference for the next couple of days. I just, ah, that is to say, we both just wanted to let you know we're wishing you success with the magazine launch. Things still going well?"

Which Valerie took to mean, "Do you still have the job?" Her mother was a corporate attorney and her father was a financial analyst, both far more at home in a boardroom than in their own living room. And far more comfortable rearing litigation briefs and stock portfolios than children. Valerie was a late-in-life accident—and a huge surprise to her very careful parents. Which was a fitting start, as she'd pretty much mystified her parents from conception onward. But she gave them credit for trying.

"Yes, Dad, things are going very well." Which was technically the truth. Her career apocalypse wasn't scheduled to arrive for another fifteen minutes. "Tell Mom I said hello when you talk to her. I'll send you both a copy of the first magazine as soon as I get one." Which might be never, but no point in mentioning that now.

"Good, good. Okay, then. Take care of yourself. And be careful. An alert citizen—"

"Is a safe citizen," she finished for him. "Yes, Dad, I know." She tried not to sigh and roll her eyes like the teenager he always managed to reduce her to in ten words or less, but it took effort. After all, she'd been raised in a succession of big cities, had lived alone in a half-dozen more since becoming an adult. She'd never once been mugged, raped, or gotten caught in the cross fire of a gang war, though she'd gotten lectures on all three. God only knows the lectures she'd get on road rage and the statistics on women murdered during roadside emergencies if she told them about the driver's license she'd recently obtained. Which is precisely why she hadn't. She said her good-byes and hung up, knowing he meant well—both of her parents did—but that didn't keep her from wishing they'd made another contraceptive error so at least she'd have a sibling to bitch with about them.

The timer went off in the kitchen, so she snagged her glass of wine and sipped her way into the small but cheery yellow kitchen. She glanced out the window, noticed it was raining, and took it as a sign. It had been a perfect, sunny June afternoon when she'd met the godmothers for lunch yesterday. Then *wham!* Eric called, dumped his big news on her. And God was now dumping the heavens on her in return. Not that she needed divine intervention to tell her that her last-gasp chance at career happiness was an entrée away from being over.

She shoved oven mitts on her hands and pulled out the tray of canapés she'd thawed and heated—thank you, Sutton Place—and slid them onto the counter. One hundred and fifty pounds of angst chose that moment to scuff into her kitchen, give her a baleful look, then flop into a boneless heap right in the middle of the narrow floor space, heaving a long sigh as he did so, just in case she missed all of his other mood indicators.

"I know, Gunther, I know." For once she commiserated with her less than passionate, overgrown watchbeast. "I should just accept that I wasn't intended to have a glossy career dealing with glossy people. Maybe I should throw it in, move to a small town, open some sort of boutique in a trendy restored building with a nice apartment right over the store. I could actually get to know my neighbors, become a member in the community, put down roots." She leaned back against the counter and crossed her ankles, sipping as she looked down into the soulful eyes of the mutant part mastiff/part Great Dane. "You don't look all that enthusiastic. You could be my shop dog, you know. Everyone would come in and say hi to you. Kids would bring treats by the store on the way home from school, stop by to tug on your ears and pet you with sticky hands. You'd become a town fixture."

Gunther merely sighed again and rolled to his side with a *thud*.

"Yep. That's pretty much how I feel. We're not cut out to grow old in Mayberry."

The door buzzer sounded. Sighing herself, Valerie straightened and, after a last fortifying sip, put her glass on the counter. "No, no," she said mildly as she stepped over her inert mound of dog. "Don't get up. I'll just tell the ax murderer not to go into the kitchen if he values his life, right? You protect Aunt Velma's hideous china. I'll cover the rest of the fort."

Gunther's only response was a snuffling snore.

" 'Single girl in the city has to have protection,' " Valerie intoned, mimicking her father. "Of course, it would help if said protection actually had a clue about his supposed duties." She'd gotten Gunther from a rescue shelter in Chicago as a puppy. Mostly to get her father off her back. And, okay, partly because he had been the ugliest, biggest one there. Those beseeching eyes and floppy ears should have been a dead giveaway even then. Forget Mercedes, Gunther totally channeled Eeyore. All the other puppies had been yapping and leaping about. Not Gunther. He'd just leaned against his gate, staring at her with that baleful gaze that followed her as she trolled the other kennels.

"I passed up three Dobermans and two Rotties for you," she reminded him. Seven years and as many cities later, they were still a team. Although she was pretty sure he still saw her as "potty provider and kibble dispenser," while his job description pretty much began and ended with "consumer of everything not put above counter level." But he was there for her every day when she got home. So what if he wasn't overly adoring? She fed him, walked him, and kept him stocked in foot-long rawhide bones. In return he kept her company with few other demands. There was definitely something to be said for that arrangement. If only men were so easily maintained, she might not still be single.

The buzzer sounded again. She paused to check her hair and lipstick in the hat-rack mirror. "Like he's going to care." Not that she'd been interested in pursuing anything personal with Eric, since she didn't mix business with pleasure. Which was severely limiting, given her hours. But he was a very attractive man and, because of some kind of biological imperative, she wanted to look her best. Even if his biological imperative was likely to be more interested in what label she was wearing than how nicely her suit hugged her body.

Of course, his lawyer might be straight, but honestly, what were the chances he'd be as hot as Eric? She pasted on a smile and opened the door. She had to work to keep the smile in place. She hadn't thought anything could top Eric's blond prince perfection.

She'd been wrong. Sort of.

The man next to Eric was no golden Adonis. Quite the opposite, in fact. Dark hair streaked with the kind of highlights no salon could create, a tanned face with chiseled features that probably required a twice-a-day shave, a bit lined as well, from extended time spent in the great outdoors. *Rugged* was the first thought that came to mind. *Damn fine* was the second. She skimmed over the pale green, ribbed knit pullover, noting how nicely it showcased the pecs and shoulders, down to the faded, perfectly aged jeans that were just the right amount of snug on his thighs, to the beat-up Dockers—no socks—on his tanned feet.

If this guy was a lawyer, she might finally get around to writing up that estate management plan her father was always bugging her about.

Belatedly realizing she was staring, she stuck her hand out. "Valerie Wagner. Pleasure to meet you." It was only when she met his eyes—an almost eerily clear shade of gray . . . and quite sardonically amused at the moment—that she felt the heat creep up in her cheeks.

"This is my friend, Jack Lambert," Eric replied by way of introduction.

But Jack didn't take her hand right away. Instead, he lifted his arms away from his body. "I'm sorry, am I supposed to pivot or something? Do you need the rear view as well?"

She raised her eyebrows. "Excuse me?" God, had she been that obvious?

Eric aimed a quelling look at his friend. "Don't start. She's too smart to fall for your lame come-ons."

Jack gave him a mock wounded frown. "That wasn't a come-on. I don't do anything as pedestrian as *come on* to women." He smiled at Valerie. "He's gay, what does he know of coming on to women, right?"

"About two million in book sales," Eric shot back.

Valerie stepped back. "Please come in," she said with a bewildered laugh. She wasn't sure what she'd been expecting, but it certainly wasn't this.

"I swear, he's housebroken," Eric assured her as he stepped inside.

Jack maintained his amused expression as he stepped past her into the apartment. Then he paused and glanced over his shoulder, catching her openly sizing him up. "And?"

She shrugged and brazened it out. "Eh. On a scale of one to ten, you're in the upper twentieth percentile."

Jack's eyes widened slightly, then he glanced toward Eric. "You know, about that paycheck we were discussing . . ."

"I told you," he said, shaking his head. "You're out of your league here. Don't even try. Save yourself the slap down."

Valerie caught the look that passed between the two men. Easy camaraderie, a no-words-necessary kind of communication that proved they went back a ways. Well, they could be chummy all they wanted if it meant Eric was going to honor his contract. They seemed pretty damn relaxed about everything. Of course, it could still be an ambush; get her to let her guard down, flirt a little, then drop some kind of legal bomb on her. But she was admittedly curious, whatever their game plan was. "Why don't you two make yourselves comfortable. Can I get you some wine? A beer?"

Jack prowled around the room, which was really both living area and dining area combined. Rather than sit, he moved toward the small tiled fireplace, pausing to look at the framed pictures lining the narrow mantel. "You have anything stiffer?" he asked, picking up a picture of her mother and father, both grinning and standing proudly in front of her mom's first law office in Boston, before Valerie was born.

She wasn't sure why Jack's familiarity with her things disconcerted her. Yes, the man was a stranger, but what difference did it make if he looked at a few family photos? Something about those clear gray eyes, she thought, as he put the picture back and turned to face her and Eric. How was it they could be so piercing and yet some-what insouciant all at the same time? He was not to be taken lightly, this one.

"In fact," Jack said, "I might want it contractually stipulated that a stiff shot of something be handy at all times."

"*Contract?*" Valerie's gaze shifted questioningly to Eric. *Where was her wine?* she thought suddenly, quelling the first little rise of panic. "What's going on?"

Eric shot a glare at his friend, then put on his most engaging smile for Valerie. "I told you I'd come up with some way to salvage things. And I have. Or, we have, anyway. I'm going to honor my con-tract."

She sighed with such deep relief she almost swooned. "That's fabu-lous!"

"I'm going to write the columns," Eric went on, sounding a bit tense, his smile looking a bit more forced. "And Jack has agreed to step in and model for the cover. Be the face of Prince Charming, so to speak."

Her smile of vast relief froze on her face. "What?" she asked, jaw stiff.

"No one knows what he looks like, right?" Jack interjected. "So I'm your cover boy."

Mouth still open, her head swiveled from one man to the other, but they might as well have been speaking in tongues. The words wouldn't compute. However, Jack's little runway-modeling exhibi-tion began to make more sense. "You can't be serious," she finally spluttered. "We can't do that." She sat down on the nearest available surface, which happened to be her coffee table, heedless of the maga-zines that spilled off the side. "Can we?"

And that was the moment she realized just how desperate she'd become to keep her job.

"Listen," Eric said, his voice all deep and smooth and reasonable, catching her before she could jump up and resolutely refuse to listen to another crazy word. "Who's going to know besides the three of us? If we want to make this work—and I think it's safe to say you and I both have too much at stake not to at least consider it—we will find a way."

She needed more wine. Hell, she needed more than that. Like a reality check. She'd be insane to consider this crazy scheme of theirs for one second. She looked to Jack and said the first thing that came to mind. "What's in this for you?"

Jack's easy smile tightened somewhat. Well, she thought, he'd just have to get over it.

"I've offered to—"

Jack cut off Eric's reply. "Let's just say I owe him and leave it at that."

"Okay, great," she said. "We're supposed to pull off the charade of the century here and I'm just supposed to trust you? I don't even know you."

Eric sat on the arm of the couch. "Does this mean you're okay with the plan?"

She stood up and paced the length of the room. "I don't know." Her mind was racing as she tried to assimilate the multitudinous and wide-ranging ramifications of their outrageous proposition. But she couldn't ignore the fact that, at the core of the matter, she had no alternative plan but to Armageddon her entire career.

But panicking wasn't going to solve anything. She took a calming breath and turned to face both men. She gestured to the couch and the two leather chairs that fronted the fireplace. "Why don't we sit down and discuss the details of this . . . proposal further."

Jack shook his head. "It's probably better if I move around. If I stop and sit for too long, I might actually realize just how insane we all are to even consider an idea like this."

She gaped. "What? You just said—"

"I said I'd do anything to help my friend." Now he glanced at Eric. "I didn't say anything about the plan itself."

"We talked about this," Eric said, then turned to Valerie. "We discussed it at length and we both agree"—he shot a look at Jack, who reluctantly nodded—"that there is no other way if we both want to salvage our careers and keep all parties involved happy."

"He's right." Jack dropped into the closest chair and looked at Valerie. "I'll take that beer now if the offer is still open."

Some prince, she caught herself thinking, half-surprised he hadn't propped his feet up on the coffee table. He was going to be America's Prince Charming?

"I'll take one, too," Eric said. "You need help with anything?"

"No, that's okay," she said, snapping to attention. Busywork was exactly what she needed at the moment. She needed something to keep her hands busy and free up her brain to figure the rest of this out. "I'll be right out." Val headed—escaped—to the kitchen. So, apparently Jack was about as optimistic as she was about this endeavor. Great. But he *was* here, she reminded herself, and she supposed his ambivalence could be a good thing. It proved he was at least attempting to think about this whole thing rationally. Still, she couldn't help but wonder why he'd agreed. Even for close friends, it was a lot to ask.

Stepping over Gunther, who hadn't moved so much as a jowl fold since she'd left, she pulled two bottles of Sam Adams from the fridge and popped the tops. She glanced into the living room as she arranged the canapés on a tray. She was struck again by how different, yet equally, well, virile they were. Sprawled in her leather chairs, all tanned arms and muscular, denim-clad legs, they looked like two jocks who enjoyed getting together on Sunday with their other jock pals to watch the game. Any game. The kind of guys who thought life was all about beer, chips, and cheerleaders in short skirts. Or men in tight, shiny pants, as the case may be.

And though she knew gay men came in all shapes, sizes, and occupations, she still couldn't wrap her mind—or perhaps hormones was more specific—around the idea of hunka-hunka Eric batting for the other team. Maybe it was because she hadn't been laid in . . . well, no sense in actually putting a number to it, right? That was still no reason to drool over a guy just because the sleeves of his polo shirt fit snugly over his seriously well-developed biceps, or because his grin was blistering hot and just as charming. Her gaze shifted to Jack as she loaded a few more canapés onto the tray. Okay, so he was a guy her hormones could also get behind. And on top of. But Prince Charming? She was having a hard time making that association. Still, those eyes of his were awfully intriguing. . . . "What's your take on sex in the workplace, Gunth?"

He thumped his tail twice. A show of great enthusiasm for him. Unfortunately, this heightened level of excitement was most likely in hopes she'd drop a canapé. Or six.

"Yes, well, thank you so much for your inscrutable canine insight." She stepped back into the living room, armed with food and a determined, all-business smile. Better to focus on saving her ass instead of getting a piece of his. She'd mourn the loss later. "So," she said, passing out bottles and hors d'oeuvres before settling on the couch across from them. "How exactly do you and Eric know each other?"

"Childhood friends." Jack popped a canapé into his mouth and washed it down with half a beer.

"We went through school together," Eric told her. "Lived near each other, lived together for a while, in fact. He—" After a quick look from Jack, Eric simply said, "We hung out. Played on the same football team."

"I bet the cheerleaders loved that," she said without thinking.

Jack smiled easily. "You'd have to ask Mr. Quarterback over there. Joe Homecoming King. He had them lining up."

"And you're telling me you were hurting for attention?" Valerie asked, a little surprised by the total lack of ego. "What, were you a late bloomer?"

Eric snorted. "Jack was the campus bad boy. Girls lined up for him, too." He grinned. "But not at the locker-room door. More like the back door of his seventy-two Charger."

"Not the kind you take home to meet Daddy, huh?" Valerie struggled to keep her tone light. But the nightmare was complete. This was the guy she was supposed to pass off as Prince Charming?

"Their loss, trust me," Eric said, even as Jack rolled his eyes. As if he enjoyed his tarnished image.

Eric leaned back, sipped his beer. "Looks, after all, can be deceiving."

He'd said it casually enough, but Valerie still felt her cheeks heat up a little. "I have a few questions to ask you. Both of you. Before we take this any further." Valerie looked to them both. "No offense, but if I agree to this little scheme, how do you know he won't reveal anything about your true identity to the media?"

"He can trust me," Jack said immediately, almost forcefully. He sat forward and put his empty bottle on the coffee table, heedless of the stack of coasters mere inches away. "If we do this, I won't betray him." He held her gaze with a very direct one of his own. "You can count on that."

Wow, Valerie thought. Serious stand-up attitude. This was some kind of childhood guy bond they shared. She found herself wondering what it would be like, knowing you had someone in your corner like that, no questions asked. She had her share of casual friends, sure, but nothing even close to that. Her hopscotch career hadn't exactly been conducive to building long-term relationships of any kind. She supposed, when you looked at it, the only truly staunch supporter in her corner was Gunther.

Well. That was a heartening little analysis.

"I appreciate that," she told Jack. "But you have to see the big picture. We really can't estimate just how intense the media reaction is going to be to this cover, and the interviews."

"*Interviews?*" Jack repeated. He turned to Eric. "You said I wouldn't have to do that stuff. I can't pull that off."

Eric looked to her. "I was hoping we could shift the print articles to phone interviews. Same with the radio plugs."

She opened her mouth to tell him he was crazy, then shut it again. "It's possible," she said at length, aware now just how thoroughly he'd thought about this plan of his. She wasn't ready to commit quite yet, but the way Eric's eyes lit up with such stark hope and enthusiasm made her realize it was probably only a matter of time. "You're also supposed to be visible as our new spokesperson," she reminded him, determined to seek out every possible glitch that could come back to bite her on the ass, before she agreed to this charade in a last-ditch attempt to save it.

"Don't worry," Eric assured her. "I've got a plan for that, too. There is nothing in the contract specifically delineating the exact nature of those duties, other than to be available to promote and advance the cause of the magazine for the first six issues. So, I was thinking, there isn't any reason we can't just expand the shoot Monday to include a number of shots of Jack in different clothes, different backgrounds. Then you'd have a portfolio to work with in upcoming issues, to go with my columns, along with shots to use for any press releases. Beyond that, we'll just say I'm not doing anything else." He shot her his hottie grin. "That way, readers will only see me in the pages of *Glass Slipper.*" He leaned back again, all manly confidence now. "The more elusive, the more exclusive."

Valerie wasn't entirely sold, but she had to admit, he might have something there.

"I'm sure you can play that angle to Mercedes, Aurora, and

Vivian," Eric assured her. "After all, I already set that standard by refusing to meet with them in person until after the contract was signed. They know how protective I am of my image, and how careful I was to make sure I controlled as much of the public unveiling as possible."

Boy, did they know, Valerie thought, thinking back to the rollercoaster ride that had been the past three months of arbitrating this whole deal. Eric hadn't simply handed himself over on a silver platter. Far from it. He didn't work with an agent or a manager, and he'd been very specific about what he would and wouldn't do. She had to admit they probably wouldn't be surprised by this demand.

"Wait a minute. What about his name?" Jack said suddenly. "I mean, they know it, right? I assume it's on the contracts. Am I going to have to pretend I'm Eric in name, too?"

"Which brings up another problem," Valerie said. "They've all spoken to you, albeit briefly, during conference calls when we put this deal together. They're going to be at the shoot on Monday to finally meet you in person."

"Wait a minute, wait," Eric implored them both. "I'm incorporated. Have been since day one. Keeps my name out of things and off copyright pages." He steepled his fingers. "Why don't I just say I'm Jack's manager? That I've been standing in for him as his legal representative until the deal was done, to ensure his privacy and make sure there were no inadvertent screwups." He waved off her immediate protest. "I know, I know, it's eccentric, but what can they really do about it now?"

"Cry foul?" Jack responded with more than a shade of cynicism. "Prosecute?"

"Not if you're standing there, making nice and having your picture taken. They'll have what they paid for, right?"

Valerie was shaking her head. "It's too complicated. These women are not gullible shills. Far from it. We're not going to pull this off without them finding out that this"—she gestured to Jack—"is not the man they've just handed half a million dollars to. They put their trust in me when they didn't have to. I respect them. And earning their respect is important to me." She looked down, then swore beneath her breath as the magnitude of what they were proposing really sank in. "We can't do this," she said quietly. "I can't do this."

"Valerie—" Eric began, but Jack cut him off.

"What happens if we don't?" he asked. "Seriously. Eric signed a contract; he'll honor it with or without me. You can put him on the cover, but he's not going to live a lie any longer."

Valerie let out a shocked laugh. "And just what exactly would you call this whopper you're suggesting we perpetrate?"

"Consider it an arrangement," Jack said. "If we do it this way, the readers still get advice from Prince Charming. The magazine gets their spokesperson and megalaunch. You get all the credit."

Eric nodded. "And I finally get to have a life. In private. With Jack's face out there, I don't have to live in fear that someone will discover that the guy who's advising women how to get the most out of their man . . . is out there getting the most out of his."

From the corner of her eye, she noticed Jack flinch ever so slightly at that comment. So, she thought briefly . . . could Eric's coming out be as recent a news flash to his childhood buddy as it had been to her? How could he not have known?

"No one gets hurt in this deal," Jack finished.

"He's right, Val," Eric said, leaning forward and reaching for her hand. He was so damn convincing. It didn't hurt that he looked so adorably gorgeous while he was doing it, either. "Everyone wins." He folded her hand between his large, warm ones. "The readers get a face to go with the name, a face I'm officially approving. And, most important, the advice inside the magazine is still mine. No one is being cheated."

Valerie leaned back. "You make this sound so rational, so simplistic."

"It is," he said. "Trust me."

She blew out a long breath. "What about Jack?"

"What about me?"

She looked at him, visualizing him on the cover instead of Eric, who, frankly, was God's gift to a magazine launch. In fact, it had taken every ounce of control she'd possessed not to bounce up and down and clap her hands in unmitigated glee the first time they'd met face-to-face. *Jackpot!* had been her thought at the time.

Now she was just getting Jack.

Who couldn't be more different from Eric. The light versus dark comparison went further than hair and eye color. Eric all but gleamed in his polished handsomeness. Jack, on the other hand, exuded something raw . . . earthy. He was more Fallen Angel than Prince Charming.

Backseat Lothario, indeed. He had *wrong side of the tracks* written all over him. The coeds had probably creamed just watching him walk by. Hell, she'd bet a few of the teachers had as well. His body was rangy, muscular, and there was a tension about him that suggested power barely leashed. His look said this was a man too busy living life to stop and analyze it. Much less write about it. This was a man who probably enjoyed women, and, admittedly, they probably enjoyed him back. But he definitely didn't come off as a guy who took the time to ponder the deeper issues that spoke to women's needs in a long-term relationship. He came off as the guy they had issues about.

How to Get Him to Commit to More Than Dinner.

Why He's Great in the Sack . . . but Doesn't Call Back.

The Man Mama Warned You About.

Those were magazine headlines *about* Jack. Not the titles for columns written *by* Jack.

"What's in it for you?" she asked him again flat out. She wanted—needed—to know the whole score here. Childhood bonds notwithstanding.

"I'm cutting him a percentage of my contract," Eric explained.

Jack shot him a we'll-discuss-that-later look, then said to her, "I owe him, okay? Let's just leave it at that."

"What about people who know you? Who work with you?" she asked. "Surely they're going to recognize you and ask questions."

"I work mostly overseas. I'm only back here a few days a month on average, if that. And, don't take this the wrong way, but most of the people I deal with probably won't be reading *Glass Slipper*."

"You'd be surprised—"

"I'm a writer, too," he said, surprising her. "So the idea of me penning a few books won't be entirely unbelievable. And trust me," he said, leaning back, folding his hands across his chest, the first hint of a real smile curving his lips, "anyone who knows me will understand why I kept my 'alter ego' a secret."

"That's just it," she said, still unconvinced. "I don't mean this unkindly, but you're not exactly . . . princely material."

"But the gay guy is?" Jack said with a little laugh. "What kind of hypocrisy is that? And what possible difference does it make what Dear Prince Charming looks like, anyway? A guy writing advice books could be a balding philosophy major with a huge Adam's apple, thick glasses, and black socks for every occasion, including sex on alternate Sundays, for all the world knows or cares. Isn't what he has to say more important than how he looks? And I don't think I'm making too big a leap here to suggest that, just maybe, that might be exactly the kind of advice he'd be dishing out to his female readership in the first place?"

Suddenly she was surrounded by rational men. Where were these guys when she was trying to find a date who was looking for more than a five-minute cocktail conversation before trying to talk her into bed?

"True," she said. "To a point. But someone who looks like Eric is going to sell a hell of a lot more magazines than someone who looks like Barney Fife. That's just the way it is."

Jack stared at her intently. "You don't think I can sell magazines?"

Valerie's throat suddenly felt a bit parched. So, maybe magazine sales weren't going to be a problem. Still, there was the issue of credibility. Readers had to believe this man knew as much about a woman's mind as his piercing gaze indicated he knew about her body. Valerie fought not to twitch a little in her seat. "What exactly do you write about? Are you published?"

He frowned now. "Yes, I'm published. And what does it matter what I write?"

"Women need to believe you. And, given your *alter ego* comment, I'm guessing your stuff is something with a more manly audience. Sports-related, perhaps? Now *that* women are going to believe."

Eric smiled. "But then, they'd believe that about me, too, wouldn't they?"

He had her there. "Touché," she said, then sighed a little. "Okay. So, you say we can trust you, that your commitment to Eric is unshakable. Before we go any further, I need you to trust me." She looked at them both with a level gaze. "I know what Mercedes, Aurora, and Vivian want from this. I know what I want from this, and what the magazine needs in order to go out big. I need to know you'll do what I tell you to do, without a lot of questions or grief. No matter what."

"I was thinking," Eric said, "why don't I just go ahead and accompany you and Jack to the cover shoot. As his manager and legal rep, I can be there to smooth things over with the godmothers, answer any questions that might come up, fill in any gaps, whatever."

"That's actually not a bad idea." It would go over ten times better if they heard the news from Eric himself that Eric Jermaine was merely the front man for the real Prince Charming. Mercedes might be a bit touchy about it, but she had no doubt he'd have Vivian and Aurora eating out of his hand. Or any other body part they could talk him into. "Except . . . what if you run into someone who knows you? Either one of you?"

"It's just for a few hours, right?" Jack said.

"I don't see where anything could go wrong," Eric added. "*Glass Slipper* readers will get everything they want."

What Valerie wanted was a handful of Advil. Preferably with a bourbon chaser.

👑

Appropriate attire

Men don't care about fashion. Not really. Oh, they'll care enough to look halfway decent when they're wooing you into bed. They'll even let you dress them up and take them out, if it makes you happy. But don't be fooled. Behind every man who's out there in killer Hugo Boss, there is a closet back at home, filled with ratty flannels and faded T-shirts. And if you've any doubt which he holds more dear . . . just try donating his college sweatshirt to Goodwill.

Chapter 4

"Come in," Jack called out when he heard the door buzzer. He remained standing in front of his bedroom closet. "I'm back here."

He yanked a few shirts from the rack and threw them on the bed behind him. Propping his hands on his hips, he stared in disgust at the clothes left dangling in front of him. He had exactly one suit. He hadn't worn it since he went to his ex-wife's grandfather's funeral five years ago. It hadn't been all that stylish then.

"I'm thinking this is why *Queer Eye for the Straight Guy* hit big," he said, hearing the front door close. "I'm definitely not the fashion-horse type. And what is up with that, anyway? What happened to my old buddy who wore sweats with the knees blown out, and that ragged-out Penn State sweatshirt of your dad's until it literally fell off of you." He looked at the clothes on his bed. "I could identify with that guy. I *am* that guy. Now I come home and you're wearing things with pleats and cuffs. You auditioning for the show or something?"

"I can't say, really," came a woman's voice from the doorway. "It could just be that he grew up after he graduated college."

Jack leaned back so he could see around his closet doors. "Valerie?" He stepped over a pile of clothes on the floor, but didn't bother kicking them into the closet. Given that his bed looked like a rummage sale at the moment, it was a little late for that pretense. "I, uh, sorry. I was expecting Eric."

She let her gaze skim over him, an amused smile curving her lips.

He didn't have to look down to know he was wearing faded Champion sweats and his old college football T-shirt. "It's Sunday. These are normal Sunday guy clothes." He folded his arms. "So, what are you doing here?"

Her only reaction to his less-than-hospitable tone was the very slight lift of one perfectly plucked brow. He'd only just met her yesterday, but he'd already neatly categorized Valerie in the Jack Lambert Ranking System. She came in as *Interesting, but not my type*.

Like last evening, she was wearing a seriously tailored suit that was all business. Although he had to admit there was a hint of that Jessica Rabbit fantasy. Something to do with the way the jacket was cut to fit at the waist, and the demure, below-the-knee skirt cupped her backside just enough to make sure a man knew she had one. Hmm.

Yet even with the help of a very good tailor, she wasn't exactly all that curvy, top or bottom. And she was a brunette. He generally went for blondes. Shelby was a brunette. 'Nuff said.

But that wasn't why he'd moved her off the *Possible* list and put her firmly in the *Not worth the grief* category. First, he was dealing with quite enough at the moment without complicating things with sex. And no matter what the women who wrote those letters to Eric claimed, sex *always* complicated things. Of course, Jack hadn't been all that thrilled to admit he'd finally discovered a situation that wasn't worth complicating. Just a little. It had made him feel . . . old.

"I'm here to help you pick out your clothes for the shoot." She glanced at the bed, then stepped forward and peeked inside his closet. "Not a moment too soon, it appears."

And then you had to factor in her mouth.

She reached past him and pulled out a faded football jersey that was missing most of both numbers, and part of one shoulder looked like it had been run over by a lawn mower. She glanced at him. "And you went to the trouble to hang it up and everything."

Case closed.

Which didn't explain why he smiled anyway as he took the shirt from her. "I'll have you know," he said mildly, as he hung the jersey back in his closet with the care one might give an outrageously expensive designer piece, "that I have had that shirt since I was in the tenth grade. It belonged to Misty Berlanger's older brother Todd, who played cornerback for the Philadelphia Eagles. She gave it to me on our third date."

"Ah," Valerie said, "a sports relic."

"Not a fan, I take it."

"On the contrary, I enjoy lots of sports. I've followed the Bulls for years. I just don't find I need to memorialize them with apparel."

"Yeah, Misty thought I took it because I was an obsessed fan." He rubbed his thumb down along one sleeve. "But, honestly? I kept it because she used to sleep in it."

It was probably unwise to provoke her—the Ranking System never lied—but Jack had to admit he enjoyed seeing that little punch of awareness when he glanced back at her. The kind of awareness that made her pupils dilate a little. Made her glance at his bed.

He tried to ignore the fact that the little punch had gone both ways. Since he and Shelby had parted ways, he'd kept things light and easy with the women who wandered into his life. He'd maxed his painful breakup quota for the decade. Maybe a lifetime. And he doubted a woman like Valerie Wagner would be either light or easy.

The interesting thing was that that was exactly what had grabbed his attention in the first place. Something about that take-charge attitude and I-know-what's-best demeanor of hers. Rather than sending him running in the opposite direction like it should have, there was some perverse element between them that made him want to shake up her carefully controlled demeanor. Muss it up. Just a little.

"The gift that keeps on giving," she said wryly, recovering quickly. So quickly he almost thought he'd imagined the brief moment. Almost. Apparently, she wasn't any more interested in the unexpected chemistry here than he was. That shouldn't have provoked him. Really it shouldn't.

She shifted past him and flipped through a few other equally ancient shirts. "I understand keeping old clothes for sentimental reasons. But you do realize that doesn't preclude a person from buying new things."

"That's one of the great things about my line of work. I don't generally have to dress for it."

"How . . . comfortable." Her lips curved a little. "You must invest in a lot of sunscreen."

Score one for the lady, he thought, intrigued and not wanting to be. So, it wasn't that he was suddenly turned on by minimally curvy brunettes in uptight suits. It was that he was suddenly turned on by this minimally curvy brunette with the sharp gaze and even sharper verbal skills. Talking with her was sort of like competing at some kind of sport.

And he really loved sports.

"I meant there isn't much I can't do in khaki shorts, jeans, and a handful of T-shirts. Which is fine by me." He glanced at what he'd flung into piles. "But I'm guessing it's not exactly cover-model material."

She looked at the messy heap on the floor, and the scatter of stuff on his bed—which he'd fortunately remembered to make. Well, he'd thrown the spread over the tangle of sheets, anyway. "Not exactly," she agreed with a little sigh. "But that's not going to be a problem. Eric already warned me about the probable status of your closet— though I see he was a bit kind in his assessment—which is why we have an appointment with *Glass Slipper* stylist Jenn Porter an hour from now."

"*Stylist?*" Jack frowned. "You know, I need to warn you, shopping— unless it's for items electronic in nature—ranks about one step above Chinese water torture on my list of fun things to do."

"I'd ask what you know about Chinese water torture, but for some reason, I'm afraid I'd actually get an explanation."

He couldn't help it, she made him laugh. "Yeah, but it would be rational and simplistic."

Her smile was wry. "And here I thought *I* was the one who could talk anyone into anything."

"So, your specialty is coercion? I shouldn't be surprised. If I didn't know better, I'd have assumed you'd used a completely different set of persuasive powers to convince Eric to ditch his mystery-author guise."

"Such a flattering depiction," she said archly. "And ever so sexist."

"Not *sexist*, just honest. And it's not exclusive to women. Men and women both use what tools they were born with to get what they want. Why waste them?"

"Why, indeed? I suppose you think I should be flattered you think I have such weapons at my disposal." She smiled sweetly and said, "But just so there's no confusion . . . or anticipation on your part, gender preference notwithstanding, I've never had to resort to that particular MO to get what I want."

He supposed he'd asked for that one. *Score two for the lady,* he thought, deciding it would be wise to call the game over now, before he did anything really foolish, like keeping her in play. His Ranking System had kept his hide—and heart—intact for three years. Not to mention what was left of his bank account.

He lifted his hands in surrender. "No offense meant, honest. A weapon is a tool is a business asset. As long as no one gets hurt and everyone understands the rules . . . no harm, no foul, right?"

"Sort of like *All's fair in love and war?*"

He smiled. "Something like that. And considering what you've got me signed up for, you're obviously skilled at deploying your arsenal."

"You're not in this because of any weapon or asset I wielded. You're in this because you owe some kind of debt to Eric." Then she flashed him a smile. "But I will thank you for pointing out that I do, indeed, have an arsenal. Just don't fool yourself into thinking they have to be sexual in nature to get the job done."

He laughed. "What I'm thinking is that you're very good at your job."

She turned her attention back to the clothes on his bed. "Well, that remains to be seen. What doesn't remain to be seen is you in anything on this bed."

There was nothing suggestive intended in the comment, but he couldn't stop the image from popping up anyway. Of her, wearing nothing, on his bed. An image that was swiftly, and far too easily, replaced with one of the two of them, rolling on the bed, tangled in his clothes and sheets. He cleared his throat. "Yeah, well, I never said I was model material. Far from it, in fact."

She caught the look he sent her way, and then held it just long enough to make him wonder if she'd suspected where his mind had gone. The worst part was, he wasn't sure if he wanted her to suspect or not.

Then her all-business smile surfaced and the moment vanished. "Well, we're about to take care of all that."

"That's what scares me."

"All's fair," she reminded him, eyes twinkling.

Her eye color was no definite shade of anything, and yet in that moment he found himself thinking they were really pretty. He shook that off and held his hands out in front of him, wrists up. "Take me to your stylist. Just be gentle with me."

She laughed. "You know, you're a very interesting man."

"*Interesting* how?"

"I'm not sure. You're like an odd amalgamation of every guy I've ever known."

"You say that like it's not a good thing."

The corner of her mouth kicked up. "I didn't say which parts you were an amalgamation of."

"Ah."

She held his gaze for another moment—a moment that once again went on a shade too long. They definitely had to get out of this room. The close proximity to his bed was radically affecting his ability to maintain rational thought. He really should have stuck around in Dubai long enough to take that WTA trainer up on her offer of some personal massage therapy. At the moment, however, he couldn't even remember what she looked like.

Valerie looked away first. "Well, why don't I just wait out in your living room while you change," she said brightly. Too brightly. "Then we'll go and see what damage we can do to *Glass Slipper*'s expense account."

"That's really not necessary."

"We're already asking a great deal of you. Trust me, we don't expect you to fund the wardrobe as well."

"No, not that. I just realized that the whole stylist thing isn't necessary." *Because there is a God,* he added with a silent prayer of thanks. "Eric is bringing some stuff of his that he thinks will work. He's a little taller, but we're roughly the same size. He should be here any minute."

Donna Kauffman

"Actually, no, he won't. I was able to reschedule the magazine interview for today, which he's doing by phone from his place right now. I'm here in his place. I have a pretty good idea what the godmothers are going to want. A very good idea, in fact." She patted the briefcase-sized satchel she wore over one shoulder. "I brought all my notes."

"*Notes?*" He eyed the bulging side pocket she'd patted. "It's just a few pictures, isn't it?"

"It's a bit more than that, but don't worry. We've got it all planned out. Fortunately, we have a number of ideas on how to achieve the look we want. I spoke with them this morning and talked over the whole idea of using this one shoot to get a number of photos for upcoming issues."

"*Them.* You mean the godmothers?"

She nodded. "I slanted my suggestion toward budget concerns and how it would be to our advantage to get as much on Monday as we could. It will give us a great deal of latitude with upcoming features, as well as allow us more flexibility with promotional opportunities if we don't have to schedule a shoot every time some prospect presents itself. Mercedes was a little skeptical, but in general I think I've got them behind me. They were definitely intrigued by the whole keep-the-mystique-going thing. We have the studio booked for four hours, but I imagine it could run longer than that, depending on how often they intervene." She gave him a wry smile. "You can count on that being fairly often."

"They're going to watch the whole shoot?" He swallowed against a little knot that had formed in his throat. This was getting more real by the second.

"You didn't think they were going to let their half-million-dollar boy get his picture taken without them calling every shot, did you? You don't know the hoops I had to jump through to get Eric signed without them actually meeting. If it wasn't for the way he charmed them on the conference calls, especially Aurora and Vivian—damn, I should have brought those tapes with me." She waved that off. "No problem, I've got them at home. Remind me to give them to you. That way you can go through them tonight, get up to speed on everything that was discussed."

"You have tapes of their phone calls?"

"Absolutely. Considering what's at stake, it was best to cover all the bases so everyone knows what everyone else said or agreed to. There's not that much to go through, really."

Jack grabbed a shirt from his bed and jammed it back on a hanger. More because he had a sudden need to keep busy, to stamp out the nerves that were climbing into his gut and forming a tight, queasy ball, than because he was compelled to straighten up. "So, Eric charmed them, huh?" He chuckled lightly. It came out sounding more like a gurgle. "He always was the smooth one." He turned to face her, mangling a sweatshirt in his hands. "Do you really think the women of America will revolt if they find out he's gay?"

She frowned. "You can't have second thoughts. Not now."

"I'm not. Not really," he added when she folded her arms. "It's just, advice is advice, right? Why should they care?"

Her mouth dropped open. "You really have been out of the country, haven't you?" She snatched the sweatshirt from his hands and swiftly folded it, placing it on the bed before picking up another one.

Bemused, he said nothing. Apparently, he wasn't the only one battling nerves. Of course, her career was on the line here, too. Only she wasn't the one standing in front of the cameras.

"You have to understand the reputation he's built up with his readers," she said. "They worship him specifically because he is a man above all men to them. The man who could sweep them off their feet and carry them over the threshold. And trust me, they want that threshold to lead to a bedroom somewhere. Even if they were willing to forgive and forget, the media certainly won't. He'd be talk-show fodder for weeks." She shook her head. "And *Glass Slipper* magazine would be a joke. Not to mention the damage it could cause to the godmothers' core business."

Jack let out a heavy breath. "I knew his books sold really well, but I guess I never really grasped—"

"He shipped five hundred thousand copies in hardcover and one-point-two million trade copies on his last title. And that's just domestic."

Jack whistled. "Damn."

"Exactly. When you couple his selling power with the mystique surrounding his true identity, well, we have no doubt he'll be worth every penny we're paying him. The sales force is almost giddy with the orders they're taking." She looked at him. "I'm surprised you didn't know all this. You two have been friends a long time."

"I travel a lot. He's holed up writing." He lifted a shoulder, but he couldn't help but feel a little pang of confusion, guilt, maybe. He knew Eric better than anyone on earth, and yet it was like they were discussing a stranger. "He's a modest guy. We don't talk business much. I knew he was doing well, but I honestly had no idea just how well."

"Do you read his books?" she asked.

He shook his head. "I buy them, you know, to support him. He knows I don't read that stuff. We joke about it."

"*Stuff,*" she repeated. "Your act being so together you don't need relationship advice from time to time?"

He'd scooped up the rest of the clothes, intent on heaving them into the closet, figuring he'd deal with them later. He paused at her question, the wry note in her voice, then shot her a grin. "With women? No."

She gave it right back to him. "And yet, you're divorced."

His smile faded. He wished that subject hadn't come up at dinner last night. But, like a bad case of chicken pox, Shelby left scars that never quite faded completely away. "We all make mistakes." He tried to toss it off, not sound curt. "I just happened to marry mine."

"Too much alcohol impairs even the most rational and simplistic minds." She said it teasingly, but it tweaked him nonetheless.

The clothes landed in a heap on the floor of his closet. He shoved the doors shut to keep them from flowing back out. "How did you hear about that?" He'd been thankful last night when Eric had responded to the swift jab he'd delivered to his shin beneath the table, and changed the subject before dragging out all the Shelby-and-Jack horror stories.

"Eric mentioned it when we spoke earlier today."

Jack folded his arms, leaned against the closet doors. "Oh, he just happened to mention it? Meaning, you asked about it. Why?"

She turned an equally level gaze on him. "I wanted to make sure no more surprises were going to come crawling out of the woodwork."

"You don't have to worry about Shelby. The only contact we have is the check that gets deposited in her account on the first of every month." He tried not to sound bitter. Or worse, hurt. Shelby was history, in his head and his heart. But the sting of failure? Not quite yet.

"What if she happens to pick up a copy of the magazine?"

He snorted. "Shelby, reading—there's something you'll never see."

"You picked a real genius, huh?"

He shot her a look. "I was young. It wasn't her brain I was trying to get into bed."

Valerie shrugged. "Hey, she got you to marry her, so she must have something going on upstairs."

"Yeah, an internal calculator. No batteries required." He sighed. "Listen, she's old news, okay? I haven't spoken to her or laid eyes on her in years, other than in magazines, and not even then if I can help it. She's from Peru, so she's never in the States anyway, unless it's for a shoot."

"Ah, she's a model."

He raised an eyebrow at the knowing tone. "Exactly when did I do something to give you such a low opinion of me, anyway? I'm doing you a favor here, you know. If it's about that MO comment earlier, I'm—"

She raised a hand. "No. And you're absolutely right. I'm sorry." She gave a little self-deprecating laugh. "I don't know why I've been poking at you." Her smile was softer, more honest this time. "I guess you bring out my inner snark." A little sparkle lit those hazel depths. "Can't imagine why."

He smiled at that, felt his body respond, and quickly backpedaled. "Yeah, well, I guess it takes one to know one."

"Partly."

He lifted an eyebrow in response.

"We each have different interests at heart here," she explained. "My job for me. Your friend for you. Maybe we're poking at each other as a way to feel each other out. I guess I can't help but be a little curious."

"About?"

"Why you're really agreeing to do this for him."

"*Suspicious*, you mean."

To her credit, she didn't deny it. "I don't know you. There's a lot at stake. I don't have any choice but to trust Eric in this."

"But you don't trust me."

"I didn't say that."

"You've pretty much been saying that since we met last night."

"Okay, maybe so. But can you blame me? Eric dropped a major bomb on me. The fact that I'm playing along with this at all is a testament to just how desperate a situation this is."

"You could sue him for breach of contract."

"I promised them a cover story guaranteed to put them on the map. Do you have any idea how hard it is to launch a new magazine and be successful in today's market?"

"I have a general idea. But it's not your fault Eric decided to come out now."

"I've been promoting the hell out of this for the past three months. Everything is set in motion. The sales staff has sold this thing based on proposed first-issue sales. A first issue with the mysterious Prince Charming on the cover. It hits the stands in less than a month. And the cover shoot with my guaranteed ticket is tomorrow. Not exactly enough time to replace him and start all over again."

He shrugged. "There are other jobs."

"Not for me."

"Publicists are in demand, especially in a political town like this."

"You don't understand. It's—" She stopped, shook her head, then pushed away a wave of brown hair that fell across her forehead. "I can't explain it to you. Let's just say I'm not taking this risk lightly. It's everything to me. Just like it is to Eric. So, yes, I guess I'm looking for some kind of guarantee from you. That no matter how hard it is, or how weird or uncomfortable it gets for you, that you don't let him down."

"Well, I can't explain it to you, either. Don't you have someone in your life you'd do anything for?" The brief flicker of hurt? envy? that crossed her face surprised him. "Well, Eric is that person for me," he said, suddenly uncomfortable, like he'd seen something private that he shouldn't have.

"I know you don't owe me anything, but—"

"I owe Eric everything," he said flatly. He didn't want to care about Valerie Wagner. His dealing-with-other-people's-shit quota was also maxed out at the moment. "That's all that matters. You'll get what you want because I won't let him down. That will have to be enough for you."

She held his gaze for another long moment, only there was no sexual subtext to this one.

The hell of it was, when she nodded, then handed him the shirt she'd just folded, and walked out of the room, he was more aware of her right then, than at any moment before. And he'd hardly even been looking at that hot little slit in the back of her skirt.

A full minute later, he was still standing there.

"The appointment is in thirty minutes," she called out, jingling her keys. "And Beltway traffic is going to be a bitch."

No, Jack thought as he grabbed his wallet and followed her out of his apartment, doing a friend a favor . . . *that* was going to be the bitch.

Indicators

You can tell a lot about a man by how he reacts during an emergency. Especially when the emergency is yours. Does he stand and give orders? Does he waste time placing blame? Or does he jump in first and ask questions later? The man who jumps is a man willing to participate. And, ladies, I don't have to tell you that participation is a Good Thing.

Chapter 5

Twenty hair-raising minutes later, Valerie squealed into the alley behind her row house, clipping her neighbor's trash can, and barely missing the tall chain-link fence that circled her minuscule backyard.

She cut the engine and Jack let out a long, shuddering breath, then crossed himself. He wasn't even Catholic. "Where did you learn to drive?"

She grinned widely, her eyes still gleaming. "Actually, a more appropriate question would be *when* did I learn to drive. If I'd known what a kick in the ass it is to play Dodgem on the Beltway, I'd have done it sooner. I've been a city girl all my life. I always used public transportation."

"D.C. is a city," he pointed out helpfully, willing his heart to slow down to something below, say, Mach 3. "They have a thing called the Metro here. Stations all over town. Buses, subway."

"The magazine offices are here in D.C., but Glass Slipper itself is headquartered in Potomac. I'd need Eric's contract to afford that cab fare. Of course, the godmothers offered me the use of a company car, complete with driver, but glamorous as it sounds, trust me, the novelty quickly wears off. My schedule is unpredictable and often frantic. I can't always call ahead and order a car. And I just can't make a guy sit at the curb all day in case I need a ride. Besides, I like to be in control of my destiny whenever possible." She shrugged. "So, I figured it was time to get my license and put a down payment on a car."

Jack opened his door and squeezed out into the narrow space between the brick wall of the row house next to hers. "That's great, really. Congratulations. But next time, I'm driving."

"Ah," she said, climbing out of her side. "A chauvinist who thinks men are better drivers than women."

"No," he said, "A preservationist." He smiled across the hood of her bug-sized bright red-and-white-striped MINI Cooper, only wincing a little as blood flow was restored to his lower extremities. "Who likes to control *his* destiny wherever possible."

"Just because that trucker tailgated us a bit too closely is no need to start making out your will."

"You cut him off. He was going to mow us down. No court in the land would have convicted him."

She blew that off with an "as if" sound. "And you claim to be a world traveler. Paris makes the Washington Beltway look like a real driver's ed course, with little orange cones pointing the way."

He pushed open the creaky rear gate for her. "You've been to Paris?"

"Several times. For the spring shows," she clarified. "I've worked at a few fashion magazines."

She tossed it off like it was nothing, but he knew immediately it was something. He thought about her earlier reaction when he'd commented that she could always get another job. The nosy journalist in him wondered just how many jobs she'd held at how many magazines . . . and why she'd moved on. Discontent on the part of employee . . . or employer?

It wasn't until he closed the gate that he thought to ask, "Why are we at your place? I assumed we'd be meeting at magazine head-quarters."

"It's Sunday, remember? I'm dragging Jenn in for some overtime on this as it is. Besides, it's probably best to keep you under wraps."

"The cover shoot is tomorrow. What difference does it make?"

"We paid top dollar to be the one to introduce Eric to the world. There are a dozen news shows and twice that many gossip columns that would kill to get any inside scoop on the man behind Dear Prince Charming. I'm not taking any chances. Even the shoot is be-ing done in a secret location, with a minimal number of people on set."

"All this cloak-and-dagger stuff seems a little over the top, don't you think?"

She tossed him an indulgent smile as she climbed the steps to the closed-in porch. "It's a cutthroat world, Mr. Lambert. When you've invested a great many more zeroes than Eric saw on his paycheck to launch a new glossy, you protect your edge. Eric is our edge. Eric, and now you."

As she fished her house key from the multitude on her key ring, he glanced back at the small but tidy yard. The grass was spotty in places, but neat enough. No flowers or garden, but a row of fir trees edged the rear and right side of the fence, affording some additional privacy. A sturdy wooden lounge chair, topped with thick, flowery print padding, and a small wrought-iron side table completed the tableau. He tried not to picture her out here in some minuscule bikini, sunning herself. Or how the privacy the bigger house and trees provided would allow her to untie the tiny top in order to pre-vent those pesky tan lines. He tried. Really he did. And failed, though in a quite spectacular, detailed fashion.

Then he spotted a chewed-up Frisbee and nasty-looking tennis ball, and his thoughts were thankfully diverted. "You have a dog?"

She unlocked the door. "No, I have a Gunther."

"What's a—" That's as far as he got before an enormous dog pushed through the door, all but knocking him off the steps. Not from any enthusiasm over having visitors, either. As far as Jack could tell, the behemoth hadn't even seen him. He'd just plowed down the stairs and headed straight for the rear corner of the yard.

"Oh, no. No, no, no," Valerie muttered, pushing through the door. "I'm going to kill him."

Jack was torn between watching the dog, who was presently relieving himself like he'd just finished running the Preakness on a full bladder, and following Valerie into the house. "Was he here last night? How did I miss a dog the size of a small European import?"

Gunther finished his duties, which had apparently worn him out. Jack watched in bemused amazement as the dog ambled across the yard, climbed unceremoniously onto the thickly padded lounge chair, and flopped down with a rumbling, chair-shuddering sigh.

Somehow, the exquisitely tailored, ruthlessly organized woman, the same one who'd hosted a dinner in her own home last night that was more board meeting than social occasion, simply did not compute with the term *dog owner*. If you could call the massive beast presently sunning himself in the backyard a dog. Valerie Wagner was the type to own a cat. Or something interesting, yet tastefully decorative. Like fish.

He took one last look at Gunther, who was now on his back, legs akimbo, tongue lolling. *Well*, he thought with a shudder, *that takes care of that little bikini scenario, anyway.*

"Careful," Valerie called out before he stepped into the kitchen. "The floor's wet."

Jack immediately moved back to the porch, imagining . . . well, more of what he'd just witnessed against that poor pine tree. But he quickly realized the floor of her kitchen was flooded with plain old water. "What happened?" he asked as he tiptoed his way across the tile floor, following the sound of her voice.

"Tub overflowed."

"What?" He stepped out of the kitchen and rounded the corner into a small hallway, which was somewhat dryer thanks to a skinny carpet runner.

Valerie was in the narrow white-and-black-tiled bathroom immediately across the hall, throwing big, brightly colored towels on the floor. The tub, still dangerously full, was now draining noisily. The sink was already full of several wet mounds. "Could you reach in that hall closet there and pull out another stack of beach towels?"

"Sure." He found the louvered doors, and opened them, not surprised to find every shelf filled with neatly folded, color-coordinated linens and towels. It was only when he looked down that he noticed the bottom compartment was filled to bursting with beach towels. He pulled out the entire stack. "You, uh, go to the beach a lot, do you?" he asked as he handed her half the stack, then moved back to the kitchen and spread the remaining half across the floor.

She didn't respond to the question, too intent on swearing under her breath. While he opened the hall closet to grab a few more towels, she was busy wedging one behind the commode. Her black wicker hamper wobbled precariously on the closed lid. "I swear to God, this is the last time I'm doing this. Damn dog. The pound *will* take you back, Gunther!" she called out. "If I have to pay them to do it."

"He's still outside, uh, sunning himself. Is that okay, or do you want me to call him back in?"

She just glared at him, then went back to work, mopping.

It was only when he bent over to help her arrange fresh towels on the opposite side of the toilet that he saw the giant plastic clamp keeping the lid forcibly closed. He glanced over at her. "You have kids?"

"No. Like I said, I have Gunther. You interested in taking him? Because right at the moment, I'll give him to you. Lock, stock, and rawhide bones. I'll even toss in a lifetime supply of beach towels."

"At the risk of having you throw wet towels at me, would you care to explain how your dog managed to flood half your house?"

"He's not a dog. He's the spawn of Satan. Put on this earth to make certain I follow him straight to hell." She tossed another sodden towel into the sink. The tub was only half-full now and draining more swiftly. Pushing her now damp hair from her forehead, she sat on the edge of the tub and halfheartedly nudged another dry towel across the floor with her bare foot. Somewhere along the line she'd ditched her heels.

Something about seeing her disheveled and not so on top of things tugged at him. He wisely ignored it and began wringing out towels. "And he's going to float you there on the River Styx, is that the plan?"

"Cute."

He shrugged. "I do my best in trying times."

"I guess I can't argue with you there," she said, and he knew she wasn't just referring to his pitching in on mopping-up duties.

"So, spawn of Satan aside, just how does a dog fill a tub to over-flowing?"

"He has a drinking problem," she said, sounding both pissed and a bit forlorn. Like she wasn't quite sure how the little world she ran so tidily had turned on her so swiftly. Given the events of the past forty-eight hours, he figured she was entitled.

"Do you fill the tub as some kind of giant water dish for him?" Considering what he'd seen outside, he thought this was a strong possibility.

She tossed a wet towel in the finally empty tub. "Normally I keep the door to this bathroom and the master bath upstairs closed. This morning was somewhat frantic, with all the calls I've been trying to make, then tracking down Eric and making sure he could be available for the phone interview. I could have sworn I closed it, but I guess it didn't click all the way shut."

Jack rocked back on his heels. "If you didn't fill the tub, you're telling me that Gunther did?" He glanced back to the baby-proofing clamp on the toilet-seat lid.

She followed his gaze. "When his water dish is empty, he drinks out of the commode. Slobbers water everywhere." She shuddered. "Not a great way to wake up in the morning. Or in the middle of the night, for that matter. I tried leaving the ring up, but I figured, hey, there should be some perks to being thirty and single, right?"

"Hence the lock."

"Which, frankly, is just as much of a pain in the ass. But if I close the door at night, he just head-butts it until I get up and either open it or fill his water dish in the kitchen."

"Doesn't he just do the same thing during the day?"

She smiled smugly. "I wouldn't know. I'm not here then, am I?"

Jack glanced at the door, thinking she was lucky Gunther hadn't taken out the whole frame. Put a helmet on him and he could play nose tackle for the Redskins. Come to think of it, the Skins might do better with Gunther on the line. "So, thwarted from using the toilet as his own personal bottomless drinking fountain, he learned how to turn on the water in the tub?"

"It was an accident," she protested, like it was something that could happen to anybody. "This past April when we had that freak snowstorm, he got filthy rolling in the mud in the backyard. The hose was frozen, so I had to wash him off in here." She leaned back and pointed to the lever that operated the shower. "All you have to do is shift it to the left or the right for the water to come on. He's so damn big it got knocked on and off over and over while I was trying to rinse him off. He's not fond of baths, but when he saw the stream of water coming out of the faucet, that got his attention. He loves to drink out of the hose. It's the only way I can keep him still long enough to get him washed outside."

"Good thing he doesn't have opposable thumbs."

She quelled him with a look. "Anyway, when I was done washing him, I turned off the water and he nudged it back on with his nose. I made the grave mistake of laughing. It sort of became a game. One I could kill myself now for thinking was remotely cute. I've been meaning to get a plumber in here to put in a different fixture, but I haven't had the time. So I just keep the door shut."

Jack wrung out another towel and tossed it in the tub. "Still, how did he flood it? Has he learned to put in the plug and take his own baths now, too?" A shame human-interest stories weren't his venue. He could think of a half-dozen ways to play this story into an article.

She leaned into the tub and pulled out another nasty-looking, chewed-on Frisbee. "He carries one of these with him everywhere. He comes in here, nudges on the water with his nose, drops the Frisbee so he can take a drink, and well, you can put the rest together."

"A shame you can't teach him to take the Frisbee with him when he leaves."

"Oh, he tries." She sighed. "But he's afraid to put his nose underwater."

Jack opened his mouth, then closed it again when her eyes narrowed. She probably wouldn't appreciate him falling over laughing right at the moment.

The doorbell rang just then. "That's Jenn. Dammit, look at this mess." Valerie jumped up as the buzzer sounded again, then slipped as her feet went out from underneath her on the slick floor.

Jack lunged from his crouching position just in time to grab her around the waist and prevent her from falling back into the heap of wet towels half-filling the tub. The momentum of her weight shift caused his feet to slip, sending them both crashing back onto the sink vanity so hard his head rapped soundly against the medicine-chest mirror.

"Jesus Christ," he swore, seeing stars as he tried to disentangle himself from her.

Valerie grappled with his shirt and shoulders, trying to push off of him, only to cause him to groan when she inadvertently kneed him.

"Sorry," she said as the buzzer rang again. "I'm really sorry." She slid away from him, but her feet hit a wet towel, sending her toppling right back into him.

He grabbed her before she could move another inch. He wanted to at least have the option of having children one day. "Just hold on there a moment, okay?"

She lifted her head and blew at the damp hair sticking to her face. "I feel like I've landed in the middle of a bad *Three's Company* spin-off."

Despite the fact that his head was competing with his balls to see which could throb more painfully, he looked into those hazel eyes and found himself grinning. "That's assuming there could be a good one?"

"You've got me there."

He was painfully aware of where he had her, all right. "Of course, my name *is* Jack."

She smirked. "I guess that makes me Janet."

"Not Chrissy?"

"My life is hard enough, thanks."

He laughed as the buzzer sounded again. "Sounds like Mr. Furley is getting impatient."

"Yeah, I imagine so," she said, but neither of them made an immediate move. "You watch a lot of late-night television, do you?"

"I log a lot of time in small foreign hotels. I can't afford to be choosy. I count myself lucky if there is one English-speaking channel."

"I didn't think it mattered what language *Baywatch* is broadcast in."

He just grinned. "True, very true."

She rolled her eyes. "Men."

"Yeah, I know. We can't help it. Ogling women in revealing red bathing suits is programmed into our DNA." Gripping her hips, he carefully set her on her feet. "But, hey, what would you do without us?"

She straightened her now damp and rumpled suit. "Well, with a big enough battery supply, probably quite well."

Choking on a surprised laugh, Jack stared after her as she left the room and tiptoed across the damp hall runner to the living/dining room area, on her way to the front door. "Not a bad exit line. Not bad at all."

He checked in the mirror to see if there was a lump at the back of his head. Sucking in his breath as blood flow was once again restored to the rest of his aching body parts, he finished surveying the damage to himself and the rest of the bathroom.

It occurred to him, as he finished mopping up and putting the remaining wrung-out towels in the tub, that spending time in the company of Valerie Wagner was quickly becoming a full-contact sport. The kind that made a guy wish for a helmet and knee pads. Not to mention a cup.

But despite being a bit on the bony side, not to mention a half-foot shorter, Valerie's body had still managed to line up quite nicely with his.

He heard her talking to another woman in the front room, which mercifully diverted his mind from the Path to Peril. True, it had been a while for him, but surely he could find some diversion other than one that entailed getting involved with the woman in whose bathroom he was presently standing. One that was more his speed of late.

Meaning blonde, built, and not prone to long discussions. Rational or otherwise.

He raked his fingers through his hair, brushed at jeans he'd pulled on before leaving his place, which were now soaked from the knee down. He smoothed out his splotchy wet T-shirt, then stopped when he realized what he was doing. Primping. He was not a primper. Besides, how he looked now didn't matter. They were going to have at him, anyway.

It was the only instance he could imagine where the prospect of letting two women do with him what they willed didn't excite him. *Three's Company*, indeed.

"Jack?" Valerie called out. "Don't worry about the mess. Come meet Jenn. She's a big fan," she added, half-announcement, half-warning.

Or perhaps only Jack had heard it that way. Whatever the case, the news had him pausing in his tracks. He'd dug out Eric's books yesterday, thinking he'd skim through them, just as a precaution. He'd yet to crack a spine. It was a freaking photo shoot. How tough a test could that be?

The first inkling of what he'd truly gotten himself into hit when he stepped into the living room and Jenn's mouth dropped open with a gasp.

"Omigod," she gushed, "I can't believe I'm meeting the real Prince Charming. Wow . . . you're . . ." She turned to Valerie, all open-mouthed smile and wide eyes. "Women are going to eat him alive." She laughed and looked back to Jack, all five feet of her quivering in excitement. "Sorry, no offense." She took out her tape measure, flipped off the rubber band, and unfurled it with a snap. "But, damn, you're going to be fun to dress." And undress, if the somewhat glazed look in her eyes was any indication.

Under normal circumstances, Jack would have been all for this apparent bonus. But even he drew the line at taking women to bed under false pretenses, which included letting them think he was someone he wasn't. Of course, there was nothing to stop him when the photo shoot was over. . . .

And that's when it hit him.

It must have registered on his face, because Valerie frowned and said, "Is something wrong?"

"Can I see you in the kitchen for a minute?" He looked to Jenn. "This won't take long." He didn't wait for her to answer, but turned and hightailed it into the other room. It was probably a good thing he hadn't driven over here today, because debt to Eric or no, he was about two seconds away from running screaming into the street, hailing the first cab he found, and heading straight to National Airport. Destination: Anywhere but here.

"What's the matter now?" Valerie asked as she stepped carefully over the wet towels still lying on the kitchen floor.

"I can never tell anyone. Ever. Can I?"

"What are you talking about?"

He paced the narrow aisle between the counters, stopping long enough to stare at lounge-prone Gunther, before pacing back to her. "Lying," he said, stopping right in front of her. "I don't make a practice of it."

"Good," she said, obviously not following him.

"I might not be the guy women take home to Mama—which is fine by me—but I'm not a cheat and I'm not a liar."

"Okay," she said slowly. "Why don't you just tell me what's bothering you specifically."

"Women. Specifically women who come to know me as Prince Charming." He folded his arms. "Just what kind of circulation do you think this magazine is going to have?"

"Wait, back up. You mean, what if women recognize you as Prince Charming?"

"This deal is supposed to be one photo shoot of me, and Eric gets to keep his job and get a personal life. Done, game over. Except, judging by your friend Jenn's reaction in there—"

He saw the light dawn in her eyes. "*Oh.* You think you'll have to pretend to be Prince Charming—"

"Forever." He waited through several seconds of silence, hating the edge of panic welling inside him when she didn't immediately say something to squash his concerns.

She bit her bottom lip. "I— Didn't you say you worked mostly overseas? In . . . remote areas?"

His eyes bugged. "*What?*"

"Quarter-million once the subscription service kicks in," she said quietly. "And that's just the U.S. and Canada. *Glass Slipper*'s circulation," she added when he looked confused. "Although, you know, Eric's only signed on for the first six issues."

"You're saying readers will forget what he looks like."

She didn't answer right away.

"What?"

"Well, yes, they probably will. Enough that you wouldn't necessarily be recognized on the street. At least not the crowded ones."

He was going to have a heart attack. Right here in her kitchen. "Except?" He'd heard the hesitation in her tone.

"Except as our spokesperson—our well-paid spokesperson—we expect to get some mileage out of his face. He's—you're—a good-looking guy. It's a known fact that women enjoy looking at good-looking guys. I think Jenn's reaction more or less proved that point. So we'd probably run a photo of you with his column."

He took up pacing again. "Okay, okay. So it's six months, then." He could get a job as a stringer somewhere overseas for that long. Hell, he'd shuck prawns in Portugal if it meant getting the hell out of here for the duration of his little lie.

"Well . . ."

He spun around. "*Well? What well?* Eric said it was six months."

"Six *issues.* We're bimonthly."

"A year?" He raked his hand through his hair. "Fine, fine. But still, it's only one cover."

"Plus the photos we'll run with his column."

"Yank those."

She just stared at him.

"It's my life here, too, Valerie. I don't want to have to lie to people outright if I get stopped in the street." He looked at her. "Eric's sold millions without ever revealing his face, surely your magazine will do just fine without mine in every single issue."

She sighed. "I don't really have control over that, but I'll see what I can do."

"You do that. Let's get this circus over with." He went to move past her, but she stopped him with a hand on his arm. It was the closest they'd been since she'd been sprawled all over him in the bathroom.

"One thing," she said.

He looked from her hand on his arm to her eyes. He wished he saw more confidence there; in him, in this whole arrangement. He supposed he couldn't blame her. "What?"

"I need you to stay here."

"Excuse me? I'm supposed to hide in your house? What for?"

"No," she said, "I didn't mean *here* as in my place. I meant *here* as in the U.S. Preferably in the D.C. metropolitan area. When the magazine comes out, I can't predict exactly what the demands on Eric are going to be. You know I'm going to do my best to deflect them, but I can't very well go turning down every promotion opportunity that might spring up. I am their publicist, after all. How would I explain that to the godmothers?"

"You said it was one photo shoot."

"I'm going to do my best. I promise." She held his gaze. "But that's all I can promise."

He lowered his arm and her hand dropped away. "Then you'd better hope like hell your best is damn good."

Character

How a man dresses can tell you a little. A man's comfort in his own skin can tell you a lot. The tux doesn't make the man. The man makes the tux.

Chapter 6

The following morning Valerie paced outside the dressing area, waiting for Jack to emerge. The photographer and his two assistants were almost done setting up. The godmothers had yet to arrive. And Eric and Jenn were taking forever to ready Jack for the first series of shots. At this rate, they'd need the use of the loft for the entire day. "What's the holdup?" she called past the screens that had been set up to section off a changing area. "Nigel is ready and waiting." *And charging us out the ass for the pleasure.*

Of course, getting the famous Nigel Cole to shoot the cover had been the second feather in her war bonnet. She'd only dared to ask him because, well, you don't get anything if you don't ask. To her shock, it turned out Nigel was a closet Prince Charming fan. Which was pretty much the only thing Nigel had left in the closet.

"No holdup," Eric assured her as he strolled out from behind the screens. "He'll be out in two shakes." He grinned. "Just don't ask me what he's shaking."

She and Eric had been working together this morning for a couple of hours, and yet Valerie still had to work not to stare. Although staring was at least a step up from the jaw-dropping gape she'd delivered when they'd met up at her place at the crack of dawn. But then, how could she have predicted such a major transformation would take place in under forty-eight hours?

Instead of the more typical Eric look of pleated Boss trousers, tan leather Shelleys, and a crisp Pierre Cardin button-down, he was wearing obscenely snug black D&G leather pants, along with a washed fuchsia Dsquared2 knit pullover that was bonded to his skin like, well, skin. His boyishly tousled mane was gone, clipped down to a close crop that hugged a beautifully shaped skull, except for a bit right in the front. The spiky-bang look lived. And worked. He'd gone from George Clooney to George Michael. During his really hot phase.

I want your sex, indeed, Valerie caught herself thinking.

Jenn's face popped into view just then, around the side of one screen.

"Please tell me you're done," Valerie pleaded. Three cups of coffee might not have been the best idea. Her nerves were humming along a live wire and she couldn't shake the feeling that the words LYING FRAUD were blinking over her head. In bright neon. She told herself she'd feel better once the shoot was under way. And better still if that could happen before Mercedes, Vivian, and Aurora showed up. As long as Jack was trapped in front of Nigel's lens, they could only admire him from afar. And the more afar, the better for Valerie.

"We're done," Jenn assured her. Even with her serious Tina Fey glasses on, she still looked like a twelve-year-old pretending to be a grown-up. "Okay, a little warning first."

Valerie's nerves twanged. "What?"

"Nothing bad, stop stressing, will ya? You know I would never let you down. He's perfect. What could go wrong?"

If only you knew, Valerie thought. But, of course, Jenn didn't know.

No one knew. Except Eric, Jack, and Valerie. Valerie and her big, stinkin' neon sign.

She and Jenn had been at *Vanity Fair* together. Jenn looked twelve, but she had the fashion sense of an industry elder. She'd been responsible for putting Hugh Grant in leather and metal mesh, shattering his casually suave Brit look for good. Shockingly, for the better. One of *VF*'s best-selling issues, landing Hugh his first action-adventure-hero leading role. Who would have guessed? Then it was Russell Crowe in Harris tweed, posed in an English day garden, and she was off to the races.

Jenn became synonymous with image-breaking covers. Photographers loved to work with her. Even Nigel. And while Valerie might be short on lifelong friends, she figured she made up for it with a list of industry contacts that would make most editors weep. So when she'd heard through her personal grapevine that Jenn was looking for a new challenge, Valerie had lobbied for her with Vivian, once a fashionista to the stars herself. A third feather and the completion of a to-die-for triumvirate.

At the moment, dying sounded like a less painful alternative to what she might be about to face. "We all know you like to tweak things," Valerie began, "and you're brilliant at it. But we both agreed yesterday during the fitting that you'd let me have my more traditional cover and then you could play with the file shots we want for upcoming features."

Frowning now, Jenn emerged completely from behind the screen. In baggy cargo pants and a tiny tee, she didn't look old enough to baby-sit. "You wanted me; you got me. All of me. Last-minute inspirations included." She held up her hand. "Don't pitch a fit until you see him."

"We've only got the space until three. Nigel's schedule is—you've worked with him before; I don't have to tell you. I thought we agreed on the fairy-tale thing. The tuxedo, the hair, the works. How hard—"

"Not hard. Boring." She lifted her hand again. "He's in the tux. But if he's every woman's fantasy, then we needed to go a step further than traditional fairy-tale, okay? *Glass Slipper's* target reader should expect more than the pedestrian." She stepped farther away from the screens. "Besides, he is too dee-lish not to play with. Val, I swear, if you take one look at him and your panties are still dry, I'll consider doing this your way. But I'll want a second opinion." She winked at Eric.

"Trust her," Eric said, and shot two thumbs up.

"Ready," Nigel called out.

Valerie waved to the pacing photographer, noting that the energy pulsing from the lanky Brit legend was almost palpable. Was it just the standard artistic preshoot vibe or excitement over meeting Prince Charming? Could she have underestimated the impact this unveiling would have on the international stage? That even the great Nigel Cole could be wound up like a three-year-old being introduced to Play-Doh for the first time?

Nigel was tapping his manicured hands on his loose-fitting Design-works trousers, craning his neck to try to get the first look of Jack when he finally came out. In his late forties, he had a flowing mane of dark hair that had silvered quite handsomely at the temples. His features were long and aquiline, his eyes a faded blue and somewhat hooded. Not exactly a hottie, but very appealing in his own enig-matic, tortured-artist kind of way. As she turned back to Jenn, she noticed Eric noticing Nigel as well.

Oh, great, that's all she needed. "This better be good."

Jenn just smiled and stepped back, then waved her hand with a flourish. "Women of the world—and men," she added, with a nod to Eric and Nigel, who'd edged closer. "I give you . . . Prince Charming."

What felt like an eternity passed—just long enough for the ten-sion inside her to climb to heart-stopping limits—then Jack finally stepped out from behind the screens.

"Damn," Valerie whispered. She would have glanced at Jenn—

who was no doubt beaming smugly—except she couldn't look away from the man standing in front of her. And neither would any other red-blooded female on the planet.

Jack was, indeed, wearing the traditionally cut Armani tux they'd chosen for him, but that was about the only thing remaining from the conventional Prince Charming look they'd decided on.

The suit was unrelieved black. The jacket had been perfectly fitted to his shoulders, and sported narrow black satin lapels. He wore a pearl-gray, starched linen shirt with flat, stitched pleats, open at the collar. Jenn had undone two buttons, just enough to enhance his tanned throat and rugged jaw. The matching pearl-gray satin bow tie was undone, draped around the open shirt collar and left to dangle, as if to showcase that little teasing view of manly chest hair.

Continuing the visual tour downward, the trousers were loosely fitted, with a thin satin stripe down the side. The cummerbund accentuated narrow hips and a flat belly, as it did the widening flare of his upper body. The cuffs shot from the edges of the jacket sleeves and were left unfolded and open over tanned, unadorned knuckles. His feet were also tanned. She noted this because they were also bare.

And who knew bare, relaxed feet peeking out from tux pants could be so damn sexy?

Jenn, apparently.

Valerie finally looked him in the eye for the first time, only to encounter a gaze that was both perturbed and amused, if such a thing were possible. And yet it was exactly that expression that pushed the entire ensemble beyond earthy and virile to palpably sexy.

His jaw bore a hint of morning-after stubble; his hair had been deliberately and artfully tousled, as if he'd just crawled from bed. And there wasn't a woman alive who wouldn't wish it was her bed he'd crawled from. Probably a number of men, too. She didn't dare look at Nigel. Man drool could be so unappealing.

Besides, she was still dialed in to those eyes. The pearl shirt and tie, set off by the black suit and tanned skin, made his gray eyes appear almost translucent. Even without proper lighting, it was as if they looked right through her.

A corner of his mouth kicked up in a sardonic grin. "Do I pass?"

And *pow!* The hint of a smile did it. Jesus. She turned to Jenn, not giving a damn how smug she was. She'd totally earned the right. "Brilliant."

She beamed. "That's why they pay me the big bucks." Jenn turned to Nigel, who was also assessing Jack quite frankly. Quite admiringly, too. "I've got more; I hope you don't mind." She scooted over to the staging area, motioning them to follow her. She scooped up a purple velvet and gold-tasseled pillow, along with the trademark full size glass slipper that the company always gave to its makeover guests upon arriving.

She handed them both to Jack. "I was thinking, instead of balancing the slipper on the pillow, or kneeling with it in your hand, as if asking the reader to let you slip it on her foot—though we definitely want those for interior shots to go with the article—" She broke off and shuffled Jack in front of the white drape backdrop where he was going to pose. She positioned him as if he were a mannequin—hips squared, shoulders just so, legs like this—heedless of the somewhat bemused look he was sending Valerie over her head.

Valerie just smiled at him, lifted her shoulder a little. Who knew, this might be more entertaining than she'd expected.

"Okay, now, hold this," Jenn instructed. She handed him the pillow. "Like this." She tucked it under one arm, so he held it in sort of a negligent manner. "Now, hold the slipper like this, by the heel." She moved his hand, positioned the slipper so it looked like he was holding a cup. "Now, we need the bottle of champagne." She turned, all boundless energy, and raced back to the dressing area, quickly emerging with a half-empty bottle.

Valerie sent a questioning look to Jack, who gave her a half-shrug, and smiled in return. Damn, but the man was sexy. Tux or no tux. Right now, no tux was definitely dominating her fantasies.

"Keep the pillow tucked, hold the bottle in the same hand," Jenn instructed. "The cover shot is you, drinking champagne from the slipper."

"Jenn—" Valerie started to interrupt. For God's sake, this wasn't *Playgirl* they were shooting.

But Jack, whose gaze had never left hers, obviously knew the direction she was going. His lips quirked a little and he continued to hold her gaze as he poured a little bubbly into the slipper. Gazes still locked, he sipped from the heel. "Like that?" he asked casually, blotting his wet lips with the jacket sleeve.

And with that, there wasn't a dry panty in the house.

Nigel startled her by running off a series of shots. She'd been so caught up in Jack's little seduction scene, she'd forgotten there was anyone else in the room.

"Perfect," Nigel said, then barked, "Music!" And suddenly Frankie Goes to Hollywood was beseeching them all to "Relax, Don't Do It." So obvious, and yet the beat pulsed and throbbed throughout the loft, in perfect counterpoint to Nigel's *clicking* and *whirring*.

"Yes, that's it," Nigel cajoled. "Keep the slipper full. Sip it, just sip it. Work your throat. Again. Fantastic! Now offer the slipper to her."

As if coming out of a trance himself, Jack finally shifted his gaze from Valerie to Nigel and his camera, suddenly tightening up.

"No, no!" Nigel shouted. "Look at *her*, lad; yes, that's it. Ignore me. Look at her, drink to her. Offer her the slipper. You want her to take it, you want her to drink from it, you want to pour it all over her— God, yes, yes! Well done. Don't stop." Nigel was almost orgasmic at that point.

Valerie could identify. She was unable to move as Jack came toward her. His smile was taunting, teasing, deliberately pulling her deeper into this charade they were mounting. Only it didn't feel like a charade, the way he was looking at her. So what if he was more Prince of Darkness than Knight in Shining Armor? Who the hell was going to care, if they saw what she was seeing right now?

The air was charged with a primal sort of energy that had her pulse humming to a beat that had nothing to do with the music. He was less than ten feet away when he stopped, poured more champagne into the slipper, then lifted it to his lips. He might as well have been right in front of her—the room shrank, the music swelled, her heart pounded. She forgot there was anyone in the room but him as she watched his throat work while he slowly sipped, never once taking his eyes from hers.

Lowering the slipper, he deliberately dragged his linen cuff across his damp lips. Her fingers twitched with the need to reach out and trace her fingers over those lips, feel the heat, the dampness.

Then he lifted the slipper to her. Frankie was exhorting her to "Relax, Don't Do It." Well, she wanted to do it, dammit. Right here, right now. Jack's mouth kicked up at the corner, his eyes twinkling devilishly, as if he were reading her mind. He took another step closer, already lifting the champagne bottle. Her feet were moving before she was even aware of it.

"Break. Reset. In five," Nigel barked, sounding exhausted.

Valerie jumped, then quickly stepped back. But not before catching Jack's wink as he swung around and strolled back to the staging area. Smug bastard, she thought, but damn if she still didn't want to follow him. And teach him to think twice before taunting her like that.

"Damn, I'm good." Jenn folded her arms in satisfaction. "And damn, he's hot." She nudged Valerie in the side with her elbow. "You're going to sell more copies of this magazine than you can print."

Valerie swallowed against a dry throat. It was the only thing left dry. "That we will," she croaked. "Christ, Jenn."

"I know," Jenn said, laughing even as she fanned herself. "Prince Charming, for sure. Look, even Stanley wants to jump him."

"Can't say I blame him," Valerie murmured as Jack handed the empty bottle to Nigel's all-but-drooling assistant.

"If I'd had any clue when I was reading his latest book that this is what he looked like . . ." Jenn trailed off and patted her hand over her heart. "I'm going to reread them all now. Hard to believe a man who looks like that can also be so cognizant of what women want."

Valerie finally tore her gaze away. "He does give good advice," she managed, neon sign blinking to life again.

"He gives good everything from the looks of it. He's the same in person as he is in his columns. Funny, witty, charming. And even more impressive, logical, rational, confident. Honestly, I didn't think a man like that really existed. And to think I almost bought into that theory that they were really written by a woman." She looked back over at Jack. "But he really exists. He really knows who he is as a man and he's not afraid to let it show." She sighed. "And I get to dress him." She looked up at Valerie. "And undress him. I should waive my fee for this." She primped her hair. "But I won't." With a little wave, she headed back toward the screens to get the next round of clothes ready.

Stanley had located another bottle of champagne. At this rate, they'd all be looped by the end of the shoot, though Valerie wasn't too sure that might not be preferable.

As Nigel posed Jack on bended knee with pillow and slipper, Eric strolled over to her. "He's doing really well, don't you think?"

"Yes," she said. "That he certainly is."

Eric smiled. "You sound surprised. I told you this would work."

"We're not out of the woods yet. This is just the first step. A baby step. He hasn't had to deal with—"

As if on cue, the godmothers waltzed, sashayed, and stormed into the loft.

"So sorry we're late!" Aurora, the waltzer, said breathlessly. "I don't know what the driver thought he was doing, taking Democracy."

"Following your directions, perhaps?" came Vivian's—the sashayer's—sardonic reply. "Helloo, darlings! Where's our cover hunk?"

"For God's sake, Vivi, can't you wait for proper introductions?" Mercedes stalked into the room, every bit the Bea Arthur of their *Golden Girls* ensemble. "Where's Valerie?"

"Over here." Valerie waved. "Brace yourself," she said to Eric out of the corner of her mouth. "Now the real fun begins."

Despite being the only one of the trio in rapier-heeled shoes, Vivian was the first to cross the airy loft space, dodging lights and stepping over cables with the finesse of a Vegas showgirl.

Valerie wouldn't be in the least surprised to discover Vivian had high-kicked on the Strip at some point in her colorful past. Lord knows, she still had the wardrobe for it. And the legs. Even if they were short. The rest of her, however, was built more like a fireplug than a showgirl, and even in spike heels, Vivian was the shortest of the three. It didn't matter. Her flamboyance made her larger than life.

A once-famous dresser and stylist to the stars in Hollywood, she still enjoyed the theatrics of an entrance made in a well-coordinated ensemble. Today, in honor of her new cover model, her flame-red hair had been teased up and sprayed. Heavy eyeliner and seriously arched brows enhanced the airbrushed blush and perfectly lined lips. Her skirt was short and made of supple soft black leather. Red heels were strapped around her ankles, matching the blouson-sleeved red-and-black slashed top that was laced, corset-style, around the middle.

While this did nothing to enhance her thick waist, it did perform a gravity-defying feat for her breasts. Which she'd be the first to tell you she had lifted and plumped every five years. Valerie liked to think that at some point she would stop being surprised by Vivian's outfits. She doubted her career with *Glass Slipper* would last that long.

"My, my, my," Vivian said, openly admiring Eric. Or, more to the point, Eric's leather pants. And how he filled them. She winked at Valerie. "I can see why you kept him under wraps, darling." She turned back to Eric. "However, I can't for the life of me figure out why you've kept your light under a bushel for so long."

Eric grinned and Vivian feigned a light swoon. "Darling boy," she said, hand fluttering to his arm, "be careful where you aim that thing."

Eric chuckled and Valerie stepped purposefully between them. "Vivian, there's something you need to know. All of you," she said, getting Aurora's attention as well. "This *is* Eric Jermaine, but he's actually Prince Charming's manager." At their confused looks, she hurried forward with her planned speech. "I know this comes as a surprise to us all, but he's also his legal representative, so everything is in order. We all know how carefully the real Prince Charming guards his privacy. He simply wanted to make sure that nothing happened to blow his cover—and your magazine launch—until it was absolutely necessary." She turned to Eric. "This is Vivian dePalma."

Eric extended his hand. "Ms. dePalma, it's been my pleasure to work with you. A greater pleasure to finally meet."

"Well, darling, it's been a pleasure listening to that voice during our conference calls." Vivian shivered a little as she took his hand. "You know," she went on, giving him another considering once-over. "We're still looking for models for future issues. Have you done any work in front of a camera?" She smiled a bit wickedly. "That you're willing to talk about, that is?"

Eric laughed, still holding Vivian's hand pressed between both of his. "I'm sorry to report I haven't done anything like that. Professionally or personally," he added with a wink of his own.

Vivian moved in closer and slid Eric's arm through hers. "Well, we could certainly change all that."

"Oh, for heaven's sake, Vivi, let the poor boy breathe." Aurora joined them, chiffon billowing, her voice warm and breathless, with that hint of Southern gentility that belied her Charleston roots. She extended both heavily jeweled hands. "Such a pleasure to finally meet you," she said, all smiles and fluttery lashes. "I'm Aurora Favreaux. We've spoken privately on the phone." This last part was surely added for Vivian's benefit. The two enjoyed an endless game of one-upsmanship.

To the untrained and uninitiated, it would often appear that Vivian had Aurora outwitted—not to mention out-manned—but Valerie had been around the women long enough to know that Aurora was not to be underestimated.

Eric smoothly extricated himself from Vivian's clutches—a feat in and of itself—and took both of Aurora's hands in his own. "The pleasure is all mine, Ms. Favreaux. However, I'm sure you would all much rather meet the real man of the hour."

"Honey, I don't ever mistake a real man."

Mercedes joined them, a flute of champagne already in hand. She gave Eric the once-over, offered him a dim smile, then turned to Valerie, clearly less than happy with her new investment. "I thought we'd agreed on a more . . . traditional look for the cover."

Eric extended his hand. "You must be Ms. Browning. I'm Eric Jermaine, but I'm not your Prince Charming."

"Depends on who you ask," Vivian murmured, quickly sipping her own flute of champagne.

Mercedes arched one sculpted silver brow. "I beg your pardon?"

"I'm the manager and legal rep for your newest employee."

Valerie once again became the target of Mercedes' displeasure. "What is going on here? Did we, or did we not, sign an agreement with this man?"

Valerie quickly explained, with Eric helping as well.

Mercedes' frown didn't budge. "Highly unusual," she said grudgingly when they were finished. "And I can't say I'm enthusiastic about this turn of events. But what's done is done. Time is of the essence here, so I suppose we should stop wasting it." She looked to Eric. "Not to offend, but we did agree that only essential personnel would be here at the shoot. Even Elaine has been kept out."

Jack came out from behind the screens just then. "Trust me, he's essential." He paused beside Eric, looking him down and up. "And a clothes thief. Ricky Martin called. He wants his pants back."

Eric grinned. "Only if I get to return them personally."

Valerie dipped her chin and sent up a silent, fervent prayer.

Vivian raised a questioning brow to Eric. "So, you're . . . ?"

"I'm afraid so," Eric said, feigning a brief pout.

Vivian lifted a shoulder. "Well, I suppose women shouldn't have all the fun."

"Speak for yourself," Aurora muttered.

Mercedes turned to Jack, obviously determined to ignore her lustier counterparts, smiled graciously, and extended her hand. "I'm Mercedes Browning. It's a pleasure to finally meet you."

To his credit, Jack didn't so much as glance at Valerie or Eric in a last-minute gut check. He smiled as smoothly as if he really were Prince Charming and took Mercedes' hand, then covered it with his other one. "Jack Lambert. Please accept my apologies for all the subterfuge. And the pleasure is all mine."

Vivian stepped in, sized up Jack, from his bare feet to his unbuttoned collar, then extended her hand. "I'm a firm believer in mutual pleasure."

Jack's smile spread to a grin as he took her hand. "Why bother otherwise, right?"

Vivian sighed, then winked at Valerie. "He was worth the wait."

Aurora stepped in and held out her hand, palm down. Only a

woman born and bred in the South could pull that maneuver off and make it look natural.

Valerie managed not to roll her eyes when Jack took the proffered hand and bent gallantly over it. They were eating this up. And so was he. Valerie should be thrilled. Everything was going beautifully.

But she would breathe a lot easier when this part was over. Jack might handle the part just fine on limited terms, but he had no idea who he was playing with here. These three were sharper than a den of foxes. Valerie had to limit their time together, never leaving him unsupervised. And pray none of them ever saw the state of his bedroom closet.

Thankfully Nigel clapped just then. "Waiting, waiting!"

Jenn came out, smiled and nodded at the godmothers, and whisked Jack back behind the screens to work her magic.

Eric followed him. "Ladies," he said, sketching a little bow before disappearing behind the screen.

Vivian and Aurora gave a collective sigh and sipped their champagne. "Personally, I don't care if he's gay," Aurora whispered. "He's quite yummy to look at."

"Downright delicious," Vivian agreed.

Mercedes ignored them both and turned a concerned look to Valerie. "We only have Nigel's services for a limited time. Is there a reason you haven't started yet?"

"Oh, but we have," Valerie assured her. "And wait until you see the proof sheets. We'll have so many good ones, it'll be a tough call on which one you'll want to use, trust me."

"But he wasn't wearing any shoes. And his tie was undone. His hair was quite unruly."

"Bed head," Vivian interjected approvingly.

Aurora nodded and sipped.

Mercedes sent them both a steely look, then to Valerie she said, "Surely you didn't have him pose like that."

Valerie laid a reassuring hand on her arm. "I know. I doubted it at first, too. But Jenn is an innovator, that's why we hired her. Trust her instincts. Once I saw him in front of the cameras, I knew we'd hit gold."

Mercedes frowned. "Be that as it may, I'll feel better when I see the proofs. This entire situation is quite unorthodox. Were you aware of their little stratagem?"

"I only just found out about it myself," she managed, then breathed a silent prayer of thanks when Mercedes' attention was diverted.

"What is he doing now?" She craned her neck a little, but didn't actually peek behind the screens.

"Remember I talked to you about shooting a portfolio, so we'd have the luxury of flexibility for future issues and promotional opportunities?" Valerie shifted the trio away from the dressing area, walking them closer to the small, food-laden table that had been set up off in one corner. "Jenn has several different looks she's selected, all based on the notes I gave her from our conversations. We'll get as many different looks and shots as we can. That way we also have the cachet of Nigel's credits in future issues as well." She bent her head closer to theirs. "Without having to pay his fee and leasing studio space."

Aurora beamed at her. "Always the smart one. Looking out for us, thinking ahead. And despite the little surprise this morning, we couldn't be more pleased." She turned to the other two. "Could we, dears?"

Valerie held her breath, but Mercedes and Vivian smiled and nodded in agreement.

Jack reemerged from behind the screens moments later.

"Denim?" Vivian said, looking doubtfully at Valerie. "And . . . plaid?"

They all started to converge on the staging area, but Valerie held

them back. "Trust Jenn. She's got great ideas. To contrast with the formal shots, you wanted something more relaxed."

"We said relaxed, not yard sale, darling," Aurora pointed out.

"He's hardly thrift shop, Aurora," Vivian scolded. "I still keep current. And if I'm not mistaken, those are Diesel—and quite a heavenly
fit, I must say—and that shirt is from Thierry Mugler's upcoming fall
line. However did you score that?" she asked Valerie.

"Talk to Jenn. She's the miracle worker this go-around." *Score two
for the Jenn-meister.*

The faded jeans hung just right on his hips, molded just enough
to his thighs. The soft, short-sleeved, green-and-white-plaid shirt
over a white T-shirt played well off his tan and brought out the
translucence in his eyes. He looked comfortable and approachable.

The staging had been changed to a pale oak window frame hung
over soft blue fabric, fronted by a potted palm. There was a padded,
dark green hassock positioned in front. Jenn was consulting with
Nigel on her ideas for posing Jack for this round of shots.

"Women want to see him as an attainable goal," Jenn was telling
him. "A guy they might actually meet on the street." She put wire-rim
glasses on Jack, who took them right back off again. There was a
short conversation, Nigel made a comment, and the glasses went back
on. An open book was laid across one knee, and Jack was instructed
to glance up at the camera, as if someone—a woman, obviously—
had called his name.

"I must say, I wouldn't mind meeting him on the street," Vivian
commented. "More champagne?" She topped off all three of their
glasses just as Nigel called Valerie over.

"We need . . . motivation," he instructed her. "He's flat."

When Valerie balked, Jack grinned at her. "Yeah," he called out.
"I'm flat. Come motivate me."

There was a quiet murmur from the godmothers and Valerie
wanted to strangle Jack for not just doing his job with as few ripples

as possible. She should have known he wouldn't handle easily. Nothing in her life seemed to come without ripples.

Sensing a problem brewing, Eric started to step forward, but Valerie waved him back. She shot the godmothers a lucky-me smile, to which Vivian winked and Aurora fanned herself. If Nigel wanted her on set, she'd be on set. There would be no scenes, nothing that would threaten to expose their carefully constructed charade. But just as soon as this shoot was over, she intended to hold a private meeting with Jack.

Judging from the palpable female reaction to Jack on set today, Valerie knew she would have to carefully select a handful of promotional opportunities they could exploit for the sake of generating good momentum after the first issue hit the stands.

And if Jack thought he was going have a little fun by playing games with her, he was about to learn otherwise.

Urges

We all have them. The problem is knowing when to act on them and when to channel that energy elsewhere. Men aren't always great at deciphering clues, so don't waste time being subtle. If the urge isn't mutual, hand us a basketball or a golf club and tell us to go play outside.

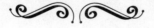

Chapter 7

'm being stood up?" Jack tucked his cell phone between his ear and shoulder and kept typing while he talked. "For a stock analyst?"

"Investment banker. Who is better-looking than you," Eric said. "More important, he puts out."

"Yeah, but would he wine and dine you with cold beer, deep dish pizza, and baseball on my big screen TV first?"

"It's not the size of his screen I'm worried about."

Jack thought he was handling this whole sexual-preference-revelation thing pretty damn well. But he was still working on the accompanying visuals. "And here I've always been told size doesn't matter."

Eric just laughed. "They were lying."

Jack shut that mental track down pronto. "Hey, I didn't say they were saying it to me."

"You forget, I've seen you naked."

Jack snorted. "Yeah, I recall that look of envy."

"Well, it sure as hell wasn't lust."

"I'm crushed," he said with mock grief. He learned early on that humor made for a great coping mechanism. Thank God for small favors, he thought. "Out of the closet two weeks and I've already been kicked to the curb." He sighed. "And you said nothing would change."

Eric chuckled. "I've been watching you get stomped on for years. It's about time you get to sit home and worry about me for a change. Besides, you're only alone by choice."

"And a damn fine choice it is, too."

"You know," Eric started, his tone turning serious, "it's been a couple of years now. Don't you think it's time—"

"For you to go primp for your date? Yes." When Eric didn't immediately shoot back a rejoinder, he sighed for real and said, "Listen, I'm fine. I've long since dealt with the whole divorce—"

"It's not Shelby you have to get over. I know you're past that. It's the fear of failing."

"Is this a performance-anxiety issue? Because if you need to talk about it—"

"Fine, fine, don't listen to me. The professional. All I'm saying is you seem to have closed yourself off too much. Life's too short."

That one hit home, and he knew Eric meant it to. They both knew all about lives not lived. "Hey, I'm out there having fun. I'm just not all that interested in anything serious or long-term."

"I'm not saying go out there and find someone to settle down with. I'm just saying to be more open to possibilities."

Jack frowned. "Is this some kind of fix-up? What, Bruce has a sister or something?"

"His name is Brice. And no, no sister. No hidden agenda here." Eric's tone turned sly. "Of course, I did happen to notice there was enough heat during that photo shoot to melt the polar ice cap, but did I say anything at the time? No, because I don't meddle."

Jack snorted again. "You're a born meddler. And that was called *acting*."

"It's called *denial*."

Jack hit SAVE and leaned back in his chair. "Are you seriously suggesting, that with everything else going on, you want me to even consider getting something going with Valerie?"

"I'm just telling you what I saw."

"Is this the same guy who always told me it's not wise to jump into anything—or on top of anyone—too quickly?"

"That was before I came out," he joked, "and realized just how long *I've* been in denial. Only I know exactly what I've been denying myself."

"I can't argue with you there." Now it was Jack's turn to be serious. "You might want to take a little of your own advice this evening, though. No point in rushing things."

"I've known Brice a long time. Wanted him even longer. I always thought we'd be great together, but I could never risk it. So I kept it casual. Now I don't have to anymore." Eric's tone went from dreamy to amused. "Don't worry, Dad, I'll practice safe sex."

"Slut," Jack shot back, glad Eric couldn't see the accompanying little shudder. He hung up with Eric's laughter ringing in his ears.

Brice, Bruce, whatever the hell his name was, didn't stand a chance, Jack thought as he finished writing his e-mail. At least he'd gotten off the phone before blurting out that Valerie was dropping by. His mind drifted to images of that photo shoot, as it had often done these past two weeks. Eric hadn't had to tell him about the heat. He knew all about the damn heat.

He attached the article he'd just written on Tomas Hernando, a dog handler who'd won Crufts flyball with a Springer spaniel named Tuffy's To 'n' Fro, to his e-mail and fired it off to an editor at *Euro-Sport*. He'd picked up some freelance work, doing human-interest stories on a smattering of athletes engaged in sports ranging from jai alai to pickle ball. It wasn't big money, but it was paying the bills until he could find something permanent that suited him.

He pointedly ignored the fact that there was a check for fifty thousand dollars lying on top of his microwave amidst a pile of bills. Eric had tossed it there on his last visit earlier this week, when Jack had repeatedly refused to discuss payment.

Heat notwithstanding, the photo shoot wouldn't hit any top-ten list he'd ever compile on how he liked to spend a free day. Playing dress-up wasn't his thing. Nor was being in front of a camera. He much preferred being the guy behind one and to the left, with a tape recorder in one hand and a notepad in the other. But if playing Fabio Lite helped Eric out of a jam, then it was a small price to pay. He just hoped they knew what the hell they were doing, slapping his mug on a magazine cover.

The old ladies of *Glass Slipper* seemed okay with it. But it was the other reaction he couldn't erase from his mind. Valerie had looked downright stunned when he'd come out barefoot in a tux. He'd felt silly with his hair all artfully mussed and his carefully clipped shadow beard. That was until he'd begun to tease her with that whole glass slipper come-on. Valerie took everything so damn seriously, it had been fun to rattle her composure a little. A bit too fun, if he was honest.

Thank God the godmothers had shown up when they did. He'd imagined them as a trio of society doyennes who'd long since become close personal friends with their cosmetic surgeon. Far from it, as it turned out. Although all three had been expertly coiffed and beautifully turned out, a more . . . unique threesome of super-successful CEOs he couldn't have imagined. Valerie hadn't been kidding about their business savvy, either. Especially Vivian dePalma. Although Mercedes Browning could scare the hell out of someone with that glare of hers.

Fortunately, Eric had fabricated an urgent meeting that required their immediate departure minutes after Nigel had taken his last shot. Jack hadn't missed the relieved expression on Valerie's face. He'd been more than willing to follow Eric's lead, especially since he hadn't ever gotten around to listening to the negotiation tapes, but it still irked him to know Valerie had so little faith in him.

She'd shown up on his doorstep a day later, and proceeded to lecture him about how important it was that he lay low, in case word leaked out from the shoot. She'd advised him to speak only directly to her or Eric if any questions or concerns arose. Oh, yes, and in his spare time, could he please please read over Eric's books. Just in case.

Just in case. Not his favorite phrase.

Her cell phone had rung incessantly and eventually she'd dashed off to put out some fire or other, leaving him somewhat bemused and, most annoying, even more aware of her sexually. Which made no sense, photo shoot or no photo shoot. She'd been all bound up in one of her business suits, her makeup understated and demure, her hair ruthlessly tamed, all combining to create what he was beginning to understand was the *Glass Slipper look*. There was absolutely nothing about her that should push any of his buttons. And yet there she was, pushing them at will. Blissfully unaware, thank you, God.

Since then, she'd called several times, wanting to get together so they could go over probable scenarios about the types of things that could occur once the magazine hit the stands. He'd put her off each time. He told himself it was because he was still irritated by her lack of trust in his ability to handle this, and because Valerie was not the kind of woman a guy gave even a toehold to when it came to invading his life. He didn't want her to get in the habit of striding in and taking over organizing his daily schedule, which he had no doubt she would do without even realizing it. But as the days went by . . . and more specifically the nights, he began to suspect he'd also put her off in the hopes that whatever was causing this more personal interest in her would die a natural death.

A knock on the door startled him from his thoughts. Which had, he noted, once again drifted to Valerie. He glanced at the clock on his computer. Seven-twenty-nine and thirty seconds. Right on time. "Gee, there's a shock."

Valerie had caught him earlier this afternoon when he'd been deep in writing his article and had absentmindedly answered the phone before checking caller ID. She hadn't bothered asking him to meet with her this time, but informed him that she'd be at his place at seven-thirty sharp, vowing to hunt him down and sic Gunther on him if he dared to stand her up. She'd hung up without waiting for a response. Which was just as well, as he'd been smiling at the time, amused as all hell by her threat and totally at a loss to understand why.

The buzzer rang again, and as he shut down his computer and got up to answer it, he realized he was looking forward to seeing her again. In a way that had nothing to do with business. And no matter what Eric and his heat theories wanted him to believe, "This is just business," he muttered. Besides, other than those few moments during the shoot, Valerie had given him absolutely no indication she was having the same concentration problems around him as he was about her.

Wishing now more than ever that Eric hadn't abandoned him to the wolves—or wolverine as the case may be—he resisted the urge to change T-shirts or check his hair in a mirror. Jesus, what the hell was wrong with him? Jack opened the door and was caught off guard for a second time that day.

Valerie followed his gaze down the length of her body, then back up, making a face when he finally made eye contact. "What, you've never seen a woman in jeans before?"

"No. It's just I've never seen you in anything other than those tailored little business suits you always wear."

His comment took her aback for a moment, but she quickly

rebounded. "I do have other clothes, you know. You don't think I sleep in my *tailored little business suits*, do you?"

Jack grinned. "Actually, I wasn't really sure." He stepped back and motioned the frowning publicist into his apartment.

It wasn't until she stepped past him that he noticed the briefcase.

"Shut up," she said, not bothering to look at him.

He feigned innocence. "Did I say anything?"

"You don't have to. Those eyes of yours speak volumes."

She'd noticed his eyes? was all he could think. Christ, this couldn't be healthy. Obviously he needed to get laid. Or something. Anything to get his mind off of where it wanted to go every time he got within three feet of Valerie Wagner. As long as it was with anyone *but* Valerie Wagner. Because that would be stupid wrong. In so many ways.

Wouldn't it?

He'd been serious earlier when he'd told Eric he was past the divorce issue, past Shelby. But he'd also been serious about not wanting to get involved with anyone right now. And okay, Eric might have hit a little close to home with the failure comment. No one liked to admit they'd failed at anything, and Jack was no exception. He could look back and know, in his head, that getting married had been an impulsive decision made by two people too jacked up on rum and each other to think clearly about the long-term consequences of their actions. But, clearheaded or no, when he thought about jumping back into the mix again, his heart still balked. He didn't have to know why. All he had to do was listen to the warning.

And Valerie was the last woman who would tempt him to believe otherwise. They were already involved in one serious situation. He wasn't about to compound that. Not even with sex. Though, damn, he'd bet it would be all kinds of hot.

She put the briefcase on the narrow bar that separated his kitchen from the rest of the room, which served as living room, dining room, and office. She popped the locks with an efficient *click*. "I might not be dressed for business, but this isn't a social call."

Knowing he'd flustered her, he wandered closer, despite just warning himself away from her. But he had to admit it was kind of fun, disrupting her somewhat prissy professional demeanor.

Her hair was still neatly pinned up and her face perfectly made up. Except for the clothes, it looked as if she'd come straight from her desk to his door. "Why the jeans? Was it Casual Tuesday at *Glass Slipper* today?"

She paused in the act of opening the briefcase, then momentarily closed her eyes. "I was coming here straight from work, but I didn't get a chance to stop by my place earlier, and I needed to let Gunther out."

"Let me guess, another flood?"

"No. Just another day with Gunther." She turned to face him. "Do you really want to talk about why I had to change my clothes? Or would you rather get down to business? I've been given the distinct impression over the past fourteen days that you're a very busy man."

He smiled. So testy. "Who was the one fielding calls every five minutes during our last conversation? At least I know when to turn the damn phone off and take a break." He moved a bit closer, leaned on the bar, and crossed his arms. "Do you?"

She shifted away, just slightly, but the movement was telling. He shouldn't have enjoyed it, shouldn't have let it provoke him. But what the hell, he was always doing stuff he shouldn't. Other than marrying Shelby, doing things he shouldn't had led to some of his best times.

"I know how to relax and have a good time. These aren't even my only pair of jeans," she said, all but challenging him to disbelieve her.

He glanced down. Her jeans were so blue he was surprised they didn't have a price tag still stapled to the back pocket. He had to stifle a smile when he noticed the knife-edge creases down the front. Who ironed denim? For that matter, who ironed? And instead of sneakers or casual sandals, she wore low-heeled leather shoes that could easily pass for office wear. "Do you own a single pair of shorts? A pair of sneakers?"

She waved a hand dismissively. "Why are we talking about this? What I do on my off time and what I wear while I do it isn't important."

"I don't know about that. I'm finding it fascinating."

She gave him a quelling look. "Trust me, it's not."

Enjoying himself more than was likely wise, Jack crossed his ankles and relaxed back against the bar. "What do you do for fun, Valerie? And I don't mean dinner dates or clubbing. I mean, like on a lazy Sunday afternoon? Or a hot summer night?"

There it was, that little spark of awareness. Is that what he'd been poking and prodding her for?

Now she folded her arms. Only she wasn't leaning on the table, she wasn't relaxing. Yet there was still a definite sexual edge to the tension arcing between them. "What are you insinuating?"

He lifted one shoulder in a negligent shrug, debating how far to push. "Nothing, nothing at all. If you're a workaholic, it's no business of mine. The godmothers are lucky to have someone so dedicated."

"I'd like to think so. Once the magazine comes out and things settle down a bit, I'll have the luxury of goofing off."

Insinuating, obviously, that he had all the time in the world to goof off. Jack just smiled.

"What?" she asked.

"You just say *goofing off* like it's some kind of dread disease."

"Maybe I haven't quite developed the knack of traipsing about the globe as you have."

Jack wasn't offended by the dig. Quite the opposite. He liked that she gave as good as she got. Promising, that. "I take my work very seriously. And I'm fortunate it allows me to travel. The difference is, I can put work in perspective, relative to its overall importance in life. I value what I do, it keeps a roof over my head, and I happen to really enjoy it, but it doesn't define my entire existence. Which means, while I'm serious about always doing my best, I know I can't take myself or what I do all that seriously."

"You're saying I take myself too seriously?"

"No. You've got a sense of humor about yourself, about life." He grinned. "Otherwise Gunther would have gone back to the pound a long time ago. But do you take your work too seriously? Maybe."

"Pretty judgmental, don't you think?"

"I'm just saying, in the scheme of things, I know that writing about the newest cricket star from Holland provides a few minutes of entertainment for my readers, and people enjoy reading about something they probably know nothing about. I also know I'm not exactly adding to the global cultural discussion. And that's okay. People need all sorts of enrichment. That's what allows me to have fun while I work. Work and play don't have to be so rigidly separate."

"How nice for you."

Jack laughed. "So, is it that you equate play while you work with questionable moral choices? Are you picturing me typing my stories from the beds of my interview subjects?" He thought about the story he had just filed. "Although I'm not exactly sure Tomas would have minded. Of course, he'd likely have wanted Tuffy involved."

"Tomas and Tuffy?"

Jack mock shuddered. "Don't ask."

A dry smile kicked at the corners of her mouth. "For once, I think I'll take your advice."

"It's a start."

She finally relented and relaxed just a little. "I wasn't questioning your ethics, you know. It's just that the magazine launch is this week. It's been a very intense, hectic schedule working to this point. A lot of people have invested a large part of the past six months preparing for this. I know we're not performing brain surgery here, but a lot of careers ride on the success of this launch. We've all had to keep our eye on the goal. I love my job as much as you do. And I've waited a long time to feel this way. Which is precisely why I take it so seriously. I want to keep it."

She resolutely turned back to the briefcase and opened it. "Which is why I'm here. You saved a lot of those very same people's hides by helping us out. Certainly mine. Don't think I don't appreciate that, or that I've forgotten. This just came in this afternoon and I wanted you to be one of the first to see it." She pulled out a manila envelope and turned to face him, smiling wryly as she presented it to him. "I thought it would be *fun* to do it in person."

He laughed as he took the envelope. "Touché. What is it?" He was already opening the clasp.

"Well, we've had the whole issue together for a while. We kept the cover shoot until last so we could keep it under wraps until the last second." She took a deep breath. "But here it is. Congratulations, Prince Charming," she said, as the very first issue of *Glass Slipper* magazine slid out into his hands.

Jack's mouth opened, but no words came out. *Holy shit* was all he could think. *Holy crapping shit.* He was looking at himself. Only that wasn't him. That was some other guy staring back at him with his carefully mussed hair and perfectly fitted tux. That wasn't him offering up a champagne-filled glass slipper, with a look in his eyes that could only be described as . . . predatory. *Jesus.*

In the moment that Nigel had snapped that shot, Jack had been intent on one thing. Rattling Valerie's composure. Hell, okay, seducing Valerie. But he'd been playing around.

The man staring back at him was not playing around.

And now that blink in time, a moment he'd thought about over and over . . . had been captured and displayed for all the world to see. He wasn't sure how he felt about that. Which led him to wonder what

Valerie had thought when she'd seen this shot. She knew exactly who he'd been offering that slipper to.

Valerie edged in so she could look at it with him. "What do you think?" she asked, glancing up at his face. It was the sound of a barely stifled laugh that brought him out of the moment, at least temporarily.

He looked up, realizing she was standing very close. "What's funny?" Did she think he looked as ridiculous as he thought he did?

"You. Speechless."

"How do you know I'm not rendered speechless on a regular basis?"

"Let's just call it an educated guess."

He continued to stare into her eyes, which were dancing a bit at the moment. He told himself it was simply a preferable alternative to looking back at the magazine cover. But maybe it was more than that. Other than those brief moments in her bathroom, she'd never been this close to him. But he'd imagined her this close . . . and closer.

He held her gaze, watched as the light there took on a different edge. Awareness sprang back between them, sharper than before. Damn Eric and his *possibilities*, anyway. "Are you ever?"

"Ever what?" she asked, and there was the barest hint of breathlessness in her voice.

His body tightened in response. "Rendered speechless."

"Not often." Her pupils slowly expanded.

Don't do it, don't do it, don't do it, his little voice screamed. *Things are already complicated enough.* But his hand was already moving. She, however, was not. Not when he cupped the back of her neck, not when he began closing the distance between her mouth and his, not when he gently bit her bottom lip before saying, "Let's see if we can change that."

She tasted like Pep-O-Mint Lifesavers. For the rest of his life, he'd remember that flavor as being the taste of Valerie.

She didn't return his kiss, or even encourage him. Nor did she move away. She let him sample her mouth, explore what it felt like to have his lips on hers.

The kiss was more sweet than hot. And not just because she'd been crunching candy. It wasn't like him, this gentle exploration. Downright shocking when you considered all the things he'd been fantasizing about doing with her, to her, over the past couple of weeks. And yet, perhaps it was just as well he'd jumped in the low end of the pool. As it was, this one soft kiss was about to blow the top of his head clean off.

Which was as good a reason as any to end this right now. Only, when he left her delectable mouth, he couldn't seem to leave her entirely. He was dropping a few kisses along her jaw when she finally put a stop to it, to him, and shifted away.

They'd made no other contact, except for their mouths, his hand on the nape of her neck. And he had to curl his fingers into his palms to keep from reaching for her when she stepped back.

"That probably wasn't a great idea," she said, trying for casual. But he heard that thready edge of need. Of want.

It provoked him, when he knew better. But what the hell. It felt good knowing he hadn't been the only one affected there. Of course, with her schedule, she probably hadn't gotten any lately, either. Which explained things. They were two people with pent-up sexual frustration, looking for a convenient outlet, that was all. Somehow that wasn't as reassuring a rationale as he'd hoped it would be.

"I don't know," he said, circling back close to the edge. Why not? He liked it there. Made life much more interesting. "I was thinking it was one of my better ones."

She held his gaze for a long moment, but when he finally gave in and took a step toward her, she abruptly turned her back on him and closed her briefcase with a sharp *snap*. The *click* of the lock was like an audible punctuation mark, ending the sentence that had been their kiss. He wondered if she'd ended it with a period . . . or an exclamation point.

There was one way to find out. He tossed the magazine on the counter and stepped closer, reaching for that trim waist of hers when she snagged her briefcase and moved around the table. "Valerie—"

She turned then, keeping the briefcase between them like a shield. "Jack, the kiss was very nice. But I—I can't play while I work. And I definitely don't play with my work. You're business. Trying to mix it with pleasure would be a mistake."

"*Nice?* It was just *nice?*"

She let out a surprised little laugh. "That's all you have to say? What it is with men and performance issues, anyway?"

"I mean, I know it wasn't a bend-you-over-the-table kind of kiss, but come on." A period. She thought it had been a period-ending sentence. For him, gentle or not, that kiss deserved at least one exclamation point. And, dammit, he knew she'd felt that, too.

She smiled and shook her head, then headed to the door. "We hit the stands Friday morning. Thursday night we're having a launch party at Bentari's. You're not—or, Eric isn't contractually obligated to be there, but he had already verbally agreed to the godmothers' request that he at least make a brief appearance. I'm hoping you'll honor his commitment."

"How big a bash is this?"

"Black-tie big." She smiled then. "Don't worry, we'll get Jenn to get that tux back."

"I'm not worried about the tux. Why didn't you tell me about this sooner?"

She paused at the door. "I believe I've tried. Have you read Eric's books?"

"Sure," he said. Skimming was the same as reading, right? "Why?"

"The party starts at eight. Why don't we meet for dinner at my place, say, six-thirty."

He was still trying to process the idea of pretending to be that guy on the cover . . . in public. Up close and personal, like. With other people. Lots of other people. "Dinner?" he repeated blankly.

"Yes. We need time to go over everything, work out a plan. I've already made a list of notes."

"I'll bet you have," he muttered, earning him a frown. But he was too busy having a silent panic attack. "Will Eric be there? I mean, can we get him in as a guest or something?"

"Already taken care of."

"And he knows about all this? Why didn't he say something to me? Never mind," he said, waving his hand. Eric had been busy embracing his newfound freedom—and God knows who or what else—with a vengeance.

Jack tamped down the nerves. After all, hadn't he been all wound up about Valerie not trusting that he could handle this? *Well, pal, now's your chance to show her.* "Sure," he said, pasting what he hoped was a carefree smile on his face. "Six-thirty, Thursday. No problem."

Her smile was far too knowing. "You need me to arrange the tux?"

"No. I can take care of the tux."

"Just make sure you do it tonight or tomorrow. Come Thursday, you aren't allowed to step foot outside this apartment until dinner. I'm sending a car, so don't worry about that. Don't answer the phone unless it's me or Eric, and definitely don't answer the door."

"Why are you saying this?" He didn't even bother to try to quell the panic in his voice now.

"Do you have any idea what's about to happen?"

"Given that look on your face, I'm not sure I want to. You're really enjoying this, aren't you? What have I ever done to you? Not ten minutes ago you were thankful that I'd stepped up to the plate."

"I still am. And I apologize. Again. I don't know why provoking you seems such a natural thing for me to do. But I get the feeling that you're used to being the guy in charge. I can't help it, I'm human. And a woman. We love seeing the take-charge types squirm." She opened the door, then rattled the knob. "Lock this. Call me if you need anything."

And she was gone.

Jack sank onto one of the barstools, averting his gaze from the magazine, from his own face staring back up at him. There was something totally unnatural about that. Nobody should have to look at himself like that.

So. What was he going to do about that kiss? Much better to think about that than about what he was going to face forty-eight hours from now. Valerie wanted to pretend it hadn't happened. He should want the same thing. He should be focusing on the party, the magazine coming out, and not getting Valerie naked.

There it was again. *Should.* He'd never been good with that word.

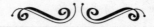

Risqué business

Business is never just business to a guy, especially if the person with whom he's doing business is a woman. Most men will be hard-pressed to pass up an opportunity to combine business with pleasure. And it's important to remember that a guy can find an opportunity for pleasure in almost any business situation.

Chapter 8

"Yes, he'll be there, Aurora. I promise." Valerie paced the length of her living room, looking out her front window, wondering where in the hell the limo was. It was already after six-thirty. The egg rolls she'd thawed and heated, then reheated, were getting a bit crispy. And Gunther was head-butting the bathroom door.

"Wonderful, dear," Aurora was saying. "I know I've said it before, but you've really helped us bring this launch off with a bang. Having Jack there will top it all off."

"That it will," Valerie agreed. *If he ever gets here.* She hadn't spoken to Jack since her visit to his place on Tuesday. Not that she hadn't tried. He wasn't picking up on his house line or his cell.

Which meant he didn't yet know about the powerhouse media blitz she'd lined up to cover tonight's event. She'd had no choice. Print and television coverage, all anxious to be the first to get access to Jack, had been hounding her nonstop since the party invites had been sent out. The godmothers were in a tizzy of excitement. All Jack had to do was step out of the limo and *Glass Slipper* magazine was guaranteed local, national, even international coverage. Even she'd been amazed at the level of clamor to which his unveiling had risen. It made her job easy. Or would have if she'd had a cooperative star.

And if they weren't lying to millions of people.

She shut that mental track down. Again. Right now she had to focus on preparing him to face the gauntlet. She was torn over just how much she should tell him. Too much information might spook him. Although, from what she'd seen so far, the man didn't rattle easily.

Still, she was relieved that Eric would be attending tonight. Just in case Jack needed additional propping up. Eric was going to coordinate his arrival with theirs, and stick by Jack's side throughout his stay. Which, she'd already determined, was going to be brief. Just long enough to make sure he showed up in Lloyd Grove's Style section column in the *Washington Post*, and that *Access Hollywood* got their promised five minutes. Everyone else was on their own. Wall-sized blowups of the cover had been placed judiciously throughout the event. Any enterprising reporter could simply stand in front of one and file his or her report.

Women all over America could switch on their evening news and get a glimpse of Jack holding up that glass slipper, offering it to them as if they were the only woman in the world, the look on his face telling them, "Not only will the slipper fit, but so will I." A look she knew very well, as it was permanently etched on her psyche.

She struggled to get her mind back on whatever Aurora was saying. This was why she should have never let him kiss her. She was in the home stretch. She needed crystal-clear thinking. One second around Jack and she was hopelessly muddled.

"Did you tell him how difficult it was for us to choose the best shot for the cover?" Aurora was saying. "A veritable embarrassment of riches. We certainly got our money's worth from using both Jenn's and Mr. Cole's services. I must say, I was a bit skeptical about that, but you really knew what you were doing there."

"I'm just glad it all went smoothly." She crossed her fingers, praying their luck would hold out a little bit longer.

"Elaine can't say enough good things about you, you know."

"Thank you," she said, feeling guiltier by the moment. Dammit, why couldn't Eric have been gay some other time?

"You know how skeptical we were about this new endeavor, but you've certainly delivered on your promises and then some. You've gone the extra mile and we want you to know we've noticed."

"I'm just doing what needs to be done. It's a pleasure." Up until three weeks ago, she'd never meant anything more.

"Yes, dear. We feel the same. Mercy and I talked after the cover proofs came in. Once we get past all the rigmarole with this party and the magazine hits the stands, we'd like to sit down and talk with you. About your future with *Glass Slipper*."

Her gut knotted. It was clear from the excitement in Aurora's voice that there was some plan afoot. She swallowed past a similar knot in her throat. "Wonderful."

"We've got big plans for you, dear," Aurora went on to say, confirming either her worst fears or her best expectations. She could no longer judge. "Now I've got to dash. It takes me a bit longer to put my party face on these days."

"You'll knock them dead," Valerie assured her, this time quite sincerely. Aurora drew people to her like moths to a flame. She had a generous spirit and a kind heart. A godmother, indeed. Which only served to deepen Valerie's sense of guilt. In addition to respecting her bosses, she truly liked each one of them. Even Mercedes had grown on her. She told herself that what she and Eric and Jack were doing was for everyone's benefit. Aurora, Vivian, and Mercedes more than anyone. But that was of little comfort.

"I'll see you in a few hours," Aurora exclaimed. "After all our hard work, this is going to be such fun!"

Valerie hung up, then pressed a fist to her gut. "Fun. Everyone is so damned hung up on having fun." This much stress couldn't be good for a person. "Well, I'm not having fun yet." She peered out the front window again, the drizzle pattering the street, matching her mood. She debated pouring another small glass of wine. She'd already had one. And there would be more than a couple champagne toasts made tonight. She hadn't eaten anything since breakfast. Too nervous. Probably more wine would not be a good idea. After one more peek at the empty curb, she managed to refrain from checking her reflection for the umpteenth time in the glass-front china cupboard and walked back to the kitchen to check on dinner. Such as it was.

She was wearing the black Chanel. Her hair had been ruthlessly gelled and spritzed into a classic Audrey Hepburn French twist, her makeup kept to a basic but flattering minimum. Her only nod to the momentous occasion was the simple strand of matched white pearls at her throat, topped by the pair fastened to her earlobes. Passed down from her grandmother, they were her best pieces. All in all, her look was one of understated elegance. And, most important, not flashy in any way.

She intended to stay out of the limelight tonight, hovering instead on the fringes of the glare that would be focused on Jack.

She slid the tray of very brown egg rolls out of the oven and onto the counter, checked on the lo mein noodles and sesame chicken she'd dumped from cartons into her own bowls and kept warm in the microwave, all the while stepping back and forth over Gunther, who'd given up on gaining access to the bathtub and had decided to play floor rug instead.

Where in the hell was Jack?

She was filling her wineglass for the third time, peering out the front window, when a short knock came on the kitchen door and Jack strolled in without further warning.

She squealed, white wine sloshing as Gunther reared up off the floor with uncustomary swiftness. "Don't let him out!" she shouted, as the juggled wine cascaded over the rim of her glass and down the front of her black dress.

Too late, Jack lunged for the door, but was flattened against the opposite wall by one hundred and fifty pounds of very intent dog. "Jesus," he yelped, pulling up one knee with a hiss when Gunther's tail thwacked him right in the crotch on his way through the screen door and down the back steps.

"No!" Valerie swore, dumped the glass in the sink, and grabbed a towel. "What in the hell do you think you're doing?" she demanded as she turned on Jack, looking out the door in time to watch helplessly as Gunther trotted happily through every mud puddle in the backyard. "This isn't happening to me."

"You need a sign on that door," Jack managed as he gingerly moved past her into the kitchen. "Maybe one for that tail of his. It's lethal."

Valerie saw her carefully planned evening evaporate right in front of her eyes. "I took him out before I got dressed, specifically so he wouldn't have to go out again until I got home tonight."

Jack moved beside her, wincing as he looked out the back door in time to see Gunther rub against one of the pine trees, making the whole thing shudder and send water cascading off the needles and onto his back. "He seems quite happy. Can't you just leave him out there?"

"It's raining."

"He's a dog. He'll be fine. Doesn't he have a doghouse or something?"

She looked away. "Yeah. I spent a fortune on it."

"Where is it?" He looked outside. "Don't tell me he's afraid of that, too."

She turned and walked back over to the sink. "He ate it."

Jack managed to stifle his little burst of laughter when she shot a deadly glare his way.

"And I can't leave him out there. He can get out."

"He jumps the fence?" Jack asked, sending a dubious glance Gunther's way. "He didn't seem all that . . . athletic to me."

"No, Gunther doesn't jump. He, uh, he opens the gate."

Jack's eyes widened in surprise. "Another little trick you didn't mean to teach him?"

She raised her hands. "I take no responsibility for this one. He became an escape artist back in his pound-puppy days. All I have to do is put an extra latch on the outside of the gate, but—"

"You've been too busy." He ignored her glare. "Interesting pet choice. Were there no other dogs at the pound that day?"

No way was she telling him what a sucker she'd been. "My father decided I needed a guard dog when I moved out on my own. Gunther was the biggest dog they had." That much was true.

Jack looked at Gunther, who had belly-crawled in the mud beneath the wooden chaise and was now lying quite contentedly with his chin resting on his paws. "Size is important. Or so I've recently been told. I don't guess anyone willingly comes into the yard or the house." He didn't have to comment on the fact that size was the beginning and end of Gunther's guarding skills.

Valerie sighed, then swore when she looked down at the front of her dress. A wet splatter stain covered most of the bodice and a good part of the midriff of her dress.

Jack closed the back door and turned to her. "I don't guess that's going to dry without leaving a mark."

She didn't even look at him. "No, I don't guess it will." Motioning to the dishes on the counter, she said, "Why don't you go ahead and move those to the dining room table while I figure out what I'm going to change into. There's a tray for the egg rolls next to the stove." She didn't wait for a response, but turned to leave.

Jack's hand closed on her arm just as she stepped out of the kitchen, stopping her. "Valerie, I'm sorry."

She turned, finally looking at him for the first time. Damn. Just when she'd finally convinced herself that it had been Nigel's magic that had turned Jack into the man currently gracing the cover of *Glass Slipper*. Even without the artfully mussed hair, or the five o'clock shadow, the man packed a definite punch.

Noticing her once-over, he dropped his hand and stepped back, holding his arms out to the sides and looking down at himself, then back at her. "Something wrong?"

It was the sincere concern in his voice that kept her from saying something snarky in order to put distance back between them. Which was the precise moment she realized that was exactly why he provoked that kind of response from her in the first place. But he looked honestly worried, and somehow that charmed the snark right out of her.

He was wearing a pale gray tux, white shirt, white silk tie and cummerbund. It played well against his tanned skin, made him look swarthy while at the same time making his gray eyes glitter. "No. Not a thing," she said honestly, damning the slight huskiness to her voice. Only then realizing her mistake as that gleam came instantly back into those clear depths. A gleam she remembered all too well. She backed up.

"I have to say, though, I liked it better when I could go barefoot." His smile faded and he took a step toward her. "I really am sorry about the dress. I'll be happy to have it cleaned for you."

"Why didn't you come in the front? I specifically told the driver—"

He snorted. "Yeah, well, we need to talk about the whole driver thing. Why don't you go change first, okay?"

"What about the *driver thing*?" She'd been so flustered by Gunther's escape that she hadn't noticed anything else. She peered out the window. "Didn't he pick you up? Is that why you're late?"

Jack took her shoulders and turned her toward the stairs. "Go change. I'll set up the table. We'll talk while we eat."

She moved quickly out of his reach, telling herself it was to thwart his controlling maneuver, not because his touch made her shiver. Dammit. But that didn't explain why she scooted up to her bedroom and closed the door instead of standing her ground and taking control of the situation. This was her place, her meeting. He worked for her, essentially. Yet she couldn't close the door fast enough. Just not before catching his amused smile at the base of the stairs. She flicked the lock with an irritated scowl. "Prince Charming, my ass," she muttered.

Valerie started peeling out of her dress as she walked to her closet. She already knew what her choices were. There were two, both handpicked and delivered by Jenn yesterday. She wasn't thrilled with either of them. Not because they weren't perfect for her. Jenn was brilliant. Maybe because they were a bit too perfect for her. One was a red silk cheongsam with a modest neckline and cut to fit her body like she'd been the dressmaker's dummy they'd used to style it on. The other was a stunning shade of aqua, soft and flowing where the red dress was formfitting. The aqua, however, had a plunging neckline, front and back. She wasn't the kind of woman who turned heads, but wearing either of these would make it that much harder to fade into the background.

She glanced at her bedroom door, helpless against envisioning Jack's reaction to either of these dresses. Her black Chanel was cool and modest, and she'd still felt the heat of his gaze on her as she'd crossed the living room. Looking back at the two dresses, she reached for the red one. Her French twist would work best with it. She'd stick in the black lacquer chopsticks Jenn had brought with her, and switch the white pearl earrings for the black ones, also from Jenn's arsenal. Thankfully, the black sandals went with both.

It took her less than ten minutes to change and make the necessary accessory adjustments. She briefly debated the red lipstick, but vetoed it. One look in the mirror had been enough to tell her she was already courting disaster. "If I have to reveal the fact that I have no curves, at least I'm keeping the little I do have all covered."

And this way she didn't have to worry about flashing her boobs or butt crack to the world every time she turned around or bent over. Not that there was all that much to flash, but when she did, she preferred to flash what little she had in private. With a deep breath, she pasted on her business smile and went back downstairs. Only to discover it empty.

"Jack?" The food was already on the table. She turned back to the hallway, cocked her head, but didn't hear anyone in the guest bathroom. "Jack?" she called out again, just in case. No response. Frowning, she went to the kitchen, only to find it empty, too. "Where in the hell did he go?"

Then she noticed his jacket, shirt, and cummerbund hanging on the dining room chair, with his shoes and socks kicked beneath it. Her mouth dropped open. He was cocky, even a bit arrogant, but this? She whipped her gaze back to the living room, then the closed bathroom door, temper already flaring. If he thought he was going to get her into bed because of one kiss and a few searing looks, well, he was about to learn that—

Her silent tirade was cut abruptly short when a commotion drew her gaze to the back door. Her hand flew to her mouth, although she wasn't sure if it was to stifle a horrified gasp, or a burst of laughter. "What in the hell does he think he's doing?" she murmured through her fingers. Although the answer to that was painfully obvious.

Bare-chested and barefooted, with his tux pants rolled up to his knees, and a towel tucked into the front to catch mud splatter, Jack was wading across the soggy backyard, hose in one hand, chewed-up Frisbee in the other, heading directly for Gunther. Who was busy doing his damnedest to scramble out from his tightly squeezed spot beneath the chaise before Jack could get to him with the dreaded water.

She watched in openmouthed shock as Jack commanded Gunther to come—and the beast listened! He held the hose so the dog could take a gulp, then stuffed the Frisbee into Gunther's mouth and led him to the back porch by the collar. Of course, Gunther could have put a stop to the charade that Jack was capable of leading him anywhere if he decided otherwise, but he lumbered along as if it was his idea all along.

"Probably thirsty," she muttered, remembering his head-butting the bathroom door. At least, she wanted to believe that was the reason. The alternative was too galling.

Jack stopped at the foot of the steps and hosed off Gunther's feet—the dog happily gumming the Frisbee, as content as if he was getting the world's best belly scratch and not a dreaded rinsing-off. She tensed when he moved the hose to Gunther's muck-covered belly, but after a good snout rub and solid head pat from Jack, the dog stood as if he'd been trained to do so since birth. Valerie knew quite well just how bogus that was. If she wasn't so amazed by the little demonstration, not to mention thrilled to be rid of the chore herself, she might have been the teensiest bit upset by the whole thing. Okay, more than a teensy bit. Was there no living, breathing creature Jack couldn't manage to seduce?

"He's not Prince Charming," she muttered. "He's the freaking Pied Piper."

Jack let Gunther have one last long drag off the hose before shutting it off. Then he grabbed one of the beach towels Valerie now saw he'd stacked on the stairs. Her hand flew to the doorknob. Gunther equated beach towel with tug-of-war. And no one beat Gunther at tug-of-war. At the last second, though, some demon inside her made her snatch her hand back. And smile. "Pied Piper, my ass," she said beneath her breath. "Let's see you go a round with him now."

Her smug smile slowly faded. She supposed it shouldn't have come as a surprise when Gunther allowed Jack to rub his massive body down, all but purring like an overgrown mutant kitten during the process. She tried to take comfort in the show Jack was unwittingly providing. It was hard not to admire the bunch and play of the muscles in his back and arms. She wasn't sure what he'd done to earn the physique, and decided maybe she didn't want to know. Somehow she doubted there were fully equipped gyms in the places he frequented. His tux pants were a bit loose in the waist without the cummerbund, and when he crouched down to rub Gunther's belly, Valerie followed the dip in the rear of that waistband unapologetically. Her eyes widened just slightly. No tan line. It was enough to make a girl drool.

Which, of course, is how he caught her when he shot her a grin over his shoulder.

Cocky bastard. Had he known she was standing there watching him the whole time?

Jack stood and held a towel up as a shield as Gunther indulged himself in a full body shake, then happily patted the dog on the head. Best buds and all that.

She opened the back door and let her very happy dog into the house, biting back the childish urge to stick her tongue out at both him and Jack, as Jack curled the hose up and gathered the towels. He'd made it all look so simple. She'd have looked like a drowned rat if she'd tried that. He'd hardly even gotten wet. Totally unfair. "You didn't have to do that," she told Jack. "You might have ruined your tux."

He smiled, unfazed by her lack of gratitude, as if he hadn't expected any. Which both stung and disconcerted her. "It's a rental."

"Still, the godmothers might have frowned on your showing up in tux jacket and jeans."

He pulled the towel off, rubbed at a few spots that had flecked the fabric. "I think they fared okay. Might need a bit of smoothing out." He looked back to her, towels in one hand, all perfect pecs and bulging biceps, sloppily rolled up pants, and a grin that was just too damn endearing. Of course he knew he was impossible to resist.

"I might need to borrow your bathroom to rinse off my feet."

It was churlish of her, especially considering what he'd just done for her, but she couldn't seem to help herself. Gunther might have rolled over for him, but she'd be damned if she would. She pointed to the hose. "You've got water and towels already."

He propped his fists on his hips, the amused gleam still in his eyes. "You have a real problem accepting help, don't you?"

"Not at all. However, I do have a real problem with people who assume they can step in and start calling the shots."

"Ah," he said, still unfazed. "Authority issues."

He was impossible. "The only issue I have is dinner and a rapidly dwindling time frame in which to prepare you for the media gauntlet you're going to face tonight."

His smile faltered the teensiest bit. "*Gauntlet?* What kind of *gauntlet?*"

"Rinse your feet off, come inside, and we'll discuss it over dinner." It was then she noticed the jet-black Mustang parked behind her little red MINI. "After that, you can explain to me why you drove yourself here instead of coming in the town car that is supposed to take us to the party."

She turned away from the door, then paused and looked back. "And thank you for taking care of Gunther." It wasn't much of an apology after her rudeness, or much in the way of gratitude, either. She knew that, but he merely nodded and began rinsing his feet.

Feeling more disconcerted than before, she fixed them both a glass of iced tea—no more wine—and waited at the table. She heard him come in, but wasn't prepared for the impact a half-naked Jack would have on her. Through the screen door, ten yards away, he'd been . . . inspiring. Standing in her dining room, he seemed overwhelming. He'd already unrolled his pants, which, surprisingly, didn't look too bad. She should have turned away, scanned her notes with an air of complete unconcern as he slid his shirt on and began buttoning it.

But she couldn't seem to stop watching him. His back was half to her, so he didn't know if she was watching or not. He didn't seem all that concerned one way or the other. Maybe he'd given up on any idea he'd had of seducing her. And, given that kiss the other day, she knew he'd at least thought about it. Well, she was pretty sure.

"So, what exactly do you have in store for me tonight?"

Valerie had just taken a sip of her tea, a vain attempt at cooling the direction of her thoughts, and almost choked. "What?"

He turned his back to her completely and unzipped.

Valerie's throat went dry.

"This *media gauntlet*," he went on, as if completely unaware of the effect he was having on her. Oh, that she could be so cavalier. Once again she thought about how unfair it was that men didn't get cellulite. They'd never learn to appreciate dark rooms and carefully lit candles. They wouldn't just unzip in a woman's dining room and stuff their shirttails down their pants, completely unconcerned about visible panty lines and the like.

He turned around then and caught her chewing on one nail, staring. It was only when she quickly pulled her hand away and looked up—because of course she hadn't been staring at the back of his neck—that the knowing smile bloomed. Just once she wanted the upper hand with him. Any hand.

He slipped on the cummerbund, but struggled to hook the back.

"If you—" To her dismay, she had to stop and sip her tea to wet her throat again. "If you hook it in front, you can spin it around to the back afterward. It's an old bra trick."

His eyes widened slightly. "I didn't know you could teach them to do tricks."

"Very funny." She got up and pushed his hands away. "Here, let me."

He held his arms out. "Be my guest."

She moved around behind him, determined to get him dressed and decent and prove to herself she could touch him and still manage to string two words together. "So, tell me about the limo."

"He showed up right on time, but just as I went to leave the lobby of my building, I noticed a guy across the street with a zoom lens. Normally this wouldn't be cause for alarm, but being part of the media myself, I know the business end of a professional camera when I see one."

Valerie straightened abruptly, leaving the last hook undone. "Are you sure he was there to get shots of you? How did he find you?" She grabbed his arm and turned him to face her. "I told you to be care—"

He silenced her with a finger across her lips. Which only served to piss her off . . . and prove she hadn't gotten past the touch thing at all. Which is why she said nothing when he dropped it and explained.

"I was careful. I think he tailed the driver. Don't worry, he didn't see me. I scoped out the rear parking lot, then made a dash for my car. No one followed me, but I circled your block a handful of times, just to make sure they didn't have your place staked out, too. I figure it was just one guy looking for a scoop." He folded his arms. "Or maybe he's part of this *gauntlet* of yours."

"Trust me, I didn't send anyone to follow the driver or you. That would make no sense."

"But you did invite every media outlet and their sister station to this shindig tonight, didn't you?"

"Well, that's what we need to talk about." She started to turn, but he turned her back.

She tugged her arm free, having had enough of his domineering ways . . . and far too little of his hands on her. Dammit. Definitely time to put some distance between them.

He just dangled his tie in front of her. "Would you mind?"

She held his gaze for a split second, trying to gauge whether this was a sincere request for assistance or some kind of test. Was he aware of the effect he had on her? Was he the kind of guy who got off on knowing he could make women want him, women who might not even like him?

Problem was, she did like him. Sort of. She didn't know him that well, but what she did know was hard to ignore. And that made him dangerous. She needed to keep a clear head and a cool body. She snatched the tie from his fingers and slid it around his neck, refusing to be affected by the forced close proximity. However, she kept her eyes firmly on tying the tie.

"How long is my appearance tonight?" he asked.

"Don't talk. Makes your neck move. Let me get this tied." It took her three tries and a few swear words, but she finally managed it.

Letting out a quiet, relieved sigh that was just a little too shaky for her peace of mind, she started to step back, but he caught her chin with his fingers, tipping it up just slightly. This close, there was no way she could avoid looking into his eyes. She'd expected some kind of smug amusement or, worse, perhaps heated desire. So she was surprised to find his gaze had turned quite serious.

"What is it about you?" he murmured, sounding as confused as he'd made her feel.

"What is it about me what?" she couldn't help but ask.

He shook his head just slightly, then let his hand drop away. It was all she could do to quell the automatic urge to sigh in disappointment.

"We'd better eat. Nice dress, by the way. Much better than the black." He moved around her and took a seat at the table, but only after pulling out her chair.

"Jenn picked it out," she responded, still feeling like she'd just been on the brink of something important, only to be left without the chance to discover what that something was.

She took her seat and the two of them ate quickly, discussing her plans for his entrance, for what he would say, what he was absolutely not going to say, all as if nothing had happened.

Nothing did happen, she reminded herself.

The problem, she was rapidly discovering, was going to be convincing herself she wanted to keep it that way.

Personal best

If you're lucky, you'll meet someone who brings out the best in you. If you're very lucky, it will be the kind of best you never knew you had.

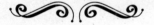

Chapter 9

Exiting the car at Bentari's, his hand at Valerie's back, Jack was smiling, confident that the night was going to go much more smoothly than Valerie was anticipating. She'd had a list as long as his arm of all the *dos* and *don'ts* he was supposed to adhere to. Like he'd been paying attention.

He'd tossed off that compliment about her dress as if it hadn't struck him deaf, dumb, and blind. She'd been attractive enough in the black one, but that red number slipping over her body like a silk waterfall had been a real shock to his system. It showed nothing, yet showcased every damn thing. How he was supposed to concentrate on a stupid list was beyond him.

They'd danced around each other every time they got close, and he was finding it harder and harder to convince himself not to push things further. After tonight, his little role in this charade was almost at an end. Valerie had promised to keep any further appearances on behalf of the magazine to a minimum. Eric, in his role as Jack's "manager," would field any and all other offers. All of which Jack would be turning down.

Which meant there was no reason not to pursue things with Valerie. *Take that, Advice Boy.* Any problems she had with mixing business and pleasure would no longer be relevant. Besides which, it was now or never. As soon as this gig wrapped up, he intended to be on the first plane to anywhere that someone would pay him to go. He was enjoying freelancing more than he'd expected, and to that end, he had a couple of feelers out. He was willing to travel, which broadened his opportunities. He'd worry about what came next when what came next got here.

Which left him with the here and now. And Valerie.

Two doormen, resplendent in top hat and tie, opened the doors for them with a flourish.

Valerie paused just briefly enough to look over her shoulder at him before entering. "Ready?" she asked with a smile that appeared both excited and nervous.

"No worries, mate," he assured her, having spent enough time Down Under to affect a dead-on Aussie accent.

She frowned slightly. "No games."

His smile widened to a grin. "Who, me?"

Her frown grew to a look of real concern and he felt bad for teasing her. This night was the culmination of a lot of hard work on her part. Everything she held important—namely her job—rode on a successful launch, which officially began tonight.

Jack slid his hand from the small of her back around to her hip, pulling her just close enough so that he could lean down and whisper in her ear. "I won't let you down. Just don't leave without me."

She looked at him, still pressed up against him—and that's the last thing he remembered before being blinded by a cavalcade of flashbulbs, followed quickly by a horde of shouts and questions and requests for him to "Look this way! Give us a smile! Who's the babe?"

It was like he'd stepped into an alternate universe. Or a rock-star fantasy. Neither appealed to him much, as it turned out.

Then Valerie's voice penetrated the blinding fog. "Smile, Jack. Nod, and keep walking." She wove her arm through his and nudged him forward, which was when he realized he'd frozen at the first wave of flashes. Snapping an insta-smile on his face, he nodded to his right and left, despite the fact that he was still temporarily flash-blind.

"You're doing great," Valerie schooled. "Just get past the throng, then we'll find the godmothers so they can formally introduce you."

"*Formally*," he repeated, still perma-grinning and nodding.

"To our guests. They'll unveil the cover, then introduce you. We'll mingle. Then you've got a five-minute one-on-one with Nancy O'Dell."

Nancy O'Dell. Even he knew who she was. *Jesus* was all he could think; this was some kind of whack dream. Or waking nightmare. Who were these people and why in the hell did they give a shit about some guy who wrote advice books? He was beginning to see why Eric had remained in hiding, sexual preference notwithstanding.

Valerie's grip on his arm tightened. "Were you listening to anything I said during dinner?" She said all this through teeth clamped into her own perma-grin. The only difference was she didn't look like a deer caught in the headlights, which he was very much afraid he did.

"I'm fine. I'm good. I can handle it," he said, trying to convince himself as much as her. For the first time he had serious doubts.

"You've got the three print interviews after that. Finally, I'll need you to mingle a bit, talk to a few of our reps, some of our bigger accounts. Then we can cut out."

"How long?" he asked through clenched teeth.

"Two hours, two and a half, max."

"Christ," he sighed. Then they were through and the world went dark, startling him.

Valerie turned to the horde and waved her arms, keeping them at bay. "Thank you all for coming. As soon as the introductions and formal presentations are done, we'll be conducting the previously scheduled interviews in a private room in the back. In the meantime, feel free to mingle. Help yourselves to the food and champagne. We've also set up stations around the fringes of the party, where you can get a sampling of what Glass Slipper, Incorporated offers its clients, and the kinds of topics we'll be covering in the magazine. Please treat yourself to a minifacial, a manicure, or a consultation with our fashion, makeup, and hair experts."

Jack's vision returned to normal during Valerie's little spiel and he was stunned to see there were only about two dozen of them. It had seemed like triple that, at least.

"What about advice?" a short woman in front of the throng asked. "Will Prince Charming be dishing up any, as some of your party favors?"

The rest of the group chuckled at the barely repressed sigh of desire in her voice. Valerie laughed easily and Jack marveled at how smoothly she'd slipped into her role. To look at her, you'd never guess she was as nervous as he was.

"You'll have to wait and read his column in *Glass Slipper*, just like the rest of us," she teased gently. "Of course, I'll be glad to supply you with the e-mail and snail mail addresses for future question submissions."

Jack gave them a short wave and nod, then let Valerie sweep him behind a dark curtain and off to a small staging room. A table had been set up with drinks and snacks. Jenn was there, as was Eric, and another man he didn't know.

Jenn rushed over to them, hands out, grin wide. "You went for the red! What did I tell you, huh? Is it perfect for your coloring or what?"

She took Valerie's hand and tugged her from Jack's side, sending her into a twirl. "Why you hide that body I have no idea," she said.

Jack watched Valerie blush a little before brushing Jenn off. "I'm only in this contraption because I spilled wine on my Chanel."

Jenn laughed and looked at Jack. "Get her to spill stuff more often, will ya?"

A slight look of alarm crossed Valerie's face, but it was only when she shot a glance his way that he realized what worried her. She didn't want anyone to get the wrong idea about the time they were spending together. Especially Jenn, who'd been around them both several times now and, like Eric, seemed quite okay with the idea of them sharing more than business. Which, of course, only served to provoke Jack.

His smile was wide and knowing as he turned to Jenn. "I'll do my best to get her out of any outfit you deem unacceptable."

Jenn hooted. Valerie gaped.

Eric tugged on Jack's arm. "So, you handling things okay, man?"

"I'll be seeing white spots for a few days, but yeah." He leaned in, punched Eric on the arm. "Who knew you were such hot shit," he said, careful to keep his voice low. "Did you see the clusterfuck of photographers out there, clamoring for a piece of you? What the hell are you telling these women, anyway?"

Eric shot him a sharp warning look, then smiled and stepped back to include the man he'd been standing with when Jack entered the room, motioning him forward. "Brice, I'd like to introduce you to Jack Lambert."

Brice was the same height as Eric, but that was where the similarity ended. He was leanly built, his black hair hanging in neat ropes down to his shoulders, with perfectly defined features and the smoothest skin Jack had ever seen on a guy. Add in eyes the color of whiskey and a set of blinding white teeth, and the dude was the perfect poster boy for the Caribbean Bureau of Tourism. He stuck his hand out. "A pleasure," he said, a hint of British-island patois in his voice.

Jack shot Eric a look that said, "Puleeze," to which Eric just smiled smugly and puffed out his chest a little.

Jack shook the guy's hand. "Yeah. Nice to meet you, too."

Brice looked at Eric, and there was no missing the flash in those eyes. Oddly enough, the byplay, rather than making Jack uncomfortable, brought forth a wave of concern. Eric was certainly enjoying his foray into the real world, but Jack couldn't help but worry that his buddy was thinking with . . . well, not with his head.

"Jack, this is Brice McGrath."

"Eric has told me a lot about you," Brice said, teeth flashing. "Amazing success you've had. Well done." He leaned in a bit. "If you ever need any investment counseling, I'd be happy to talk."

"Thanks. We're pretty happy with the way things are set up." Eric's smile dipped a little, and Jack relented. "But I'll be sure to keep your offer in mind. Listen, do you mind if I borrow your, uh . . . Eric, here, for a few?"

Impossibly, Brice's smile brightened further. "I don't mind at all. Wonderful to meet you. Congratulations."

It took Jack a second to remember what he was being congratulated for. "Right. Thanks."

They stepped to the corner. Jack glanced past Eric's shoulder. "Where did you pick him up, anyway? Club Dread?"

"You're just jealous of the accent."

"Yeah, that would be it. Where's he from?"

"British Virgin Islands."

Jack gave Eric a deadpan look, then shook his head. "It's too easy." Eric grinned. "You can beat him up if he breaks my heart, okay?" He backed down a little. "I'm sorry. I'm sure he's a nice guy. It's just—I'm not used to having to worry about you. And I've lost enough people in my life, okay? Be careful."

"You don't have to worry. I'm not going to do anything stupid." Eric glanced at Brice, who immediately beamed. And Eric lit up like a rainbow-coalition Christmas tree. "For now, at least." Before Jack could do more than roll his eyes, Eric nodded toward Valerie. "Besides, you've got your own love life to worry about. The lady looks good in red."

Jack agreed wholeheartedly, but the last thing Eric needed was encouragement in the matchmaking department. "I don't have time for a love life." He motioned to the insanity presently taking place beyond their curtained-off area. "I've been a little preoccupied, re-member?"

"Yeah, I know," Eric said, immediately contrite. "And I owe you big." His gaze flicked once again to Brice and his excitement couldn't be contained. "Bigger than you know."

"*Now* we're venturing into the too-much-information zone."

"That wasn't a euphemism, Mr. Evolution."

"Fuck you," Jack said.

Eric grinned. "Get in line."

"Okay, I'm leaving now. The press is all yours, buddy boy," Jack said, turning away.

Laughing, Eric pulled him back. "Okay, okay, I'm sorry. It's just—" His whole face was illuminated in a way Jack could never remember seeing before. "I'm sorry, I know I sound giddy. But it's so damn in-credible. Being free, for the first time. If it wasn't for you—"

"Enough with that, okay?"

"Fine. But do one more thing for me. Cash the check, Jack. If that crowd out there is any indication, you're going to earn it."

Jack ignored that.

Eric wisely didn't push. "Back to your love life. What's the deal with you and Valerie? And don't give me the song and dance about working the crowd. The crowd was the last thing on your mind when you two walked in here."

"I'm telling you, there is no deal," Jack said, his gaze drifting automatically over to her and Jenn. *Yet*, he thought, watching as she laughed at something Jenn said, even as she checked her watch and looked at the door. Always working. Speaking of which. "Are you staying for the duration? Or have you made other plans?"

"No, I'm here for you tonight, for us," Eric said, mercifully turning his attention back to business. "Val said you read the books. Do you have any questions, anything you're worried about? As your *manager*, I can stick pretty close by and no one would question it. Any hesitation in fielding any kind of off-the-wall query, all you have to do is look to me and I'll step in. Maybe we should come up with some kind of signal. . . ."

"God, now you sound like Valerie. It's some pictures and a few questions. It's not going to be that tough."

"Wasn't that you blinking like Mr. Magoo when you walked in here?"

"I was caught off guard. I won't be again. I'm a journalist. We're great observers. We think on our feet. I'll be fine."

Just then the godmothers bustled in, a swirl of stiff linen (Mercedes), fluffy silk (Aurora), and snug black satin (who else?).

Mercedes took in the measure of the room and the people in it with a quick but thorough once-over. Aurora rushed over to buss Valerie on both cheeks. Vivian headed directly to a tray filled with champagne flutes. Before Jack had a chance to do more than straighten his tie, they all descended on him.

"There he is," Aurora cooed. "Our man of the hour."

Vivian sipped her champagne and gave him a critical once-over. "Very nice, darling." She tipped his clean-shaven chin between two lethal-looking fingernails. "My, you do clean up well." Only Vivian could so blatantly invade the personal space of someone she barely knew and make it seem completely acceptable.

"I'm very sorry we weren't here to greet you when you arrived," Mercedes said, her mouth still pulled down at the corners. In fact, Jack was beginning to think that was her permanent expression. "We were unavoidably delayed."

"Now, Mercy, don't start in," Aurora began immediately.

"Yes," Vivian chimed in. "It's hardly her fault that she needed another fitting. This night is special and it wouldn't do to be seen in something less than perfect." She sipped her champagne. "So, how *did* Johannes fit, hm?"

Aurora blushed furiously as Vivian adopted an innocent expression that no one over the age of ten would have bought.

"Really, the both of you are enough to tax me into a migraine," Mercedes grumbled.

Valerie had already rescued two flutes from the nearby tray and was handing one to Mercedes. She kept the other for herself. "Here. This evening is going to be wonderful. The turnout is spectacular. Rob just stuck his head in to say that everything is set. Jack, are you ready?"

He didn't dare do anything other than nod.

"If you three are ready, we can commence with the unveiling."

Aurora fanned herself. "Oh, this is so exciting." She pinched Vivian's arm. "Our own magazine, Vivi. Way would turn over in his grave if he knew what I'd gone and done this time."

Jack knew from Valerie that Aurora had been married many years back to Senator Way Favreaux, and that it was after his death over a decade ago that the three women, all at a crossroads in their lives, had teamed up to start their own business, which operated out of what was once Aurora's home. A palatial spread in tony Potomac.

"Nonsense," Mercedes said. "He'd be proud of you."

Aurora merely snorted. "Now, now, you know as well as I do that he believed women were meant to serve mint juleps and make small talk. Not turn their ancestral home into a business empire. Or start up a periodical." She took Vivian's champagne glass from her. "Just because he's gone doesn't mean we have to nominate the man for sainthood." With that, she downed the remainder of the flute's contents. Smiling brightly, she said, "Shall we go turn the world on its ear?"

Snatching a fresh glass from a passing tray, Vivian toasted her. Mercedes merely sighed, but finally nodded and moved toward the rear exit from their little staging area. Aurora linked arms with Vivian and they followed in Mercedes' wake. Jack imagined that that was probably the normal pattern for the three of them.

Valerie peeked through the black shimmery curtains, then back at the trio. "Wait right here. I'll have Rob escort you up the stairs, onto the dais." She ducked out, but was back in a blink with the ubiquitous Rob, who was apparently some sort of stage manager for the event. For all Jack knew, Valerie could be racked with nerves, but she didn't show it. Her eyes were gleaming and her smile bright and confident as she ushered the three women into big Rob's manly care.

As soon as they were safely climbing onto the small stage that had been erected for the presentation of the cover, Valerie motioned Jack over. "Okay, let's go over what you'll be doing." Gone was the confident smile and assured air. "What?" she demanded when he smiled.

"Nothing. You just put on a great show for them."

She didn't pretend not to understand. "That's what I get paid for. To put a good public face on any situation. Hopefully, to my employers' increased advantage."

"They're lucky to have you, you know."

The sincere compliment caught her off guard, judging by her reaction. Which was fine by him, as it had caught him off guard, too.

"We'll see if you still feel the same way a couple of hours from now."

"Your faith in me is so underwhelming."

Her lips quirked a little, but she quickly shook that off. "It's not that I don't have faith. I just don't want you to take this so . . . cavalierly."

"I owe too much to Eric for that to happen. But it's a party. I'm great at parties. Trust me."

Before Valerie could say another word, there was a group gasp from the collected guests, then a roar of applause and cheers. The cover had been unveiled.

"And now, the moment you've been waiting for," Vivian announced. "Dear guests, media friends, and world at large. You've read his books, you've taken his advice—or not, much to your peril," she added with a sly wink. "But now he's all ours. And we've convinced him to share himself with you. At least for the next hour or so. So get ready. I give you, for the first time in public . . . Mr. Jack Lambert. Our very own Prince Charming!"

Jack's gut squeezed into a tight fist and he was pretty certain he was going to throw up. So he did what any self-respecting man who was about to pull off the world's most ridiculous charade since Milli Vanilli would do to quell his nerves.

He pulled the nearest woman into his arms and planted one on her.

Valerie's arms flailed for only a moment before grabbing onto his lapels and steadying her mouth beneath his.

Her eyes were a bit glassy, her lips soft and open, when he lifted his own. "Thanks. I really needed that."

"Uh . . . yeah. Right. Anytime," she managed, still disoriented.

"Be careful, I might hold you to that. In fact, holding you felt pretty damn good."

She recovered swiftly, already frowning. "Jack—"

He stroked a quick thumb across her lip. "That's Prince Charming to you." He shot her a wink, then strode through the parted curtain.

A blitzkrieg of flashes blinded him, the delirious applause and cheers roared over him. The world was waiting.

And all he could think about was kissing Valerie Wagner.

With a wry smile that was pure Jack Lambert, he bounded onto the stage.

Synchronicity

It's easy to say it was the right person at the wrong time. Harder to go for it, anyway. And we all know there is truth to the saying that harder is better.

Chapter 10

"He's something else," Aurora said, leaning in close so Valerie could hear her over the continued din of the party.

"He is that," Valerie murmured. Jack apparently hadn't been kidding about his people skills. But then, her lips were still tingling and their kiss had been hours ago.

"And tireless," Vivian added with an appreciative sigh. "Always a good thing."

Valerie shared her smile, but privately she wasn't too sure about that. Her plan had been the media exclusives followed by the hand-picked queue of print reporters, questions kept to a bare minimum. Everyone would get just enough to ensure a mention in every market and hopefully make people want to buy the magazine to learn more. She'd planned ninety minutes, two hours tops, then Jack would be whisked away, back to his carefully protected privacy, where all would assume he was back to work, soothing the needs of many—and spiking the desires of more—with his witty and timely advice.

Three hours later, and The Jack & Eric Show was still in full swing.

Valerie had hung on to at least a thread of control through his five-minute chat with Nancy O'Dell, monitoring every syllable uttered between them from her post five feet behind the cameraman. Jack had handled himself almost too well, she had to admit. He'd managed to turn the tables on Nancy, teasing her, feigning disbelief that she had ever required his advice assistance—flirting, basically—just enough to deflect answering anything but the most basic of questions. The answers to which they'd hammered out ahead of time.

The print interviews had been more nerve-racking, with Valerie worrying about what angle each reporter planned to take. Some of their questions had been unexpected, but Jack never faltered. In fact, he'd tried to wave her off several times when she'd stepped in to warn the reporter their time was up. She'd ignored him.

Yes, he was a journalist himself, and knew all about hidden agendas and predetermined angles, but he was enjoying himself way too much, a fact he conveyed with the occasional wink sent her way, the cocky grin, the quick shoulder squeeze and "Chill, would you? I'm fine," that he handed her between interviews. But she knew that when you relaxed too much, you let your guard down. So she made sure they stuck as close to the schedule as possible, giving him as little rope to hang them all with as possible.

After the last reporter left, still dreamy-eyed—she'd purposely selected mostly female reporters, but did they all have to fall for good looks and an easy line?—she'd told Jack they'd make the rounds of the room once, say their good-byes to the godmothers, and call it a night. A very successful night, she'd finally started to allow herself to believe.

Oh, it was successful, all right. Everyone was having the time of their lives. Except her. For her it had been a three-hour roller-coaster ride. She'd crunched through an entire roll of antacids already.

Eric, who had been by her side all through the interviews, had stepped in during the chitchat, schmooze-the-room part of the night, and somewhere along the way, the duo had taken on a life of their own. Much to the guests' delight. You'd think they'd rehearsed, except it came much too easily to be an act. No, those two were the real deal, friends with a special bond that can only develop over time. They worked the room like seasoned party-circuit veterans.

For all her cynicism, the odd pang of envy came as a surprise. Just because her friends were scattered over the course of her career path, sort of like the trail left by a streaking meteor, it wasn't as if she was a loner. But it was hard to watch the two of them, with Jack's all-work-and-no-play speech still echoing in her ears, and not start to question things.

Eric was laughing over some verbal jab from Jack, which had the small crowd around them hooting. That was what she'd missed out on. That thing where you fit with someone so seamlessly that you finished each other's sentences, had such a wealth of shared experiences that the most innocuous comment would trigger the same memory, the same in-joke. It was intimate without being sexual. Familial.

She thought about her family. Parents who were both professionals, who admired her work ethic even as they despaired of her ever finding her niche. She always thought she was lucky; they hounded her about settling down, but into a career, not a marriage. Oh, they'd be happy enough if she found the right man and started a family, but their marriage was more a business partnership than a grand love affair.

She tried to picture them with grandchildren and smiled when the visual proved to be beyond her. Workaholics, both of them, she'd come by her own tenacity and drive honestly. Howard and Evelyn had many friends, every one of them a business associate first, friend second. Despite the more bohemian nature of her collection of pals,

Valerie had to admit it was the same for her. Not one person in her address book had come to be there through any other path than a professional connection.

That had never bothered her before. At the moment, however, watching Eric and Jack, it felt just the tiniest bit hollow.

"Why the long face?" Aurora asked, pressing another flute of champagne into her hand. Valerie took a small sip, knowing she'd discard it shortly, as she had the last half-dozen they'd plied her with. She wasn't ready to celebrate a victory. The night wasn't over yet.

"Just keeping an eye on our investment," she told Aurora, uncomfortable with the woman's awareness of her moods. And quite aware of the irony there. Pining for the intimacy of real friendship, yet uncomfortable and unsure when a chance to find it presented itself.

She was too strung out on nerves and an empty stomach to analyze that at the moment.

"We definitely got our money's worth," Vivian chimed in, joining them. "And my, my, that Eric? How yummy can you get?"

"Vivi, hush," Aurora admonished her, then turned sparkling eyes on Valerie. "They are quite something, though, aren't they?"

Mercedes joined them, happier than Valerie could recall ever seeing her. She couldn't help but think that it was the three women who were quite something. Despite their innate personality differences, it was clear they were as successful at maintaining their personal relationships as they were at expanding their business endeavors. Again she felt that tiny pang, but rather than feel sorry for herself, she counted herself lucky to be on the periphery of their friendship. Who knew, if she stuck around long enough, maybe she'd learn something.

"I think we can call this evening an unqualified success," Mercedes announced. Lifting her glass toward Valerie, she waited until they each lifted theirs as well. "To a stunning launch."

Vivian beamed and lifted her flute higher, angling it toward Valerie. "To the woman who bagged us a prince."

"We're in the magazine business, ladies," Aurora chimed in.

Glasses *clinked*, and they all sipped. All except Valerie, who pretended to sip, but couldn't get a drop past her lips. She'd bagged them something, all right. *Please just let this night be over.*

Valerie looked over the rim of her flute just as Jack glanced across the room at her and winked. She lowered her glass, frowned, and tapped the slim watch on her wrist.

He mouthed the words *party pooper*, then Eric caught the byplay and flashed her one hand. Five minutes.

She nodded, then pointed to the staging area, where they would make their exit. She turned to begin her good-byes to the godmothers, but Mercedes spoke to her first.

"I know this has been an exhausting marathon for you," she began. "We've all put in a great deal of time on this and I'm sure we'll all enjoy a breather this weekend. But we'd like to schedule a meeting early Monday morning. I know Elaine already has you busy working on the next issue, but it's important we talk."

Valerie hadn't thought her stomach could tighten up any further. Mercedes' tone was perfectly modulated, with nary a negative vibe to be found, but Valerie couldn't help but feel the portentousness of the request. Probably that was the guilt screaming inside her head. "I do have several meetings scheduled early Monday, but I'm sure I can rearrange them."

"Let one of us know what you arrange, dear," Aurora said. "We'll meet in our regular offices, if that's okay. We'd come into the magazine, but we don't want to take away from the team's efforts. Elaine is doing a wonderful job and we don't want her to feel overshadowed. Now that the first issue is essentially launched, we'll be stepping back to the advisory role we'd agreed upon."

"Will you need Elaine to attend this meeting as well?" Valerie asked, wanting some clue as to what was up.

"Oh, no, darling," Vivian said. "Just you."

Valerie managed to swallow and smile and nod. "Okay, then. Monday it is." She said her good-byes, found Elaine and Jenn and told them she'd be leaving and taking their guest of honor with her.

"Fabulous success," Elaine said, toasting her with what appeared to be one flute too many of champagne. "You and I need to talk."

Valerie wanted to tell her to take a ticket and get in line. "Yes, of course. Anytime."

"Clear a block for lunch next week," Elaine said, still managing to speak in that staccato, rapid-fire way of hers, despite being at least two sheets to the wind. "Lots to go over, much to discuss."

Valerie nodded, then let Jenn pull her aside as Elaine was tugged back into her conversation with a bunch of suits.

"So, how did you get to be the lucky one to take Prince Charming home? You know, if you'd rather stay and party, I could selflessly make myself available for that lowly chore."

"You're so generous."

"I know. It's one of my more endearing qualities."

Jenn was joking, but Valerie thought she was, indeed, very endearing. And open. She wished that kind of joie de vivre came more naturally to her. It just shouldn't be so damn awkward. She thought about the godmothers, how they shared the highs and the lows of their business, and found herself wishing for the first time that she had a trusted friend, someone she could confide in. The burden of the secret was growing heavier by the day. How great would it be to have someone to unload it on, discuss it with, or frankly, just bitch about it to? Not that she could tell anyone about this . . . but it would be nice to know there was someone there anyway.

Jenn glanced past Valerie's shoulder. "I think you're being signaled."

Valerie looked back and saw Eric herding Jack in the general direction of the staging area. "My cue to leave." *Thank God.*

"Yeah, yeah, rub it in. You tall chicks get all the hot guys."

"I'm not tall."

Jenn looked up. "Val, in my world, everyone is tall."

Valerie laughed and finally started to let her neck and back unkink just a little. *Almost home, just a few more minutes.*

"Do a short girl a favor. See if he has any single friends. Hell, I'm not choosy. His gay friend is pretty damn fine."

"Jack is single."

Jenn just looked at her. "Technically, yes."

"What does that mean?"

Jenn just took her glass and pushed her toward the black curtains. "Go. And every once in a while, just for kicks, don't think of everything as a business opportunity."

Valerie frowned. Was it really so obvious that all anyone had to do was take one look at her and see her for the No Social Life Loser she was? She knew the answer to that. The question was, what was she going to do about it?

Jenn drained the rest of Valerie's champagne, waving her away with her free hand. "Go, already. He's waiting."

Valerie took a couple of steps, then suddenly turned back around and blurted, "Jenn, do you, ah, do you want to get together for dinner sometime? Or something? Outside work?"

To her everlasting credit, Jenn didn't hoot over the absolute awkwardness of Valerie's invitation. Instead, her face lit up. "Yeah, I'd love to. I'm still finding my way around town."

"Me, too." The only places she knew were restaurants where she'd conducted power lunches, and business dinners. She hadn't even gone down to the Mall and wandered around the Smithsonian yet. "We can wander aimlessly together."

"Good deal. Why don't we match up schedules after the magazine hits?"

Valerie smiled, feeling ridiculously triumphant. It was just one step, but maybe Jenn could help her figure out how to keep taking more of them. "Great."

She met Eric and Brice at the staging-room curtain, still smiling. "Hi, guys. Are you two going or staying?"

They exchanged a look that screamed barely restrained anticipation.

"Leaving, then," Valerie filled in for them.

"It was a wonderful party," Brice said. "Thank you for letting me tag along. I think your magazine is going to be a smash hit."

"Thanks." She hadn't spent more than five minutes with Eric's date, but what little she'd seen, she really liked. Respectful, natty dresser. Cute as all hell, and with an accent to die for. Eric had done pretty damn well for being on the market all of three weeks. "It was a pleasure meeting you."

"You'll make sure Jack gets out of here okay?" Eric asked her.

Valerie nodded. "We've got it covered. After that photographer followed the Glass Slipper town car to Jack's apartment, we're not taking any chances. I've got a second town car that will hopefully lead anybody who didn't get an invite and wants to scoop those who did on a wild-goose chase to the Glass Slipper headquarters in Maryland. By the time they figure it out, Jack will be safely home." *And so will I*, she thought.

Where she would lie in bed, stare at the ceiling, and relive tonight in minute detail. Then pray for a big media blitz for one or two news cycles, before they all moved on to feed on something else. And try not to have nightmares about the whole sordid truth ending up on *The Smoking Gun.*

"I think it went okay," Eric said, looking relieved. "You?"

She smiled and gave him a quick hug. "Yes. And thank you for sticking by him during the schmooze-and-booze part of the evening."

Eric held onto her arms, not letting her step entirely away. "Thank you," he said, his eyes conveying everything he wanted to say, but couldn't with Brice standing so close.

"Just keep your fingers crossed it all goes okay over the next three or four days." She glanced past him to Brice, her smile widening. "In the meantime, go enjoy your new life." She leaned in close. "He's a hottie."

Eric's smile flashed to a grin. "Lucky me."

Lucky Eric, indeed. He looked happy and excited. A man who understood the power of friendships, and was willing to risk everything for the chance to build new relationships. A month ago she'd have thought he was crazy to risk it. At the moment, all she felt was a deepening sense of respect. "And here I was thinking he was the lucky one. Just, you know, be careful."

"Suddenly everyone is my mother."

Something else occurred to her. "You know you can't tell him—"

"Of course I know. As it turns out, the compromise is a small price to pay. I'm beginning to think I should have backed myself into a corner years ago. Playing the manager of Prince Charming is actually a relief. Who knows, after my obligation to *Glass Slipper* is over, I just might retire."

It all sounded good. Too good. Valerie had learned fourteen *perfect jobs* ago that when something seemed too good to be true, it usually was. But she had faith that Eric wanted his freedom badly enough to protect the ruse. He wouldn't screw Jack, and she didn't think he'd screw her.

"You can reach me on my cell if anything comes up," Eric assured her. Then he winked. "Let's just hope the only thing that comes up in the next forty-eight hours is—"

"Got it," Valerie said, blushing despite herself. "Emergencies only."

Eric bussed her on the cheek, then turned to Brice. "Shall we?"

Brice nodded, his perfectly styled dreads all but vibrating. "Absolutely, dovie."

Valerie's heart bumped a little as she watched them leave. She told herself the little ache accompanying it was perfectly natural for a person witnessing two people falling in love.

She ducked behind the curtain herself, expecting Jack to be there already. The small room was empty. Shit. Eric and Brice had already gone out the back, but she ran to the service hallway anyway. No Jack there, either. Had he already gone out to the limo?

She stepped into the damp night, drizzle lightly misting the air. Two town cars were lined up, the drivers inside and out of the rain. She leaned down as the front passenger window lowered on the first one. "Jack Lambert?" she queried.

"Haven't seen him come out, ma'am."

She looked to the second car, but the driver was already shaking his head. "Well, where in the hell—"

Just then came the purr of a racing engine. A midnight-black Mustang tooled up along the other side of the limos. The passenger window lowered. "Want a ride? Or are you taking the town car?"

It was Jack. Sans tux jacket and tie, sleeves already rolled up. With impossibly sexy shades on.

"It's past one in the morning, why the sunglasses?"

He tugged them down and wiggled his eyebrows. "Incognito, baby."

She couldn't help but laugh. "You are so full of it." Just then the skies opened up, making her gasp as the fat raindrops soaked through the silk of her dress.

He leaned over and pushed the passenger door open. "Get in. Jenn will never forgive you if you ruin that dress."

She glanced at the driver of the nearest limo, who grinned and shooed her in. He cracked his window and called out, "We'll head out anyway, just in case," he told her, then winked and raised the tinted window before she could correct his very wrong assumption.

"Val, get in."

One limo pulled out, the other fell in behind him, each heading in a different direction when they left the lot.

Valerie got in the car and closed the door. She'd barely reached for the seat belt when Jack pulled a one eighty and backtracked behind the building, in the opposite direction from the exit the limos had taken.

"Didn't we leave this car at my place? And we agreed on the town-car diversion just in case—"

"We're clear. Brice knew one of the guys who works at Bentori's. He took a buddy and they went and picked it up and brought it down when they got off their shift. Made some ready cash on the deal. Trust me, this is fine." He edged into the alley, then into another back parking lot, skirting that building, and finally ending up on a side street. After a quick look, Jack turned and went two blocks in the wrong direction, but just when Valerie started to comment, he whipped down another side street, then pulled into the first available space and killed the engine.

Heart thrumming, Valerie looked over her shoulder, but the rain-swept street was quiet. "Were we being followed?"

Jack slid his sunglasses off. "No, I've just always wanted to do that."

Valerie didn't know whether to smack him or laugh. So she did both.

"What was that for?"

"Do you have any idea how stressful this night has been for me? And you're playing games."

"You? Stressful for *you*?" Jack hooted. "All you had to do was stand around and take turns glaring at your watch, then at me."

"Well, if you had followed the timetable I set up, I wouldn't have needed to."

"So now you're saying I'm a loose cannon? Did I or did I not talk to every person you put in my path?" He held up a finger, stalling her reply. "And did I or did I not get every bit of information out that you wanted me to reveal, with our own spin on it? They now know I was a sports reporter. They know I kept the Prince Charming thing under wraps because I wasn't sure how to combine my two *images*. And they know I came *out* because my real job ended and I was tired of the charade. No surprises, no skeletons to come back and bite me or you on the ass later. In fact, I think between Eric's natural charm and my bullshitting capabilities, you scored big tonight. And you want to deny me one little moment of fun?"

Valerie just stared at him, letting the drumming rain on the soft roof of the convertible fill the silence. Finally she sighed and said, "Okay. You're right. I just—" She stopped when he suddenly turned and began searching for something in the backseat. "Now what are you doing?"

"Looking for something to write that down on. You admitted I was actually right about something."

"Very funny. You know how much is at stake here tonight. You were all over the place, talking to any and everyone. If the situation was reversed, you can't tell me it wouldn't have been nerve-racking for you to watch me work the room like that."

The streetlamp illuminated his smile. "Watching you do anything would have been a hell of a lot more fun than glad-handing congressmen and pretending I thought they married their trophy wives for love."

"So cynical," she said with a surprised laugh.

He shifted his gaze to the front windshield. "Yeah, well, everyone's entitled to his opinion."

She knew he was referring to his divorce. At least, she assumed that was what had left him so bitter. "So, no trophy wife for you, I see."

He laughed a bit harshly. "No. I did that the first time around and got it out of the way."

"How long were you married?" She knew it had been brief, but had never asked specifically.

"Eighteen months and ten days longer than I should have." He looked at her. "A long time ago; it's history, okay?"

"Sounds like you're determined not to let history repeat itself."

"We're supposed to learn from our mistakes, aren't we?"

"I guess it depends on what lesson you thought you learned. If you're going to let one person ruin what could be an enriching life experience with someone else, then I don't know. Maybe that's not learning. That's avoiding."

"And you've been married how long now?"

Valerie's damp cheeks flushed a little. "Just because I'm not married doesn't mean I can't look around at those who are. I would hope that I wouldn't let one mistake jade me for any future possibilities."

"Have you ever come close?"

Now she wished she'd never brought it up. She shook her head. "I've moved around a lot since I was little. It's hard enough to maintain friendships, much less a committed relationship."

"Ever had your heart broken?"

She smiled a little. "You say *broken* like you mean *chewed up and spat out*."

He paused for a moment, then nodded. "That's a pretty fair assessment, I think."

She settled back in the seat, shifting so she could see him more clearly. "I'm sorry," she said quietly.

"For?"

"Poking into your personal life like that. You're right. I have no idea what you went through, or how I'd feel if I went through it. Maybe I'd be as cynical about love as you are."

"I'm not cynical about love," he said, sounding honestly surprised.

She lifted one eyebrow, her lips quirking. "Okay."

"No, really. I think the concept of falling in love, being in love, is wonderful. Marriage, on the other hand? Not so much."

"Why?"

"Both parties have to give the same level of effort, want it to work just as badly. Even with good communication, there's a lot of guess-work, a lot of assumptions."

"I think that's what they call *having faith*."

"Maybe. But faith is supposed to be rewarded with faith, right?"

"And yours wasn't?"

He looked away, didn't answer immediately. "It was a lot more complicated than that."

"Relationships usually are."

He shrugged and she could tell he regretted getting into such a se-rious discussion. "It just seems like a setup to me. Someone isn't go-ing to live up to the expectations of the other, which in turn brings pain to them both."

"But you're totally open to love," she said dryly.

He laughed a little. "It wasn't wrong to fall in love with Shelby. Blind, maybe, but not wrong."

"So one woman's actions have turned you off the entire institution of marriage?"

"It sure as hell made me a lot more wary of it. But, hey, who knows, maybe someday I'll find a woman who'll make me crazy stupid in love enough to consider it again."

She laughed. "Meaning, it's a decision no one in their right mind would make?"

"All I'm saying is I'm not hanging my hopes, or my happiness, on being married. Maybe you've been around more successful partner-ships than I have, but I figure mine's a pretty healthy outlook on life."

Valerie shifted her gaze out the window. "Probably." It sounded to her like his narrow views on marriage had begun long before he'd hooked up with Shelby. It made her curious about his childhood, his parents, his family. But she'd probed enough for one night.

"What about you?"

She darted a look at him. "What about me?"

"You say you've moved around a lot. You landed this job with *Glass Slipper* and you're very dedicated to it, to making a success out of it. I don't know, I just get the feeling that career success is listed at number one on your Palm Pilot's little to-do list. Hell, it's probably the whole top ten." He lifted a shoulder. "It just seems like relationships and marriage aren't uppermost on your mind, either, or even bottommost. You said yourself you don't even have the time to form friendships."

He was right, but put like that it sounded so . . . well, pathetic. "I'm working on that. And you make it sound like I've sacrificed having a life for having a career."

"Have you?"

That stung. "You don't even know me." Which wasn't entirely the truth. In fact, she was beginning to think he knew her too well. "For all you know, I go out clubbing five nights a week, and end up with a different man in my bed every Saturday morning."

Jack laughed. Valerie scowled.

"Maybe you do," he said, barely making the attempt to placate her.

"And just because I don't, doesn't mean I've given up on love and marriage."

"You're just what, then, postponing it for a while?"

"I'm doing no such thing. Unlike you, I'm perfectly open to the idea of falling in love."

"I never said I wasn't."

"And," she added pointedly, "I assume at some point a marriage would follow. I don't want to just fall in and out of love forever. Besides, you're not even talking about falling in love. You're talking about screwing around. Not that I have anything against that. But it's totally different."

"So, you're saying that if I was really in love, I'd automatically want to get married."

She waved her hands dismissively. "Live together as a committed couple, then, whatever you want to call it. But I don't think that's what you're saying."

He sort of shrugged.

She laughed. "You're so full of it. You no more want to settle down again than you want to pose for another magazine cover."

"Thank you, Dr. Phil. I think you've been reading too many of Eric's books."

She arched one brow. "Unlike you, who was supposed to but hasn't."

At least he didn't try to deny it. "I skimmed."

She wagged a finger. "I caught your careful nonanswers in there tonight. I bet that bullshit routine came in handy back in school, too."

He reached out and snagged her wagging finger. "You think you've got me all pegged, don't you," he said tauntingly. "Is that what you do? Categorize people, so you can keep everyone in their tidy little places?"

She forced a laugh and yanked her hand away. "No, that's what you do."

He grinned widely, surprising her. "Yeah, but at least I admit it."

"So I'm right," she said, carefully steering them away from discussing her . . . and how clearly he'd pegged her. "You aren't looking for commitment, you're looking for a good time."

He cocked his head. "You want to know what category you fall into?"

He caught her badly off guard with that one. Her mouth opened, but nothing came out.

"Interesting. Not my type. Possibly worth it anyway."

"I guess I'm supposed to be flattered that you considered making an exception in my case," she said dryly, trying to find her footing. It didn't help that his teasing brought her back to that kiss earlier tonight, and the one before that, in his apartment. Obviously they hadn't meant anything to him. Nor had they to her, really. But she had a feeling she was the only one having a hard time believing that.

"I thought about it," he went on, "but decided you'd be too much work."

Her mouth fell open again, this time in affront. She folded her arms across her chest. "Which is why you've kissed me. Twice. You'd think someone like me would be right up your alley. Focused on her career, not wanting any sticky entanglements. Perfect for a roll, but not for a ring."

That wicked grin flashed again. "You trying to talk me into it?"

"You really are incorrigible."

Whatever Jack might have said in response was cut off when he glanced in the rearview mirror. "Shit."

She started to turn around, but he reached out to grab her. "Don't."

"What?"

"Get down." He started to shove her down. "No, wait, that'll just look worse."

Valerie struggled. "What in the hell are you talking about?"

"Dammit. Come here."

And the next thing she knew, he was dragging her across the seat and into his arms. She pushed against his chest.

"Don't fight me," he said against her mouth, "someone is watching."

She fought harder. "Well, this isn't going to help any!"

"Just turn your face to mine," he hissed, then grabbed her chin and pulled her mouth to his.

She fought the kiss for about a second, then sighed and gave in to it when he stopped punishing her with his mouth and started really kissing her, too. Vaguely she heard a car rolling along the wet street, but it barely registered.

He stroked his fingers back along her jaw and tilted her head so he could slant his mouth and take the kiss even deeper.

It was only when someone moaned, and she realized it was her, that she finally came to her senses and pushed away. "What were you thinking?" she demanded, albeit a bit breathlessly.

She was still in his arms and they only tightened when she tried to move away. "I was thinking that turning our faces toward each other would keep them away from the camera."

She stiffened. "Camera? What cam—"

Just as she turned her head, a blinding flash emanated from the side window of a car idling about five spaces down the opposite side of the street. He was already squealing away before Valerie could stop gasping.

"That camera." Jack easily kept her in his arms to prevent her from leaping from the car. "Do you want to hand the guy more ammo?"

"What guy?" She looked at him. "You know who it was?"

"Same dude who was outside my house earlier. I recognized the car. If you'd just stayed the way I had you, all he'd have gotten was two people kissing in a rain-covered car. He wouldn't have had either of our faces."

"But I was looking right—" She hung her head. "Shit."

Jack just shook his head and sighed.

She punched him in the arm. Hard.

"Hey!"

"*Hey* is right. If you hadn't pulled the Neanderthal act, all he'd have gotten was us sitting in the car, a respectable distance apart, talking."

"Honey," Jack admonished her, "it wouldn't have mattered. No one sits on a dark side street, miles from home, to talk. At least, that would be the angle they'd have played, anyway."

"Well, now they won't have to work that hard at it, will they?"

He shrugged. "I was just trying to protect your identity. He knew I was in here, but seeing me with an unidentified woman was hardly going to tarnish the Prince Charming image. I could have spun that ten different ways. Eric's readers, waiting for their prince to come, would have been tickled pink to know that Jack Lambert, aka the real Prince Charming, was on the prowl. Trust me, I know how women think."

"Oh, please," she said, snorting in disgust. "You haven't a clue." She'd never admit he was completely right on one score, though. Now that he was out in the open, he was fair game. "You probably see this whole thing as a gig to fill your dance card. And we both know I'm talking about the horizontal tango here."

His smile was unrepentant. "I'm just doing a friend a favor. If there's something positive in it for me, then so be it. It's not like I'm getting paid here."

She frowned. "I thought Eric said—"

"Never mind what Eric said. And never mind what I just said." He switched on the ignition. "We'd better get out of here before Peeping Tommy and his zoom lens make a reappearance."

Valerie retreated into her thoughts as Jack wound them through the streets of D.C., ending up in a back alley, one block from the party.

"Now what?" she asked. At least the rain had finally stopped.

"One of the limos is back. Maybe you should let them take you home instead of me. Just in case."

"Right. Okay." She unlocked the door, but his hand on her arm stopped her from opening it.

"Listen, I'm sorry."

She looked over her shoulder. "For?"

"For doing anything back there that might cause trouble for you," he clarified. "Although that kiss was almost worth it."

"*Almost?*"

"You need to relax more next time. Enjoy yourself."

"Oh, for God's sake." She slid out and closed the door, then leaned back down when he lowered the window. "There won't be a next time."

He pouted and somehow managed to look entirely too endearing. "And just when you'd convinced me."

She knew she shouldn't take the bait, but she couldn't stop herself. "About?"

"Being the right woman at the right time."

She laughed at that. "I couldn't be more the wrong woman for you if I tried. And this is possibly the worst time."

His grin only widened. "I know. That's what convinced me."

Natural selection

How do you know when you've met The One? You realize that no matter how long your Reasons-Why-I-Shouldn't list gets . . . you still keep coming back for more.

Chapter 11

"Shit. Shit, shit, shit." Jack tossed the tabloid onto the counter and sank onto one of his barstools.

"What in the hell were you thinking?" Eric paced Jack's apartment. "You sure as shit don't have to tell me what you were thinking with."

"Oh, like your mind wasn't on Brice's virgin ass the whole night. And I use the term *virgin* strictly geographically."

Eric paused, smiled briefly. "It is a sweet ass, isn't it?"

"Please. No visuals before my first cup of coffee, okay?" Jack picked up the paper again, swearing as he raked a hand through his hair. "Has Valerie seen this yet?"

"I tried her house and her cell on my way over here. Nada."

"Great. Just fucking great." He stared at the grainy photos that had been blown up and plastered on the front page, providing checkout-line denizens everywhere the opportunity to ogle and discuss. One shot was of two people in the throes of a passionate kiss. The second, to erase any doubts as to the identity of at least one participant, was a surprised and very mussed Valerie. Of course, Jack knew her hair was like that because of the rain, but the photo made it look otherwise.

The headline read:

PUBLICIST PAYBACK FOR PRINCELY DUTIES?

The short write-up speculated that *Glass Slipper*'s ruthless new publicist had relied on a certain time-honored tradition to secure Jack as their cover boy. The writer—and Jack used that term loosely—wondered just what kind of favors Valerie had promised that had to be paid off in his car.

"Damage control," Eric was saying. "We're going to have to do serious damage control. For the magazine, the godmothers, and Valerie. If she hasn't already been canned. That might be where she is right now. It would explain why she's not answering her cell."

Jack flung the paper toward the couch. It landed on the book he'd left lying open last night. To think he'd actually been so unsettled by his little conversation with Valerie that he'd thought he'd find some answers in one of Eric's books. Obviously he needed a hell of a lot more help than any book could give him. He'd really blown it. The whole evening had gone without a hitch, then *wham!* one second of bad judgment, and it all went to shit. "What are you suggesting I do?"

Eric's response was drowned out by the sudden pounding on the front door. He waved Jack back to his seat. "I'll get it. Who the hell knows what might be out there at this point." But after a quick peek through the fisheye, he immediately unlocked the door. "Hey," he said as Valerie strode into the apartment. "We've been trying to reach you."

"Yes, well, I haven't been able to take calls all morning. I've been too busy making them." She slapped a copy of the newspaper on the table, then noticed Jack's copy strewn across the couch. "I see you've already been made aware of the happy little results of your brilliant strategy."

"Have you talked to the godmothers?" Eric asked.

"Oh, yes," Valerie responded. "At length." She paced the room, alternately taking gulps from a Starbucks grande and glaring at Jack. "I've also talked with more reporters than I knew existed. All of whom apparently have nothing better to do on a Friday morning than read the goddamn *Star*."

Jack pushed off his stool. "Valerie, I'm—"

She swung around to face him. "Don't you dare. You weren't sorry last night when you were playing your cavalier little game of cat and mouse with that reporter, so don't insult me now."

"I didn't intend—"

"Too late," she shot back. "Go grab a shower and put on something decent." She turned to Eric, leaving Jack looking down at the old sweats and T-shirt he had on. "Help him coordinate something that says *average guy with potential*. I'm thinking jeans and a nice polo shirt, something like that. Blue if you have it, to bring out his eyes, but soften up that face." She looked back at Jack. "And shave."

"Am I allowed to ask why?"

"Because we don't want you looking like a rake this morning; we need you to look like the nice guy next door."

"And who am I looking like a *nice guy* for?"

She slapped her day planner down on the counter next to him and flipped it open. "Where would you like me to begin?" she asked, running a carefully manicured nail down a handwritten schedule. It was blocked off into half-hour and hour segments. Every one of them was filled in.

"Jesus." Jack took the coffee cup from her hand and drained it.

She snatched the cup from him. "He can't help you. But I can. Go clean up. Then we've got battle strategy to go over." She looked at Eric. "We're going to need more coffee. And food. Have you guys eaten? I've been up since five and I'm starving."

Eric waved a hand. "I'll take care of it. How does it look outside?"

"Who the hell cares about the weather?" Jack demanded, his hair standing on end now that he'd raked his hands through it so many times.

"I'm not asking about the weather," Eric explained.

"No one I've seen so far," Valerie told him. "Did anyone follow you home last night, Jack?"

He blew out a sigh. When had this gone so wrong? He already knew the answer to that. The moment he'd kissed Valerie. Hell, before that. The moment he first decided he wanted to kiss Valerie. "Our happy paparazzi guy was here when I finally got home."

"Finally?"

"Yeah, finally. I drove around for a little while, okay?"

She didn't press him and he was perfectly happy to let her believe he'd been trying to throw anyone else with a camera off his trail. In fact, he'd driven the streets of D.C., trying to figure out what he was going to do about Valerie. Specifically, what he was going to do to make sure he kept his hands off of Valerie. Shouldn't have been that big a deal. As far as he knew then, save for a possible appearance or two, professionally speaking, he was done with this job. Problem was, personally speaking, he wasn't ready to be done with her.

"No one else?" she asked.

"No. When he saw I was alone, he lost interest. Probably ran off to zap the picture in so he could get the big payday." He shoved off his stool. "Listen, I want to—"

She held up her hand. "You want to go take a shower. Eric, I'd kill for a sesame bagel and cream cheese. I've got more phone calls to make, and I have to check in with the godmothers." She tossed him a look. "Why are you still standing here? We've got approximately"—she looked at her watch—"fifty-five minutes. And we've got a lot of ground to cover."

Jack saluted. "Yes, sir, drill sergeant, sir."

"You really don't want to be cocky with me right now."

You have no idea the things I want to be with you right now, Jack thought, surprised to discover that rather than dampening his desire for her, watching Valerie march around in her plum-colored suit, with her hair ruthlessly combed up into one of her tidy little twists, just made his fingers itch all the more to rip off that jacket, yank the pins out of that twist, run his fingers through all that hair, and—

Eric cleared his throat, jerking Jack's attention away from Valerie. He slung an arm around Jack's shoulders and herded him toward the bedroom door. "Dude, you might want to kill the whole smoldering routine," he said quietly, out of Valerie's earshot. "Or at least take it down, say, a hundred degrees or so."

Jack shrugged Eric's arm off his shoulders. "What in the hell are you talking about?"

Eric just grinned. "You know damn well what I'm talking about. You look at her and it's like flames shoot from your eyes. I'm just saying that might not be helpful to your cause, or hers, when you go on camera."

"Camera?"

Eric nodded. "So make the shower a cold one. And save the hungry looks for after this is all over."

"There is nothing going—"

Eric cut him off with a look. "Please. Pictures don't lie. Neither does the way she shoots those flames right back at you."

"That was her wanting to fry me where I stood."

"Yeah. But only after she devoured you."

Jack swore beneath his breath, but didn't bother to deny the hot little thrill Eric's observation sent rocking through him. "So, you think she wants me, huh?"

Eric rolled his eyes. "Maybe you two should just spend the next fifty-five minutes in the other room, getting each other out of your systems. It might be the only prayer we've got."

Jack slung an arm around Eric's neck and they both stole a look back at Valerie. "It's going to take a lot longer than an hour."

"Then you better find the OFF switch, my friend. At least for now." He shifted out from under Jack's arm, his expression turning sober. "She's got a lot riding on this."

Eric didn't have to add, *And so do I.*

"Yeah. I know. Best behavior." Jack crossed his heart and held up one hand, fingers folded. "Scout's honor."

Eric shook his head with a rueful smile, and reached out and re-arranged Jack's fingers. "You'd have made a lousy Boy Scout. Just do your best."

By the time Jack got out of the shower, Valerie and Eric had set up a base of operations that had taken over Jack's living room. All that was missing was an overhead screen and a PowerPoint presentation. Although the idea of Valerie with one of those whiplike pointers did give Jack a few lovely visuals. She'd need spikier heels, though....

"Jack, finally," Valerie said, giving him a quick once-over. Apparently the jeans, along with the short-sleeved blue cotton shirt over a white Fruit of the Loom met with her approval, because all she said was, "Coffee is on the kitchen counter. Grab one and have a seat. I've got today's battle strategy mapped out."

"Yes, master," he murmured as he grabbed a cup of blessedly hot coffee and snagged a bagel from the bag sitting beside it. "Where's Eric?"

"He said he had a few things he had to do."

"Yes, and the first one is probably named Brice."

"Jealous?" She didn't wait for an answer. Apparently, that was as close to teasing as he was going to get from her this morning.

Except she'd hit a little closer to home than she could have known. Because the responding little twinge had surprised him, too. Maybe part of the reason he'd been so quick to pick on Brice was because he saw him as a form of competition. Which was ridiculous. If his marriage and subsequent divorce, along with years spent trotting all over the globe, hadn't diminished their bond, Eric's new boy toy certainly wasn't going to be a threat.

"Don't worry," she told him, misreading his frown. "He'll meet us for the first interview."

That got his attention. "First? Of how many?"

She motioned to the couch, then flipped through her notes. "Five."

Christ. "Why so many? Can't we just do one or two and let everyone else lift from them?" He perched on the arm of the couch and took a bite of bagel. "And what are we wanting them to find out, anyway?"

"We do all five." She was busy making notes and not looking at him. It was then he noticed the sexy glasses. Okay, so they were dark-rimmed and not remotely sexy. But with her hair pulled up in a bun, lips pursed, pen flying over paper . . . well, she was hot as hell, really.

"Because as it turns out," she went on, "yours and Eric's little party act was something of a hit last night." She flicked a glance at her wristwatch. "The magazine hit the stands two hours ago and early indications are that sales are brisk."

"How in the hell can you know that already?"

She looked at him over the rims of her glasses. "We have ways."

Damn, he wanted to yank them off and push her back on that couch and—

She frowned. "What?"

"*What*, what?"

"Why are you looking at me like that?"

He shrugged and quickly took a bite of his bagel, forcing his mind back to the topic at hand. Because it was where he wanted to put his hands that had gotten them into this fix in the first place.

She sighed and went back to her notes. "We've got people running to their newsstands, which is a good thing, but we also have this minor furor over the photo in *Star*."

"If it's selling magazines, then who cares?"

"It might be good for sales, but we have to contain it. We want to control the impact you—or Prince Charming, anyway—has on the public. We can't let this take on a life of its own."

Jack wasn't interested in that, either, but ever the devil's advocate, he asked, "Why? What difference does it make what the tabloids or anyone else says if it means more *ka-ching* for *Glass Slipper* at the cash register? In another news cycle it will be some movie star getting divorced, knocked up, or falling off the wagon again, or the latest sighting of an alien baby. We'll be old news."

"Yes, but the magazine goes on, as does Eric's column. Image and perception are powerful tools, and *Glass Slipper*'s public image is important." She took the glasses off and sent him a pointed look. "Hitting the cover of a sleazy tabloid, right out of the gate, is not what we had in mind."

He had the grace to be at least a little abashed. "Yeah, okay. You know I'm sorry." He nudged her over and slid from the arm of the couch to sit next to her. Looking at the notes she had spread over the coffee table, he said, "What's our plan of attack?"

She didn't say anything right away, so he turned to look at her, only to find her staring at him, a somewhat perplexed expression on her face.

"What?" he asked. "What did I do now? I screwed up and I'm

ready to take my medicine like a good boy. What else do you want from me?"

Bafflement flickered briefly to a smile, then she shook her head and looked back to her notes. "Nothing. Just your cooperation today."

Intrigued, maybe a little irked, too, he reached out and touched her chin with his fingertips. She jerked away, but looked at him, serious now. "None of that."

"None of what? I just wanted—"

"That's just it, you don't get to do whatever you want. Including touching me." She shifted a little on the couch so their legs were no longer brushing each other. But it was a love seat with pillows at either end, and there wasn't a lot of extra space. "We've got enough problems."

Despite knowing better—or maybe because he knew better—he wanted to push. "What was the little smile and head shake about? What did I do that was so damn amusing? I hate it when women do that."

She smiled again.

"See? That's exactly what I'm talking about. Explain the smile."

"Okay, you want to know? At the risk of inflating your ego further, you have this . . . way about you. You are admittedly cocky, a bit arrogant—"

"*Arrogant?* I'm not—"

She raised a hand. "You asked me to explain, I'm explaining. Like I was saying, you can be cocky, a *bit* arrogant, Mr. I'm-in-Charge-I-Know-Best." She sighed with feigned resignation. "Then, as most cocky, arrogant men do, you screw up, proving you're not in charge and you don't always know best."

"Date a lot of *cocky, arrogant* men, do you?"

"No, but I've worked for my fair share. And though there is a small moment of smug satisfaction in observing your failure, we're mostly resigned to it, because you don't learn, and we know you'll be just as cocky tomorrow."

He laughed.

"See? Right there? You don't even try to deny it. You can pull the most frustrating stunt, then shoot one innocent little smile, give us a sincere 'I'm sorry,' and we're helpless not to sigh and go, 'Okay,' because you're so damn cute about it. That's the reason for the smile." Again, she lifted a hand when he grinned. "But it's a momentary, somewhat fatalistic reaction, and is not meant to encourage more acts of stupidity."

He leaned closer. God, she was something.

She stilled, caught her breath for just a moment, then abruptly shook her head. "From either party. Jesus." She went to stand up, but he stopped her with a hand on her arm. "Jack," she said warningly.

"Can I ask one thing?"

She sighed. "One thing."

"What would be the harm? I mean, really. There's a spark here. Don't deny it," he said quickly when she looked like she was going to. "We're both single, consenting adults. And you said yourself that women want to see Prince Charming available and out there dating."

"Did you read the headline? Did you read the story? The speculation on exactly how *Glass Slipper* managed to snag you? I'm sorry, but I'm not real fond of being called a whore in print, and I don't care if it's a stupid, sleazy tabloid printing it, okay?" She yanked her arm back and shoved herself to a stand. "My parents will see this." She paced across the room, stopped, leaving her back to him, but saying nothing.

This is why you don't push, idiot. Jack put his coffee on the table and walked across the room to her, but stopped short when she stiffened. "Did you talk to them?"

"Not yet."

"Do you want me to talk to them?"

The offer seemed to surprise her. Which made sense, because it had surprised him, too.

"Thank you," she said after a moment, "but no. I'll—I'll deal with them; they'll understand." She gave a short laugh, but there was no humor in it. "Who am I kidding? They've never understood anything about me."

He couldn't help it. He smiled. He reached out, wanting to turn her around, say something, anything, to restore peace and goodwill, but pulled his hand away. She'd clearly made herself off-limits.

"Well, then, they need to try harder."

She stilled but didn't say anything. And he couldn't tell if he'd just made things worse.

"What I want . . ." she began, stopped, then said, "No, what I need is for you to promise me you'll do it my way today. Please."

There was a slight quaver to her voice, and he swore under his breath. "Val, I'm sorry."

She turned around. "That only works once. You've used up your cute quotient for the day."

"Does that mean I get another shot at it tomorrow?"

"Let's hope we won't need to worry about it tomorrow, okay?" she said with forced good nature and a suspicious glisten to her eyes that made him feel lower than slime. He didn't imagine a woman like Valerie was shaken too often.

"Okay," he said, sincerely chastened. "But if you change your mind about the mom-and-pop chat, the offer stays open." He stepped away from her then, before he promised her anything else. Usually, when a woman got emotional or exhibited any signs of being trouble, he was more than willing to walk—hell, run—in the other direction. He was not in the market for the rocky ride, not when there were so many short, smooth ones available. But Valerie wasn't turning out to be someone he could dismiss so easily.

He snagged his coffee and moved behind the counter that separated the living room from the kitchen. Perhaps a physical barrier was wise at the moment. He admired how quickly she gathered herself. There was a slight hitch in his resolve when she slid those glasses back on, but he manfully persevered. "So, what's our battle plan, *ma générale?*"

"We have three radio call-ins, the first in about forty minutes. One is the Washington market, just local. The next is New York, for a syndicated team. We'll have to talk about that one. I want you to be very careful with those two, they'll try to get you going and—anyway, I have notes there. The final one is northern California. A Bay Area afternoon team, but that's later today."

"Call-ins? Why not have Eric do those?"

"We discussed it, but since you'll be doing several interviews today, we feel it's better to keep the continuity going, get you in a groove, so to speak. After the first two radio shows, you're doing a print interview with *US Weekly*." She tugged her glasses off and looked from her notes to him. "Then, before the Bay Area call, you'll do another personal appearance for the early evening news. Local station, but Washington is a major market. So we're going to have to be prepared. It should be a fluff piece, but we can't afford for you to get too cocky or self-assured."

"Somehow I don't think you'll let that happen."

"I'm going to do my best," she said evenly.

His instinct was to tease, to push again. He wasn't used to this, to not being in the driver's seat when it came to casual flirtation, to the little dance two people did around each other when attraction reared its beguiling head. Maybe because there was a sense of urgency to it that he wasn't able to explain away. Logically, rationally, or otherwise.

He glanced down, caught the cover of the tabloid again, the screaming headline. Thought about her parents, two people he didn't know and would probably never meet, looking at this, knowing everyone would be murmuring about it. And found the motivation he needed to get over this blinding attraction thing. She didn't deserve this kind of press, and she most certainly didn't need him to make it worse for her.

His game face on, and determined to keep it that way, he left the kitchen and took the seat across from her. "Tell me what you want me to say. And what you don't want me to say."

She looked up, pausing, as if expecting him to follow that up with some kind of punch line. When he didn't, she seemed to relax. Like maybe she was beginning to trust him a little. Or was at least willing to try. It was a start, anyway.

He flashed back to their conversation in his car last night, how communication, assumptions, and matching expectations could make or break a relationship.

Interestingly, he could state with unequivocal certainty that she would work tirelessly in dealing with and fixing this little fiasco. More interestingly still was the fact that he was hell-bent on making sure she knew he would, too. Trust being a two-way street and all.

To that end, he curled his hands around his coffee cup, leaned back, and propped his ankle on his knee. He watched her go over her notes, absorbed a synopsis of Eric's column highlights, listened as she fired orders at him, let her coach him in how to deflect questions they didn't want answered and work in the information they did, no matter what the direction of the interview. He paid attention, made mental notes, committed the game plan to memory.

And the entire time, in the back of his mind, all he could think was that somewhere along the way she'd blown his neat little category system all to hell. There was no category for a woman like Valerie Wagner.

But he had a feeling he was in the midst of creating one.

Crazy stupid, indeed.

Anticipation

Just when you think you have it all under control, something happens. Expectations are exceeded. Curiosity is piqued. And then you're in that lovely holding pattern between Do I Dare? . . . and Dare I Don't?

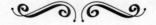

Chapter 12

"Sorry I'm late," Eric said as he shouldered his way through the cluster of people watching the taping.

Valerie spared a quick glance at him before returning to the action, as it were. "Where in the hell have you been?" she whispered furiously.

"I got caught up."

Judging from the ebullient smile on Eric's face, she could hazard a guess at what—or more likely, who—he'd been caught up in.

"How's he doing?" Eric asked. "Knocking them dead, knowing Jack."

Valerie wished she'd been as confident as Eric seemed to be. She watched as Jack made the Channel 4 reporter laugh. And blush. Again. "He's holding his own."

"I'll say. I caught the radio call-in earlier. He kicked ass."

Valerie had to grudgingly agree. Both radio spots had gone better than she could have hoped. Jack was well-traveled, a sportswriter, and a jock. That combination worked to his advantage with the morning-drive boys. Whatever they tossed at him, he tossed right back.

The US Weekly reporter had been female. Jack's combination of good looks and boyish charm, with just an edge of wolfishness, had the woman panting. Valerie was fairly sure the coverage would be flattering.

So why was she feeling so, well, pissy? It was almost as if she felt a bit jealous or something. Which, of course, was absolutely insane. She had no claim and wanted none. And even if she did, Jack was putting on the good show to save her hide. And Eric's.

But did he have to do it so damn effortlessly?

"Looks like he's enjoying himself out there," Eric whispered.

"Yeah," she murmured. Almost too much. Which at least explained the anxiety she was also feeling. Shades of the launch-party animal haunted her. But, true to his word, he'd stuck to their battle plan. More or less. It was that subtle shift from more to less that concerned her.

Eric squeezed her shoulder. "Don't worry. Women love him. And from the looks of things, today isn't any different."

"So, Mr. Lambert," the newswoman was saying.

"Jack, please," he interrupted, all jaunty smile and casual demeanor.

"You started the Dear Prince Charming column as an on-line endeavor, then went on to parlay that modest beginning into a syndicated column and several national best-sellers. Hasn't it been difficult hiding your alter ego from friends and family all this time?"

He'd handled this question many times now. Valerie could practically mouth the response with him.

"I don't have any living relatives, just a few close friends. I travel a great deal with my regular job, so it really hasn't been all that tricky."

Valerie glanced at her watch. Five minutes, then she was cutting him off. They had plenty of tape to fill the ninety seconds of airtime they were going to give him during tonight's six o'clock news coverage.

"Did those close friends know you were Prince Charming?"

"My manager did. I've known him since we were kids. And there were a few others. They respected my request to keep it under wraps."

"And why did you? Did you think a sportswriter would be ridiculed for dispensing relationship advice to the lovelorn?"

"My readers aren't lovelorn. They're smart women who enjoy the ongoing discussion on the mating rituals between men and women."

"What do you know," Eric whispered. "He was listening to me."

Jack was grinning now. "We all read advice columns in the papers, regardless of how our own lives are going. It's human to be interested in other people's problems and concerns, don't you think? Sometimes it puts things in perspective, helps us feel like maybe we've got it better than we thought."

The reporter smiled, a bit more thinly this time. She'd apparently thought he'd be a bit of a pushover. "I suppose. So why keep it a secret?"

"Honestly? I thought the air of mystery would enhance the appeal of an advice column written by a man." The grin again. "And I was right."

The reporter was persistent, though Valerie suspected she'd respected his straightforward answer. "And now?" the woman asked.

Jack's gaze flicked very briefly beyond the reporter's shoulder to the spot off set where Valerie and Eric stood. "Nothing works forever. I'd been thinking about lifting the veil, so to speak, but was unsure how to do it."

"Meaning, you wanted to exploit it if you could."

So much for this being an all-fluff filler, Valerie thought.

Now Jack's smile grew a bit tight. "From a marketing standpoint, it made sense to tie in revealing my true identity to a book launch or something like that. Then the lovely ladies of *Glass Slipper* approached me with an offer to be their spokesperson." He shrugged, all guileless charm. Or so it appeared. "It seemed the perfect way to help us both."

The reporter's smile was wide and predatory.

What she didn't know, Valerie thought, was that Jack had played this interview to this exact moment, wanting the question that was surely about to follow. So she could afford to let the reporter feel smug. Just as long as she managed to fit this next bit into their ninety-second spot.

"Speaking of the lovely ladies of *Glass Slipper*, you were spotted leaving the big launch bash with their publicist. What's the story there?"

"Ms. Wagner has done a dynamite job bringing together the magazine launch. I know the owners are very happy with her work."

"I would say, given some of the photos we've seen, that you've been pretty happy with her performance as well."

Jack gave her an admonishing smile. "The last I checked, we were both single, consenting adults. Beyond that, it wouldn't be very gentlemanly of me to speak of private moments, would it?"

"So, you two are an item, then?"

"I didn't say that."

The reporter leaned closer, trying for that it's-just-you-and-me vibe. "Well, what are you saying, then?"

Valerie tensed. *Come on, Jack,* she silently telegraphed. *Finish it up so we can get out of here.*

"My reasons for signing on with *Glass Slipper* were and are strictly professional. That hasn't changed."

"But your relationship with their publicist has, perhaps?"

Valerie willed Jack to keep his gaze locked on the interviewer and not risk even a hint of interest in her. It was clear the reporter was on the hunt now and would detect the slightest hitch in his response.

"Ms. Wagner puts her job first. She's a consummate professional."

The reporter's smile turned knowing. "You're very good at evasive answers. Is this how you counsel your readers?"

Jack's smile was just as knowing. "I wouldn't characterize my advice that way. Why don't you read my column in this month's issue of *Glass Slipper* and judge for yourself?"

The reporter laughed and nodded as if to say touché, then turned to the camera to begin her prepared wrap-up. Jack shot Valerie a quick wink, all relaxed and smiling.

Was she the only one whose stomach was in knots?

"When is the Bay Area interview?" Eric asked.

"We'll have an hour after this. We're taking that call at Glass Slipper, Incorporated. We're meeting with the godmothers afterward."

"Tabloid notwithstanding, they must be happy with this heightened exposure." Eric waved to Jack as the techs unhooked his mike.

"They weren't too happy this morning, but the tide should be shifting by now." She faced him. "How about you? Any regrets?"

"Only the stress and strain this has added to your life."

"And Jack's?"

Eric laughed a little, looking past her to where Jack was amiably chatting up the reporter, off camera. "It was a lot to ask of him, yes. But it looks like he's holding up all right." He glanced back to Valerie, his expression serious now. "How about you? Are you holding up all right?"

She managed a smile, a little nod. "I'm getting there."

"I know Jack would have never intended to put you in this situation," he told her. "He's a stand-up guy. His heart may be a little bit battered, which is understandable given all he's been through, but it's still in the right place."

"He's told me a little bit about that." Eric looked surprised, and her smile deepened more naturally. "I guess it's not all that surprising he's a bit cynical. I might be, too, in his place. But his heart is definitely in the right place when it comes to your friendship. He doesn't take that for granted. He knows he's lucky to have you in his life."

"We're both lucky," Eric said, considering her a bit more thoughtfully. "You know, I wouldn't have picked you two for each other, but the more I see you together . . . You're good for him." His lips curved a little. "And, whether you want to hear it or not, I think he's good for you."

Valerie blushed a little, tried to cover it with an eye roll. "Suddenly everyone is my mother," she teased, tossing his words of the night before back at him.

"Just don't be too quick to dismiss him," Eric said, grinning, though his tone was sincere. "The timing might suck, but he's worth the effort."

Valerie really didn't want to be having this discussion. Things were too confusing to think about this, much less discuss it with Jack's best friend. "Speaking of timing, how are things going with Brice?"

Eric's eyes sparkled and his answer came with no hesitation. "Fantastic. I'm having the time of my life. Finally. He's really amazing."

Jack came up just then, slung an arm around Eric's broad shoulders. "Ah, young love. It's so disgusting."

Valerie shot him a look. "Careful what you say there, PC, there's a lot of microphones around. If you're all set, let's get out of here. We have to make the drive to Maryland." She looked at Eric. "We're in the company town car. Do you want to leave your car here and go with us, or follow?"

Eric's cheeks colored ever so slightly. It was actually becoming on his beautiful face. "I'll, uh, meet you there. I know the way."

Jack made a show of rolling his eyes, but it was clear he was just joking. "Oh, Jesus, he's got loverboy tucked away in the Jag."

"Brice has been considering buying one, so I'm letting him test-drive mine," Eric explained happily, not remotely put off by the teasing.

"Looks like Cabana Boy is test-driving all kinds of things," Jack commented, with a little shot to Eric's shoulder.

Eric caught Jack's fist in his own and easily twisted his arm, his smile smooth and beguiling. "Stop calling him that, okay?"

Jack was chuckling as he shook his arm loose. "Pretty touchy. Must be true love." He feinted just in time to avoid a jab to the ribs.

Valerie just shook her head at their horseplay. Eric was right about one thing, though. Jack was a stand-up guy. Not every man, especially one as alpha as Jack was, would handle their best buddy's coming out so well.

"At least I know it when it's staring me in the face," Eric said pointedly.

Valerie felt the heat rise in her cheeks and pushed them both in the back, careful to avoid eye contact with either of them. "Can we please at least get to the parking lot before we ruin what little credibility we've managed to build today?"

"Hey," Jack protested, "I think I've done pretty damn well, if I do say so myself."

"Which, considering you caused this mess in the first place—" Eric began, but was cut off by Valerie.

"Let's not go there, okay? What's done is done and I think we've turned it to our advantage." If she ignored the part about the tabloid headline staring her in the face for the next week, that is. She'd already decided to just order takeout until the paper disappeared from her grocery store. They paused beside the town car. "Don't lag too far behind," she told Eric. "The godmothers want you at the meeting, too."

Eric's brows lifted. "Any particular reason?"

"No. I think it's just that as Jack's *manager*, they think you should be present." Her lips curved. "Personally, I'm pretty sure that after seeing you in those Dolce and Gabbana pants at the photo shoot, Vivian has made your presence mandatory at all future meetings. And trust me, her opinion only strengthened after seeing you in Prada last night."

Eric grinned. "Well, then, I'll be there with bells on."

"Okay, let's not take this gay thing too far," Jack deadpanned.

Eric laughed. "We'll see you there."

Eric waved and trotted across the lot toward his shiny XK8 and even shinier new love. She wanted not to worry about Eric, she had enough on her plate handling Jack. But she liked him. A lot. Despite the havoc he'd wreaked on her life, she knew he was a good, decent man. And she couldn't help but wonder if he was jumping in too deep, too fast. Or maybe she was just projecting, she thought, her gaze shifting to Jack as he opened the door for her.

"So, are we going?" Jack asked, a droll smile curving his lips. "Or are we going to lust after what we can't have?"

"I could trade up if I wanted," she quipped, rebounding fast.

"I wasn't talking about the car."

She smiled and slid into the backseat. "Neither was I."

He just gave her a yeah-right look as he slid in next to her.

"Just because a guy is gorgeous does not automatically make a woman lust after him."

They moved away from the curb and set off down Nebraska Avenue. "So you're telling me that when he first walked into the room, you didn't want him? Not even a tiny little tingle?"

"No," she lied. "Did you?"

Jack laughed. "I've known him since we were both pimply and sprouting faux whiskers. Even if I were gay, I would be long over him."

"Somehow I can't see either of you as awkward adolescents."

"Trust me, all guys are awkward at that age, no matter how smooth they think they are. In fact, the smoother they think they are, the more vulnerable and dorky they probably feel."

"Speaking from experience?"

He just shrugged, then made a truly dorky face.

She laughed despite herself. "I guess it was more awkward for Eric than you knew."

He sobered quickly and glanced out the window. "Yeah, I guess it was."

"So how did the two of you meet? You said, or he said, that you lived with his family for a while?" She told herself she was probing for business reasons. The more she knew about him, the fewer surprises could be sprung on them all. And as she held her breath, waiting to see if he'd answer, open up a little, she knew that for the half-truth it was. She wanted to know more. As a publicist . . . and as a woman.

"I spent some time at his house," he said casually. Too casually.

He didn't elaborate and she spent a few seconds deciding how much to push. "Trouble at home?" she asked, figuring that was general enough.

"More or less."

He shifted a little, clearly uncomfortable. At least it was clear if you knew what to look for. His jaw was tense, which she knew wasn't the norm for him. His shoulders were a little hunched, when he was usually the epitome of relaxed and unwound. At least outwardly.

"What about now?"

His gaze flicked from the window to her, and the intensity she found there surprised her. "What about now what?"

"Your family. Did you ever sort things out?"

A moment ago she'd had to look to see the signs of his discomfort. Now? Not so hard.

"I have no family, remember? Eric is as close to family as I have."

"I meant before . . . never mind. It's none of my business." She realized then that she didn't know nearly as much about him as she should, considering the heightened interest in him. Most of the interviews thus far had been focused on his career and the shroud of secrecy he'd worked under. No one had probed much into his past, beyond how he'd gotten his start. And since it was clear he wasn't too thrilled about her poking around in it, either, she elected to let it drop. For now.

"So," he asked at length, "do you think we contained the damage?"

They crossed the Potomac, heading toward Maryland. How much of the truth should she tell him? Did he need to know just how spectacularly well he'd done? If he'd needed the confidence boost, yes.

But Jack Lambert's confidence was never in danger of being anemic. "I think we're on the right path," she told him.

His lips curved knowingly. *The right path. Huh.*"

She wasn't sure she liked how easily he saw through her professional demeanor. Most of the people she dealt with were so caught up in themselves, they were willing to believe whatever image she chose to project. Jack, as she was so quickly learning, was not most people. But his shoulders had relaxed, his jaw had lost that harsh edge, the twinkle had returned to his eyes. And they still had one interview to go, and the godmother showdown. So she figured it was worth the responding dangerous spike in her libido. Surely she could control herself for the duration of a thirty-minute car ride.

His smile grew as he held her gaze.

Okay, maybe not so sure. She cleared her throat and slid her glasses on, pulled out her notes. Not caring if he saw right through her quickly erected shield. She just prayed he'd honor its intent. "There are a few things we should probably go over."

"Do you think the Bay Area DJs are going to toss me anything I haven't already dealt with?" he asked, his tone serious now, sincere.

"Probably not. But I wasn't referring to that, actually."

"You're worried about the godmother meeting, then? Do you

think they're still going to be pissed about the tabloid after today's blitz?"

"Let's hope not. I doubt they'll hold any of this against you, anyway."

"Meaning, you're taking all the heat. Why? Didn't you tell them that I was the one who suggested—"

"It's okay. And frankly, although Mercedes wasn't thrilled, I don't think Aurora and Vivian were all that upset." In fact, she knew they weren't. Vivian had privately given her a high five and Aurora had winked and patted her on the arm as they'd left their early morning meeting. "But they are well aware of the double standard the public applies to two people caught in a compromising position." Her smile was dry and tight. "Notice that the assumption was immediately made that I had lured you into the deal. Not that you had seduced me into offering it to you."

"Well, I think we effectively cleared that up, don't you?" He lifted his hands when she snorted. "Okay, I know how the media operates. Hey, don't give me that well-duh look. Just because I'm a journalist does not mean I'm a muckraker. I write about curling and bocce ball, for God's sake. Trust me, my subjects would love to be exploited, if for no other reason than to bring the hot glare of attention to their obscure sport. But that's not what I'm about."

Valerie chewed on the end of her pen. "All I'm saying is, the journalists who are involved in this story may not share your integrity. They'll put whatever spin on it that will sell papers, tune in viewers, or gain a wider listening audience. We can only hope that some of what we've put out there today can do that, with little or no embellishment on their part."

"So if it's not the interview and it's not the godmother meeting, what else is there to talk about?"

"The fallout from the fallout. This round of media will be disseminated to the public over the next several news cycles, likely petering out after forty-eight hours. It's the weekend, news will be slow on Capitol Hill, and the major entertainment news shows are off until Monday. By then, movie premieres will have occurred, someone will have announced a new world tour, whatever. Prince Charming will be yesterday's news." She lifted her gaze from her notes. "And no matter what the godmothers say, that's exactly how I'd like it to play out. Our new mantra is: 'We got more exposure than we could have hoped for, but we don't want to wear out our welcome.' Overkill can be deadly. Besides, if I can't do something with what we've already got, then I deserve to lose my job. Eric is already writing the column for the next issue, and I'm sure you'd like to get on with your life."

He held her gaze with a far more serious expression than she'd expected.

The limo bounced a little as they pulled off the main road and began winding down the long drive toward the stately Victorian house that was home to Glass Slipper, Inc. He was still staring at her when they glided to a stop.

Mercedes, Vivian, and Aurora all descended the wide front steps leading from the shaded front porch, looking excited (Vivian), concerned (Mercedes), and anxious (Aurora).

"Promise me you'll follow my lead," Valerie said, feeling the tension start to ball up inside her again, which was mixing uncomfortably with the sexual tension Jack had somehow re-ignited during the last few minutes.

"I'm not so sure."

Her mouth dropped open. "What do you mean you're *not so sure?*" She shot a fast glance at the approaching trio, then back at him. "You've been doing great all day. Don't play around with me on this, okay?"

"I'll handle the godmothers just fine. That wasn't what I was responding to."

"Hellooo," Aurora trilled as the driver rounded the front of the car.

Valerie waved and forced a breezy, confident smile. "What are you talking about, then?" she asked out of the side of her mouth.

"Whether or not I'm ready to get on with my life," he responded calmly. "I'm sort of enjoying this one at the moment."

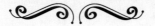

Impulses

Even the most commitment-phobic guy will occasionally leap before he looks. Of course, this is rarely relationship-related. It's usually an attempt to prove some misguided manly point. You'll earn points by not rushing to point that out.

Chapter 13

Tea was postponed until after Jack completed his phone-in interview to San Francisco. It was admittedly more nerve-racking shooting the bull with the afternoon-drive boys while the godmothers looked on. All in all, he thought it had gone well. In fact, somewhat surprisingly, for a guy who preferred to write the story rather than be the story, he was having a pretty good time.

He looked over at Valerie, scribbling notes on her ever-present pad of paper, and wondered how much of that good time was due to his growing fascination with a certain wry, aggressive, workaholic publicist.

"Tea is served on the rear veranda, Ms. Browning," a young man in a lemon-sherbet-colored linen blazer—a Glass Slipper, Inc. trademark, Jack had quickly discovered—announced from the doorway.

"Shall we?" Aurora asked brightly.

Valerie finished whatever notes she was taking, probably a critique of his performance, with a sidebar of suggestions for any future interviews he might give. He didn't know what it said about his burgeoning feelings that he was actually looking forward to whatever private harangue she was preparing to deliver. As long as he got the private part. Whatever the reason for this attraction, he knew one thing: Now that he was done mopping up his mess, he intended to start working on those hair-trigger defenses of hers. He wanted some alone time with Valerie. No notepads, no schedules, no rules. No Prince Charming.

Which meant he had to work fast. If she was right, and his function in their little deception was due to end shortly, he'd be catching a flight out of here as soon as he could book himself some work. *EuroSport* was pushing for more from him and he was fairly certain he could end up with a full-time gig there if he played his cards right. He'd probably end up giving up his apartment in Alexandria, find more permanent digs on the other side of the pond, but hell, why not? He had no business or family ties in the States. Eric certainly had the means to travel. That is, if he could fit in a visit to an old friend around his newfound social life.

Jack had considered relocating overseas before, but figured it was a knee-jerk reaction to his divorce. Pride had kept him from tucking his tail and hiding in another country. That was Shelby's way, not his.

Had Jack dated her longer than a nanosecond before marrying her, he'd have learned that and more about his ex-wife. They were both the same age, but Shelby's childhood in Peru had been a far cry from his own. Her father was fairly well-to-do and she'd led a very sheltered life, used to being given everything she wanted. When she'd been discovered by a talent scout for a European modeling agency, her family had ordered her to refuse the contract. She was supposed to stay home, marry, begin a family. Headstrong and not used to being told no, Shelby had taken off and had quickly found work all over Europe. But where she'd triumphed on the runways, she'd failed spectacularly in understanding the ways of the world.

She knew nothing of managing money and had no head for business, nor did she care to learn. She missed being taken care of, but she was stubborn enough that she refused to run home to Papa. So she did the next best thing: She found someone else who would take care of her and make her the center of his world. A string of them, Jack later learned. But he was the only one fool enough—or drunk enough—to actually marry her.

Thinking about it usually pissed him off, renewed those feelings of remorse and guilt. *Remorse*, for being so foolish and leaping before he looked. *Guilt*, no matter how misplaced, that he hadn't been able to do right by Shelby and make her happy, even though he knew she'd never worried that much about his happiness, or doing right by him. He'd like to think he was over it because he'd matured, moved on. Not because another woman had entered the picture and he was fool enough to forget the lessons he'd learned. Number one being that you never knew what you had truly gotten yourself into until it was too late.

Valerie wasn't going to be part of any big picture where his life was concerned. They were quite literally heading in two different directions. But a snapshot in the big picture? Well, he didn't see how that could hurt anything. His eyes were wide open this time. There would be no foolish mistakes. He could certainly look without leaping.

"You were quite fabulous, darling," Vivian purred, linking her arm through his and steering him from the small office they'd been using and out toward the rear veranda. She squeezed his bicep and sighed a little. "Have I thanked you for saving your little coming-out party for us? We're truly appreciative, you know."

"I'm being fairly compensated," he managed.

"I must admit, I still don't understand why you waited so long." She gave him a quick once-over, lingering momentarily on his backside before smiling up at him again as he paused to let her step out onto the veranda.

"Marketing. Habit," he said easily. She'd heard all the answers during this latest interview, so he didn't elaborate.

"Still, you must realize how much stronger your impact is going to be on sales now that you've emerged from your cocoon to show the world that Prince Charming is truly a prince in every way."

Jack flashed her a grin. "I wouldn't say every way."

Vivian hooted. "And you prove my point. No woman wants a prince who's not capable of being a rogue on occasion."

Fortunately Jack was saved from responding to that when Aurora floated through the door on a cloud of flowery perfume. She paused long enough to buss him on the cheek. "You'll have to pardon the familiarity, but you are just so adorable, I had to express my affection for you." She wiped off the lipstick smudge with heavily ringed fingers. "Besides," she added with a surprisingly sly wink, "I'm simply not forward enough, or young enough, to try anything else." She shot a look at Vivian. "Unlike some others, I try to maintain at least a modicum of decency."

"Indecency has its incentives," Vivian shot back with a sly smile of her own. She moved to the edge of the awning-covered veranda and carefully wedged a cigarette into a slim-stemmed, ebony holder that Bette Davis would have wept for. Knowing Vivian and her Hollywood connection, it just might be Bette's, Jack thought.

"Must you, dear?" Aurora asked her disdainfully.

Vivian blew out a long stream of smoke, then sighed appreciatively. "Absolutely."

Aurora gave a little sniff, then surprised Jack with a private wink. "I can hardly blame her really," she whispered. "Great sex is a lovely way to spend the afternoon."

Jack choked on a shocked laugh.

Aurora's cheeks pinked quite becomingly as her eyes twinkled. "I said I believe in decency, but I'm hardly dead."

"No, ma'am," he agreed. "You most certainly are not."

Aurora flicked the silk scarf she held toward him, then went over to examine the display of fresh fruit that had been laid out on a side table along with a variety of breads, crackers, cheeses, and cut vegetables.

"Quite a spread," Jack said, maintaining his post at the door as Valerie finally made her way in.

"At Glass Slipper, afternoon tea is an event."

"So I see. Where is Mercedes?"

"She was waylaid by one of the staff. Something to do with a guest having a conflict with her linguistics coach."

"I hate it when that happens," he deadpanned, happy to see the dry smile replace the worried frown she'd been sporting since their arrival. "So, how long do you expect this to last?"

"I have no idea. Not too long. Why? Hot date?"

His lips quirked. "I don't know. What are you doing later?"

She rolled her eyes. "Please. We've just spent all day killing rumors."

"Actually, we killed rumors about how I got the job. Not whether or not we are an item. It was you who said not to try to deny what the pictures clearly showed."

"To the uninformed. They didn't clearly show what was really happening. Only you and I know that was just a ruse on your part."

"And yet, I think the media seemed to like the idea that there might be something going on between us. Of a romantic, not salacious, nature."

"Rather ironic, isn't it? Given your views on romance. Honestly, though, they just like the idea that Prince Charming is on the prowl, because they know their readers will like it. We've done what we set out to do. I'm not about to provoke another firestorm."

"Valerie? Jack? What's got your heads together?" Vivian called out. "Come share with the group. Mercedes can catch up when she gets here."

Valerie looked past Jack, a smile on her face. Only Jack was close enough to see the tic in her jaw. "We're just waiting for Eric. He should be here momentarily. I'm not sure what delayed him." So only Jack could hear her, she added, "Although I'm sure the key word there is *laid*."

"At least somebody is allowed to have some fun."

She smiled more naturally now. "Well, he's been waiting a hell of a lot longer than you have. Besides, I figured you'd be happy for him. It can't have been easy on him all these years."

"No, I don't imagine it was."

Her smile faltered. "You've known he's gay for a long time, right?"

Jack shook his head. "Found out the same day you did."

"Wow. I would have thought—" She stopped, shook her head. "Never mind."

It pricked a little, her assumption. Probably because it was still a bit of a sore spot with him. "Yeah, well, I would have thought so, too. He had his reasons."

Her expression turned as serious as his tone. "I guess so. I'm sure it wasn't easy for either of you."

Her understanding shouldn't have made an impact one way or the other. Maybe it was because he hadn't been able to tell anyone, to discuss the shock waves that were still rippling through him over his best friend's stunning revelation. He really had thought he was handling it pretty damn well. Who the hell needed to talk about it? It was what it was, right? Deal with it. Move on. End of story. Kind of like his divorce.

Which did little to explain why he held on to her compassionate gaze, and said, "No, it wasn't. It's still not. But I'm working on it."

"You're doing an amazing job, then. I'd have never guessed you hadn't known all along. You're a good friend, Jack. Anyone can see it."

"Thanks. He's earned whatever I have."

"You've referred to that before. That you owe him. Are you—don't take this wrong—but are you sure there isn't something else I might need to know?"

He sighed, wishing he'd never said anything. Would he ever learn? "Are you ever not working?"

He went to move away, but she took his wrist and tugged him back inside the house and away from two very avid pairs of eyes. "I'm sorry," she said, sounding both contrite and sincere.

"It doesn't matter," he told her, though it did. He just didn't want it to. He wanted to get her into bed, sure. But that was the only place he wanted her. Not in his head, and sure as hell not mixed up in any other part of his life. "You said this was probably all over, anyway. Since I don't plan to stick around any longer than I have to, you have nothing to worry about."

"What do you mean? Did you get a job already? Because—" Just then her cell phone went off. "Dammit." She unclipped it and read the text screen. "Wait just a second, don't go back out there." She flipped it open. "This is Valerie," she said, all professionalism. "Yes. Right." There was a pause, then her gaze shot to his, eyes wide. "You're kidding!"

Jack turned to go back outside and leave her to business. He had no desire to pursue this conversation any further. In fact, if he was smart, he'd get this meeting done, then start to concentrate on getting the hell out of Dodge. Permanently. Valerie Wagner was too much trouble. He'd known that from the start. A good reminder never to ignore the Jack Lambert Ranking System.

"Holy shit," Valerie breathed. "No, no, I'm right here. Static. Yes, go ahead. When? They want to do this when?" She snatched his arm and held on, shaking her head furiously at him. "Don't go," she mouthed.

Just then Eric strolled up, mercifully Brice-free.

Donna Kauffman

Jack extricated his arm from her grip. "We'll talk when you're done." He didn't wait for a reply, but ushered Eric out to the veranda.

"So, what did I miss?" Eric asked jovially.

Jack spied what looked like razor burn on Eric's neck and throat. "I don't know," Jack said, motioning to the open neck of Eric's polo shirt. "Not much from the looks of it."

"Yeah, well, we, uh, took the scenic route through Potomac and . . ."

"God, you're such a tramp," Jack exclaimed in mock disgust.

"Hello, Pot, meet Kettle," Eric shot back. "I have years of catching up to do before I can even begin to compete with your vaunted past."

"Well, you might want to button up the shirt and keep your face in the shade. Those two don't miss much. And I'm sure they would be quite happy discussing every last detail."

Eric had just done the last button and flipped his collar up a little when Mercedes joined them. "Sorry for the delay." She looked at Vivian and Aurora and made a small moue. "Celeste."

The other two made faces. Clearly Celeste, whoever she was, had had problems with more than just her linguistics coach.

Smoothing her face into a polite, social smile, Mercedes turned to Jack and Eric. "Nice to see you both. I trust the day went smoothly?"

"Yes, ma'am," Jack responded. "I think we can safely assume we worked things to your—our—advantage."

"Why don't we all have a seat. Valerie should be done with her business call in a moment." She gestured to the spread. "Help yourselves. Would you rather have tea or a glass of wine?"

"Nothing for me," Jack said.

"I'll have wine. White," Eric said. "This looks wonderful."

Jack plucked a fat strawberry from the mound and popped it into his mouth as Eric loaded up a small salad plate.

He noticed Jack noticing his growing heap and smiled, unrepentant. "Refueling is important, I'm discovering."

{226}

Jack held his hand up as he forced the lump of strawberry down his throat. "Thanks."

Eric just chuckled, and reached for a strawberry, or three.

Valerie stepped onto the veranda just then, easily drawing Jack's complete attention. He told himself it was the nervous smile she shot him that did it. But he was starting to suspect it wouldn't have mattered. *Definitely need to see about that job with* EuroSport. *ASAP.*

"Why, Valerie, dear, you look like a cat who's not quite sure about the canary she just swallowed." Aurora motioned to the table. "Would you like some tea? Wine?"

She shook her head. "I—actually, I have some news. Why don't we all sit down."

The godmothers gathered at the lemon-yellow, linen-covered table, each perching in one of the white wicker chairs.

"What is it?" Vivian asked.

"Pray God, it's not another horrid tabloid story, is it?" Mercedes asked.

"No." She shot a quick glance at Eric and Jack, who had taken positions against the white pillars that fronted the covered veranda, then put on her best publicist face and smiled at the godmothers. "It seems our media blitz this morning accomplished even more than we'd hoped."

Uh-oh, Jack thought. This could not mean good things for him. It was only a matter of how badly he was about to get screwed. He felt Eric tense beside him, but didn't say anything.

"*US Weekly* had planned a small sidebar in their Faces and Places column. We were just hoping for a picture. Well, it seems that one of the editors from *People* was in town today and caught part of Jack's radio show this morning. They discussed doing a small tidbit on him for their Insider column, then somehow got wind that *US* had beaten them to it. Never to be outdone, they've asked if they can do a feature."

Jack noticed she didn't look at him or Eric.

"Well, that's fabulous, dear!" Aurora exclaimed.

"There's something else, isn't there?" Mercedes asked.

Valerie nodded. "A couple of things, actually."

Aurora clapped her hands together. "Isn't this exciting, Vivi?"

"Tell us the rest," Mercedes directed.

"The entertainment business is a small world, as you all probably know. Well, somebody's assistant from *People* told somebody on *Live with Chuck and Vicki*." Now she looked at Jack, a quick beseeching look. "They contacted Elaine an hour ago, trying to get in touch with me or Eric. They want you on the show. This coming week."

Vivian hooted. Aurora clapped again. Mercedes frowned, as if she couldn't quite let herself believe it was good news.

Jack understood that sentiment entirely.

Valerie took a seat and opened her notebook. "Before we get ahead of ourselves, we need to talk about this." She motioned to Jack and Eric. "Our agreement is that Prince Charming's exposure be limited. We've already pushed our contractual boundaries in one day. We also have to be careful of overexposure. We don't want people to tire of seeing him."

"Surely a spot on a highly rated talk show would be good exposure?" Aurora shifted in her seat to look up at Jack and Eric. "You wouldn't mind a few more little interviews, would you? You've done so magnificently, it's a surprise you haven't gone before the camera sooner."

"You certainly photograph well," Vivian added.

It only took one look at her for Jack to immediately understand that Valerie didn't want him to do this. He could see the nerves all but roiling beneath her perfectly polished surface. He realized that a feature in *People*, with their massive subscription base, coupled with a spot on the most popular morning talk show in the country, were quite different on the exposure meter from a local news spot and fifteen minutes on drive-time radio.

Of course, he had no desire to prolong this circus, either. In fact, he was opening his mouth to explain why he agreed that it would not be a good idea to overexpose the whole Prince Charming thing, knowing Eric would jump in and back him up—when Valerie nervously *clicked* and *reclicked* her pen and said, "Yes, he's got great presence, but we've hired him to dispense advice exclusively for *Glass Slipper* magazine. It's why people will buy it. It might not be smart to just give that away right off the bat. His platform should be the magazine, not a talk show."

It dawned on Jack then that, even though today had gone so well, she still didn't trust him. She didn't think he could handle this without screwing up and giving away the charade. Had he spent a few more minutes thinking it through, he might have realized that she was more concerned that prolonged media exposure invited prolonged media scrutiny. Then again, if he was the kind of guy who took the time to think things through, he wouldn't have been in this spot in the first place.

Which is why, before Eric could step in and help her out, he jumped right out of the frying pan without so much as glancing at the fire. "Well, you did hire me as your spokesperson," he said.

Eric's mouth dropped open. "Jack—"

Valerie's reaction time was a bit slower. She turned to stare at him.

He smiled, all benevolent and helpful as he looked at the assembled group. "It's just one interview, a few pictures, and a couple minutes talking to the talk-show hosts, right?" He shrugged. "I don't see why this should be a problem." He turned to Eric. "Do you?"

Eric all but drilled holes right through Jack's forehead despite the grin he kept on his face. "Maybe we should discuss this," he said tightly through the smile. He looked past Jack to Valerie, who was looking very relieved at the intervention.

Which only served to piss Jack off more.

"When do they need a response?" Eric asked.

"Right away, I'm afraid," Valerie said, obviously hoping the tight time frame would work in her favor. "The booking agent from the show is waiting for a call back from me right now."

As if they were seated at Centre Court, Wimbledon, the god-mothers' heads turned in unison, from Valerie to Eric and Jack, then back again.

"Do you mind if we talk this over privately?" Eric asked, already reaching for Jack's elbow.

Jack neatly sidestepped him. "No need. Honestly, I don't see the big issue here. As your spokesperson, I expected to do the occasional media function. I feel responsible for the situation we found our-selves in this morning and I'd like to do what I can to make it up to you. I'm sure it will help boost your magazine sales, and it can't hurt my book sales, either. As far as I can tell, we all come out winners."

The godmothers breathed a collective sigh of relief. Valerie, on the other hand, used that brief moment to glare at him. He smiled. She was going to have to learn that he didn't do well with being micro-managed. Or underestimated. Besides, it wouldn't affect his time-table too much. He could still be out of here in a week or two. Then Valerie wouldn't have to worry about what he might say or do, would she?

"This is simply fabulous," Vivian gushed. "If *People* is foolish enough to let us build our subscriber base on the backs of their es-tablished mailing list, then more power to us, I say."

"Exactly, dear," Aurora concurred.

"It does seem to be a good opportunity for us both. Thank you for going the extra mile," Mercedes said, finally giving in to a small smile.

"Not a problem," Jack assured them.

"Dear, why don't you go make your calls," Aurora suggested to Valerie.

"Thank you for your hospitality," Eric broke in, "but if it's okay with you, Jack and I should also take our leave now. We've got to go over the revised schedule and make plans accordingly."

Both Aurora and Vivian looked crestfallen, but not wanting to upset the coup they'd just scored, they all quickly agreed. "Of course," Mercedes said with a nod of finality. "Naturally, *Glass Slipper* will take care of whatever expenses are incurred. Valerie will schedule your transportation and accommodations."

"Of course," Valerie agreed with a fixed smile as she gathered her cell phone and stacks of notes and crammed them into her satchel.

"Would you like us to fix you a plate to take with you?" Aurora asked. "You didn't get tea."

"Don't go to any trouble," Valerie answered for all of them. "We have a lot to go over." Turning so the godmothers were behind her, she shot Jack a death glare. "We'll be sure to have a long dinner while we go over every last detail."

"You do that, dears," Aurora said. "It's been a whirlwind that appears to continue, so you have to take care of yourselves."

"Oh, we'll be taken care of," Valerie assured her. Under her breath, as she passed by Jack and Eric, she muttered, "All the way along our descent straight to hell."

Sexual attraction

Hunger is a powerful thing. It can make you deaf, dumb, and blind to reality. Hunger is sneaky. It can make you believe that feeding it is more important than anything else. Hunger is also vital. But indulge at your own risk. Or it will come back to bite you on the ass.

Chapter 14

Valerie Wagner was a woman on the verge.

The question was, of what? Her career was taking off. And yet, every time she looked into the smiling faces of the godmothers, the guilt factor increased. And every time she looked into the grinning face of the source of that guilt, her lust increased despite the irritation.

This was not good.

Her intercom buzzed. "They've arrived," Tracy, her new assistant, chirped. "Should I direct them to the conference room, Ms. Wagner?"

"Yes, please. And it's Valerie, okay?"

"Yes, Ms. Wagner." She stopped, giggled. "I mean, Valerie."

Valerie sighed and gathered her notes. Had she ever been that young? Probably. But hopefully she'd never been that vacuous. When Elaine had told her to hire someone to take on the day-to-day increase in traffic she was now having to handle, Valerie had been secretly thrilled. She had staff! She'd immediately planned on hiring someone with verve, attitude, and a hunger to get in on the ground floor of something good. Much as she saw herself back in the early days. And the middle days. For that matter, all the days leading up to taking this job.

Instead, she'd gotten Tracy. Well-meaning, klutzy, heavily mascara'd Tracy. Who also happened to be Elaine's niece. Nineteen, fresh out of high school, and *taking a break* before starting college. Valerie got the feeling she was being used as incentive to make Tracy want to end her *break* early. After only two days on the job, Valerie was totally on board with that program.

She stopped by the teenager's desk on her way out. Tracy was busy blocking out her schedule with a variety of colored highlighter pens. Valerie could only hope there was actually some sort of method being employed, but a quick glance at Tracy's Sponge Bob screensaver reminded her that *methodical* and *forward-thinking* were two adjectives she'd likely never employ when describing her new assistant.

She put a short, neatly printed list of numbers on Tracy's desk. "I need you to contact these people. It's just a confirmation list, so you should be able to get through it quickly. If anyone hedges, put them through to me. If there are any changes, tell them I will call them back."

Tracy looked up from her artwork, beaming like a puppy who'd just figured out how to use the paper for the first time. "I hope you don't mind," she said, nodding to the desk calendar as she uncapped a fresh pen. "Color makes me happy. I think the world needs more color."

"Very Peter Max of you."

"Who?"

Valerie swallowed the urge to sigh. "Never mind. Just take care of the call list first, okay?"

Tracy recapped the pen and bobbed her pert blond head. "Sure thing, boss." She fanned her liberally applied M•A•C foundation with the call-back list. "You know, I still can't believe you scored Prince Charming."

I can't believe I want to score with Prince Charming, Valerie thought, but managed not to say.

"And who knew he was such a hottie?" Tracy burbled. "All my girl-friends are going to drop a total brick when I tell them he was stand-ing not two feet away from me and actually spoke to—"

"Tracy, the calls?" Valerie broke in, smiling faintly.

Her assistant immediately adopted what she probably thought was a serious, businesslike demeanor. Renee Zellweger would have been more convincing. "Yes, Ms. Wagner." At Valerie's short sigh, she quickly cleared her throat. "I mean, Valerie. I'll get this done right away."

Shaking her head, Valerie strode quickly toward the conference room. How was it that for every minute she spent with Tracy, she felt five years older? She shifted gears and mentally tried to prepare her-self for the upcoming meeting with Jack and Eric.

She'd waved them off when they'd all left Glass Slipper, Inc. less than seventy-two hours ago, but only after she'd made sure Eric was aware it was his job to explain to Jack exactly why she wasn't very happy with him. She'd spent every minute since then with a cell phone in one hand and her Palm Pilot in the other.

The calls they'd gotten Friday morning had turned out to be the mere front wall of the avalanche. "God forbid he play by the rules and just say no, like we'd agreed," she muttered. Because then she might be able to sleep at night and stop using Rolaids as condiments with every meal. When she had time for one, that is.

She pushed into the conference room, intent on taking charge from the get-go and not letting up an inch until she was certain they were all on the same track. Meaning her track. Which was to bull their way through the now white-hot glare of media they'd attracted—or, rather, that Jack had attracted—pray they didn't slip up, keep him from basking in the glow for even one second longer than was absolutely necessary, then mercifully close the door on this charade. Then maybe she could settle into the slightly more sane and humane pace of playing publicist for a bimonthly publication. And at some point, she might even stop feeling guilty, and start believing in, and enjoying her success.

Who knew, she might even be able to figure out a solution to her totally unreasonable attraction to Jack.

Her blossoming optimism was swiftly extinguished by the sight of Jack sitting at the conference table, talking with a woman Valerie had never seen before.

"I think women are as perplexed by men as we are by women. Myself included," Jack was saying, quite amiably and somewhat flirtatiously, if you asked Valerie. Of course, Jack was just being Jack, but the result was the same.

"So I can't help the guys out," he went on, "but I try my best to demystify my gender for the opposite sex when and where I can."

Once Valerie dealt with the totally uncalled for pang of something that felt the teensiest bit like jealousy, she simultaneously assimilated two vitally important pieces of information. One, Jack was giving relationship advice. And two, that little recorder in front of the woman indicated she was taping his comments. Meaning, she was a reporter.

When Tracy had said "They're here," she'd assumed her assistant meant Jack and Eric. "Where's Eric?" she blurted, thinking only that she had to stop this farce as quickly as possible. And she needed backup.

"Valerie, good, you're here." Jack swung his feet off the black conference table, where he'd been making himself very comfortable. "Eric was unavoidably detained." With that damnably amused smile, he stood and gestured to the woman, a polished, slim blonde with a wide, attractive smile. "Petra Mackaby, this is Valerie Wagner. Valerie, this is Petra. She's the stateside correspondent for *Okay!* magazine in the U.K." He smiled, quite pleased with himself.

That's about to change, Valerie thought. "Hello," she managed through a partially clenched smile.

"A pleasure," the pert British woman responded. As she pushed to a stand, her bobbed hair and gravity-defying boobs bounced pertly in unison. Everything about her was pert.

Valerie had had it up to here with pertness.

"Valerie is *Glass Slipper*'s publicist," Jack explained.

The younger woman's cleverly sculpted brows rose as the light of recognition dawned in her—of course—sparkly blue eyes. "Ah."

She didn't need to tack on "The one from the front page of the tabloid," as it was clearly a given.

Petra extended a hand. Valerie took pleasure in noting the bitten-down nails, knowing it was small of her. She didn't care.

"I hope you don't mind my tagging along here," Petra said in her lovely British lilt. "I assure you, I plan to report only the good things." She smiled adoringly at Jack. "As if there could be any bad."

Jack grinned. Valerie barely refrained from rolling her eyes.

"Yes, well, I certainly appreciate the interest in our spokesperson, but at the moment his contract is somewhat restrictive when it comes to giving interviews. Jack, I'm afraid I have you promised to a number of other outlets and we're in danger of overextending the boundaries of our agreement." She looked back at Pertra. "I'm sure you understand."

The gleam in Petra's eyes turned somewhat more speculative. "Ah, yes. I believe I do." She glanced between the two of them, then began gathering her things.

Jack stepped in. "Now, Valerie, don't be hasty. Petra is doing a sort of day-in-the-life article. I thought you'd approve of expanding *Glass Slipper*'s exposure to an overseas market."

Petra didn't pause in stowing her recorder and scooping up her trendy Gucci white leather bag. "It's quite all right, Jack. I believe you've given me enough to work with." She smiled at Valerie, and there was a definite smugness to it now. "More than enough, I'm sure."

"At least let me arrange transportation for you," Jack offered, reluctantly accepting the abrupt change in plans.

Petra waved him off. "I've taken quite a bit of your time and I don't want to delay your meeting with Ms. Wagner here another moment. It appears she's got important things to discuss. I can take care of myself." With one last knowing glance at Valerie, she slipped on a pair of red Boomslang sunglasses and was gone.

"I'll just bet you can," Valerie muttered, definitely done with everyone calling her Ms. Wagner. It made her sound as bitchy as she felt. "*Day-in-the-life*, my ass. More like, *night-in-my-bed*."

Jack closed the conference-room door and turned back to a still cross-armed Valerie. "What was that all about? I honestly thought the article was a good idea."

"I have the feeling you'd think anything that presented itself in body-hugging black knit would be a good idea."

His lips quirked. "Ah."

"Don't you *ah* me." She slapped her notebook down on the table. "And you can wipe that amused smirk off your face while you're at it. Didn't Eric explain anything to you? Do you realize what just happened?"

"I don't smirk." He lifted a hand when she growled. "I will cop to being amused."

"At some point during all this, you've begun to believe you really are Prince Charming, haven't you?" She folded her arms again. "Well, you might think you can charm your way through a few interviews and a few reporters, but you forget that I know the real deal. The real you."

Jack came closer, his gaze suddenly very focused. It took considerable willpower, but she managed to remain rooted to the spot.

He stopped mere inches in front of her. "You don't know the real me," he said calmly and very intently. "You don't know anything about me except the bits and pieces I've had to reveal to pull off this farce."

Valerie struggled against the almost hypnotic tone of his voice, the tugging tractor-beam pull of his gaze. "What I know," she told him, damning the faint quaver in her tone, "is that you just handed that woman an article better suited for *Page Six* than some human-interest story that might have done us some good."

"I didn't hand her anything. We were getting along just fine until you came in."

"I bet you were," she said, realizing as she heard her own words what she sounded like. The brief kick at the corners of his mouth told her he thought the same. "What you do on your own time is up to you. But you don't have any of your own time until we're done with this fiasco."

"What *fiasco?*" he asked, honestly perplexed. "I mean, I know none of us planned this, but as far as I can tell, the magazine is selling like hotcakes, and Eric's popularity is multiplying just as fast."

"Is that why you jumped in and said yes to the godmothers, even though you knew I didn't want you to? Even though we'd agreed you wouldn't? To help Eric's career? Because I don't think he—"

"No, I did it because you looked like you were about to have a stroke at the idea of putting me in front of a camera. Honestly, Valerie, you worry too much. And, frankly, I don't think you give me enough credit."

"*You?* I don't think you give *me* enough credit! You said after that little tabloid-making stunt that you'd do things my way. But did you, at any time, think to clear this little chat through me? No. You have no idea what I've been dealing with over the weekend, or how hard I've worked to safeguard our little secret and yet still appear to do my job." She knew she had to rein it in, get herself under control. Jack was far too calm about this whole thing, which only served to make her look even more like a screeching shrew than she already felt. "And dammit, where is Eric this time? He was supposed to—"

"Baby-sit me, I know," Jack broke in. "I know you think I'm a little slow on the uptake, but yes, I managed to pick up on the fact that you apparently don't trust me to be able to string more than three sentences together that you haven't vetted and preapproved." He leaned closer, smiled. "Believe it or not, up until a few weeks or so ago, I was doing a pretty damn good job of policing myself."

He was not going to worm his way into her good graces. Or anything else, for that matter. That frisson of awareness she felt every time he invaded her personal space? A perfectly normal reaction to the heightened tensions running between them. She could certainly control herself. And would. "Well, a few weeks ago, your face wasn't plastered on the cover of a national magazine. And based on your performance today with Perky Petra, I'd say my instincts are pretty much dead-on."

His eyes twinkled. The gall.

"*Perky Petra*, huh?" He reached out and traced his fingertips along her clenched forearm.

She tried very hard not to react. Not to shiver in awareness. To absolutely refuse to acknowledge the way the hairs lifted from her arm as her entire body prickled. He was frustrating, irritating, and a major pain in her ass. She had no business wanting him to touch her.

"I wasn't really paying attention," he went on.

She snorted. "Oh, please." But she didn't move away. Simply proving to him, of course, that his touch didn't affect her. Nope. Not at all. Totally immune.

His mouth curved more deeply. "Although I do think that for all her supposed perkiness she was pretty perceptive. In fact," he continued, retracing his path down to her wrist again, "I'd say she was pretty much spot on with her assessment of the undercurrents that were really swirling in this room. Undercurrents, by the way, that didn't start until you stepped through that door."

It was only when he leaned forward that Valerie conceded defeat and turned away. "Believe what you want," she snapped, flipping open her binder and trying to focus on her notes. On anything except whatever the hell it was he did to her every time they were alone. "Because Petra sure as hell will. And she'll make damn sure all of her readers believe it, too."

Jack allowed her to retreat, leaning back against the table, crossing his legs and arms. "I think you're making too much of it. I understand the grocery-store tabloid wasn't the vehicle we wanted. But this is different." He tried one of his trademark cocky smiles. "Besides, it will be in British grocery stores. What do we care?"

Before she could begin to enumerate that list, he went on. "People are going to speculate about something no matter what. Might as well reap the attention for *Glass Slipper*."

Valerie ground her teeth. "I think we've garnered enough positive attention not to have to pander to people's more prurient interests, don't you? Never mind, don't answer. And for God's sake, stop smiling at me like that."

He chuckled. She huffed and took a seat. To think she'd spent even two seconds considering the idea of sleeping with him when this was all over. Obviously, sleep deprivation was getting to her. Although, admittedly, sex deprivation might be equally to blame.

"We have a lot to go over." She nudged out the chair opposite her with her foot and gestured him to it, not caring what conclusions he drew.

To her relief, he circled the table and sat. "Shoot."

"Don't tempt me." She sorted through her notes, careful not to look at him. She really needed to find a way to stay more balanced around him. She was never like this, testy and shrewish all the time, except around him. Jack Lambert set her off faster than anybody in recent memory. Of course, he could probably get her off faster than anyone in recent memory, too. That was half her problem. Two thirds, even.

"Is Eric planning on making an appearance today?" she asked.

"Actually, Eric seems to think he can trust me. I know, wacky concept," he said with a mock-surprised shrug. "He said something about an appointment with a real estate agent. I have no idea what that means, or what he's up to, but since I've never seen him this happy and excited, I decided maybe I could trust me, too." His expression softened a little, and Valerie was struck by how sincerely pleased he was when he talked about his best friend. "And, okay, maybe I wasn't thinking clearly when I jumped in and agreed to do this *People* thing and the talk show. I shouldn't let you provoke me."

She sat back. "I didn't *provoke* you. We'd agreed you wouldn't do anything else. That's not provoking, that's expecting you to hold up your end of the deal. And if I recall, you were all for that yourself. Even Eric agreed. He was all prepared to back us up, too, but nooo, you go and jump in, save the day, be a—"

"Prince?" he supplied helpfully.

She threw her pencil at him.

"Hey!" He lifted a hand and it bounced off his arm.

"That's provocation, okay?" she said. "Now let's talk about the upcoming schedule."

"Valerie—"

She lifted her hand. "I should have said, let *me* talk about the upcoming schedule. You talking is what got us here in the first place."

"Just exactly what is it you think I'm going to do wrong?"

She folded her arms on the table. "I don't know. When I came in here you were dispensing advice. Just because you read Eric's books doesn't mean you're qualified to—" She broke off when she noticed Jack was suddenly having trouble keeping her gaze. She let out a short, harsh laugh. "Oh, my God. You still haven't read any of them?"

"I skimmed. Heavily," he added quickly, then sighed and slouched back in his seat when she continued to scowl at him. "I have your synopses of his books. And Eric and I talk all the time. I wasn't supposed to give advice anyway, so why read hundreds of pages of it?"

"Oh, I don't know. So you might have a clue what it is you've supposedly made buckets full of money writing about? You know, just in case someone *asks about it!*" She shoved out of her seat, more angry with her own lack of control than anything, and paced to the long bank of windows, keeping her back to him. "Dammit," she swore under her breath, then stiffened as she felt him come up behind her. "I don't know why I let you get to me like that."

"I don't know, either. Maybe the same reason I let you get to me." He very gently took her shoulders and turned her around.

She couldn't bring herself to meet his eyes quite yet.

"I know I haven't been a model stand-in. I'm not even sure why I've pushed things the way I have." He tightened his grip on her shoulders. "But you get all bossy and controlling and the next thing I know I'm agreeing to do this, stepping up to do that. Pushing things."

She finally lifted her gaze. "Oh, so it's all my fault."

"I didn't say that. Maybe we're both not dealing with this as well as we could be." His grip turned into a caress as he massaged her shoulders a little. "You're very tense."

"I've got a lot on my mind." She gave him a pointed look.

He pushed his fingers deeper into the muscles of her shoulders and it was all she could do not to groan in abject pleasure as the knots slowly unwound under his clever ministrations. Okay, so maybe she was just a little tense.

"I wasn't dispensing advice, you know," he said quietly.

She realized she'd let her eyes drift shut as he continued his massage. She didn't say anything. They weren't arguing, and at the moment she wasn't willing to give up the moment of blissful relaxation.

"I was just repeating what Eric said when he described his occupation to me."

"Somewhere along the line, you're going to get tripped up," she said, her voice having taken on a heavier note. "You can't be so blasé about this. Readers take Eric's advice seriously."

"I know they do."

She opened her eyes, lifting her hands to cover his, stopping him. "Do you really?"

He held her gaze for a few long moments before finally saying, "I don't know. I don't usually turn to a book for answers to my personal problems." He tried a little smile. "But then, I have Eric, so I don't need to. But I don't dismiss it as a recourse for others, if that's what you're afraid of."

She didn't say anything. She didn't know what to say.

"I think you know, deep down, you can trust me," he said. "If for no other reason than that I wouldn't do anything to hurt Eric."

"I know you don't want to. I just think you have a cavalier attitude about this, and it worries me because there is so much riding on it."

"Is that what you're really afraid of? Losing your job?"

She closed her eyes briefly, then sighed as she looked at him again. "I'd be lying if I said that's not part of it."

"But?"

"But the part that keeps me awake at night, and maybe a big part of why I'm so testy all the time, is the dishonesty. I'm not a good liar, Jack. And I can't enjoy any of the success we've gotten from this because it's all based on a lie."

"Eric's books exist. That's not a lie."

"But Prince Charming doesn't. Not like we're pretending he does." He wouldn't let her disengage her hands from his. Instead he turned them and wove his fingers through hers. "Eric *is* a real Prince Charming. He just happens to be gay. So we're giving the public a Prince they can handle. That's all."

Valerie couldn't help the dry smile that curved her lips. "I'm not sure they can handle you, that's the other part of my problem."

Jack smiled briefly, then, when she looked away, he dropped one of her hands so he could tip her chin up, turn her face back to his. "We're not hurting anyone. And we're giving Eric a chance at a real life, without sacrificing everything he's worked for. You said people take that advice seriously. Well, that's because it's damned good advice. Why ruin that? Why make them doubt what he's told them over the years? Who is that going to help?"

"I don't know." She let him trail his fingers along her jaw, knowing she should move away now. But it felt too damn good, and she'd been carrying this guilt for what felt like ages. It was nice, just for a moment, to share the burden a little. "I just don't want this to blow up in our faces. Not just for my job. But for what it will do to the godmothers. To Eric." She pulled his hand away then. "I've come to care for them all a great deal. And I guess I'm just scared that what we're doing could end up hurting them all very badly."

His lips quirked. "Well, that explains things a little."

"What do you mean?"

"The tension between us. Why you see me as the bad guy, or potential bad guy. You're setting me up as the fall guy. The one who can take the blame, at least in your mind, if this all blows up."

She opened her mouth to tell him he was totally off base, then stopped. Because maybe he wasn't. Not totally. "Well, you're certainly not helping matters any there."

"Meaning?"

"This," she said, stepping away. "You provoke me, irritate me, then you step in and start being all reasonable and nice. Touching me and—"

"I like touching you." He pushed his hands into her hair, walked her so her back hit the window.

She gasped as his body came right up along hers. But she didn't squirm free. She could have told herself it was because he wouldn't have let her go anyway. But that was one lie too many.

"And for the record, you provoke me and irritate me, too."

"Then why do we keep ending up like this?" she asked, frustration creeping into her voice.

"Screaming sexual tension?"

She grabbed his forearms, but didn't push them away when he ducked in and kissed her. It was a short, fast kiss that he followed up with a trail of softer, sweeter kisses along her jawline.

"We can't do this," she said a bit breathlessly.

"I wish like hell you were right," he said, nibbling at the side of her neck.

"Then you don't want this, either?"

"It complicates things. I'm not one for complications." His breathing grew more ragged as he pinned her arms up against the glass.

"So why don't you stop?" She gasped as his body pressed more fully into hers.

"Maybe it's more than sexual tension."

She wasn't sure about that, and he didn't sound all that sure, either. It felt pretty damn sexual at the moment. In fact, if her skirt weren't so narrowly tailored, she'd be inching her thigh up his hip, shifting that hard body right where she needed it most. "How could it be? I drive you crazy," she panted. "You make me nuts."

"Insane. I know."

"So?"

He lifted his head to look at her. His gray eyes had gone all glittery and silver. The desire she saw there packed almost as powerful a punch as what he'd been doing to her with his mouth and hands.

"So," he said, quite seriously, his chest rising and falling against hers. "I can't seem to stop. And I don't want to. I think about you, wonder about you. All the time. It's making me crazy." He traced his fingertips with surprising tenderness down the side of her face. "Maybe we just need to get each other out of our systems."

She smiled just a little at the earnestness in his words. "You think?"

He smiled a little, too. "I don't know what to think. And I have to tell you, that's not like me. But then, I haven't been me for a while now, have I?"

"You know," she said, more seriously than she intended. "I'm beginning to think you're right. I don't know the real you at all."

"Well," he said, his smile slowly growing. "Here's your chance." He started to lean in again.

"What if it's a chance I'm not willing to take?"

"Then just tell me to stop."

Now her smile widened. "I believe I've been doing that all along."

That bad-boy grin that made her pulse leap. "And yet here you are, letting me put my hands all over you. Again."

"I guess I'm going to have to work on that."

"You do that," he said, then leaned in and put his mouth on hers.

And just when she gave in, just when she lowered her arms to circle his neck, to fall completely into his kiss . . . that, of course, was when the door to the conference room swung open.

Foreplay

Men are generally a bit slower to realize that the "F" word should be more than some groping mixed in with a little tonsil hockey. Ladies, these men can be trained. Eventually. However, never underestimate the power of a man who needs no training. This is a guy who can have multiple flaws, and still steal your heart. This is the man who understands that the most powerful aphrodisiac in the world . . . is shared laughter.

Chapter 15

"ell, well," Eric said, his voice filled with amusement. "And here I thought I was the only one who couldn't keep it in his pants."

Valerie scrambled away from Jack. "This is exactly why I can't do this. I lose all perspective around you. Jesus."

Jack didn't try to stop her as she moved around the end of the table, scooping up her ubiquitous notepad along the way. As if they'd been deeply involved in their meeting and had, for no apparent reason, just paused suddenly for a deep soul kiss. Shaking his head, he turned a rueful smile on his friend. "Your timing still sucks."

Eric's smile was unabashed. "Oh, like Jill Lockerman was going to let you get past second base."

"She might have," Jack retorted. "I'd been practicing my moves."

"*Moves.*" Eric snorted. "Women aren't like pillows. They actually respond."

"Like you'd know."

"True," Eric conceded.

Valerie just looked at them both as if they'd lost their collective mind. "Can we please get back to business?" She glared Jack into silence when he opened his mouth. "And I don't mean monkey business."

"She's comparing you to an ape," Eric said. "I'm thinking you still need more practice."

Valerie glared at Eric. "Do you have any advice on how a woman is supposed to deal with two grown men who can't be around each other for five minutes without reverting to frat-house humor?"

Eric scratched his closely cropped hair, pretending to give it serious consideration, then grinned unrepentantly and said, "Nope. I'm afraid there is no cure for that."

For once, Jack wisely stayed out of it and took his seat. Valerie and Eric did the same, and they spent the next hour going over the list of media outlets vying for a piece of the Prince.

When Valerie finally closed her notebook, Jack drained his second cup of coffee and slumped back in his chair. "No offense to you, man," he said to Eric, "but what in the world is wrong with these people?"

"Never underestimate the power of a pretty face," Eric said dryly.

"Oh, yeah. I'm downright adorable," Jack said.

"He has a point. Eric, I mean," Valerie added quickly. "Seriously, though, maybe it's because you're not exactly what everyone expected. Don't let this go to your head, but I think the general consensus is that you are a better-than-average-looking guy."

"Now there's gushing praise," Jack said, propping his feet up on the chair next to him.

"What I mean is, everyone was hoping for a handsome prince, but we're all cynical enough to know that's probably not going to be the case. Then you come along. Not exactly princely," she said. "A bit rough around the edges. More of a guy's guy than readers expected. With the kind of edge that gets a woman's attention."

Jack let his mouth curve as he held her gaze.

She didn't fluster so easily this time, holding ruthlessly to her all-business demeanor. "You held your own with your interviewers, both male and female. And I think that helped boost your desirability." She tapped her pencil on the table. "But now that we're getting into lengthier interviews, that means meatier interviews. A sparked public is a nosy public. Someone is going to go digging; they're going to find out you've been married. So we have to be prepared to deal with and respond to the fact that the guy dishing out advice couldn't keep his own marriage together."

"Hey now—" Jack started, smile fading, but Valerie cut him off.

"You might think it's none of their business, but I'm here to tell you they're going to think everything you've ever done, thought, or said is their business. It's ridiculous the things they will find to be of the utmost importance."

Jack shot a look at Eric. "I begin to see the need for secrecy."

Eric shrugged. "Hey, even I had no idea it was going to blow up to something of this magnitude."

"Which is exactly why I wanted you to get out. You were supposed to make your little splash, then dive right back into hiding. Keep the mystery quotient there, give them just enough to whet their appetite and spike sales, but not so much that they became obsessed."

"What are the godmothers' opinions?" Eric asked.

Valerie sighed. "Are you kidding? Vivian is eating this up. Aurora thinks Jack is just the next best thing to a mint julep. And Mercedes is hearing the *ka-ching* of the registers in her sleep."

Jack toyed with his coffee cup, tearing long strips off the curled rim. "I don't guess it would help at this point to say I'm sorry." He smiled, abashed. "Again."

Valerie looked at him. "What would help is you taking this seriously. Eric and I are going to spend however long it takes between now and the next interview drilling you on how to respond to the questions that will probably come up now that the public has caught the Jack Lambert bug. That means questions about your marriage, your past jobs, your childhood—"

Jack's feet slid to the floor with a *thump*. "No. I'm not discussing that."

"If you avoid it, they'll just dig deeper," Valerie said, watching the two men exchange glances.

"I'm sure we'll come up with something that will work," Eric said. "Leave that part to me, okay?"

Valerie looked as skeptical as always, but she must have sensed she was going to be outvoted. "Okay. Just make sure you have something other than 'no comment.' "

"Don't worry."

Valerie laughed without humor. "Yeah. No problem." Just then a knock came at the door.

"See how well that works," Jack said to Eric. "Knocking first?"

Tracy poked her freckled nose in the room. "Um, Ms. Wagner—" She broke off to roll her eyes and giggle. "I mean, Valerie? There are, like, some conflicts in the schedule?"

Jack had been around her less than ten minutes and had already noticed her penchant for ending every sentence with a question mark. She noticed him, then Eric, and turned a most alarming shade of scarlet.

"Thank you, Tracy. Just put the notes on my desk. I'll be there in a minute."

The teenager opened her mouth, but nothing came out. Her gaze was transfixed on the two men. She finally managed to nod, and with a final sigh, she clutched the legal pad of notes to her chest and backed out of the room.

"Maybe we should call it Prince Charming Fever," Eric suggested, chuckling as the conference-room door shut and they heard a *thunk*, as if Tracy had barely managed to close it before swooning.

Valerie was already standing and collecting her things. "Let me go see what the latest drama is, and, Eric, you can begin coaching Jack."

She fished out a sheet of paper. "Here's a list of some questions I thought might come up. Vicki, the talk-show hostess, will definitely try to push things to the more personal angle. It's her trademark."

Then Valerie's cell phone and pager went off simultaneously. "Here we go again." She left the room, muttering, juggling her notes in one hand, squinting at the readout on her pager, and pressing the phone between ear and shoulder, all while maneuvering the door open with her heels.

"She really is something," Eric said as the door swung shut behind her before either of them could get there to help her out. "Very take-charge." He turned to Jack, smiling. "Not your usual type, as I recall."

"I don't think I'm her type, either. I'm not predicting a long future. Hell, it might already be past, thanks to you."

Eric gave a short laugh. "Don't underestimate yourself. Or her. But what were you thinking, putting the moves on her in the workplace? What if I'd been her simple-headed assistant? My God, it would be tabloid city all over again. They wouldn't even have to offer her money to tell all."

"It's not like I planned it, okay? It just sort of seems to happen between us."

Eric sat back down. "You don't seem as blasé about that as you'd normally be." A slow smile spread across his face when Jack didn't immediately respond. "This might be getting serious."

"It's some kind of weird chemical compatibility. Trust me. In any kind of real relationship, we'd be at each other all the time."

"Sometimes that can be a good thing." Eric folded his hands behind his head and sighed in utter satisfaction. "A very good thing."

Jack groaned. "Please, spare me."

Eric chuckled. "All I'm saying is that sometimes it's just pent-up frustration that makes things seem rocky at first."

"Is this the advice columnist, or my finally-getting-regular-sex friend talking?"

Eric cocked his head. "Would it matter?"

Now Jack laughed, then shook his head. "Hell, I don't think there is advice out there for what we're doing. Or not doing, as the case may be."

"Is it just the subterfuge that's keeping you two from just going for it?"

"On her part? Yes."

"And you?"

"What are you all of a sudden? Dr. Ruth?"

"Just answer me. If it weren't for our charade, do you think you would just have at it and see where it goes?"

"Honestly, if it weren't for all this, I doubt she and I would be involved at all."

"So it's proximity."

"I told you, it's chemistry. Something she's got is combustible with something I've got. Under normal circumstances? I don't think she and I would even give each other a second glance."

"But you have. So that's moot. People always think they know what's right for them. Until they find it. You know, this media thing won't last forever."

Jack folded his arms. "If there is a God."

Eric just looked at him pointedly.

"I know, I know. I'll be good from now on, promise."

Eric just laughed. "So, then what? You're going to pursue things, aren't you? When I said be more open to possibilities, this was exactly what I was talking about."

"I need to go back to work. When this stunt is over, I'll get a real job and take off. If anything is going to happen between me and Valerie, it would be during. Not after. She's already putting the major brakes on, and since you blew my one go-with-the-flow moment, I'd say this entire conversation is moot."

Eric just smiled knowingly.

"You know, for a guy who only started getting laid again—"

"A couple of hours ago?"

Jack scowled. "Don't rub it in."

Eric just laughed again. "Listen, I may not have been personally involved in a long-term relationship. But I've been quite the student in observing, discussing, and dissecting others." He leaned forward, turning serious. "All I'm saying is, chemistry is easy. Happens all the time. In my experience, when it's not convenient to act on it, it's pretty easily dismissed. And despite not being each other's type, combined with incredibly bad timing, you two still seem to be having a very difficult time walking away from it."

"Maybe we're both just hard up and horny."

"And maybe it's more than chemistry."

Considering Jack had all but said the same thing to Valerie not an hour earlier, it shouldn't have been so disconcerting to hear Eric say it to him. But the way his stomach did funny little things and a cold sweat threatened to bead up on his forehead told him otherwise. "Now I remember why I don't talk to you about women. You're too analytical, wanting to see things that aren't there."

"And yet, who was the first one to tell you that Shelby—"

Jack raised his palm. "Please," he pleaded, "can we have one discussion about women without her name coming up? I'm begging you."

"Fine, fine. But now that she has come up—"

Jack groaned, but Eric pushed on. "I'm serious. Unrelated to this other discussion, but I've been wondering if it might not be a bad idea to contact her, or let me contact her, and make her aware of what's going on. Just in case."

Jack looked at Eric like he'd lost his mind. "You know, maybe you should stay on the sidelines. Because love, or lust, or whatever the hell you're in right now, has surely fucked up your brain. Are you insane?"

"Just trying to cover all the bases."

"You know damn well that she's either on some island location wearing next to nothing while seducing her photographer, or in some other exotic locale banging him. What she's not doing is paying any attention to the American press or television. Trust me on that."

Eric seemed to shrug it off. "It was just a thought."

"Well, it was a shitty one."

Eric laughed. "Awfully touchy about the topic of women these days."

"Cut me some slack. I've done more talking about relationships, with perfect strangers, mind you, strangers with microphones stuck in my face, than I have personally discussed with anyone, ever. I don't know how you do it."

Eric smiled, shrugged. "What can I say? I find human relations fascinating."

"Well, let's relate about something else, okay? Like where in the hell you've been these past couple of days? And I'm not asking for sordid details. But even a guy routinely getting some for the first time in his adult life has to come up for air sometime. So what else is going on with you? What's this about a real estate agent?"

If it meant getting his increasingly confusing personal life out from under the microscope, Jack would risk hearing details about Eric and Brice that no straight male would ever willingly choose to hear.

Eric was all too happy to accommodate him. "Remember I told you Brice and I had really enjoyed our drive around Potomac on our way to Glass Slipper? Well, we both really love the peacefulness and privacy out there. So we've been talking, and we're, um, looking."

Despite his obvious excitement, Jack could see that Eric was also a bit nervous. "So, you're looking . . . together?"

"I know what you're thinking. It's way too soon. I know that better than anyone." He paused, then sighed, his expression wreathed in such joy and happiness that Jack couldn't find it in him to rip at it. He grinned. "I'm my own worst advice nightmare."

Jack thought about the parallels to his whirlwind fling with Shelby. Only there were no palm trees and mai tais involved. As far as he could tell, Eric wasn't drunk on anything but love. "Just be careful. Don't sign anything right away. I mean, if it's for real, what's the rush, right?"

"If you're worried that Brice is just after me for my money, don't be. He's got more to be worried about in that department than I do."

"Meaning?"

Eric fiddled with his coffee mug. "Well . . . I've been thinking. These past couple of weeks have been incredible. Not just because of Brice. But the freedom of being myself, of not worrying anymore about a readership judging me. Don't get me wrong, I care about them deeply. And they've given me a great deal. But when it comes down to it, they're strangers. And I've given them total control of my life. Now that I have it back . . ." He trailed off, lifted a shoulder. "It's better than even I realized it would be."

"You're thinking maybe you don't want to write anymore?"

He didn't look at Jack right away, but kept fiddling with his cup. "Maybe." He glanced up. "Am I crazy to consider it?"

Now it was Jack's turn to shrug. "It's your life."

"But?"

"I don't know. It just seems like you finally have it all. Out of the spotlight, able to do the work you love without fear of discovery. And with all this media frenzy, you're more popular than ever. Guaranteed best-sellers."

"I know, I've thought about that, too." Eric glanced at his watch and pushed to a stand. "We've got a shuttle to catch. Then we have to prep for the *Chuck and Vicki* taping."

Jack stood, perfectly willing to let the topic go, like Eric obviously wanted. But, as his friend, he felt obligated to say the rest of what was on his mind. "You should do what makes *you* happy. You've more than earned that right. But it's only been a few weeks. And we're still in the middle of all this. Just don't do anything rash, okay?"

Then Valerie bustled back in. "You guys ready? Car's waiting. Did you go over everything?"

"Everything important," Eric said. "And I won't if you won't," he told Jack, cutting a meaningful look at Valerie.

Jack scowled, then held the door open while they all shuffled out. So much for his ability to give advice. Or take it, he thought as he watched Valerie walk ahead of him. Because of him opening his big fat mouth, they were going to be joined at the hip for the next three days.

Question was . . . would he be able to keep himself from trying to get her to join other, far more pleasurable body parts?

Seven hours later he was in the makeup room of Studio A, getting his hair moussed and his face deshined, while watching Valerie flip through the wardrobe Jenn had sent up to New York with them. Due to a heavy thunderstorm, their flight had been delayed leaving Reagan National and delayed again upon arriving at LaGuardia. They hadn't had time to check in at the hotel, instead coming directly to the studio, luggage and all. Valerie had pulled out the garment bag with Jack's clothes—not the ones he'd packed, mind you, for those had been sent on ahead to the Plaza with Eric, along with the rest of their bags.

Speaking of which . . . "Where is Eric? Shouldn't he be back by now? I mean, Brice isn't the biggest dude in the world, but I'm pretty sure Eric didn't pack him in with all the rest of his clothes."

That got a short smile from Valerie, but she quickly went back to sorting and muttering. She'd grown increasingly tense during their flight, until both Jack and Eric had buried themselves in the in-flight magazine to avoid saying anything that might provoke another worried lecture.

"And did you see how many of those bags were his? My God, you'd think it was him making the media rounds. I never knew he was such a clotheshorse. And here I thought that was just a cliché."

The male hairdresser finished one last primp on the front of Jack's hair, then smirked. "Honey, sometimes the clothes do make the man." He glanced meaningfully at Jack's faded jeans and rumpled shirt, then turned and packed up his tools.

The makeup artist finished patting his forehead with a large poufy thing filled with powder, then leaned in a bit closer. "And sometimes it doesn't matter what a man is wearing. Or not wearing." She winked at him as she moved back and began stowing her stuff in an enormous black canvas bag. "They'll be ready for you shortly, okay, hon?"

"Thanks for your help," he said with a smile and a wink, catching Valerie's eye roll from the corner of his eye. The two left and he turned to face the mirror for the first time. "Maybe I was too hasty. Is this really the style? Because I could have just not combed my hair when I got out of bed and pretty much pulled this off."

Valerie looked over at him long enough to say, "Keep your fingers out of it. And don't smudge the makeup. Men. You're worse than a toddler."

"Funny, I was thinking you're worse than a stage mother before her child's first recital. So I guess it all fits." He slouched back in the padded chair and crossed an ankle over his knee. "So, Mommy, what should I wear for my big number?" He clasped his hands. "Do you think they'll like me? Will they really like me?"

"Not to make you nervous or anything, but you do realize that millions of people will be watching you today. You might want to consider that and stop screwing around."

"Jeez, forgive me for trying to lighten things up. You might want to consider that your uptight, nervous attitude isn't doing me any favors."

She pulled out a pair of black pants and a blue, short-sleeved, button-up cotton shirt with monochromatic blue embroidery that gave it a kind of Hawaiian flair, and turned to face him. "Yeah, I can see how stressed you are. Kibitzing with the production staff on your way in, flirting with the makeup artist. You're just a bundle of nerves, all right."

"I only *kibitz* when I'm anxious," he said with mock earnestness.

She finally cracked another smile. "Okay, okay. I'm sorry. But I'm just afraid you're not taking this seriously enough. This is big. Huge."

"I love it when women say that to me."

"See? This is exactly what I mean."

Jack pushed out of the chair. He took the clothes from her hands, hung them back up on the rack, and reached for her.

She stepped back. "Oh, no, uh-uh. No touching. I can't handle touching. Not now, and most definitely not here. Besides, you have to get dre—"

That was as far as she got before he yanked her into his arms and kissed her. She fisted her hands in his shirt, but he wasn't sure if it was to push him away, or pull him closer. All he knew is that she didn't fight the kiss. And when he lifted his head, a few moments later than he'd originally planned, they were both breathing a bit harder.

"You really have to stop that," she informed him, her freshly kissed mouth making it hard for him to take her too seriously.

"I was trying to give you a different outlet for all your pent-up stress."

"Ah. Arrogant, cocky, sexy . . . and selfless. It's no wonder I can't resist."

He tilted his head and grinned. "You think I'm sexy?"

She groaned and pushed him away. "Here," she said, grabbing the clothes off the rack and pressing them against his chest. "Go change. You're going to be called to the wings in about five minutes."

He tossed the clothes on the chair and pulled off his shirt, then laughed when she spun around. "Hey, I like a good-luck kiss as much as any red-blooded guy would before going off to do battle. But even I have my standards." He shucked his pants, waited a beat, then grinned when he caught her peeking in the mirror. "I need at least ten minutes for an actual sexual encounter."

She sniffed with all the dignity she could muster, and turned to face him as he zipped his pants. "Just as well, then. A ten-minute man doesn't usually make my list of things to do."

Jack hooted as he shoved his arms through the sleeves of the shirt, and was still chuckling as he buttoned it up. "Touché, Ms. Wagner, touché."

A quick rap came at the door, followed by a young woman with her hair in a messy topknot, wearing a headset, poking her head in the door. "We're ready for you, Mr. Lambert."

He glanced over at Valerie, surprised at the sudden invasion of butterflies in his stomach. It was just another interview. That's what he'd been telling himself all day. But as he nodded to the woman and could only manage a tight smile to go with it, he was forced to admit that Valerie wasn't the only one a little wound up about this next step they were about to take. He just handled his stress a little differently than she did. Although, thinking back on the kiss, he still thought his way was better.

"You're going to be great," Valerie whispered as she passed through the door in front of him.

"Oh, *now* you give me the confident pep talk."

She gave it right back to him. "Now is when you needed to hear it."

They followed the young woman to the wings of the set, where he

Donna Kauffman

was fitted for his mike. "Now," the production assistant said, "it's just like we went over during the preshow warm-up. We're in commercial break at the moment. When we come back, they will do your intro. You wait until you hear your name. Audience goes clap, clap, clap, you walk to center stage, greet Chuck and Vicki, then take the stool between them. You'll be out there for approximately eight minutes, answer a few questions, then we go to commercial break again and you're done." She smiled brightly. "You got it? Any questions, now's the time."

"I'm good," he assured her, absently wondering if he had time to throw up real quick.

The assistant stepped back and talked into her mouthpiece. The band started to play, the audience cheered as the camera lights went back on and the hosts began to speak.

Jack's entire life flashed before his eyes. What in the hell had he been smoking to think he could pull something like this off? *It's just another interview. It's just another interview,* he murmured silently, wishing his heart wasn't pounding so hard. He couldn't hear his own thoughts, much less them announcing his name.

And then the production assistant was waving him to go. But his feet wouldn't move. Then he felt Valerie step up behind him, followed by a very sharp pinch on his ass.

His mouth dropped open with a surprised laugh.

"Knock 'em dead, sweet cheeks," she whispered in his ear.

And so it was that he took the stage with a wide, somewhat naughty grin that had the women in the audience cheering.

Risk

Some guys will risk their job, their pride, even their life, before they'll risk their heart. Especially if they've had it handed back to them already. So it always comes as a surprise to them when they find out their heart has a mind of its own.

Chapter 16

Only two minutes to go. Valerie curled her fingers into her palms to keep from biting her nails down any farther. She wasn't cut out for this kind of knife-edge tension.

"So," the perky hostess was saying, "we understand you were married once."

"Yes, I was."

There was a communal holding of breath from the audience. Vicki smiled and put her hand on his arm, all girl-next-door-you-can-trust-me.

Very convincingly, too, Valerie thought, hoping Jack hadn't forgotten this was being seen and heard by far more than this intimate little recording-studio audience.

"It didn't last that long, correct? What happened?"

"Didn't the advice man have any advice for himself?" Chuck, the more biting, acerbic half of the talk-show duo, inserted, to growing titters in the audience. "What a prince, hey ladies?" The chuckles grew and the tension in the studio shot up as the audience murmured and rustled in their seats, waiting for their Prince to shoot Chuckie down.

Valerie had been waiting for this, knew Jack was properly prepped. The audience had loved him from the moment he hit the stage. "All you have to do is give the stock answer, and we're home free," she murmured, willing him for once, to do things the way they'd planned and end the interview without stirring anything else up.

"Well, Vicki, where the heart is concerned, you don't always want to listen to advice. Even your own."

The women in the audience—who were easily ninety-five percent of the whole—sighed and clapped. Valerie held off, waiting for the finish.

"We reacted to the moment, didn't wait until cooler heads"—he shot a look directly into the audience—"or other body parts, for that matter, prevailed."

The women swooned, laughed, cheered.

"Jesus," Valerie muttered, "he can even seduce them en masse." But her heart started to speed up. He was actually going to pull this off. She should trust him more. Then she remembered his maneuver in the dressing room and realized that she couldn't dare give him so much as an inch. Or he'd be giving her every one of his. And judging by how his body had felt, pressed up against hers in the *Glass Slipper* conference room, she knew he had a few to spare.

"I think it was to both of our credits that we did give it an honest go," Jack was saying. "I think we both knew early on we'd made a mistake, and when we couldn't ignore that reality any longer, we ended things."

"Nasty divorce?" Chuck asked, obviously hoping to dish some dirt.

Jack chuckled, shifting effortlessly from intimate pal talk with Vicki to mano-a-mano talk with Chuck. "No. Never make an enemy with a lawyer on retainer."

The ladies in the audience groaned a little, but the few token men cheered, making everyone laugh, including Chuck.

Perky Vicki butted back in, all concerned for women everywhere. "So, do you still talk?"

Jack switched back up once again. Smiling tenderly, with a hand over his chest, he said, "When emotions have ricocheted as wildly as ours did, that can be pretty tough. But I wish her nothing but the best and hope she feels the same. Sometimes that's the best you can hope for."

The audience "Awwwed" and Vicki patted him consolingly on the arm. And Valerie allowed herself a little fist pump. He'd done it. She counted herself lucky they hadn't mentioned Shelby by name, looking for the added notoriety of her celebrity. She'd counted on them bypassing that potential hook, anyway, since Shelby wasn't known to the American public, all her success coming on the European runways and print ads.

"Well, our producer is signaling we have another minute or so before we have to go to break." Vicki turned to Jack, all chipper, encouraging smiles. "You up for taking some comments and questions from the audience?"

Valerie froze. They were supposed to clear that kind of thing with her. She craned her neck and glanced around, trying to pinpoint just which assistant she could threaten most effectively. Except it was too late for that. Jack had already been put on the spot. She gave a quick little head shake, in case he glanced to the wings where she was standing. Only, of course, he didn't. In fact, he didn't so much as blink.

"Sure, why not. After all, without them, Prince Charming wouldn't be such a success."

A rousing cheer from the crowd, complete with whistles and hoots. A staffer popped up in the audience with a handheld microphone, which Vicki directed to one of the women raising her hand. Valerie held her breath as the woman stood and was asked to introduce herself.

"Hi, Vicki and Chuck, I'm Pam. I don't really have a question, but I want to tell Jack how much his books have helped me."

There was an immediate round of confirming applause.

"I was having a hard time getting my boyfriend to commit. I knew what I was feeling and your book, *Dear Me*, just confirmed what I already knew. Using your suggestions, I tried to tell him, but it wasn't getting through. I knew if he just read your book, he'd understand, but you know guys. There was no way he was reading an advice book by anyone, especially one by some guy claiming to be Prince Charming. Women all around her were nodding, collectively disgusted with their macho counterparts.

"Then he heard you on the radio and saw you on the cover of the magazine." She blushed a little. "Honestly, we were both a little surprised by how, you know . . ." She broke off, covering her face.

"How hot he is?" Vicki offered, oh so helpfully.

Pam nodded, hopelessly embarrassed as the whistles and hoots started up again. "My boyfriend was, well, he was probably both impressed and a bit jealous, maybe. But he did end up reading the parts of the book I wanted him to." She looked around the audience. "So, ladies, I just want you to know. If you can get your guy to read one of Jack's books, it might not make him a prince, but it sure was the *charm* we needed to make our relationship work."

She sat down to rousing cheers, leaving a still-smiling Jack looking endearingly humbled. "Thank you," he said, but was mostly drowned out by the continued wave of adoration gushing from the audience.

For her part, Valerie sighed once again in relief. The man was part cat, but he was quickly using up his nine lives. Just then her cell phone hummed at her hip. She stepped back as far out of the way as she could and still keep her eye on the stage, before flipping it open. "Valerie Wagner," she said, keeping her voice low. "Elaine, hi, I can't—

what? *You're kidding!*" Her mind went blank for a moment as the news sank in, then she quickly juggled the phone and pulled out her Palm Pilot as Elaine continued to reel off information.

"They want him tomorrow. Dave's doing a top ten Prince Charming list."

Dave. As in David Letterman. "I'm not sure we can work it in," she said, trying hard to think on her feet. Trying harder not to pass out.

"They want Jack to read the list himself," Elaine went on.

"Okay, okay. Let me talk with him. Give me the number." She punched it into her Palm. "When do they need to know?"

"Yesterday."

Shit. "I'm on it." She flipped her phone shut, adrenaline and tension spiking once again as she tried to analyze the possible ramifications of this latest wrinkle. It was in that moment that the inescapable truth finally hit home. This was never going to be over. It no longer mattered what Jack did or didn't do. The train had left the station . . . and they weren't getting off anytime soon.

"Time for one more question," Vicki called out to the audience. "Anyone need advice from the Love Doctor here?"

Oh, for the love of God, Valerie thought, as her attention careened back to the moment at hand. *Love Doctor?* They'd never hear the end of that one. She could only pray Dave's people weren't still watching. She could see the *Late Show* list right now. *Top Ten Things the Love Doctor Would Prescribe to Mend Your Broken Heart!*

Of course, Jack would love it. She could already see his cocky grin when she told him he'd landed a spot on *Letterman*. Valerie wondered how many Rolaids a person could chew up before their kidneys turned to compressed chalk.

Another woman took the mike. Valerie focused on her, shutting out everything else, willing her to make it short and quick, so she could hurry up and start obsessing over her next potential heart attack.

"Hi, I'm Marci. I just wanted to tell you—" She paused suddenly to press her fingers to her lips as her eyes welled with emotion.

Valerie held her breath along with the rest of the audience. *Please, we've come this far. Don't screw it up for him now.*

Marci took a breath, then plunged on. "I spent two years in an abusive relationship. I'm smart, educated. I never thought I would get trapped in that kind of vicious cycle. I even recognized it for what it was, but I couldn't seem to find my way out of it. I knew I had to end it, but I was afraid . . . and I was ashamed. The wedding was planned, all this money had been spent, and to everyone else he was my Prince Charming. I knew differently, but I couldn't bring myself to tell anyone else."

She took another breath and Valerie could feel the audience silently willing the woman to continue.

Through a sparkle of tears, her voice gone hoarse, she continued. "I'd read your books. I knew you were right, and I should hold out for a man who would love and respect me. A real Prince Charming. But I confess, a part of me didn't believe they . . . or even you really existed. And then, there you were, on the cover of that magazine. Proof the right guy really does exist. It probably sounds silly, but that's the moment I found the courage to tell my friends and family the truth. And with their love and support—and a restraining order," she added with a dry if watery smile, causing the audience to laugh through their own tears, "I found the courage to end it." She sucked in a shuddering breath. "And I'm just so grateful I have the opportunity to thank you in person." Tears were streaming down her cheeks now, and Vicki stood up and beckoned the woman to come down the aisle.

There was nothing else Jack could do but go and accept a hug from the woman. The audience cheered and sniffled through the whole thing. And as the woman made her way back to her seat, they gave both her and Jack a standing ovation.

Valerie was wiping away a few tears herself. Vicki was sniffling and even curmudgeonly Chuck pretended to wipe away a few tears as he finally sent them to commercial.

Vicki rebounded quickly, and knowing she had a hit guest on her hands, invited Jack to stick around for the cooking segment they were going to do with their other special guest, Emeril Lagasse.

Valerie edged closer to the stage, trying to catch Jack's eye and motion him to talk to her first, but to her surprise, after giving both hosts a heartfelt thank-you, he politely declined without so much as glancing her way. He shook Chuck's hand and hugged Vicki. Both hosts, clearly knowing they'd bagged a winner, gushed that they'd love to have him back as a guest, maybe do a full hour on advice. Jack just kept nodding, smiling, giving them vague responses, waved to the audience one last time, then finally left the stage.

Valerie was stunned. He'd actually played it exactly as she'd have wanted him to. And here she was, certain he'd want to bask in his triumph as long as possible. It was all she could do to keep from yanking him into a huge, relieved hug. Hell, she'd been more or less expecting one from him. He had to be pumped over the amazing victory they'd just scored. But instead of the cocky swagger of a guy who'd just delivered a lethal one-two punch to national daytime television, Jack took her by the elbow and immediately steered her toward the dressing room.

He was still smiling as they wound their way through a host of other staffers, all of whom were congratulating him and patting him on the back. To anyone else, he appeared to be a bit rushed, but sincerely pleased. Only Valerie was close enough to see the tense set to his jaw, to feel the fingers digging a bit deeper into her arm with every pause they had to make to nod or speak to someone.

Once inside the dressing room, he quickly closed the door and immediately began gathering the few belongings they had with them. "Is the car waiting?" he said, no longer smiling. He sounded almost angry.

Valerie stopped stock-still in the middle of the room and propped her hands on her hips. "What's wrong? Even I have to admit that you were freaking brilliant out there. That was amazing. Admittedly, you had me worried for a few moments there, but you totally nailed it."

He said nothing. Well, there was a brief snarling sound, but his back was to her. She tugged him around by the arm. "You were barely even done and I was already fielding a call from Elaine, telling me the talent booker for David Letterman's *Late Show* called her, trying to reach you or Eric. He's doing his Top Ten list on you tomorrow night and he wants you to read it."

"I hope you said no." Jack's face was set in stone, his eyes cold, totally cut off and inaccessible. For all that they'd bickered before, there'd always been an element of teasing, of knowing they were each capable of giving as good as they got. She couldn't recall ever seeing him like this.

In fact, she wasn't sure she'd have thought him capable of it. Mr. Trust Me & Stop Worrying.

"You're turning something down? Am I to believe what I'm hearing?"

He jerked his arm free, then balled up and shoved the clothes he'd worn to the studio earlier into the bottom of the zippered garment bag. "I thought you'd be thrilled," he said, somewhat caustically. "I've finally come to my senses." He yanked the bag from the rack. "Is this all we have? Let's get out of here."

"But—"

"No *buts*. Tell them whatever you want, but get me out of it. That's what you're paid for, right?"

Her mouth dropped open.

"Haven't you been telling me I've more than kept up my end of the bargain?" he said. "You're right. In fact, I'll go so far as to say you've been right all along and I've been a complete and total ass about this. The world has seen enough of Prince Charming. Time to go recapture a bit of Eric's mystique." And with that, he tugged open the door and ducked out. Leaving her to follow or not, apparently not caring which option she chose.

She barely caught up to him in time not to be left standing curbside. She slid into the limo and they were pulling away even before she shut her door. She tossed her satchel onto the seat and swiveled to look at him, but he was stone-faced and looking forward, as if alone in the car. Or simply wishing he were.

"What in the hell is wrong with you? Will you at least grant me the courtesy of telling me that much? Why the sudden change? What's with the attitude?"

He didn't say anything right away. "It's not a game anymore," he said tightly. "Okay?"

"Okay," she said carefully. "And this pisses you off, why?"

He finally looked at her. "Didn't you hear that woman? She thinks I saved her from a fate worse than death. She saw my face, heard me talk, and decided men could be the good guys."

"You are a good guy."

He looked like he was going to explode. "I was *lying* to her! She's telling me I saved her, and I was fucking lying to her. That's . . . wrong. I know what it feels like to be deceived, okay? And it sucks." He glanced away, turning his gaze out the window. "It was a harmless game," he muttered. "Now it's not."

Valerie sat back, a little stunned by the sudden outburst. She assumed he was talking about Eric. And though she realized Jack understood Eric's reasons for keeping his sexual preference a secret, she didn't blame him for feeling somewhat betrayed by it, too. Of course, for all she knew, he was talking about Shelby. But now wasn't the time to get into that. "Wasn't it you who said we're not hurting anyone? Well, we aren't. You aren't. That woman got the help she needed."

"She believes Prince Charming is real. And it's all some big sham."

"*She* doesn't know that. And Prince Charming *is* real. We just put your face to him rather than Eric's. Eric does exist; his advice is valid."

He turned to her again. "And do you think if she found out Prince Charming was a gay man who'd never had a relationship longer than a one night stand before last month that she'd still have run to her family and confided in them?"

"I don't know. If she saw Eric's face and heard him talk, it's possible." She shifted to face him more fully. "Listen, I feel awkward about this, too. You know that better than anyone. But what just happened back there was a positive thing. No one was hurt by it."

He swore, then blew out a heavy breath. "Okay, fine. But it ends there. We go out with a bang. No more. We've pushed it far enough."

Her lips curved slightly. "How did this happen?"

"What?"

She nudged him with her elbow. "Here I've been begging you to rein it in, keep the profile as low as possible while still promoting the magazine. And you've been the renegade bad boy. Somehow that got all turned around."

He looked at her. "Color me confused. I thought you'd be relieved. Are you telling me you actually *want* me to do *Letterman*?"

She shook her head. "An hour ago? No. But as I watched you, the audience, and fielded that call, I finally had to admit that you're out there now, a public commodity that the public hasn't gotten enough of yet."

"So I'm doing *Letterman*." He still didn't sound convinced.

Oh, the irony. "You don't have to, no. Dave is going to do his Top Ten no matter what. We'll get the publicity, Prince Charming will stay in the public eye. I can try to withdraw you from the market after that, but it'll be much harder now. Honestly? You're going to be hunted. For a while, anyway."

His gaze narrowed.

"Don't worry. I'll do my best to get you out, but the godmothers will want a say. Contractually, you—or Eric—will have a say, too. And the public will have their say. I'll juggle. But you've walked pretty far out on that rope." She smiled briefly. "We just have to keep from hanging both of us with it."

He looked out the window. It was clear he understood the situation, that his anger was directed at himself. Surprisingly, for all that he'd been driving her crazy over the past couple of weeks, her first instinct was to try to smooth him out, take some of the guilt off his shoulders.

"We have that stockpile of photos," she assured him. "When we need to trot you out, I'll do it in print media. Eric can provide the rest."

"I wouldn't be so sure about that."

Now it was her turn to frown. "What are you talking about?"

Jack sighed, finally relaxed a little, even if it was more of a slumping. "This probably isn't the best time to mention this, but he's thinking about retiring. Settling down, as it were."

"What? He made a vague reference to that, but he knows he signed a contract, he—"

"Whoa. He'll finish out his commitment. But he's . . ." He trailed off, shrugged. "Happy. Content. I think he's ready to hang it up, move on."

"Is it Brice? How did that get so serious so quickly?"

"He thinks he's in love," Jack said. "I think it's infatuation. This is his first time being able to commit his heart and I think maybe he's in love with being free to express his emotions."

"Do you think he'll figure it out before he does anything foolish?"

"I don't know. They're looking at real estate."

"Jesus."

"Yeah. I know. I'm a little worried about him. Speaking of which, where the hell is he?"

She'd completely forgotten about that part. "He called from the hotel earlier. There was a little problem with the rooms. Well, room."

Jack finally looked at her again. "I beg your pardon?"

"The show's producer put us up in a two-bedroom suite. I forgot to mention that your *manager* was traveling with us and would need additional accommodations."

"So we book him another room."

"That's what he was trying to do. Some convention is there and all the rooms are packed, as is most everything else in town. He was working with the concierge to find something suitable when I last spoke to him."

"It's a suite. It has a couch or something, right? Tell him he can bunk in. We'll figure something out."

"I suggested that, but he said he'd handle it. You were doing so great I didn't think you needed his support at the studio, so I told him to do whatever he thought he had to do."

The limo pulled up to the hotel and the liveried doorman stepped forward to open the door. They had barely emerged from the backseat when Eric came through the rotating doors . . . with Brice behind him.

"Ah," Jack said as he came around the back of the car to where Valerie stood, waiting for their garment bag to be removed from the trunk. "Now I understand," he murmured. "Doesn't that guy have a job?"

Valerie smiled at that, relieved to be back on somewhat even footing again. Teasing banter she could handle. But she also couldn't help but note the real concern underlying it. Despite his protestations, and her occasional frustration with him, Jack Lambert was a good guy.

Eric stepped to the curb and took the garment bag from the driver. "So, I'm guessing the show went smashingly well?"

"You could say that," Valerie said, lifting her cheek for Eric's obligatory buss. "Hi, Brice," she added, nodding, thinking she understood the infatuation. The man was truly beautiful to look at. And listen to.

"Hallo, Ms. Wagner," he said, taking her hand as she stepped up on the curb. "I hope you don't mind the intrusion," he added, with that lovely island lilt to his voice.

"Call me Valerie," she told him, unable not to smile in the face of his impeccable manners. Somehow, being called *Ms.* wasn't so bad when there was an accent involved. "I didn't know you were coming up."

He glanced at Eric, who was busy talking to Jack, and the emotion in his eyes was surprisingly powerful. "We thought a few days apart would cool us down a little." He looked back at her and there was no doubt about it. The man was a total goner. Love, apparently, looked the same, no matter the genders involved. His smile was both sweet and sexy as hell. "We didn't last eight hours before I was on an Acela for Penn Station."

Valerie laughed. "I can't say I blame you." She looked at Eric, who was smiling and laughing at something Jack was saying. "Tall, tanned, and gorgeous," she agreed. "What's not to love, right?"

Brice sighed a little, nodding. "Smart, funny, generous, and kind, too. I know he's only recently outed himself, and I should let him go and experience life." He looked back at her, and she saw the sharp, caring man behind the gorgeous surface. "But I've been dating a long time, and I'm finding it hard to do the right thing when he is my right thing. We've been friends a long time. This feels perfectly natural to me." His eyes flashed. "I've waited long enough."

"So you go for it. You're both grown men. And there are no rules when it comes to how you feel." She smiled at the emotions that played across his face. Love could be a beautiful thing. So what if there might be some heartache at the end of their run together? It was worth it for that heady rush they were experiencing right now. Wasn't it?

Her gaze shifted to Jack. She wished the feelings that surfaced there were as easily categorized. Heady? Yes, even when they were arguing. And when he was touching her? Definitely.

Brice moved in beside her, following her gaze. "So what about you? Maybe you should take your own advice, eh?"

She couldn't help but wonder what would happen if she allowed herself, like Eric, to just fall into it and not care about the outcome. She shook her head. "I don't know." Something about Brice's soothing, gentle demeanor made her uncharacteristically blunt. "I've spent so long worrying about my career, about finding my niche, that I've shoved my relationships into a kind of temporary-only holding pattern. Not on purpose, really, it just happened somewhere along the way." She shrugged. "I guess I just assumed that if something more important or long-term came along, I'd figure out what to do with it when it happened."

"And has it?"

She smiled, albeit a bit sadly. "I'm not sure. But Jack's made it clear he's not going to be here long-term, so I guess—" She shrugged and Brice squeezed her shoulder, giving her his most blinding smile.

"Don't be so fast to toss it away," he said. "You never know what life might have in store for you, right around the corner."

If he only knew, she thought. She'd had just about all the surprises she could handle.

"It's cliché, but true. Live for today," he told her. "Let tomorrow take care of itself." He turned as Eric and Jack approached.

"Wow, *The Late Show*, huh?" Eric asked Valerie. "Impressive."

Valerie couldn't believe how sincerely happy Eric was. There wasn't the faintest hint that he wished it was him getting the attention he'd earned. But then, with gorgeous and understanding Brice standing beside him, she supposed Eric was getting all the attention he needed.

She glanced at Jack. "Does this mean you changed your mind and you're going to do it?"

"No." Jack ignored Eric's look of surprise. Apparently they hadn't gotten that far during their little chat. "Listen, can we take this inside?"

He looked at Eric. "What did you work out with the rooms? Because we could probably—"

Eric's cheeks colored a little, while Brice's smile could only be termed *naughty.*

"What did you do?" Valerie and Jack demanded simultaneously.

"Don't be mad," Eric said.

"Too late, I think." Jack looked at Valerie. "Don't worry, whatever it is, we can change it."

"It's a two-bedroom suite," Eric began as they entered the expansive lobby. "And, well, given what I walked in on the other day—" He put a hand on Valerie's arm. "Sorry to be indelicate. It's just that the two of you sharing the same suite . . . well, I asked myself, what were the chances you'd end up using both bedrooms?"

Valerie choked a little—though frankly that thought had crossed her mind. Live for today, indeed. And tonight.

"Eric—" Jack began, only to be cut off.

"And when Brice surprised me—" He shot Brice a blistering hot look that made both Valerie and Jack flush a little. "I just figured, hey, problem solved. We'll take one room," he looked back at Valerie and Jack. "You guys can have the other."

Valerie and Jack both had that deer-in-headlights look.

"Eric, really, I—" Valerie began.

"Don't worry. Jack is a gentleman," Eric assured her. "He'll take the couch if you want him to. Right, man?"

Jack stood there with his mouth open, apparently incapable of speech.

"Listen," Eric went on excitedly, "here's the key." He pressed it into Jack's hand. "It's the Vanderbilt Suite."

"Where are you two going?" Jack asked, finally finding his voice.

"Brice surprised me with reservations for Aigo. You don't need me tonight, do you?"

"No," Valerie managed. "I think we'll be fine."

Eric just winked. "We'll probably be late. There's a club I read about that I want to try."

"New York City, with a stunning man on my arm?" Brice stated. "Have to show him off a bit."

Eric grinned. "God, I love my life."

Thankfully they were both spared from commenting as Eric and Brice exited the lobby, heads bent together, laughing and talking.

"You're right," Valerie said. "They do seem very happy."

Jack moved closer and watched with her as Eric and Brice by-passed the line of taxis and hopped in a white stretch limo instead. "I wish I could say I was hip and liberal enough to be okay rooming with those two. But I'm pretty sure I'd feel just as weird watching him be that goo-goo ga-ga over anyone of either gender. I swear I thought they were going to revert to baby talk any second."

"Look at it this way, they'll probably be out until four in the morning. With any luck, we'll miss them entirely."

They turned toward the bank of elevators, careful not to look at each other. Jack tucked the key in his pocket. "About my schedule—"

"There are some things I can't get you out of," Valerie warned him. "We've got two days here. Two and a half, actually. I'll get you out of *Letterman*, but—"

He punched the UP button. "I'll do it."

"Do what? What part of it?"

"All of it, whatever we already agreed to. Just promise me that when we leave New York, I'm done."

"You're sure?"

"Of course I'm not sure. But—" He broke off, shrugged. "Eric was pretty cool about the whole thing on the show. In fact, he sort of seemed excited and flattered by it. I figure I can hack a few more days."

"If you're sure."

He glanced at her, smiled wryly. "What the hell? We've gone this far. What else could happen?"

The doors to the elevator slid open. As a throng of people flowed out, Jack pressed his hand to the small of her back to guide her out of the way. Something about his touch, how natural it felt, yet made her body start to clamor . . . and for once Valerie ceased to think about business.

There was a sudden return of the tension that spiked between them every time they were alone together. She trembled slightly and his hand slid up along her spine. "Nervous?"

She thought he was teasing her, but there was something else threading through that deep voice. Wasn't there? She didn't dare turn around and look at him to find out. Were his feelings for her— assuming he had any—more than simply physical in nature? He'd implied as much before, back in the dressing room. But . . . And what about her? Sure, she was fighting some pretty randy hormonal surges where Jack Lambert was concerned, but could there be something more than that?

Well, now they were headed up to a fabulous suite in the Plaza Hotel. An empty fabulous suite. Alone. Together.

What else could happen, indeed?

Compatibility

Sometimes it's not about finding what you have in common. It's about sharing your differences and discovering something new about yourself in the process.

Chapter 17

"Wow," Valerie breathed as Jack pushed open the door to the suite.

"Chuck and Vicki know how to treat their guests right." Jack walked over to a large fruit and cheese spread that had been laid out for them, along with two bottles of wine. He smiled as he picked up the card. " 'With our thanks for being our guest,' " he read, then snorted.

"What?" Valerie asked, popping a cheese cube in her mouth. "Looks like Goldilocks has been here and helped herself to some of this lovely food."

"It was Goldi-Eric, who added his own postscript to the note."

Valerie slipped the folded card from his fingers.

"Wait, there's a—"

She just smiled and shoved a cheese cube in his mouth when he started to protest. " 'Leave me some of those strawberries,' " she read, " '. . . or don't fall asleep on your stomach. Love, Eric.' "

"Present attached," Jack finished, after swallowing the cheese.

Valerie unfolded the card and two packets of condoms dropped into her palm. She laughed. "Well, at least he'll protect you. That's love right there."

"Please," Jack said. "You know, I can never say 'Fuck you' to the guy ever again. His being gay takes a lot of fun out of things."

He was teasing, of course, but Valerie's expression turned thoughtful as she munched on a carrot stick. "You really had no idea, huh? Although he is a pretty macho guy. I'd never have guessed. It must be a major adjustment for you."

"You could say that."

She paused for a moment, then said, "About what you said earlier in the limo, about feeling deceived. You *were* talking about that, right?"

"Listen, don't worry about—"

"Because I understand why you'd feel that way, even if you understood why he didn't tell you earlier. But that's not the same thing as what happened with his reader, in the audience."

"Close enough," he said, appreciating that she was trying to help, but not wanting to get back into it. "What's important is that Eric seems to be adjusting pretty well. I'll catch up." He took the card from her and tossed it back on the table. "What's on the schedule for this evening?"

Thankfully, she let the subject drop, but surprised him by tucking the condoms into his shirt pocket and patting his chest with a little smile. "I've got some calls to make. We need to go over tomorrow's schedule. Prep a little. We also have to figure out your wardrobe for *The Late Show* since we weren't prepared for that." She plucked a grape from the tray, but Jack took it from her before she could eat it. "Hey."

Maybe it was time he took a page from Eric's book. Throw a little caution to the wind and go after what he wanted, when he wanted it. And what he wanted was Valerie Wagner. And when he wanted her was right here, right now. So bad he could almost taste her.

He shut out the little voice in his head shouting, "Slow down; think about this; don't do anything stupid!" Because he knew if he stopped now, he'd never start up again. And he also knew he'd always regret it if he did.

He moved in close, then closer, backing her up step by step, until she came up against one of the tall pillars separating the foyer area from the sunken living room. "So what you're saying is, we have the evening to ourselves?" He fed her the grape.

She caught it between her teeth, holding his gaze steadily as she braced her hands on his arms. Only when he lowered his hand did she eat it. "What I said was we have to prepare for tomorrow. And I have some work to do. Then you have the rest of the night off." She smiled. "Maybe you can meet up with Eric and Brice and go clubbing."

Jack's grin turned wry. "Well, I would, but it seems I forgot to pack my leathers." He enjoyed the slight widening of her eyes, the way her pupils dilated a little. "Hmm," he said, lifting his hand once again, this time to slip through the hair at the back of her neck. "You like leather, do you?"

"Jack," she began, only to moan in pleasure as he kneaded the nape of her neck, then slid his fingertips up her scalp.

"You're a little tense."

"Gee," she said, managing a sardonic look. "I can't imagine why."

"Well," he said, moving in closer still. "I don't know about you, but one of the ways I could prepare for the rest of our busy schedule here in New York would be to unwind as fully as possible tonight."

"I bet," she said, her tone still dry as dust. Her body, however, was relaxing, her hips pushing slightly into his. "You know," she said idly, as he slid his other hand down her arm, then tucked it behind her waist. "At this rate, we're just going to give Eric the satisfaction of being right."

Jack's grin turned downright wicked and he finally leaned his mouth down to hers. "Yeah. But he's used to it. He's always right. At least this way we can all be satisfied." Then he finally claimed those lips he'd been dreaming about since the moment they'd been interrupted the last time. And it was better than he remembered. Worth every risk he'd decided to take and more.

She relaxed immediately, all those soft curves pushing up against his hard ones. Some growing harder by the second. *Thank you, God*, was all he could think. She fitted too perfectly in his arms, the sense of rightness almost overwhelming him. *Finally*, as if he'd been waiting for this exact moment a whole lot longer than a couple of days. In fact, it felt like he'd been waiting for this his whole life.

The warning bells wanted to go off again, but he blocked them out. He wasn't drunk, and he was no longer foolish or stupid. He could satisfy his needs without feeling the need to marry the reason behind them.

But he could sure as hell make it take as long as possible to satiate his hunger. And yet it was all he could do to take his time. Especially when what he wanted was to strip that tidy little suit off of her and begin a very thorough exploration of the body that had begun to haunt him somewhere along the way. In fact, he couldn't remember ever feeling so . . . well, *desperate* was the word that came to mind.

She ran her hands up his arms and he pulled her more fully into his. Their kiss went deeper, and deeper still, until his head was swimming. God, he was so incredibly gone for her it was ridiculous. But it felt too damn good to care. It wasn't alcohol clouding his judgment this time. Oh, he was buzzed all right, but it was on pure, unadulterated Valerie. He was finally, mercifully right where he wanted to be.

He'd sort the rest out later. After. Surely after he'd tasted her, had his fill of her, he'd finally be able to get his head on straight where she was concerned. It was really just a matter of supply and demand. He'd be back on an even keel once he'd gotten the balance back in order.

He slid his hands down her back, cupped her sweet backside and pulled her tightly into him, the softness of her making him groan deep in his throat. She moaned, too, arched her back a little, and he had to fight not to beg. *Don't make me wait any longer.*

Her thoughts seemed to be traveling along a similar path. She ran her fingers up over his shoulders and into his hair, and—

"Ow!" He pulled back instinctively when her fingers tangled in his gelled and sprayed hair.

"Hold still. My ring is—" She carefully unwove the offending piece of jewelry from his hair and he swore he heard her snicker.

As soon as he was free and could lift his head, he caught the glint still in her eyes. "Pain is amusing? I didn't know about this side of you."

She shook her head, not remotely put off by his comment, judging from the mirth still glinting in her eyes. It was one of the things he liked best about her. They understood each other, always giving as good as they got. Damn, but that turned him on, too.

"Well, there's a lot of things you don't know about me," she said. "But no, inflicting pain isn't funny. It's just that I've never made out with a guy who has more products in his hair than I do."

He smiled a little. "Ah, well, I can see where that could be faintly amusing." He tugged her arms around him again. "So, is that what we're doing? Making out?"

The humor in her eyes faded incrementally and the sass factor in her tone turned a hair more wry. "Well, it sure felt like that to me. What would you call it?"

Her body was pressed into his and he was so hard it hurt. So, what *would* he call it? It shocked him a little that he'd called her on it, even teasingly. Yet he couldn't deny it had bugged him. Because why? Did he want this to be more than making out, more than getting it on, more than a hop in the sack? Which begged the question, just what in the hell did he want it to be? Making love? Surely he wasn't that wigged out over her. He was just horny as all hell. Right? And after their prolonged foreplay, what red-blooded guy wouldn't be?

His pulse spiked a little, and this time it wasn't because of the way she was pressed up against him. The first faint thread of alarm crept past his carefully erected barriers. He knew what he was doing here. They both did. Valerie was finally in his arms, and if he was any gauge of things—and he was—she was about five minutes from being naked. He was not going to screw up what might be his only chance for simultaneous nudity because of some stupid emotional surge that could easily be chalked up to lust-crazed confusion. "Just sounded a little high school to me," he joked. He moved his hips. "And what I was feeling was a whole lot more adult."

She scanned his eyes for a brief second and he found himself holding his breath, hoping he hadn't ruined things.

"Well," she said after what seemed an eternity, the teasing glint returning. "I have a very adult idea."

He resumed breathing. "Do you?"

She ran her hands down his chest, then flicked open one shirt button, then another. "Actually, it's a confession."

Her fingernails were lightly grazing his bare chest, so it took him a second to find his voice. *"Confession?"* He shuddered a little as her nails raked over his belly, pausing at the waistband of his pants.

She spun them around so his back was now against the pillar. And for once, he was more than happy to let her take over and run things.

She pushed open his shirt, then leaned in and nipped at his chin as she slid her hands around the bare skin of his waist, once again letting the sweet pressure of her body align itself with his. A sensation that could only be improved if she weren't wearing so many clothes. Which he started to explain, but she spoke first.

"My confession is that I have wanted to run my fingers through your hair since that day we were mopping up water in my bathroom."

He'd been rapidly sinking into a hormone-driven daze, but her revelation jerked him out of it. His eyes snapped open—he hadn't even been aware they'd closed. "You have?"

She nodded, looking faintly embarrassed now. "So," she forged on, "I was thinking. Why don't I grab a bottle of wine, and you go find a bottle of hotel shampoo and the shower in this place. Set it on steam."

His lips curved. "This would be the adult part of the idea?"

"What better way to get my fingers in your hair than to lather it up?"

He hadn't thought he could be any harder. But he twitched at the idea of the two of them naked, under a hot spray, all sudsy and slippery. "What better way, indeed," he said, his voice almost hoarse.

Just then there was a knock on the suite door.

"Oh, no, not this time," Jack said, taking Valerie's hands. "No more interruptus." He pulled them both farther into the suite.

"Delivery," came a voice from the hall.

Valerie slid her hands free. "Go find the shower."

Jack huffed. Just a little. Their track record was lousy when it came to interruptions. "If you're not there in five minutes, I will come get you. I won't be dressed. And I won't care who I embarrass."

Her grin was wicked. "I might wait six minutes, just for the show."

He laughed. How was it she always said just the right thing? He debated stripping down right there, but the rap on the door repeated. She reluctantly shoved him away and turned to get the door.

It actually took him a few minutes to find the bathroom. Their bathroom, anyway. Each bedroom had its own master bath, and the first one he'd entered had already been taken over by Brice and Eric, as was obvious by the tousled sheets. Not wanting any stray visuals to dampen his, uh, spirit, he quickly moved to his and Valerie's bedroom and their very own, very private master bath.

It was huge, ornate, with a sunken whirlpool tub on one side and a roomy walk-in shower with multiple nozzles on the other. The walls were covered with mirrors. "Hmm. Which would be more fun?"

"Does it matter?"

He turned to find Valerie holding a bucket of champagne. He grinned. "Apparently not." He took the bucket and set it on the floor by the Jacuzzi. "Let me guess, from Eric and Brice?"

Valerie shook her head. "The godmothers. They saw you on the show today and this is their way of saying thank you."

"Very nice of them." He noticed she was looking a bit more tentative. He knew he shouldn't have let her answer the damn door. He didn't want to admit that his frustration went deeper than being upset at the possibility that he wasn't going to get any after all. Because admitting that would be admitting he needed Valerie for more than just a few hours of earth-moving sex. "What's wrong? Did the note say something else?"

She pasted on a smile. "They're coming up."

Jack froze. "*Up?* Here? To our room? Now?"

Valerie laughed. "No, no. To the city. Tomorrow. For the taping. God, you should see your face."

He went back to working the cork, making Valerie jump and squeal just a little when it shot off and ricocheted off one of the mirrors. "Let's just say, with our luck, I wouldn't have been surprised." He took the two flutes she'd wedged in the ice and poured champagne into each before handing her one.

She smiled and took a sip, crinkling her nose a little as the bubbles assaulted her. "To making New York your own," she toasted him, eyes dancing as she wiggled her nose a little.

To making you my own were the words that immediately flashed through his brain. Followed by a brief flicker of panic, and a longer flicker of wonder. He *clinked* glasses and sipped to cover his momentary lapse. Making her your own *for the night*, he mentally corrected. Maybe both nights if he was lucky. Although with the arrival of the godmothers tomorrow, he had a feeling this was his best shot. But it was a shot. Not the beginning of something else. Something long-term.

Something like a . . . a relationship.

He was definitely going to go light on the champagne, however. Just to be safe. There was that phrase again.

"If we're shampooing," she was saying, "then maybe we should start with the shower."

"Start?"

She moved in closer. "Some suds, followed by a relaxing dip in the whirlpool. . . ."

All thoughts of exactly where this was leading, beyond the shower, anyway, floated away as he slipped an arm around her waist and pulled her tight up against him. "For once, I'm perfectly happy to let you organize my immediate schedule," he told her. "Just one question . . ." *Fool! Take what she's offering, be thankful, and shut the hell up.* Of course he couldn't. Note to self: This self-help crap is ruining your life. Ignore it. Revert to former, insensitive macho-pig status immediately.

Sure, he'd be lonely, but probably not as horny and confused.

"Yes?"

Lonely? Where the hell had that come from? He wasn't lonely. Alone, yes. Big difference. So what if he was starting to like knowing she would pop up in his life all the time. Temporary insanity. Two days alone together and they'd be climbing the walls instead of each other. Probably. Maybe. But he still had to know one thing. "Why?" He shot her a grin, going for insouciance, and likely missing by a mile. "I mean, I know we have this amazing animal attraction to each other, but—"

"But while my body keeps saying yes, my mind keeps saying no?"

"Pretty much. Why are they both saying yes now?"

"I tend to get very focused, very goal-oriented." Her lips quirked. "It's killing you not to make a comment here, but because you want to get laid, you're being good."

He just pressed his lips together and shrugged. Then grinned and nodded.

She laughed. "Well, you did make a point the other night, when we were talking about having friendships and fun and a life outside of work. I have put things off, things that aren't goal-related."

"Like great sex, you mean?"

"Actually, yes, although I'm not a nun. But you've made me step back and ask myself some tough questions." Her lips curved in a knowing smile. "Yes, you make me want to go AWOL from the convent on a regular basis. But you're . . . complicated."

"Me? Nah, I'm very simple. Simple guy, simple needs."

She cocked her head. "You said I didn't know you. But I'm starting to. And there's so much of you I admire. I'm serious," she said when he snorted. "Your friendship with Eric, for starters. The way you look at life, put things in perspective relative to their overall importance, and though it has caused me endless loss of sleep, the way you don't take everything so damn seriously."

"Sounds like you summed things up pretty well. What's so complicated about that?"

She lifted a shoulder. "This situation we've been somewhat forced into, for one thing. That's complicated."

"Because it gets in the way of those pesky goals."

"Yes," she said.

"And now?"

She sighed. "Now we've just had a very successful day. Things are going incredibly well. It looks like we've pulled off the coup. And I'm trying to get over myself a little, just let things be for a change."

"Because your goal is finally in sight. Valerie Wagner, *Glass Slipper* executive publicist."

"Well, I'm at least allowing myself to think it might end like that."

"Instead of the Armageddon you've been so certain I would wreak."

"Pretty much," she said with a laugh. "But you might also be interested to know you're not my only tentative step toward having a life. Last Thursday night at the party, I invited Jenn out to lunch. A non-business lunch."

She said it with such obvious pride, but he knew he couldn't tease her.

"Although I guess, in a way, I have you to thank for that, too."

"Me? What did I do?" He smiled. "Although, if it will help my case here, then I'm all for taking credit."

She smirked, but her eyes were dancing. "It wasn't anything specific. Mostly watching you and Eric together, realizing that I miss not having that close friendship. For the first time, I found I wanted to share the burden with someone, you know? Just having a bitch buddy would be really nice right about now. Not that I'm going to tell her anything," she added quickly.

It was then that his heart began to teeter. Dangerously. There was no bullshit with Valerie. He'd never met anyone so up-front and direct. Sure, she drove him crazy, but she was self-aware enough to know it, and she could laugh at herself. And she made him self-aware, so they laughed together. Which made all the difference.

He tugged her closer, leaned in so his forehead brushed against hers. "I know it's not the same thing, but as far as this charade we're pulling goes, you can feel free to bitch to me—notice I said *to* me, not *at* me," he added with a playful smile. "Anytime you want."

Now those eyes turned dangerously glassy, and he wondered what he'd said wrong. "Hey, I didn't mean—"

"I know what you meant." She lifted up and kissed him softly on the lips. "And thank you. You really are a good guy, you know?"

"Yeah, well, don't let it get out, okay?" His heart went from being tugged to being yanked. He worked hard to get back on ground that wasn't so shaky. "So, is that why I'm getting so lucky here tonight? Because I'm a *good guy*?"

"Well," she said, playing along with him, giving him a considering look. "I am in a gorgeous hotel suite, with fine champagne, a steamy shower, and a pretty-okay-looking guy who apparently wants me naked. And I was thinking . . . well, maybe I deserve a little AWOL time. Maybe we both do. After all, who better to understand what's at stake here? It's not like we're going to do anything stupid to put our hard work at risk. No one has to know about this . . . but us."

She was every man's dream. A woman who wanted him now, with no promise of later. So how perverse was it that it just made him want later even more?

"Good, because I don't really want to share this, or you, with any-one else." *Ever.* He backwalked her to the shower, then reached in and flipped on the showerheads.

She tipped her glass to his lips as steam slowly began to rise. She pushed his shirt from his shoulders, then guided his glass to her lips and took a sip. She leaned down, and made him gasp as she trailed cold, fizzy kisses down the center of his chest. She rolled her chilled glass over one nipple as her tongue flicked over the other. He groaned and let his head fall back. And decided right then that one night was definitely not going to be enough. Not even.

Who knew she'd be so . . . adventurous? Although he supposed he shouldn't have been surprised that she liked to be the one taking charge. Made him wonder just how spontaneous Ms. Organized & Carefully Planned could be.

He took one last sip, then took both glasses and fumbled them onto the sink counter. He tipped her chin up so he could take her mouth, letting the chilled champagne slip from his lips, into her mouth. She moaned and opened her mouth against his, urging him to take the kiss deeper. He angled his mouth, wrapping her more tightly against him . . . while walking them both right into the water.

"Jack," she sputtered against his mouth, trying to stop him. "We're still dressed."

"Yeah," he said. "Come here."

She was laughing as he pulled her under the jet sprays. They were instantly soaked.

He pushed her back against one tiled wall. "I've been dying to peel you out of one of these suits almost since the moment I met you."

"*Peel* is exactly what you're going to have to do now," she told him, laughing.

"Darn," he said, smiling, dropping kisses along her jaw. "It could take a long, torturous time, too." He slowly freed the top button on her blouse.

"Could it?" she asked, somewhat hoarsely, as her smile faltered. She moaned a little when his fingertips grazed her damp skin. Her breathing became a bit jerkier as he popped another button, then another.

"Definitely," he said, peeling open the white silk blouse. The water had made it all but transparent, so he already knew what he'd find beneath. Her bra was delicate, silky, small, as was she. Curves always caught his eye, the lusher the better. So it was somewhat surprising to discover just how arousing it was to uncover those tight little buds, to close his mouth over one, hear her gasp, feel her arch away from the wall. He moved to the other, fair play after all, then peeled both blouse and bra the rest of the way off, draping them over the top of the glass-paned enclosure.

He covered her breasts with his hands and her eyes flickered shut. She moaned and arched when he caught her nipples between his fingers. Her frame was narrow and he mapped every inch of it as he slowly ran the palms of his hands down her torso. He sank to his knees, then took her hips, making her gasp when he rolled her so she faced the shower wall. She twitched hard, gasping again as her nipples pushed into wet tile, and he wasn't sure how he kept from just shoving her skirt up right then and there.

He ran his hands down her hips, then cupped her backside. How many times had he watched her walk away from him? How many times had he imagined doing exactly what he was doing right now? It still felt unreal, dreamlike. Except this was a damn sight better than any dream he'd ever had.

He tugged the zipper down, then slowly pushed the skirt and slip down over her hips. Now it was his turn to gasp. Hell, he almost swallowed his tongue. "Jesus," he breathed as he uncovered the slim white garter and matching panties. Panties she wore over the garter, so he could just slide them off and . . . Dear Lord have mercy.

Despite the fact that his every touch made her twitch and push into his hands, she laughed a little. "I hate panty hose with a passion."

"So do I," he murmured devoutly as he helped her step out of the skirt. He ran his fingers up her silk-covered thighs, letting them drift along the soaked silk panel that ran in between them.

Laughter was replaced by a long, low groan. He rolled her again so her back was to the tile and her hands immediately went to his head. He chuckled against her inner thigh. "Did I mention that there are times when your single-minded drive turns me on?"

"I know we're supposed to be shampooing you," she managed,

then jerked almost violently when his mouth closed over the wet silk. "But I guess that can wait."

She sank her fingertips into his wet hair as he slid one finger beneath the silk, while never lifting his mouth. He shuddered hard, almost came when he slipped his finger inside her and she tightened around him immediately. He pushed the fabric aside so he could taste her as he pushed deeper inside her. He groaned as she tightened further, his body hardening painfully. She climbed the peak slowly, digging her fingers into his scalp. "Jesus," he moaned, reveling in the taste of her, enjoying the scrape of her nails against his skin as it spiked him up higher. She pumped against him, faster, harder, groaning, then almost lost her balance as he finally wrenched her over the top.

They were both panting as he yanked her panties off. He stumbled a little before he managed to stand up, wishing like hell he'd gotten himself naked first. Getting his wet pants off now was going to be a bitch, and in his impatience he wanted to claw them off. Water streamed down his face and body as he forced himself to slow down. He steadied himself by planting a palm on the tile beside her head.

Her eyes were huge, sexy, drowsy with pleasure. Her smile was slow and even sexier as she dropped her hands to his waistband. "Let me help."

He was never so thankful they were both on the same page. He wanted her with a force that was literally painful. "Right now, I'll let you do anything you want."

She merely lifted one eyebrow. Her hair, always so neatly twisted, had started to come loose. While she carefully worked his zipper, he gently pulled the pins free from her hair, letting it fall to her shoulders in wet ropes.

"You're so beautiful," he murmured, kissing her forehead, then the tip of her nose.

She laughed a little, though her voice was low and a bit rough. "Only a man who desperately needs to come would say that at the moment. I'm sure my mascara is dripping off my chin and my hair looks like—"

He cut her off with a kiss. A deep kiss whose ferocity surprised him as much as it did her. He wondered if she realized it had more to do with showing her exactly how she made him feel . . . than it did with shutting her up so they could get on with getting him off. And it was just as well he'd chosen to express himself this way. Because he had no idea what words he'd have used to describe the powerful, almost possessive feelings that roared through him as his body covered hers.

Never, not ever, had he felt such an intense need to . . . to protect, defend. And all those other archaic primal things men were supposed to feel about their women. All of which would have been laughable if he'd had even half a working brain at the moment. Not only was he no Neanderthal when it came to women, but the very last woman who'd ever be in need of his supposed male imperative was the one currently in his arms. He'd never met anyone more capable of taking care of herself than Valerie. Perversely, that only made the feelings that much stronger.

She managed to work his zipper down, then carefully peeled both pants and snug boxer briefs over his hips, finally, mercifully, freeing him. And just as mercifully distracting him from that very disconcerting track of thought he'd been on. He pushed away from the wall enough to shrug out of his shirt.

Valerie caught it, then unwadded it again.

"What?" he teased, amazed he could do so given his current state. "Somehow me in only a wet shirt doesn't seem to carry the same hot factor as you in that garter and stockings." He glanced down at her and sighed. "Which will be forever immortalized in my brain." He found a smile. "In fact, how in the hell I'm going to ever look at you in those suits again and not get, well—"

"Like this?" she said, reaching down and circling him with her hand.

He jerked hard, almost fell against the tile, managed to nod as he was suddenly incapable of speech when she began to stroke him. His shirt dropped to the shower floor, leaving her holding the condom packet she'd pulled from the front pocket.

"Oh," he managed.

She smiled. "Yeah. Oh." She tore one open with her teeth.

He groaned, praying like hell he'd make it until she put the damn thing on. Just the idea of her hands smoothing it— "Jesus," he groaned as she did just that.

Maybe it was the satisfied little smile, or the glint in her eye as she smiled up at him, but whatever the case, his last thread of control snapped. He grinned . . . and growled, though he couldn't say which one made her gasp a little in surprise. Maybe it was the way he grabbed her wet, silk thighs and pushed her up against the tile as he wrapped them around his hips and pushed himself inside her in one deep stroke.

She gasped, then dug her nails into his shoulders and held on as he took her. And took her. He tried to slow down, but it was like something wild had been unleashed the moment he'd buried himself inside her. *Home* was the word that echoed through his mind, over and over, with each thrust. He felt such a strong sense of belonging, of . . . safety. Of absolute trust. Insane. He knew there was no such thing. And yet, he let it wash over him, rush through him, no longer questioning this thing he'd become with her. He'd come to his senses later. Surely.

Right now, all he could do was pull her more tightly around him and hold on for what felt like dear life as he rushed up and screamed over the edge. But even as the shuddering rage subsided, he held on. He didn't want to let her go now, either. And he suspected he could stand here until the water ran cold, and that wouldn't change. Exhausted and spent, his barriers deserted him. He could no longer claim that this need she'd spawned inside of him was about sex.

He pressed his lips against the curve of her neck, telling himself not to leap. Knowing it was already too late.

Love

Women think men look for sex, not love. But men want to love and be loved. It's just hard for them to admit it. Admitting they want sex is easier.

Chapter 18

Valerie nudged at his chest, and Jack finally rolled to his back as he carefully let her slide off him. But when she began to stumble away from him, he tugged her back into his arms and held her there tightly against him.

Too tightly, she thought, with not a little wonder.

"I'm sorry," he said hoarsely, nuzzling her neck again.

"For?"

He gentled his hold, but only so he could tuck her more comfortably against him. The tenderness of his touch after the way he'd just taken her mixed her up even further. But it felt good to stand in the shelter of his embrace, let the water beat against her back, let the dazed whirlwind of feelings and emotions swirling inside her hopefully settle back down into something that resembled rational thought.

He nudged at her jaw with his nose until she lifted her head enough to look at him. God, he was beautiful, was all she could think. Dark, wet hair and flushed skin, his gray eyes glinting almost silver as water droplets clung to his thick lashes. Her heart bumped painfully at the same mix of confused emotions she saw mirrored in his eyes. She didn't need to fall for this man. Hot shower sex: yes. Dear God, yes. Anything more serious: Was she nuts?

"Did I hurt you? I didn't mean to be rough; I've never just lost it like that. I don't know what came over me. I—"

"It's okay," she told him, willing herself not to read anything into his sincerely stunned-sounding confession. "I might have tiny tile-print marks permanently imprinted on my back—" She'd meant to tease, pull them out of this postcoital emotional overload they were both apparently feeling, and get them back to where they belonged with each other. Which was simply as two consenting adults who'd figured out how to have mind-blowing sex the first time out of the gate.

But the look of concern that flickered immediately to life in those eyes stopped her, surprised her . . . made her heart squeeze even tighter. She had to get out of here, get away from him, get her shit together before she did something really, really stupid. Like imagine herself starting some kind of real relationship with him. "I'm kidding. It was . . . You were . . ." She heard the awe in her voice, the wonder, and fought to curb it. She reached up, kissed his chin. "No complaints," she said, hoping her grin was cheeky. Not adoring. "Now, what did we do with that shampoo?" She went to pull from his arms, only he wouldn't let her go.

"Valerie—"

She couldn't let herself hear whatever it was he was about to say. Which, judging from the look in his eyes, was something serious, something emotional. He'd thank her for saving him the embarrassment of recanting later, she told herself, as she firmly disengaged herself from his arms. Because surely whatever it was he was feeling, or thought he was feeling, was simply a by-product of what they'd just done with each other. So what if it had felt like something beyond explosive sex to her, too? She'd calm down with time. Stop feeling that way. Stop thinking about the look that had come into his eyes when he'd lost control and just taken her. Dear God, had he taken her.

She shook that thought free and turned to gather up the soap and shampoo. "You first, okay?" she said brightly, as if she always showered with a guy while wearing a garter belt and stockings.

He caught her elbow, tugged her back around. No teasing smile curved that wickedly gifted mouth of his, no cocky glint lit up those eyes. Still serious, still emotional. "Come here."

"Jack—" she began, then stopped. She had no idea what she wanted to say to him.

"Just let me . . ." He trailed off as if he wasn't quite sure of himself, either. He tugged her gently against him and it was that uncertainty they were both feeling that caved in whatever resistance she had.

Neither of them said anything, just stood there and let the shower beat down on them. After a while, he reached behind her and grabbed the soap and shampoo. Neither of them tried for light and playful as they soaped and sudsed each other. The mood was distinct for its quiet intensity, and though she suspected she'd regret it later, she allowed herself to sink into it, revel in the unique power of it. This was something she'd never felt, never experienced.

They used fluffy white towels, warmed on racks, to dry each other off. And when he scooped her up and carried her to the bedroom, leaving stockings, pants, and garter lying sodden and unheeded behind them, it felt like the most natural thing in the world as he dragged the comforter off the bed, laid her amongst the white sheets and pillows, then joined her there. Their lovemaking this time was slow, gentle, almost unbearably sweet. All the things she'd have never imagined Jack Lambert capable of being. She raked her nails slowly up his back as he pushed inside her, arched her back, and couldn't help but remember how angry he'd been, feeling like an imposter to those women in the audience.

If they only knew, she thought before letting go completely.

Prince Charming, indeed.

She wasn't sure what time it was when she woke up, but the room was dark, as was the sky. She felt the warm heat of him next to her even before it all came back to her. She turned her head to find him propped up on one elbow, watching her. It was too dark to read what was in his eyes. Valerie thought that might be just as well, hoping he couldn't read hers, either.

"Hungry?" he said, his voice rough and husky.

She wanted to stretch, revel a little in how languid and fulfilled she felt, then grin to bursting before yanking him on top of her again. She managed to refrain. Barely. "I could probably eat something."

At any other time, Jack Lambert would have most likely shot her a cocky grin and made something suggestive out of that. But this Jack Lambert was someone she didn't know as well, and surely couldn't read. "I can order from room service. Or we can get dressed and head out if you'd like."

"What time is it?"

"Does it matter?"

Now she smiled. "In New York? Probably not." She was stretching and grinning before she realized she'd given in to the instinct. "What do you want to do?"

She glanced at him and her vision had adjusted to the dark just enough to catch the glitter in his eyes. She shivered a little as pleasure raced over her and through her. Surely he wasn't suggesting he

could . . . again. But the mere idea of it had her toes curling in anticipation.

He drew a lazy circle around her navel with his fingertip. "I don't
have the stamina to do what I want to do."

She grinned now. "Meaning, going out on the town after such
a . . . workout, or staying in to work out some more?"

"Yes."

She laughed, and caught the flash of his smile right before he kissed
her. And felt her heart teeter on the edge . . . and fall off.

Damn.

"Actually," he said, the mood shifting more effortlessly back to
teasing than she'd expected, "I was debating whether it was worth the
potential embarrassment, not to mention that squicky feeling, of going over to beg, borrow, or steal more condoms from our room-
mates."

"Ah," she said with mock sobriety. "I can see the dilemma." She
rolled to her side and propped herself up on one elbow, mirroring
him. "I could go."

He laughed, then made her squeal when he suddenly pulled her
on top of him. "I want to take you out," he said. "Do the town, see the
sights." His arms came around her. "And I want to keep you here, all
to myself."

Just in case. He didn't say it, but she heard it nonetheless. Just in
case the world intruded on this perfect little bubble in time. And
burst it. Which it would, in any case. They both knew that.

Their gazes caught in a stream of moonlight. "Room service," they
both said at the same time, then laughed.

Jack ordered while she slipped off to the bathroom. Seeing their
clothing strewn carelessly on the tiled floor should have embarrassed
her. Instead, it brought back a wave of memories. The way he'd
teased her, the way he'd taken her. And the gentle, almost protective

way he'd treated her afterward. She sighed and splashed water on her face, not sure she wanted to look at herself in the mirror.

She groaned when she did. Her cheeks and nose were flushed, her neck all red from his five o'clock shadow. Her still-damp hair was a wild nest and her makeup was completely gone. Thoroughly ravished, yes. "Ravishing . . . hardly." Their bags hadn't been unpacked, so there wasn't much she could do about it at the moment. She raked her fingers through her hair, but it was just dry enough that she was only making it worse. Sighing in defeat, she wrapped herself in one of the hotel's fluffy white robes, hoping Jack had left the bedroom dark. Morning would come soon enough and the cold light of day would likely end whatever it was they thought they'd begun. And though she knew she'd already gone way too far over the line, she wasn't in any hurry to end it sooner than she had to.

As it turned out, Jack had left the bedroom dark. Mostly. He'd lit two tall candles that had come with the room-service cart. And there was soft music filtering in from somewhere. But she didn't have time to appreciate the ambience he was striving to achieve. She was too busy watching the way his body moved as he shoved the heavy love seat away from the wall. He'd pulled on gym shorts, and she noticed his suitcase was spilled open on the bed. "What are you doing?"

"Being romantic."

"Ah."

He paused in his manly endeavors to glance her way. "I realize Prince Charming would be smooth about this and all, but some of us regular guys have to work at it a little."

Smiling, she folded her arms and leaned against the bathroom doorway. "I think you're very charming without even trying."

He'd gone back to grunting and shoving. "I wish I'd known that before I started this little endeavor. Jesus, what did they build this thing out of, anyway? Cement?"

She went over to the other end of the couch. "Let me help you. Exactly where are we pushing this?"

He nodded behind him. "There. In front of the window. No," he corrected when she began to swing her end around. "Facing the window. For the view." He stopped and moved over to the heavy curtains, pulling them the rest of the way open, sheers and all.

Valerie walked up behind him. "Impressive," she said, looking out over the city. They were high enough to see both a good deal of the area and the night sky, and be above most of the street noise. She turned to him. "Very nice." She was more touched by the effort than she wanted to be. And yet she was hopelessly gone, too hopeless to fight it.

"I thought we could sit here and eat. Unless you'd rather sit out—"

"No, this is perfect." And it was. Too perfect. Who'd have thought Jack would be a romantic? Or even try? From the corner of her eye she saw the beads of sweat trickling down the side of his face and swallowed the urge to laugh. Probably not Jack, she couldn't help but think.

He tugged her against his hips as they looked out the window. "What's so funny?"

"Nothing, really. You're not exactly how I'd thought you'd be. But then I guess . . . well, I guess I don't know you well enough to judge." *But I want to.* She managed to keep that last part to herself. Not that it helped much. She thought about the way Brice had looked at Eric . . . and suspected she was close to looking at Jack the same way.

He didn't push, or respond. Instead, he shifted her away from the window, and tugged the couch the rest of the way, before rolling the cart to one end. "Madam, your table is ready," he said in perfect French.

"Pretty decent accent," she noted. "Do you speak many languages?"

She curled up on one end of the couch and he flipped a linen napkin across her lap. He slid the coffee table into the narrow space between the window and the couch, and laid out their food before taking a seat at the other end of the short love seat. Her toes brushed his thigh and he reached out to massage her ankle. It was casually done, and yet so natural, as if he touched her all the time. Which is what made her heart catch. Jesus, she'd better get a grip, and fast.

"I pick up some wherever I go. Enough to order food and get directions, anyway. You?"

"I'm decent with French and Spanish, a handful of Italian. That's pretty much my limit."

They took the lids off their plates and spent the next ten or so minutes eating in surprisingly companionable silence. Eventually, Valerie leaned back into the corner of the cushions and sipped her wine.

"Food okay?" Jack asked.

She nodded, liking the way his hair dried all wavy and messy, yet still looked sexy as hell. His body was a good one. Not overly musclebound, but lean and defined. She'd loved every minute she'd had her hands on it. All over it. "I'm not so much hungry for food at the moment."

He glanced over at her as he cut into the last piece of his steak. "No?"

She smiled and shook her head, sipped her wine.

"Hmm," he said, his mouth kicking up as he chewed, swallowed. "Dessert, then?"

"Later, maybe," she said, not realizing she was going to broach the subject until the words were already coming out. "I'm more interested in learning more about you." She hadn't known how he'd react, but she'd suspected he might turn a bit wary, perhaps even close himself off. Knowing what little she did about him, she knew he wouldn't be curt about it. No, Jack would more than likely tease her on to another subject, make her forget whatever it was he didn't want to talk about.

So he surprised her by using the linen napkin to dab at his mouth, then settled comfortably back in the cushions with his glass of wine, turning so he could rest his back on the armrest, and tangle his legs with hers. His gaze was direct, and though he was very relaxed, there was a definite intensity in his eyes. "Like what?"

Of course her mind went completely blank. She didn't want to get too personal—well, she did, but not right off the bat—and she wasn't sure where that line was drawn at the moment. "How did you get started in sports journalism?"

He just looked at her. "You mean, other than what I've told every reporter who's asked?"

"I know the story about helping that girl—"

"Candy Kenner." He said it with a sigh, then lifted his glass in a mock toast.

Valerie just rolled her eyes. "—on your high-school newspaper write an article about the football team. Surely there was more to it than that."

"If you're expecting me to kiss and tell on what I did with Candy—"

"No, I don't want your sordid high-school adventures, especially with a girl named Candy."

"She *was* sweet."

Valerie groaned and shook her head. "Stick to sportswriting."

"I'd be more than happy to," he said with such heartfelt sincerity that it tugged at her heart. She and Eric had turned his life upside down. How easy it was to forget that during her all-about-me moments.

"But you went to college on a partial athletic scholarship and majored in physical education," Valerie said, pushing onward, not wanting to dwell on the real world at the moment. Beyond making sure tonight was all about him. About them. "Obviously, Candy didn't alter your entire life's path."

"Well, yes and no. She was my first love . . . and my first, you know."

"Ah. Well, that is special, I guess. Or it must be for some people, anyway."

Jack grinned. "Your first time wasn't so hot, huh?"

"Apparently I shouldn't have been looking for love on the year-book committee."

"The football team wouldn't have been any guarantee, either," he said with a laugh.

"Like I'd have had the chance to find out. I was not cheerleader material. Jocks did not lust after me. I'm not sure guys in any clique did."

Jack slowly sipped his wine. "I find that hard to believe."

"Let's just say I was in my *experimental* phase with finding myself. I think I scared most guys off." She laughed. "No, I know I did. I wasn't too concerned with being attractive to the opposite sex. While most girls were twirling their hair and popping gum outside the boys' locker room after practice, I was in the art hall, immersed in fashion and the world of glamour and figuring out what the next hot runway trend would be."

"Hey, guys dig models. Even teenage guys aren't that stupid."

"Well, let's just say I was usually a trend or two ahead of myself. And though I was gangly and scrawny, I never really managed to make a good hanger."

He nudged her leg with his toes. "But you showed them in the end, huh? Look at you now."

She laughed outright. "Oh, yeah, I sure did."

He cocked his head. "What's that supposed to mean? You know, you've commented several times about this being your last chance. Eric mentioned that, too. What does that mean? You seem pretty damn good at your job as far as I can tell. You're an incredibly capable woman."

It surprised her how much his opinion mattered. So naturally, she had to push it away. Dangerous territory. "I thought we were talking about you."

He smiled over the rim of his glass. "Were we?"

"Okay, fine. I'll tell you all about my failures, lay myself bare, then you must reveal something personal and awkward."

"What *failures*? Somehow, you don't strike me as someone who would tolerate failing. At anything."

She lowered her glass to her lap. "I can't decide whether to thank you for what is perhaps the best compliment I've ever received. Or laugh hysterically and say, 'Boy do I have you fooled.' "

"Come on," he said seriously. "What do you define as failing, then? We probably have different ideas on—"

"I'm thirty years old. I've been fixated on the glamour industry since I was nine, and working in some form of it since I was sixteen. And I've never held a job more than eighteen months."

He didn't try to hide his shock. "Meaning, you got canned? Or bored? Bored isn't failing; it's just admitting you haven't found what's right for you yet."

"It wasn't always boredom. And it's taken me twenty years to find what's right for me."

"Being a publicist?"

She nodded. "Being part of this world is the only thing I've ever wanted to do. And I've done and tried pretty much every job you can imagine. I did recognize early on that I wasn't cut out to wear fashion, design fashion, or even take pictures of fashion. So I ventured into the world of fashion magazines, and hitched my star there. Then, after another dozen years, I was humbly forced to admit I wasn't cut out to write about fashion, assist those who write about fashion, edit, lay out, or market fashion. In fact, I was pretty much at the brink of giving up altogether." She paused, staring down into her wineglass as she ran her finger around the rim. "Have you ever wanted anything really badly? So badly you just refused to believe it was totally wrong for you?"

She glanced up, and he held her gaze for the longest time. The shift in the tension was subtle at first, then grew in intensity the longer he stared directly at her. Then, very quietly, he said, "Until recently, I would have said no."

She didn't know quite how to interpret that, or what to say. And she was just chicken enough not to try. "Well, that was me and fashion. It caught my full attention early on, and I don't even really know why. But it's a fascination that just refuses to die."

"I think I understand that more than you realize," he murmured.

Her body quickened at the heat in his voice, the surety. It made her nervous as hell to think he could be talking about . . . what she thought he might be talking about. And secretly, it thrilled her at the same time. "Anyway," she said quickly, "I stumbled across this opportunity, and almost the instant after I talked my way into it—"

"Meaning, you've never done this before."

"Meaning, I've never had proper training for anything I've done before. But I'm observant, a quick learner, and willing to work hard."

"So, you're telling me you talked your way into this job—and God knows how many previous jobs—with no direct experience, no references?"

"I didn't say I didn't have references. I have loads of references. From every possible corner of the fashion industry." She dipped her chin, smiled wryly, and added, "Just never for the actual job I'm applying for."

"So you're a bullshit artist." He raised his palm when she opened her mouth to argue. "An artist with a passion for what she's bullshitting about. I can get behind that. It's pretty much exactly what I do. I write about things I know nothing about but find fascinating nonetheless. So I learn just enough to find an angle that can connect this oddball sport with the common readership. It's challenging, personally rewarding. The pay's not stupendous, but I get to travel to the four corners of the earth and see things, talk to people I'd otherwise never meet. Well, I used to, anyway."

She frowned, no longer miffed at his summation. In fact, admittedly, he was pretty much right on target. "Surely you'll find another job. Eric told me you were already moonlighting for some wire service in Europe."

He nodded. "Trying. And there might be a full-time position for me with them when this hoopla is over. If they still want me, that is."

"You think this whole Prince Charming thing would keep them from offering you a job?" It was shaming to realize that throughout all of this, she hadn't really considered the future impact on Jack. Eric had told her he would compensate Jack generously for his help, and she knew he was already working freelance. It just had never occurred to her that he might be permanently affected by agreeing to help his friend. And her.

"I don't know," he said quite frankly. "Hopefully not."

"But Eric told me he'd worked something out with you, and so at least you have that to—"

"I'm fine," he said, his expression tightening somewhat. "I don't need Eric holding my hand. I agreed to do this and while I might not have known what I was getting myself into, I've also done my share in making it a bigger deal than it had to be." He shrugged. "I'll be fine when it's done."

"This is an awfully big favor to do for a friend."

"He's earned it."

"You've alluded to that before. What did he do for you that earned such a blind sacrifice?" She lifted her hand. "I swear this won't end up in some press release or interview bio. This is just between you and me."

Now it was Jack's turn to stare into his wine. And just when she thought he was going to shut her out, he said, "He saved my life."

"Literally?"

"Close enough." He looked up then. "My mom died when I was eleven. Car accident, drunk driver."

"I'm sorry." The idea of a motherless Jack tugged hard at her heart. "I can't even imagine."

"Are you close with your parents?"

She half-shrugged. "My mom and dad never planned on having children, and they sort of ended up treating parenting me more like a business decision, with corporate policies and managerial strategies. And I still grew up to be someone so different from them that they never really knew what to do with me. But they supported me, still do." Her lips quirked. "Though I know they'll be much happier when I—"

"Let me guess, settle down and give them grandchildren?"

She laughed. "Heavens no, are you kidding me? They didn't know what to do with me; the last thing they want is a grandchild they don't know what to do with. No, they want me to find my niche in life and prosper. Not necessarily even monetarily, although both my parents do very well in the corporate world, but they want me to find something that excites me and that I enjoy and that I can succeed at." She sipped her wine. "What about your dad? What does he think of you traveling all over the world?"

"My, uh, my dad didn't do so well after my mom died. He sort of had a breakdown."

"Jack, I'm sorry. You don't have to—"

"When I was sixteen, he killed himself."

She gasped, horrified.

"I'd been hanging out at Eric's house a lot by then. His dad had died when he was young, so we had that in common. And even though his mom was never all that healthy, she was great about letting me hang around. My dad had pretty much checked out in terms of parenting, and there was no other family to speak of. Mrs. Jermaine wasn't exactly the mother figure I was missing, but their house was bright and cheerful, very different from mine. And when she was well enough, it smelled like fresh-baked bread. I'll always love that smell."

He smiled briefly. "She was addicted to soap operas and if Eric or I weren't careful, she'd have us wheel her into the living room, then make us hang out there and watch a few of her 'stories,' as she called them, with her." He shuddered in mock horror, then shook his head and laughed. "I know Eric spent a large part of his formative years watching *As the World Turns* and *One Life to Live*, so maybe that's where he honed those advice skills of his. Anyway, I used to go home with him after school, help him with his chores, then we'd hide out together in the tree house his grandfather had built for him in their backyard when Eric was little."

He trailed off, then tipped his chin down again. "I slept out there many a night, and Eric covered for me with his mom. She probably knew, I think now. But at the time, I knew I'd never be able to repay him for giving me that place to escape to. After my dad died, they more or less took me in. I had a job after school with the local parks and rec department, so I wasn't around much, but I pitched in as much as I could. We both graduated a year later and went off to college together. Eric had a full ride and I got a partial scholarship and qualified for some assistance. But there is no doubt that if Eric and Mrs. Jermaine hadn't been there for me, I'd have never kept my shit together. God knows how I'd have ended up. Probably as lost as my dad. It wasn't easy and I wasn't always easy, far from it, but Eric stuck it out with me." He looked at her again. "So in terms of payback, this is a drop in the bucket."

She set her wineglass on the table, her hand a little shaky. "I don't know what to say," she said quietly. She wanted to hug him, rock him, something. But she knew he'd take it as pity, when she merely meant it as comfort. Like she could do anything to erase what had happened to him, or soften it. "I'm in awe of your bond with Eric," she said finally. "Maybe even a little jealous. Envious, at least. I've never found that." She held his gaze. "What you're doing for him now is no small thing. It's not just about being the face of Prince Charming. It's about accepting him for who he is and not judging him. I imagine telling you was probably the hardest thing he's ever had to do. And you didn't blink. You're both very lucky."

Jack set his glass on the table as well, and when he leaned forward and reached for her, she saw his hands weren't completely steady, either.

"Come here," he said quietly, taking her and pulling her back with him until she was lying on top of him. He settled her so her head rested beneath his chin. He tucked his ankles around hers and looped an arm around her waist, stroking her back with one hand, her hair with the other. They lay in silence like that, his heartbeat thrumming beneath her ear. Thank you," he whispered against her hair, so softly she wasn't sure she'd really heard him.

In response, she just pressed her palm over his heart, and left it there. And as time continued to pass quietly, while the candles flickered beside them and she lay in his arms, she knew she'd made possibly the biggest mistake of her life. She'd fallen in love. At precisely the wrong time, and with precisely the wrong man.

The morning after

Guys can royally screw it up, but not always for the reason you think. Sure, there are those who are awkward and tentative because it was just one night and they don't want you to assume too much. But sometimes he's awkward and tentative because it meant more to him than he thought it would . . . and now he's afraid you won't assume enough. Only he's not sure how to let you know that. So stick around, give him a chance to do it right.

Chapter 19

With one towel wrapped around his hips and using another to dry his hair, Jack emerged from their bedroom the following morning to find Valerie already seated at a table in the main room, a phone at one ear and a pen poised over a legal pad.

Rather than interrupt, he leaned against the doorframe and took the opportunity to simply observe her in her natural habitat. Hair swept up in a neat twist, another perfectly tailored suit—this one the color of a mango—adorning her trim body. A body he now knew intimately. Every curve and dip. His body stirred . . . and so did his heart.

He'd woken up alone, sprawled on the love seat where they'd fallen asleep. The guttered candles and half-eaten dinners had been removed, and the comforter from the bed had been thrown over him. He'd heard the shower running and his immediate instinct had been to join her there, pick up where they'd left off the night before.

Only where they'd left off hadn't been the let's-get-it-out-of-our-systems-sex it had started out to be. That had changed almost from the moment he'd touched her. They'd shared far more than their bodies. Stories had been told, revelations made, and even the silent moments had shifted things. Between them, inside him. If he was honest, he'd admit that shift had started even before they'd begun peeling each other's clothes off.

In fact, lying there alone . . . and for the first time not at all relieved to have avoided morning-after conversation . . . he'd been forced to admit that it had probably never been about the sex. Without even realizing it, he'd been poised to leap from the moment she'd delivered that first wry smile. He just hadn't been willing to admit it until now.

So he'd purposely waited for the shower to end, then gave her another healthy chunk of time to dress before he'd gotten up and headed to the bathroom door. A chickenshit response, perhaps, but it was simply too much to handle all at once. He needed to sort things out first, decide what in the hell it was he was feeling, and what he wanted to do about it.

And part of him wanted to gauge where she was this morning, too. Maybe it had been the darkness, the wine, the explosive sex making him feel this way. *The laughter, the quiet whispers, the way she'd laid her hand over his heart.* He shut that path down. For all he knew, she'd come buzzing out of the bathroom, peck him on the cheek, or worse, make some kind of joke, then settle into work as if nothing earth-shattering had taken place last night.

Which was when he'd sat down hard on the edge of the bed. Because it had been for him. Hard to escape that conclusion.

So . . . which reaction was he hoping for, then? Did he want her to come out and be mushy all over him? Or would it be better if they both just agreed that it had been fun, but now it was back to business? He didn't know which conclusion terrified him more.

She'd come out of the bathroom before he could decide. And she'd seemed startled to see him there, sitting on the bed, watching the door . . . and now her. As if she weren't quite prepared for this moment, either. Which, somehow, had settled him better than anything else could have. If they were both screwed up over the right way to handle this, then there was no wrong way to handle it.

So he'd gotten up off the bed, walked over to her, and brushed a finger down the side of her face. She was dressed, but her hair was still wrapped in a towel, her face free of makeup. "Morning," he'd said.

"Morning," she'd managed.

And it had taken every last scrap of will he'd owned not to haul her up against him and kiss the daylights out of her, then strip her out of that tidy suit and drag her back to bed. What stopped him was that the motivation behind the need wasn't about getting some. It was about not letting go of her.

"I, uh, thought I'd do my hair and makeup out here so you could have the shower." She shifted away, just slightly, but enough that he dropped his hand. "I ordered up some coffee. I never made those phone calls last night . . . and we still need to go over today's schedule."

So . . . he'd thought. It was going to be back to business. And though it made no sense whatsoever, given his own personal confusion, that pissed him off. Maybe because she'd managed to get her shit together better, or faster, than he had; he wasn't sure.

He'd stepped back, held on to his temper, and said, "So, what am I wearing today?"

She had sensed the shift in tension, but merely motioned to the bathroom. "I hung a few things on the back of the door." And then the bell had rung, announcing room service, and she'd escaped.

The long, hot shower hadn't pounded any answers into him. Neither was standing here, staring at her. He still didn't know what he wanted. Well, that wasn't entirely true. He wanted Valerie. But how, and for how long? At the moment, he was thinking forever. But then, he'd been in that place before. And look where that had ended up.

As soon as he thought that, he discarded it. No. He'd never been in this place. He'd never felt such powerfully strong emotions for anyone. He'd never once felt such a strong sense of rightness. He'd wandered the world without ever really knowing what it was he'd needed to feel whole, until he'd stepped into her arms and found himself in that one place he'd always belonged. And that was the true source of his fear. Because those feelings intensified every self-doubt he'd ever had. Would he figure out how to make it work this time? Would she be willing to work just as hard?

Jesus, listen to him! Here he was, pondering eternity, and she didn't even know how he felt. And if he got up the nerve to tell her? He couldn't help the smile that curved his lips. Knowing Valerie, she'd come up with a laundry list of reasons why he had no business feeling that way. And though she'd probably be right, it wouldn't change anything. The real question was, how did she feel about him? And could he shove away all his insecurities long enough to risk finding out?

He glanced across the main room to the other bedroom door. It still stood wide open. "Where are our roomies this morning?" he asked, startling her.

Her cheeks flushed instantly, making him wish he'd been paying attention to what she'd been saying . . . and to whom.

She ducked her chin and lowered her voice. "Yes, it was. And I can't tell you anything else. Because he's standing right here!" She glanced up then, and grinned through her embarrassment. "A towel. Uh-uh. Better than that. I know!"

Jack's eyebrows lifted when she actually giggled. It was deep and throaty, kinda sexy, even if it was at his expense.

"I really have to go," she said, not bothering to whisper now. "*No,* because we have work to do. Mind outta the gutter." She laughed again. "I know. I'm having the same problem. I'll try to catch you later, after the taping." She finally hung up, then cleared her throat and took a deep, dignifying breath before looking at him.

He leaned against the door, folded his arms. "Who was that? It sounded very, I don't know, slumber party."

Despite her attempts at reasserting her professional mien, her face lit up. There was a touch of wonder and maybe a little yearning in her expression. And what little piece of his heart he might have still controlled slipped swiftly from his grasp. He didn't even try to stop it.

"That was Jenn, actually."

"Ah," he said, as if that explained it all. Which it did. "You two are getting tight, then?"

She cocked her head. "Yeah. I think maybe we might be." Her smile turned a touch sly. "Why, feeling threatened?"

He pushed away from the door and stepped into the room. "Hey, she might be five-feet-nothing, but hurricanes could take energy lessons from her. And team her up with you? I'm thinking we need to warn the Western Hemisphere that life as they know it is about to change."

She laughed and rubbed her hands together. "Ooh, what power we wield." As he continued to close the distance between them, she went back to straightening her pads of paper and her pens, more out of habit than anything. Jack enjoyed watching her fuss . . . and try to come to terms with her fledgling new friendship with Jenn.

But he couldn't help wanting to redirect her thoughts to her other fledgling new relationship. With him.

"I, uh, talked to the booker for *Letterman*," she said, her expression shifting a bit as she appeared to be trying to read his thoughts.

He wondered what she surmised, wondered if she'd be shocked to know the truth.

"They went ahead and tapped someone else to do an appearance, but they'd still love it if you'd read the Top Ten," she told him. "The taping is scheduled for later this afternoon."

She was nervous, he realized, and for once he didn't think it was about his appearance as Prince Charming. Which intrigued him, and gave him the edge he so desperately needed. "Sounds like a plan." He nodded to the opposite bedroom. "Where's the darling duo this morning?"

Valerie glanced at the open door and shrugged. "I don't know. The door was open when I came out, and no one's home. I'm not sure they ever made it back last night. There are no messages, either." She tapped her pen on her legal pad. "You look surprised."

"Not surprised, really. Not that they didn't come back, at any rate. I guess I'm still getting used to the gusto Eric is charging into this new life with. It's not like him to be wild and irresponsible." He sighed. "Though maybe he's due for a little of that." He stopped across the table from her and leaned on one of the chairs. "I'm sure they'll pop up when we least expect them. Or where."

"You're probably right. If it makes you feel any better, I worry about him, too. I know he and I have only just forged a friendship, but . . ." She trailed off, smiled briefly as she reached for her coffee mug. "He kind of grows on you really quickly. I care about him. I want him to be happy."

Jack had to bite his tongue to keep from asking her what would make her happy. He already knew the answer to that: getting this early media blitz over and done with so she could settle into her job. Into her newfound success, her niche. What he didn't know was where he might, or if he even could, fit into that.

He was happy for her, cared enough to want to make sure this went smoothly for her sake now as well as Eric's. She'd worked hard; she deserved the success they'd achieved. As for him? His plan had been to finish up what was left, then head off for parts unknown.

Probably overseas. He'd considered selling his apartment, although he'd since reconsidered. At the time, because he'd wanted to stay more connected to Eric, do a better job at maintaining that friendship. And now? Well, Alexandria was quite close in proximity to . . . a certain row house he'd grown fond of, complete with a monster dog in the backyard. Maybe crossing paths when he was in town was all they'd ever have. He didn't think that would be enough. But maybe it would have to be.

It was then he realized the silence had spun out a bit, and that they were both staring at each other. And just like that, the air between them became charged, tension arced, and only part of it was sexual.

Valerie spoke first. "Jack, I—about last night—"

Whatever she'd been about to say was aborted by the sudden opening of the suite's double doors and the bustling, unannounced arrival of the godmothers.

"Hello, hello, darlings," Aurora gushed as she wafted in, in a cloud of White Diamond.

"Hello, indeed," Vivian added, pausing just behind Aurora as she caught sight of Jack, who immediately realized he was still wearing a towel, and only a towel.

"Excuse me, ladies," he said with a slight bow. "The black one, then?" he directed to Valerie, as if they'd been discussing wardrobe and nothing more.

"No," she said, picking up right on cue. "The khaki and navy." She crossed the room as Mercedes entered last. "What a nice surprise."

"Are you sure?" Vivian cut a glance at Jack as he walked into the bedroom and shut the door.

He leaned against it and blew out a deep breath. There was nothing he could do about the other bedroom door being open. Hopefully they'd see the tumble of sheets and assume Valerie had slept in there. Forced explanations would only complicate things. Silently praying Eric and Brice stayed put wherever the hell they were, he shaved and dressed.

The godmothers were still twittering about when he came back out. Well, Aurora was. Vivian had turned on the big-screen television and was watching the news. Mercedes was sitting at the table across from Valerie, going over a list of something or other.

"There you are," Aurora said, coming immediately toward him, hands outstretched. She took both of his hands in hers and squeezed tightly, making him wish she wore slightly fewer rings.

He hid the wince with a smile. "Here I am, indeed."

"I was just telling Valerie that you've spawned quite the fan club."

"*Fan club?*" He shot a quick glance to Valerie, but she had her head bent with Mercedes'.

"Yes, there is an absolute throng of women outside the hotel," Aurora went on, almost giddy with excitement over this latest development, and apparently assuming he would be, too. "I guess it's common knowledge where Chuck and Vicki put up their guests. Anyway," her eyes sparkled as she squeezed his hands again, "they have signs and everything. I can't decide which was more adorable. The one that said 'Be My Prince' or 'Charm Me!' "

"Personally, I liked the one that said 'Prince Hottie,' " Vivian chimed in, winking at him from her perch on the armrest of the couch. She was wearing a typical Vivian outfit: a wild zebra-print, loosely flowing top over a pencil-slim, short black skirt with a slit up one side. Tinted stockings and dagger-heeled silver sandals completed the ensemble.

"Honestly, Vivi." Aurora shot her a quelling look, then beamed at Jack. "We were just saying that we can't begin to express our thanks for all you've done. I know this is beyond the boundaries you initially had Eric establish for you, but you've done such a magnificent job."

Vivian waved her gold-stemmed cigarette holder in his direction. "Absolutely. You're so at home in front of the cameras. Which gobble you up, by the way," she added, followed by a brief perusal of him that left no doubt she'd have likely gobbled him up, too, had there not been so many years between them. At least he hoped she'd consider the age difference a deterrent.

"Thank you," he finally managed.

"I'm surprised you've waited so long to come out of the closet, as they say."

Jack felt Valerie's gaze jump to him, but he carefully kept his expression casual. "Well, it's all worked out to everyone's advantage, so I guess the old saying is right. Everything happens when it does for a reason." Keeping a smile on his face, he carefully withdrew his now numb fingers from Aurora's grip and moved to the silver tea cart, where he poured himself a mug of coffee. "Can I get you ladies anything?"

"I'll have tea," Aurora said, as Vivian merely sent him a suggestive little smile before turning her attention back to the television.

Mercedes cleared her throat. "Valerie was telling me about the *Letterman* deal, Jack. Well done, and again, please accept our thanks for going above and beyond. We're already getting amazing reports from the distributors." She smiled and Jack found himself thinking she should do that more often. It softened her in ways he hadn't thought possible. "It's been a far more successful launch than we could have dreamed of. And we owe a great deal of that to you. In fact, I've just told Valerie that once we're back in Washington, we'll have to sit down with you and your manager and discuss an adjustment to your contract. You should be compensated for—"

She was cut off by a gasp from Vivian, who was clasping her gold "wand" to her chest. "What the hell?"

"What is it?" Aurora asked, hurrying over. "It's Margo Fontana and that cute Benjamin Styles, isn't it? I told you that marriage wouldn't last a month. I'm telling you, you'd think Hollywood couples would realize it doesn't work when the man marries someone more famous than he is. Their fragile egos simply can't take it." She glanced at Jack. "No offense, mind you."

Jack just raised his mug to her, quite happy to have the focus shifted away from what a great guy he supposedly was. "None taken."

"Hush, Aurora!" Vivian exclaimed. "Everyone, come here. I think we should all look at this." She looked at him. "Especially you, Jack."

A familiar name blared from the TV set, and they all froze.

"Prince Charming. Is he a prince? Or a pretender? Tune into *Brock Sullivan Live* this morning at ten as we discuss the nation's latest heartthrob . . . with his ex-wife. The former Mrs. Jack Lambert, international fashion model, Shelby Lane, will be here live in our studio to tell us why her ex is no prince."

Jack could only hear the ringing in his ears that had begun the moment Brock had spoken Shelby's name. *Jesus freaking Christ.* What, wrecking his life once wasn't enough?

Just then, both the suite phone lines and Valerie's cell phone began going off. "Don't answer them," she immediately instructed. "Not until we find out what's going on."

Jack looked at her as if she'd lost her mind. He knew exactly what the hell was going on, or about to, anyway. And from the slightly wild look in her eyes, so did she. The shit appeared to be one step away from officially hitting the fan. And hail, hail, the gang was all here, too. Lovely. Just fucking lovely.

"Do you know anything about this, Valerie?" Mercedes asked, her frown so deep there were grooves on either side of her mouth.

"Oh my!" Aurora exclaimed, her hands fluttering to her mouth. "What on earth do you think she's going to talk about?" She turned to both Valerie and Jack. "What possible scandal could there be? I mean, you've discussed your first marriage with Chuck and Vicki."

"I'm sorry," Valerie said. "I'm as surprised as you are. The last we knew, she was somewhere overseas doing a photo shoot."

Vivian tapped her cigarette holder against her thigh. "I wonder how much she's getting paid for this little revelation. No offense, Jack, but she must have some motivation for traveling halfway around the world just to rat about you and your marriage."

Aurora reached out to take his arm. "Is there something we should know about, dear? Some rift in your relationship that she might blow out of proportion?"

"I wasn't the perfect husband, but there was nothing between us that would be considered scandalous." Jack's mind was spinning like a hamster wheel, trying to get one step ahead of what was happening, or about to happen, trying in vain to figure out if there was anything he could do to stop it before the whole truth spilled out.

Shelby had known and disliked Eric, mostly because the feeling was mutual, and because she had wanted Jack's attention exclusively on her and no one else. Everyone was a threat, but none so much in her mind as her husband's best friend. But she didn't know Eric was a best-selling author. She'd never bothered to ask what it was he did for a living. For that matter, she wasn't all too interested in what Jack did for a living. If it wasn't all about Shelby, she wasn't interested.

Admittedly, it would sound implausible that a wife didn't know about her husband's alter ego. But it was still speculation. She might not want to believe he'd written more than sports columns, but she couldn't prove he hadn't. He glanced at Valerie, wishing he could take her aside so the two of them could figure out just how to play this.

Just then his hip buzzed. He reached down to unclip his phone from his belt. Eric. The women were all glued to the television, waiting to see if any other teasers for *Brock Sullivan Live* aired, so he turned his back and flipped the phone open. "Listen," he said quietly and without preamble, "you need to get your ass back here right away. Shelby is in town and—"

"*What?*" Eric said, sounding more than a little freaked out. "Holy shit, so that's why they called."

"There's nothing she can do to hurt us, really. She can't prove anything. We just have to figure out how to counterpunch. Just get back here so we can begin damage control. And, warning, the godmothers are here." Jack paused as Eric's words sank in. "Wait a minute. Who called? What's going on? Where are you?"

"The Village. Listen, I need to tell you something. Brice is, uh . . . he's gone."

"Gone where?"

"Gone, gone, as in he wasn't here when I got up. But now I think I know why."

He knew Eric was upset, and rightfully so, but right now he was more worried about Shelby's impending television debut. "Listen, that totally sucks, but I really need you to—"

"No, you need to listen." Eric broke off, swore, then said, "I—last night we . . . last night was—" He broke off again, then heaved a deep sigh and said, "It was incredible. I—I told him everything."

Jack gripped the phone. "You told him what?"

"I love him, Jack. And I—I couldn't lie to him. I can't. So, I told him. Everything."

"*Everything?* You mean—"

"Yes," came the almost hushed reply. "Only, I just got up and . . . he's gone."

"Shit," Jack said.

"It gets worse. I picked up my cell phone to call him, only to see that I'd already gotten a call this morning. I—I was asleep and Brice must have answered it. I checked it out. It was a producer from the *Brock Sullivan Live* show. I thought it was someone calling me, wanting to book you for the show."

"Holy fu—you don't think he's—"

"That's exactly what I think. I mean, I wouldn't think he could do something like that to me. Last night he seemed really touched that I'd confessed, and I was shocked to wake up alone. I just—" There was another pause, then, "Wait! I just found a note taped to the bathroom mirror. He's gone to the taping. But not to rat us out." His voice went hoarse. "He, uh, he went to protect me. Jesus." The emotion was thick in his voice, even as he chuckled weakly. "I guess I have a Prince Charming of my own."

Jack's mind was racing. "You have to get back here. We have our own live interview to give. I'm sure we can come up with some way to fix this."

"I'm on my way. And . . . I'm sorry."

"Hey, none of this is your fault. Don't bother coming here. Just meet me at the studio, okay?" He flipped the phone shut and took a deep breath, then blew it out slowly. He looked at Valerie first and gave a very slight shake to his head, then looked at the godmothers. "I think we should all sit down. There's something I have to tell you."

"Jack," Valerie said, alarmed, "why don't you and I talk first. I'm sure whatever crisis Eric is having can be dealt with. No need to bring everyone into it." She tried to smile encouragingly at the godmothers. "Besides, we need to get downstairs. I'm sure the car has arrived and you're due on the *Good Morning* set in less than thirty minutes."

"But what about *Brock Sullivan?*" Aurora asked. "Shouldn't one of us stay to see what happens?"

But no one was listening to her, they were all watching Jack. "I think you might want to call and cancel the taping."

Now the godmothers looked truly alarmed, Aurora included. "What is the problem?" Mercedes asked him.

"Does this have something to do with your ex?" Vivian asked. "Because I'm certain we can defuse anything she might bring up. In fact, you can use your spot on the *Good Morning* show to do just that. Although if you suspect you know what she's going to say, I think you might want to explain that now."

Valerie had shifted behind the three women and was shaking her head, making cutting motions at her throat and motioning toward the bedroom. *We need to talk. NOW,* she mouthed.

He appreciated that she still wanted to salvage this, but the jig was up. They couldn't stop Shelby and they couldn't stop Brice. They should have known this was going to blow up. But even he couldn't have predicted just how spectacular Prince Charming's downfall was going to be. But Vivian's comment had given him an idea. He couldn't salvage this, but there was one princely thing left to do. It wouldn't save him or Eric, but it would spare the godmothers from suffering the fallout from the bad press that was sure to follow. And, more important, it would preserve Valerie's job. All she had to do was play along.

"Please, have a seat," he said, searching for the right way to tell them. By the time they'd all arranged themselves on various chairs and couches—except Valerie, who'd chosen to remain standing—he still had no clue where to begin. "This is going to come as a shock to you all," he said, with emphasis on the word *all*. He sent Valerie a brief look, imploring her to just play along with him. "But I'm not the real Prince Charming. Eric is."

Mercedes' mouth dropped open. Aurora gasped. Vivian, however, just smiled. "Well, well. I wondered what was going on."

"You . . . you knew?" This from Valerie, who was looking heartsick, and when she glanced at him, a whole lot angry.

Vivian shrugged. "Let's just say I had my suspicions about how Jack here wrote those touchy-feely advice books." She smiled at him. "No offense, darling, it's just that you're a man's man. But trust me, we women like you just fine that way."

Valerie merely gaped, along with Aurora.

Mercedes, however, was frowning deeply again. "What possible explanation could you have for perpetrating such a ruse?"

"First I need to tender my apologies. To all of you." Again, he shot a quick look at Valerie. If she'd play along as if this was just as much of a shock to her as it was to the godmothers, she might be able to salvage her job. "We never intended to hurt anyone. It's just that Eric has been in the closet about, well, everything. For years. And he wanted a way out."

"You mean, he's just now come out?" This from Vivian. "How interesting. He's certainly done it with flair. I rather like his friend. What was his name? Bruce?"

Aurora and Mercedes looked at Vivian as if she'd sprouted a third eye. "Good heavens, Vivi," Aurora stated, "this is hardly the time to discuss the man's love life. We've a full-fledged scandal on our hands!"

Jack glanced at the clock and began to sweat. "It's Brice. And, yes, he certainly did. He just wanted a personal life, but with the whole mystique surrounding the Prince Charming thing, he didn't dare. He'd spent years convincing women their prince really did exist and—"

"He knew they'd give up if they found out Prince Charming was gay," Aurora said with a soft sigh as she clasped a hand to her bosom. "Oh, how tragic for him. And he's such a nice man."

Mercedes was still glaring at him. "More likely he knew book sales would plummet."

"He doesn't care about book sales," Jack said. "In fact, he wants to retire altogether, but he cares about his readers."

"So he decided to lie to them?" Mercedes demanded.

"No, he just . . ." Jack didn't know how to explain, but he knew he was running out of time. Valerie began to open her mouth, so he jumped back in before she could reveal she'd been part of it. "He was just trying to find a way to make everyone happy. What he wasn't planning on was falling in love."

Aurora's face softened. "Eric is in love?"

"With Brice?" Vivian asked. "Well, well."

"Let's not get sidetracked here, ladies," Mercedes instructed. "It's all well and fine that he's found someone, but our integrity is on the line."

"Yes, well, that's why I'm telling you this. Eric's, uh—Brice is getting ready to defend Eric's integrity."

"Excuse me?" This from Valerie, who'd been watching the discourse like a Ping-Pong match. "He's *what*? How exactly does he plan on doing that? And why?"

"Eric told Brice everything. Last night."

"Everything?" Valerie repeated, going a bit pale.

Jack nodded. "The *Brock Sullivan Live* show called this morning, apparently trying to book me on the show with Shelby, to do a point-counterpoint kind of thing. Only Brice got the call, and when he heard Shelby was going to trash me and Eric, he took off—"

"To defend the honor of the man he loves," Aurora finished, clasping her bosom once again with a little swoon. "How romantic."

Vivian hooted. "Oh, I love this."

"*Love this?*" Mercedes demanded. "We're going to be ruined! On live national television."

"Oh, stop being so melodramatic, Mercy," Vivian shot back.

"You haven't begun to see melodrama," Mercedes huffed. "That show is nothing but a viper pit of melodrama. They're going to turn *Glass Slipper* into a laughingstock."

"They're going to try," Jack said. "But I'm not going to let them."

"What are you talking about?" Valerie asked. "What are you going to do?"

"We can't control what Brice and Shelby say to Sullivan, but I have my own live interview in about thirty minutes. Which airs before Brock goes on." He looked at Valerie, then at the godmothers. "I'm going to go on and explain the whole thing. We'll pull the rug right out from underneath them. It might still blow up in our faces, and for that I'm truly, truly sorry. We never intended this. But you have my word that I will do everything to minimize the damage to you, the magazine, and your business. I'll make it clear you had no knowledge of this. When it's over, we'll come straight back here. Eric can get his lawyers, or whatever, together and hopefully come to some agreement on how to handle this."

"Jack, listen, we need to talk about this," Valerie said, panicking.

He looked at her. "I want you to stay here, okay? You'll have phone calls to field, and damage-control fallout to work on. Just wait until I'm done, okay? Before you talk to anyone."

"Jack—"

"Promise me, Valerie."

She paused then, holding his gaze, and he knew she understood what he was trying to do. For *Glass Slipper*. And for her.

"I need to handle this one," he told her. "Trust me."

She nodded but said nothing. No rules, no suggestions, no unstoppable need to control. And though the apprehension and dread were there in her face, the look in her eyes was one of trust, and faith.

He hit the elevator running, praying he was doing the right thing, that now that he'd earned her trust, he wouldn't fail her.

Praying that he wouldn't lose the one thing he knew he couldn't afford to let slip away.

Trust

You can ask for it. You can be asked to give it. You can even believe you're feeling it. But real trust has to be earned. And you won't truly know if it has—until it's put to the test.

Chapter 20

Valerie wanted nothing more than to sprint after Jack. Not because she didn't trust him. After last night, she had no doubt whatsoever that he would do everything he could to minimize the damage and pain this fallout was going to cause.

"Valerie, dear," Aurora said gently. "Did you know about this?"

That was why she wanted to run. She didn't want to face the godmothers, face telling them her role in this. Jack had made it very obvious he was trying to pretend as if he and Eric had hatched the whole plan by themselves. If she told the godmothers she'd had no idea they'd pulled a fast one on her, she knew Jack and Eric would swear to it and she'd probably keep her job. Of course, that might be an appropriate punishment right there, considering the damage control she was going to have to try to spin over the next several days.

But if Jack could face down all of America on live television, she could certainly face down the three women who'd given her a chance at something special. A chance she had no one but herself to blame for blowing.

So she held their gazes squarely when she said, "Yes. Yes, I did. I know I've let you down. I've let us all down, including myself. I wanted this job more than you can understand, but I'll tender my resignation immediately. I know it's not enough, and that it comes too late, but I'm sorry. So very sorry."

Mercedes looked deeply troubled. Aurora appeared more hurt than anything. It was Vivian, whose expression was more of deliberation, who spoke first. "We'll discuss resignations in a moment." She motioned to the seat across from the couch on which they were all perched. "Why don't you sit down and start at the beginning." She checked her watch. "We have time." She gestured to the chair again when Valerie hesitated. "Go on."

"Okay, but first, do you think we should somehow alert the *Sullivan* show to Jack's appearance on *Good Morning?*"

"I'm sure they're well aware of his appearance," Mercedes said. "It will be more explosive to go on directly after he's been on a competing network, all smiles and charm."

"But maybe if they know Jack is going to go on and spill the beans, robbing them of their exclusive, they'll scrap their plans to sling mud. The damage will still be done, but at least they won't have the opportunity to add insult to injury, or to fan the flames of indignation."

"You might have a point," Mercedes said thoughtfully.

"No, no, no," Vivian admonished. "I say let the old fool go on with his ridiculous show. Jack will have his say, screwing an unsuspecting Sullivan out of his tawdry scoop. And Shelby will just look like a bitter witch out to milk her fifteen minutes of fame off her ex-husband."

"I don't know," Valerie said, "it could just amp up the whole thing."

Aurora looked at Valerie, the disappointment still clear in her faded blue eyes. "Brock Sullivan will go on with his program no matter what. If he's given advance warning, it will just allow him to adjust his slant. Best to let him scramble to catch up."

Mercedes sighed. "She's right, of course."

"How did you let this happen?" Aurora asked plaintively. "Why?"

Valerie felt like gutter slime, but at the same time, it was an immense relief to finally get it all out in the open, no matter the consequences. She finally sank down into the chair across from them and folded her hands in her lap. "We'd already signed the deal with Eric when he told me he was coming out of the closet." She explained the entire chain of events. "We were so close to going to press, it was either lose our launch, or come up with some other idea. Eric proposed getting someone to stand in for him. It was just supposed to be for the cover."

"Why did Jack do it?" Aurora asked.

"For the money, of course," Mercedes said.

"Actually, no, he wouldn't take any money," Valerie told her. "Eric offered to compensate him, but this wasn't about money."

"Then what was it about? Why would he do something like this for nothing?" Mercedes asked.

Valerie bit her lip. She couldn't reveal the very personal, painful information Jack had given her last night. "It wasn't for nothing. They've known each other a long time. Eric was there for Jack during some difficult times in his life. This was his chance to give something back."

Vivian pursed her lips, looking intrigued. "And you know about Jack's history?"

Valerie nodded. "But I'm afraid it's personal. You can ask Jack about it if you want, but he told it to me in confidence and I don't feel right speaking for him."

"*Confidence*, hmm?" Vivian tapped her cigarette holder against her fingers. "You two have grown close through this, I would imagine."

Valerie wasn't sure where she was headed with this, but this was no time for evasion. "Yes," she said directly. "Yes, we have."

"And that photo in the tabloid . . . you explained that away as a minor slip. A heat-of-the-moment kind of thing. Can I take it that you've had other heated moments since then?"

Valerie felt her cheeks burn, but was spared from responding when Aurora swatted at Vivian.

"Oh, isn't it enough we're dealing with this whole shocking mess? You don't have to go and dig up every salacious detail." She looked at Valerie. "He duped you, didn't he, dear? Led you on? We certainly understand. He is quite the charming rascal. Much like my Way was."

Mercedes rolled her eyes. "Oh, for heaven's sake, Aurora, Way's idea of charm was to tell the same horrendous Senate war stories over and over." She turned to Valerie, still stern. "I understand that desperate situations can lead to desperate acts. I can't say I condone what you've done, but I'm trying my best to be impartial until we hear Jack out."

"Oh, oh!" Vivian called out. "The show's starting!"

Vivian moved faster than Valerie would have thought her capable of in those spiked heels. Everyone scrambled from their respective seats and gathered around the television, as one of the *Good Morning* hosts, Steve Sutter, introduced his cohost, Julie Nash, and the "surprising, very special live interview" she was about to conduct with Jack Lambert. They cut to a camera showing a sea of the show's fans milling outside the studio, many of them carrying signs touting their admiration for Prince Charming.

"Oh, there's the one I liked!" Aurora exclaimed. " 'Charm Me!' "

"Hush, Aurora," Vivian told her, edging closer. "Oh, there's the 'Prince Hottie' sign!"

"He's really drawn quite a following," Mercedes observed.

Aurora pressed her ringed fingers to her lips. "I hope they don't turn into an angry mob when he tells them the truth. It reminds me of those horrid sale days at Garfinkels back in the seventies." Her expression anxious, Aurora gripped Valerie's arm and squeezed.

Angry mob, indeed, Valerie thought, feeling like she was in a living nightmare. One of her own making. She wanted to cover her eyes, plug her ears, but then Jack's image blared on screen. He was sitting in a comfortable chair across from Chirpy Cohost Girl. Julie Nash, who usually gave a whole new meaning to perky, was looking abnormally somber. Or as close as Julie could get to somber, she supposed, which was actually a cute kind of grimace. What was slated to be a fluff interview had now turned into something serious. *What a break for Julie*, Valerie thought morosely. At least someone's career was going to get a shot in the arm because of all this.

"So, Jack," Julie began, unable to completely rid her voice of its natural chirp, "we were originally going to talk about your books and the incredible buzz that's erupted since you revealed yourself to the public. However, I understand you have something important you would like to discuss with me and our viewers." She leaned forward, all chummy and you-can-trust-me, obviously a graduate of the same girl anchor school as the rest of them. "What's on your mind?"

"Good morning, Julie, and thank you for giving me this opportunity to reach your viewers and hopefully a number of my fans. Or should I say, a number of Prince Charming's fans."

Julie worked hard to present a serious girl reporter expression. "Wouldn't those be one and the same, Jack?"

Valerie bit her lip, her entire body tense as she watched Jack resettle himself in the chair. "I should have gone with him," she murmured. "I should be the one taking the heat. This wasn't his idea, he shouldn't have to be the one to fall on his sword." On national television, no less.

Aurora squeezed her arm. Vivian shot her a brief, considering look. Mercedes just hushed her.

"Actually, no, they're not," Jack said. He shifted to face the camera.

"I have a confession to make, and I'm hoping the viewers out there will hear me out before judging me, or Prince Charming, too harshly." He looked back at Julie. "You see, I'm not really Prince Charming."

Julie struggled to keep her game face on. "Really."

Okay, maybe this wouldn't result in a career shift for the bubbly cohost after all. Valerie absently wondered if Steve Sutter, veteran news anchor turned morning-show cohost, wasn't chewing nails over losing this opportunity to such an airhead. But she was thankful Steve had lost it, because he'd have turned it into something hard-hitting whereas Julie would let Jack steer this pretty much any way he wanted.

"Exactly who are you, then?" Julie queried. "And where is the real Prince Charming?"

"He's here," Jack said. "In fact, they're mike-ing him up right now, and if it's okay, he'd like to join me on the set."

"Oh, dear lord," Mercedes whispered.

Valerie held her breath. Eric was going on with Jack? The phones started going off again, but Valerie was too riveted to shut them off.

Vivian simply turned up the sound. "This should be good," she said, and Valerie noticed her eyes were gleaming. Was she enjoying this?

"But before he comes out," Jack went on, "I'd like to explain what's happened. And why we've done what we've done."

"Please do," Julie said, ever the sharp interviewer.

"I am a sports reporter, and everything I've said in my previous interviews is true. Except for one thing. I didn't write the Dear Prince Charming advice column, or books. My best friend, Eric Jermaine, did."

"Eric Jermaine," Julie said, looking as if she were pondering one of the universe's deep mysteries. "Why does that name sound familiar?"

"He's been acting as my manager, when in fact, he's the real author."

The cameras cut to the throng outside, who were all standing, riveted, as they watched the huge monitor that broadcast the show to the street. They didn't appear angry so much as shocked. Valerie hoped this was a good sign.

"So why the duplicity?" Julie asked as the camera switched back inside the studio.

"Wow," Vivian said, "I wouldn't have thought she'd know a word with so many syllables."

Valerie would have laughed if she wasn't so close to tears.

"Vivi, hush." This from Aurora. "She's trying her best."

"Listen," Mercedes instructed.

"For years, Eric has been advising women how to find their Prince Charming, demystifying the guy's point of view of relationships and hoping it would help women communicate better with the men in their lives."

"He's been quite successful at it, too," Julie said. "I'm a fan of his books myself." She leaned forward again. "Is there some reason he felt he couldn't reveal himself?" She struggled to shift from serious to concerned and sympathetic. "Is there . . . something wrong with him?"

"Oh, good lord," Vivian snorted in disgust. "Where did they find this Twinkie?"

"You know, she would benefit from our services at Glass Slipper," Aurora commented. "Mercy, you should see what we could do in getting her to come out for some help. Poor dear. We'd keep it confidential, of course."

"Not in the way you mean." Jack grinned. "Actually, he's a darn sight easier to look at than I am."

Now Julie flushed, abandoning *serious* altogether and reverting back to total fluff cohost. "I think our viewers, especially the female viewers, would agree it's been no hardship watching you."

Jack ducked his chin, his smile fading. "Well, thank you, Julie, but I don't imagine they're going to feel quite so generous now."

"So, tell us why you agreed to stand in for your friend. Your best friend, did you say? How long have you known Eric?"

"Most of my life. We grew up together. He's been there for me through thick and thin. And there were some pretty thin spots along the way. When I found out the position he was in, and how miserable he was, I agreed to help him out. I realize that it was wrong, but we honestly didn't feel we were harming anyone. In being the public face of Prince Charming, I was allowing Eric to finally have the private life that he, like anyone, deserves, but never felt he could have."

"Why is that?"

"He was afraid his readers would unfairly judge him and the advice he'd been giving all this time if they found out the truth."

Julie all but chewed on her microphone. "The truth about what?"

"If it's okay, he'd like to come out himself and talk about that."

"Oh, this is fabulous," Vivian hooted. "Wait until this bubblehead gets a load of Eric."

"Wait until all the women out there get a load of Eric," Aurora murmured.

Vivian grinned smugly. "I bet Brock Sullivan is ready to pee his pants right about now!"

Valerie frowned. Did they think they were out of the woods here? Mercedes still looked upset, but the other two . . . Well, the actual repercussions would come soon enough, she thought, stomach still churning as she turned her attention back to the screen.

"But first," Jack told the host, "there is something else I'd like to say. I stepped into this to help out a friend, to put a face to a brand name. I didn't really take it all that seriously, was just happy to help Eric. But having done these talks, and listened to some of his readers, I've come to realize just how important he is to people. And with good reason. He has good insight and good people instincts, and maybe if I'd listened to him more, I wouldn't be a divorced guy stumbling through a string of meaningless flings."

Valerie went stock-still. *Meaningless flings?* Her throat closed over. Was that what she was? Aurora's grip tightened on her arm, but Valerie didn't dare look at any of them.

"We all could use some help, and the benefit of outside advice from time to time," Jack went on. "I guess I just never thought that applied to me. I thought that was for people who wanted to blame someone other than themselves for their problems, or people who simply refused to take responsibility for themselves and wanted someone else to come along and make their messes okay. But I've changed my mind on that."

"Why is that?"

"Listening to his readers, for one. Seeing the strong, amazing women out there who, when confronted with a problem they didn't know how to solve, went looking for solutions instead of whining about their situations. I never saw it like that. And I think a lot of guys out there are just like me in that regard. Too proud to admit they need help, afraid to realize their problems might be their own faults, something they need to work on."

"And do you need help?"

"Yeah, in fact, I do. It took two people to ruin my marriage, but rather than face that, to face what I thought a marriage was, what a relationship should be, I chose to avoid serious relationships altogether."

"But that's changed?"

"Yes. During this, well, this charade, I met someone."

Valerie tensed. Vivian gripped her knee.

"Given that I hadn't done so hot in my one shot at serious commitment, I certainly didn't think this was the best time to get involved on any serious level with anyone. Certainly not with someone who had a stake in all this as well."

Julie was all but salivating. This was right up her alley. "And would that someone be the woman you were photographed with in that tabloid a week or so ago? Didn't she work for the same magazine you do? Or that Mr. Jermaine does. Or . . . whatever?" Clearly this was taxing Julie's limited resources.

"I'd rather not drag more names into this. She knows who she is."

Julie tried not to look too crestfallen. Valerie felt like she might throw up. Or pass out. What in the hell was he doing?

Jack looked at the cameras. "But I guess you don't always get to pick when you fall in love. Or with whom. You can only pick what you want to do about it."

All three godmothers gasped. Valerie choked.

"The timing stinks. And our careers, well, such as they were," he said, his infamous grin ghosting his lips for the first time, "were heading in different directions. At any other time in my life, I would probably have taken the easy route. The same route I always took. Enjoyed it while it lasted, then walked away."

"But now?"

"All this talking about relationships and seeing how others have fought for what they wanted has made me rethink everything." He looked to the cameras briefly. "It's still just as terrifying. But this time I don't want to walk away. I want to make it work." He smiled, looked back at Julie. "She's worth fighting for."

Cut to the cameras outside, and as they panned the crowd, the women were alternately clutching their hearts or sniffling.

Aurora sniffled and pulled a hankie from her voluminous sleeve. "Oh, this is so sweet."

"This is brilliant." Vivian once again sent a calculating glance at Valerie, but said nothing else as she returned her attention to the screen.

Valerie was still reeling. Her head, and her heart. Had Jack Lambert really just proclaimed, on live television, that he'd fallen in love with her? The very idea was both terrifying and exhilarating. Was he being honest, or, as Vivian seemed to think, was this just another angle he was playing to win viewer sympathy? Would Jack assume she'd realize that and not take his proclamation seriously?

Julie was beaming. "Well, maybe we should get you some advice from the real Dear Prince Charming." She turned to the camera. "Please help me welcome Mr. Eric Jermaine."

Then Eric was striding out onto the set and Valerie dragged her scattered thoughts and emotions together once more so she could pay attention to the drama unfolding onscreen.

Julie stood and there was no doubt about her reaction, as her mouth dropped open the moment she got a good look at the real Prince Charming.

His hair was tousled, only this time Valerie was pretty sure it was natural. He was wearing black jeans and a loose weave shirt. Despite the slightly anxious expression, he was completely mouthwatering.

Cameras cut to the crowd. They all seemed to agree. A wave of *oohs* and *wows* swept the throng.

Julie motioned to the third seat that had been shoved up next to Jack's. "Mr. Jermaine, a pleasure to meet you."

"Eric, please," he said, his voice even deeper and rougher than usual.

"Turkey's done," Vivian noted.

"I beg your pardon," Aurora sniffed. "He's understandably nervous, but that hardly gives you the right to—"

Vivian pointed her cigarette holder at the screen, specifically the front of Julie's tight sweater. Where her nipples were obviously at attention. "Baste her and taste her. She's ready for—"

"Vivian, really," Mercedes exclaimed. "Must you be so crude?"

"Oh!" Aurora said, coloring slightly as she got the point. Or points, as the case might be. "I see."

"So does the rest of America," Vivian said dryly, "and I'm betting

Julie isn't alone." She turned to Mercedes. "Ten dollars says most women won't care which way his pendulum swings."

"We're hardly in the position to be betting," Mercedes said, but her scowl had shifted, her expression had turned to one of consideration. She folded her arms and settled more comfortably on the arm of the couch.

Valerie didn't know how much more of this she could take. She couldn't read the godmothers, the phones were still ringing off the hook, she had no idea what was going to happen when Eric dropped the bomb. Except that perky Julie was certain to respond with something typically ridiculous.

He loves me. He loves me not.

The words kept repeating over and over inside her head. Her entire world was not only falling apart, but exploding in a magnificent destructive display. And that was all she could think about.

Jack Lambert might be in love with her.

"So, Eric, welcome," Julie was saying. She smiled beneficently as Jack and Eric shared a quick hug and clap on the back.

"You didn't have to do this," Eric said quietly to Jack, but it was picked up on his mike anyway.

"Yeah, I did," Jack said, and smiled.

"Together through thick and thin," Julie interjected, perky smile back in place. "So, Eric, to be frank, looking at you, it's hard to see what possible reason you might have had for getting your friend Jack here to play you in public. No offense, Jack," she gushed, "but I think the ladies out there would be quite happy to play Cinderella if Eric here were to come riding up on his proverbial white horse, huh?"

Cut to the crowd. The women were jumping up and down, cheering and whistling their agreement. Valerie's nails dug into her palms as she waited for the other shoe to drop.

A blushing Eric grinned a bit sheepishly. "I appreciate that, Julie. Really I do."

"Oh, the camera is just gobbling him up," Aurora said. "Don't you think, Vivi and Mercy?" She sighed. "So handsome."

Eric's expression turned earnest. "You see, the thing is, I'm not looking for Cinderella."

"Cinderfella, maybe," Vivian murmured, merely smiling when Aurora swatted her with her scarf.

"No?" Julie tried to look earnest, but the end result was more confused than anything. "Do you mean the man who has been working for years to help others with their relationships . . . would rather be alone?"

"Actually, I'm not alone. Not anymore." Eric blushed a little, and shot a quick glance at Jack for support.

Only rocket scientist Julie interpreted the glance entirely differently. She gasped, then scooted forward on her chair. "Are you telling me that you two are—"

"No!" Eric and Jack said in unison.

"Oh, for heaven's sake!" Mercedes exclaimed. "That woman is a complete idiot."

"What that woman is, is our savior," Vivian stated emphatically. "She's making this whole circus into exactly what it should have been all along. A fluff piece. Women clearly love Eric, and between him and Jack, they'll run circles around this bimbette. It will run two news cycles, three at the most, then be done with."

"I just hope our magazine isn't done with," Aurora said plaintively. "I was rather enjoying our little endeavor."

"We'll be fine." This from Mercedes. And the certainty in her tone pulled Valerie's attention from the television in a way that nothing else could have at that moment.

As much as she'd love to believe Vivian, she knew better. She was surprised Mercedes didn't.

"Jack and I have both found someone," Eric was saying, pulling their attention back to the television. "In fact, it's because of my significant other that we're here today. I thought it was best for everyone if I perpetuated the myth that seemed to grow up around my mystique. I figured if I gave my readers what it seemed they really wanted, I could be free to do what I really wanted. Which was to find that special person and settle down, to begin living the life we all dream of."

"And why not do both?" Julie asked. "What was it you thought your readers wanted that you couldn't give them?"

Eric paused, then Jack punched him on the shoulder. "Go ahead, man. It's love." He grinned. "And I can honestly say now, it's worth it."

Aurora sniffled again. Vivian sighed appreciatively.

Valerie's heart stopped in her chest. *So he'd meant it? He was really in love with her?*

"What my readers want is the right man to love and be loved by," Eric began haltingly, "and . . . so do I."

Julie's mouth dropped open. A collective gasp rose from the outside crowd.

"What I've realized," Eric forged on, "is that there is a bit of Prince Charming in every guy. You just have to find the one who makes you strong enough to embrace it. For me, that person is Brice. When he thought I was threatened, when he thought I was in danger, he went charging off to defend me. Without a thought to what it might mean for him, or what repercussions he might suffer. And I knew that if I was even half the man he thinks I am, I had to step up and defend us, too." He looked at the cameras. "I love you, Brice."

"Oh," Aurora sniffled. "This is just the most beautiful thing."

Vivian dabbed at the corners of her eyes. Even Mercedes' eyes looked a bit moist.

The crowd outside looked both stunned, and moved. The camera panned, but there were very few expressions of disgust or antipathy.

Eric turned back to Julie, and though his hands were clenched tightly on the arms of his chair, he was clearly more in control now. "So that's my secret. I'm gay. And I was afraid that if my readers found out, they wouldn't trust me with relationship advice. I let that fear keep me locked up like a virtual prisoner for years. I didn't have enough faith in myself, or in my readers, to hope they'd trust that issues surrounding relationships and love are the same for us all. That my insight was valid because we're all looking for the same thing."

"I guess what it boils down to is that we all just want to connect with that special someone, don't we?" Julie simpered.

"Exactly. I hope my readers out there will understand and accept my apology for not giving them the credit they all deserved."

Julie reached out to take Eric's hand in a tight grip. "I'm sure if they're anything like me, they all will," she said, her voice full of emotion. Then she turned to the camera herself, sighed, and laughed a little at herself. "Well, that was something, wasn't it? We'll be back right after this break, when Steve will be talking with Dr. Edmund Friedman about the ten best ways to protect your pet from the summer heat."

Vivian muted the television and tossed the remote on the table. Aurora reached for a tissue and noisily blew her nose. Mercedes stayed where she was, deep in thought.

Valerie merely steeled herself for what came next. "I know how disappointed you are in me, in all of this. I should have come to you when Eric first confessed."

"Yes," Mercedes said. "You should have."

Valerie ducked her chin. "I know. It's just . . . I know this is no excuse and I'm not offering it as one, but . . ." She looked up again, and held their gazes directly. They deserved that much at the very least. "I've been bouncing around the fashion industry since I was a teenager."

"We know," Aurora said quietly.

"You . . . know?" Valerie's train of thought stumbled badly. "But—"

"Go on with what you have to say," Mercedes instructed. "Then we'll say our piece."

Scrambling for the right words, Valerie forced herself to continue. "I've dreamed of fitting in someplace, finding my niche. I never thought it would be so hard. I was almost ready to give up when I answered your ad. And from the moment I stepped foot in Glass Slipper, the moment I met you, talked with you, took over the job, I knew I'd finally found it." She clasped and unclasped her hands. "I know I was less than truthful during the application process. But I also knew I could do this job and do it well. When you chose me, I was bound and determined to do whatever it took to prove I was worth your trust." She faltered badly then, as the enormity of what she'd ruined really hit her for the first time. It was truly over. Everything she'd worked for. And she had no one to blame but herself.

She worked hard not to cry, but the sniffle came anyway, as she once again held their gaze. "When I landed Prince Charming, I knew I was on my way. So when Eric told me the truth, I panicked. We both did." She couldn't do it; she couldn't look at them a moment longer. The disappointment in their eyes was so keen it was like a dagger in the heart. "I'm sorry. I know it doesn't amount to anything. And if I'm criminally responsible in some way, then I'll face that, too. But . . ." She trailed off. "No, no *buts*. There is no excuse. I'm so sorry."

Vivian huffed a sigh and pushed off the couch. "For pity's sake, are we done torturing the poor girl?"

Mercedes shot Vivian a hard look. "I think recanting her sins is not only the very least she owes us," she turned to look at Valerie, "but the least she owes herself."

Aurora came to Valerie and took her hands. "Dear, we truly adore you. And we know how hard you've worked to bring off the launch of this magazine. We've been mightily impressed by the job you've done, so much, in fact—"

"Not now, Aurora," Mercedes said.

Aurora frowned at her, then patted Valerie's hand and sighed. "Yes, we're disappointed in the choices you have made, but we all make mistakes, darling." She glanced at Mercedes. "Well, most of us."

Vivian stood. "I'd like to talk with the two of you, alone, if you don't mind, Valerie."

Valerie wasn't quite sure what she was hearing, or what was happening. Her gaze flicked from Aurora, to Vivian, to Mercedes. "Certainly, I—"

"I know what you wish to discuss, Vivian, and it will have to wait," Mercedes stated flatly.

What was left to talk about? Valerie wondered. She'd tendered her resignation. Unless it was to discuss the legal ramifications.

"Right now I believe we have some phone calls to make," Mercedes continued. "To our advertisers, for starters. And we'll need to call a staff meeting immediately." She glanced at her watch. "We'll need to book flights for all of us. I'd like to be packed up and heading back as soon as possible. I'm sure there are numerous calls coming in from other media sources, but I don't want to hold any interviews or do any press of any kind until we see what that ridiculous Brock Sullivan plans to do now, and certainly not before we've convened the rest of the magazine staff. From now on, all decisions should be done by committee." She finally looked at Valerie. "Well, don't just stand there. We're paying you to handle these details, aren't we?"

Valerie swallowed, but it was hard to get past the lump in her throat. "You want me to handle this?" she croaked out.

"Did you not just get done telling us this was your dream job?"

"I—well, yes." Valerie straightened her shoulders, her heart beating so hard she was sure the thumping was visible. "Yes, I did."

Mercedes waved her perfectly polished, sparingly decorated hand. "Then dream on. We haven't got time to waste."

Valerie didn't know whether to burst into tears, or hug her. So she did both.

Mercedes didn't know quite what to do, but Valerie was already moving on to hug Aurora, squeezing her tight, tears leaking from the corners of her eyes.

"There, there, dear," Aurora told her, patting her back. "We'll see this through as a team. We progressive women have to stick together."

"I won't let you down again, I swear it."

Then Vivian stepped forward and said, "I believe there's one detail you have to take care of first, honey. A man just professed his love for you. It's been my experience that it's hard enough for them to do that in private, let alone on national television. That takes guts." She eyed Valerie speculatively. "What about you? Do you have the guts?"

"Vivian, honestly, don't interfere," Aurora chided.

"She's needed here at the moment," Mercedes added.

Vivian snorted and waved her hand at both of them. "Jobs come and jobs go." She looked at Valerie. "And this one isn't going any-where, at the moment, at any rate. We'll handle what needs handling. We run a multimillion-dollar corporation, for God's sake. We're not exactly helpless females here. If we can't handle a little scandal, we're not the women I thought we were." She waved her gold wand and her lips curved. "Love, on the other hand, is a rare and wondrous thing that doesn't always come along at the most convenient time. And, I've learned, it doesn't always wait." She turned Valerie by the shoulders and pushed her toward the door. "A career doesn't keep you warm at night, either. But I'm betting Jack does. Now go find him, al-ready."

"But—" Valerie turned around. "I'm sure he'll understand."

Aurora and Mercedes came to stand beside Vivian. "I'm sure he will, too, dear," Aurora said with a soft smile. "You hang on to the un-derstanding ones."

Mercedes gave a short nod. "Jack and Eric both might need your publicist skills to extract them from the studio in one piece."

Stunned by this second turnaround, when she was still reeling from the first, Valerie didn't exactly know what to do.

"We've got a lot to discuss," Vivian said meaningfully to the other two women. "Why are you still standing there?" she said to Valerie. "Your prince awaits."

And with the blessings of her most unexpected trio of fairy godmothers, Valerie fairly ran out of the hotel suite and went after Jack.

Now all she had to do was figure out what she was going to say to him when she found him.

👑

Commitment

Women think men are afraid of it. And they are. But not for the reason women think. Men think women view commitment as a guarantee. There are no guarantees. Only a promise. To have faith, trust, and hope. And a willingness to find a solution, even when it seems impossible.

Chapter 21

Jack stood by the limo in the rear alley while Eric sat inside it, on a private call with Brice. Thankfully the mob out front hadn't discovered their hiding place. Judging from the reaction of the people on set, and the monitors stationed around the studio showing scenes of said mob, it appeared as if they'd pulled off the miracle. At least on the face of it. Jack knew Valerie was likely handling a landslide of calls, not to mention the fallout of the godmothers. All he wanted to do was get back to her side, which he planned to do just as soon as Eric finished talking to Brice.

Thankfully Eric had gotten word to Brice before he'd gone on the program, which had left Brock Sullivan with Shelby as his only guest . . . and no big exposé to expose. Jack imagined she hadn't been happy to have her all-about-me television debut ruined, but he couldn't seem to care all that much.

And as if his thoughts had conjured her, the studio door opened and out she stepped. In fact, he had to blink twice to make sure he wasn't imagining things. She pulled out a cigarette then stopped when she saw him standing there. If she was surprised to see him, she didn't let it show.

Her dark hair was slicked back into a tight bun, her makeup was heavily but expertly applied. A lanky five-feet-eleven, she was wearing a slip dress that hung on her frame as negligently as it had on the hanger. She was gorgeous in an almost offhand manner. Stunning without having to do anything to make you aware of it. Her impact on a room full of people was immediate. "Hello, Jack," she said, her accented voice a soft caress. He'd forgotten how beautiful it could be, seeing as the last time he'd heard it, it had been at a high screech.

"Hello," he said, surprised to discover that he wasn't feeling all that much one way or the other about seeing her again.

"What are you doing here?"

"Looking for you. They said you'd already gone."

"How did the taping go?" he asked.

"Now, now, you're not angry about that, are you?" She tried her little pout and poor-beautiful-me smile, but he wasn't buying. To her credit, she'd matured enough that she quickly dropped the pretense. "I hope you aren't taking it personally. You know I wouldn't have said anything bad about you."

Jack just laughed. "So why are you here? If you needed the money—"

She looked affronted. "It wasn't for the money. Enrique, my manager, got a call from the show." She lifted an elegantly slim shoulder in an absent shrug. "I've been trying to break in to the American market, and we thought this would be good exposure."

Jack shook his head, knowing she spoke the absolute truth. Some things hadn't changed. Shelby would always be the center of her own world.

"You're not angry with me, I hope," she said. "If anything, I should be angry with you for stealing my thunder." She smiled a little. "Although I guess you think I deserved it."

Jack thought about his carefully constructed responses to all the questions he'd fielded about his first marriage. About how they'd just been two people who were wrong for each other and who'd been fortunate to figure that out before causing each other too much pain. Funny how it wasn't until right now, looking at her again, talking to her, that he realized the absolute truth of that statement. It didn't negate the pain he'd gone through, or the confusion and subsequent closing off of his emotions. But it finally put to bed the blame issues, his guilt over the marriage's failure.

"No," he told her. "I think you deserve whatever happiness you can find. We all do."

Her carefully sculpted eyebrows lifted. "Well, well. How mature of you."

"I guess the best we can hope for is to not hurt anyone needlessly."

"I suppose I could say you hurt me today, but considering your very public profession of love, I guess you were only doing what you felt you had to." She smiled, and for once it was sincere, if still somewhat calculating.

But that was who Shelby was. If he'd only accepted that years ago, he could have saved himself a lot of heartache.

"I hope you realize I was only doing the same thing."

Jack nodded, finding it easy to be magnanimous now that the crisis had been averted. "What are your plans now?"

She shrugged again. "Enrique is meeting with people. I'm sure my trip to New York won't be wasted."

"No," Jack said, lips curving. "I don't imagine it will be."

The limo window lowered behind him. "All done here," Eric said. "Oh, hello, Shelby. Long time."

Shelby's smile tightened. "Not long enough, apparently."

Eric simply put the window back up without further comment. Jack couldn't hide his grin. Some things, it seemed, were never going to change.

Shelby turned her attention back to him, then lifted up on her toes to kiss his cheek. "Best of luck to you, Jack. I hope you are happy." She wiped the lipstick off with her thumb. "I have to find Enrique." Then, with a little shimmy to straighten her dress and a quick hand to smooth her hair, she turned gracefully and reentered the studio, much in the same way a queen would enter her castle.

"She's all yours, America. And don't say I didn't warn you," Jack said, smiling and shaking his head as he climbed into the limo.

"Wow, bet that was fun," Eric said wryly as he closed the door. "Like root canal."

"It wasn't so bad, actually. And maybe it was just as well. You know, put the last of the ghosts finally to rest."

"I guess," Eric said, not sounding remotely convinced. "You going back to the hotel to talk to Valerie?"

Jack nodded. "If nothing else, I want to make sure the godmothers don't bring this down on her head. I think we did a good job of keeping the magazine out of this."

Eric slumped back in his seat. "I can't believe what I just did."

Jack smiled a little. "It was for the best."

"I should have done this in the first place before I dragged you, Val, and *Glass Slipper* into things."

"What's done is done. And hey, look what you got out of the deal." For that matter, look what he'd gotten. He was still coming to terms with the fact that he'd basically told Valerie he loved her on live television.

Eric smiled dryly. "Now all we have to do is not screw that up, too."

"Yeah." Now that they were out from the glaring light of the public eye, the real tension was starting to creep in. And Jack hadn't thought the ball in his gut could squeeze any tighter.

He wished he had a clue what to do next, what to say to her. He supposed he could look for a job in D.C. It might not be the kind of sports coverage he wanted to do, but it would keep him close to Valerie, at least until they figured out if things were going to work between them. Of course, Valerie might not have a job at this point. Which pissed him off. But it also left him pondering the alternatives. "What do you think my chances are of convincing Valerie to head off to Europe with me?"

Eric grinned. "Really?"

"I don't know. I just know I don't want to walk away."

He shook his head. "I don't know. She's pretty career-oriented."

"Yeah, well, she might not have a career at the moment."

Eric's expression fell.

"Hey, now, she knew the risks. We all did."

"What do you think the fallout is going to be? I've already called my lawyer, and he's pretty sure we can beat a fraud rap."

Jack's eyebrows rose. *"Pretty sure?"* He'd been so caught up in thinking about Valerie, he hadn't stopped to think about the legal repercussions of their little performance today. "Do you think the godmothers will sue?"

"I guess we're going to find out." Eric motioned to the curb in front of their hotel. "We're here. Brice should be here shortly. I can deal with it if you'd rather not—"

"No, I'm in."

Eric started to say something, then suddenly pointed at the taxi in front of them. "Hey, isn't that Valerie?"

Jack looked out the limo window just in time to spy Valerie climbing into the yellow cab. It pulled away from the curb before he could get out.

Eric flung his door open. "I'll go up and deal with the godmothers, you go after her."

"But—"

Eric slammed the door shut and slapped the roof of the limo.

Jack couldn't believe he was going to say this, but what the hell else could he do? He leaned forward to the partition separating him from the driver and said, "Follow that cab."

For ten agonizing blocks, they wove in and out of traffic. Where was she heading? Was she leaving town? Leaving him? Without talking to him? Maybe he'd totally freaked her out with his on-air confession.

Stupid, stupid! And here he'd been feeling all smug about what he'd learned about women and relationships. Only to lose the only woman he'd ever truly loved enough to fight to keep. He realized as he watched her cab buzz from one light to the next that he didn't know quite how he'd handle it if she walked out of his life forever. It felt . . . wrong. Simply and completely wrong.

Well, it didn't matter. This time he wasn't going to run and hide because things had gotten a little rough.

Traffic knotted up completely when they hit Forty-fifth Street. Jack couldn't take it any longer. "I'll be right back." And he bailed out of the limo and hoofed it three cabs up. "Valerie!" He banged on the window.

Only, the woman who jumped and glared at him from the backseat wasn't Valerie. He waved an apology and immediately jogged back to the cab behind it. Empty. How had he lost track? He went in the other direction, but past the cab he'd first approached was a truck and two cars. He turned around, looking up and down Fifth Avenue, at the sea of cars and cabs, clueless about how he'd lost her. Or worse, how he'd find her again. Traffic started to move and he had no choice but to jog back to his limo.

"Jack?"

Even with all the street noise, the car engines gunning, the honking, he had no problem recognizing that voice. He spun around to find Valerie weaving her way back through traffic, oblivious to the blaring horns and streams of curses directed her way as traffic shifted to move around her.

Skirting two cabs and a truck, he met her in the center lane. They stopped just short of each other, as if suddenly wary about what to do next.

"I thought I'd lost you," he said, as horns kept blowing, people kept cursing. He didn't care. What mattered right now was standing in front of her. He didn't care if he clogged traffic all the way to New Jersey.

She looked past him as his limo angled its way to the curb. "You were following me? But I was coming to find you."

There was a sudden weightlessness to his heart. "You were?" He wanted to ask what she'd thought of the show, but that was tantamount to asking her if she loved him back. All his insecurities reared up inside him again. Suddenly he wasn't that brave.

"The godmothers thought you and Eric might need some help extricating yourselves from the mob at the studio," she said, looking as uncertain as he felt.

Funny how quickly weightlessness could turn into a gravity-sucking vortex. "Oh." It was the best he could do. "You still have your job, then. Great." And it was, only he knew he didn't sound enthusiastic about it.

"I don't know what I have," she told him. The racket from the horns and the screaming drivers was making it hard to hear her.

"Maybe we should get in the limo. Talk."

She nodded, and he led the way to the limo, helping her in, then closing the door behind him. "The Plaza," he told the driver.

The sudden silence that followed, devoid of all the clattering chaos, seemed to overwhelm them both for a moment. Jack had to curl his fingers into his palm to keep from reaching for her. They both ended up speaking at the same time.

"What did the godmothers think of the show?" Jack asked.

"Did Eric talk to Brice?" Valerie wanted to know.

"He did," Jack answered first. "Brice didn't go on. I talked briefly to Shelby." Valerie's eyebrows lifted in surprise, but she said nothing, so he went on. "She was a little pissed off that I'd pulled the rug on her big American debut. Seems her manager saw the call from Sullivan as a means of launching his client into the hearths and homes of America."

Valerie gaped. "On the *Brock Sullivan Live* show? Some manager. Next thing you know, he'll tell her posing for *Playboy* will be the break she needs to be taken seriously as an actress or something."

Jack laughed, even as his heart was about to pound its way out of his chest.

She smiled briefly, but he noticed she was twisting her hands in her lap. He wasn't sure if the sign of nerves was a good thing or a bad thing.

"The godmothers were impressed," she said finally. "Moved, even. Of course, I'm not sure they realize that not all of America might respond like your adoring fans outside the studio did. We'll know soon enough."

He watched her look worriedly out of the limo. "But they sent you to help me and Eric, so that means you're still in the game, right?"

She looked back at him. "I told them everything. I know you tried to protect me, my job, and I appreciate that. But it was wrong, what I did. And I couldn't let you take the fall entirely. Nor could I go on and keep my part in it a secret. It's been eating me up."

Jack could identify with that at the moment. "So . . . what is the plan? With them, I mean. With your job?"

She held his gaze, twisted her fingers, swallowed hard, and finally said, "I'm not sure. Mercedes seemed willing to have me stay, do my job, see what comes of this mess. But Vivian and Aurora . . ." She shrugged a little. "I don't know. There seemed to be something else going on." She shook her head. "I really don't know what it is. It might have something to do with that meeting they'd wanted with me this week, which of course got shoved aside with all that's been happening." She glanced at her hands, out the window. Everywhere but at him.

He felt like he was dying by inches. She'd obviously seen the show, but hadn't made any mention of it, or even hinted at what his declaration meant to her. He wanted to drag her into his arms, remind her how powerful things could be between them. But he couldn't seem to make the first move. It was like he was frozen to his seat, stuck in some kind of stupid limbo, unable to act, or speak.

Finally she looked at him. "What . . . what are you going to do now?"

That pretty much depends on you was what he wanted to say. But she had enough riding on her shoulders at the moment. It didn't seem fair to put all of his expectations on her, too. She was on the brink of getting what she always wanted. If he truly cared about her, he wouldn't force her to deal with him and his untimely emotions right now.

"I'm not sure," he told her. It was the truth.

"You said you were looking at a job overseas." More finger-twisting.

"I can find a job anywhere. It's just a job."

She looked at him sharply, as if wondering if there was a hidden jab or message there.

"What I meant," he said, "was that, fortunately, I can find a job I enjoy. Overseas, or here. It's important to love what you do."

"Yeah," she said, ducking her chin. "It is."

He itched to reach over, lift that chin, look into her eyes, and ask her if she ever thought she could love him back. Tell her he'd work doing anything, washing dishes, whatever, if it meant they might have a chance together somewhere down the line. It was terrifying how close he was to begging. The urge to flee, to just get out and start walking, was strong.

But he wouldn't be able to outrun these feelings. And he didn't want to run from them. He wanted to explore them, wallow in them. Because, terror notwithstanding, this was the best feeling he'd ever had in his life. One worth fighting for. He just wished he knew how in the hell to go about it and be fair to her at the same time.

"What—" He had to break off, clear his throat, which had suddenly closed up. "What would you say if I took a job here? I mean, not here in New York, but something around D.C." He realized he was looking down at his own fisted hands, and forced himself to look at her.

Her chin was trembling. "I'd say that after all you've already done, you shouldn't have to do anything else you don't want to do."

"But I want to. I—"

She stopped him. Her eyes were getting glassy, and he felt his heart begin to sink lower, if that were possible.

"What I mean is, you're right. I've come to realize that while you should love your job, it's not as important as other kinds of love."

His heart stopped sinking. In fact, it stopped altogether.

"Love shouldn't mean sacrifice," she went on, choosing her words carefully. "But maybe . . . maybe it does include compromise."

"Staying here wouldn't be a sacrifice," he said hoarsely.

Her wobbly chin lifted, her gaze stayed steady on his, despite the quaver in her voice. She took a deep breath, and said, "Neither would me finding a job overseas." She smiled. It was a bit crooked, but he'd never seen anything so beautiful in his life. "I'm qualified to do a lot of things. Not that that's always a requirement for me."

The enormity of what she'd just offered was not lost on him. "I don't think I could ever ask you to do that. Your work means more to you—"

She smiled more fully now, more in control. She always did prefer to be in control. If he could have calmed down enough, he'd have grinned at that.

"It's exactly because I knew you wouldn't ask me that makes me want to," she told him. "I've never had anyone care about me like that." She reached for his hand then, and he tried not to crush hers when he took hold of it. He was pretty sure he was never going to be able to willingly let it go now. "And," she went on, smiling even as tears formed, "I've never cared about anyone so much that what I do isn't as important as who I'm with while I'm doing it." She sniffled a little. "Vivian told me that a job is just a job. But that—" She broke off, her voice suddenly gone hoarse.

Jack couldn't stand it any longer. He tugged on the hand he held, pulling her from her seat across to his. But not content to have her sitting beside him, he pulled her onto his lap. He closed his eyes and sent up a silent prayer as his arms came around her, vowing right then and there to do whatever he had to, to keep her there.

Her eyes were bright and shiny, and he kissed the trickle of tears that leaked from their corners. *"But that* what?" he asked softly.

"But that love doesn't come around too often. If ever."

"I know," he said, and never before had he invested two words with such meaning.

She lifted her hand to his face, and he had to work not to sigh at her touch. "Jack . . . "

"We'll figure it out," he told her. "Okay? Trust me. We'll find something that works for both of us. I know we can."

"I do trust you." Even with the tears, that wide, wry grin spread across her face. A face, and a grin, he hoped to see for years to come. "I trust you with something a hell of a lot more important than my career."

He gave her the smile right back. "There's something more important than your job?"

"Yeah, smart-ass." Suddenly she sniffled again. "My heart."

There was a sudden stinging in his own eyes. "Yeah?" he said, his voice barely more than a croak as his throat tightened.

She nodded. "Yeah. And I've never trusted anyone with it before, so you'd better take good care of it."

He pulled her head down to his. "I'll guard it with my life." And he finally, blessedly, kissed her. Held her tightly as he poured all the love, fear, and joy he was feeling into it. "I love you, Valerie. I should have told you in person. The first time should have been private."

"Well, maybe I can make up for that. A little, anyway. I love you, Jack Lambert." She grinned. "Boy, that felt even better than I thought it would."

"Not as scary when you go second," he said with a laugh.

"Oh, it's petrifying. Trust me."

He pulled her close. "I do trust you." It came out more seriously than he'd intended.

Her expression sobered in turn. She cupped his face, traced her fingertips over every dip and contour. "I know you didn't plan on this. Ever. And I won't ever take this—or you—for granted. I know how special it is." She kissed him. "And I know how special you are."

He would have laughed at that, except the stinging sensation was back behind his eyes, and he was very much afraid if he said anything, he'd be the one crying.

As it turned out, they were both saved from further declarations when the limo pulled up to the Plaza, and the godmothers were all waiting at the curb.

"There they are!" Aurora trilled, waving a silk scarf to get their attention. As if they could possibly go unnoticed.

"Our greeting committee," Jack said as he helped Valerie slide from his lap while she smoothed her hair. Somewhere along the journey it had fallen from its neat little bun. "Don't," he told her as she tried to pin it back up. "It looks good down. All soft and touchable and— What?"

"You're such a guy."

He grinned. "I'm glad you noticed."

"Oh, I noticed. What do you think our chances are of ditching the trio out there and finding another room in the city? Any city?"

"Don't tempt me."

The car pulled to a stop and the godmothers descended on them. "Oh, and here I was planning to do just that." Now she grinned. "Often." She didn't wait for the driver to get the door, but opened it herself.

Jack figured he could get used to loving a woman who liked to do things for herself. In fact, he looked forward to the challenge of showing her that it could be fun to relinquish control every once in a while, let someone else take care of her for a change.

God, was love strange or what?

Life

Just when you think you have it all figured out, life presents you with a new plan. It keeps things exciting and challenging. Especially if you're flexible enough to trust in new things. And share that with someone you love.

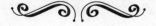

Epilogue

"Gondola races."

"Yep."

Valerie looked out the hotel window, down to the canals of Venice below. "Well, if anyone can introduce the world to the wonders of gondola racing, it's you."

Jack wrapped his arms around her waist, and kissed her on the back of the neck. "I'm so glad you could come with me this time."

"Me, too. Things are running pretty smoothly— Hey, don't laugh, they are. Compared to ten months ago, anyway."

"Anything would be smooth compared to the chaos that was the grand opening of Glass Slipper, Incorporated, the U.K. version."

She turned in his arms, smiling, still a little giddy every time she thought about it. "I'm still in shock whenever I remember Vivian making me the offer that afternoon in New York. Me, managing a life-makeover business." That had to have been the single best day of her life. And to think it should have been the single worst. Jack told the world he loved her, and the godmothers had offered her a chance to live out a real dream.

"Vivian's a smart cookie," Jack said. "She knew from the beginning it was the perfect job for Miss Jill-of-All-Glamour-Trades. And you're proving them right."

"Trying to. Thank God for Jenn. I don't know what I'd have done if she hadn't taken my job offer and uprooted her whole life." Jenn had become her right hand at work. And her best friend all the time. Valerie felt rich beyond words. "I still can't believe it's real."

He grinned. "I still can't believe you're real."

She laughed as he scooped her up in his arms, stepped over a prone Gunther—Jack's stalwart traveling companion these days—and dropped them both to the bed, rolling her beneath him. "Why is it your reality checks always seem centered around sex?"

"Are you complaining?"

He raked his fingers through her hair, which had grown below her shoulders over the past months, and which she wore down whenever they were together. It made him happy. And to be honest, she loved the feel of his hands in it. She groaned and shifted beneath him. "No complaints."

He nuzzled at her neck. "Good."

"Oh, I almost forgot to tell you," she said, her voice deepening as he continued his exploration, unbuttoning her sundress. He liked those, too. So, as it turned out, did she. "I heard from Eric and Brice. They're going to try to make it over to London, to join us for the holidays."

Jack lifted his head from where he'd been tugging at the edges of her lace bra. "You mean, they're going to take time out from their busy, busy life of leisure to actually stop in and say hi?"

She rolled him so he was now beneath her. "Hey, they're happy." And they were, deliriously so. Which was a good thing, because as it turned out, the rest of America hadn't been as forgiving as the women gathered at the studio that day, so long ago. *Glass Slipper* magazine had done very well, as the scandal had only served to sell even more magazines. And all was forgiven when Elaine managed to snag George Clooney for their next spokesperson and cover model.

All was not forgiven for Eric, however. While he had his fans, he also had his detractors. Including his publisher, who had withdrawn his option offer. So, after fulfilling his obligation to *Glass Slipper*, he'd chosen to retire from the advice-giving life. Brice invested Eric's contract earnings, and the two of them were presently on an extended holiday that showed no signs of ending anytime soon.

"It couldn't have happened to a nicer couple," she said.

"Well, except for us."

She rolled her eyes, then popped open the buttons on his shirt. "If only we could sail around the world without a care to our name. I'm lucky if I get to spend two weeks in a row with you."

"Yeah, but it just keeps you wanting me bad."

She gave up and ripped the rest of the buttons off. "That it does."

about the author

Once upon a time, Donna Kauffman was born in Washington, D.C. Alas, there were no glass slippers in her closet, but fate was kind, and a trustworthy (and totally hot) knight did cross her path. No fool she, Donna didn't need a fairy godmother to point out a good thing when she saw it. Their happily-ever-after is currently taking place in Virginia.

Just couldn't get enough?

Turn the page for an excerpt from

Donna Kauffman's

next exciting book

Sleeping
with Beauty

Coming soon
from Bantam Books

Sleeping
with Beauty

Coming Soon from Bantam Books

"How is it that Debbie Markham still manages to come across petite and blond on an e-mail loop?" Lucy straightened from her hunched position behind her friend's shoulder. She didn't want to read any more reunion posts.

"You're just projecting," Jana told her, stuffing the last of her Sun Chips in her mouth. "For all you know, she's turned into a leather-skinned skank with overprocessed highlights, saggy tits, and a flabby ass."

Lucy's smile was decidedly unkind as she clasped her hands beneath her chin. "Do you think?" Then her shoulders drooped. "Nah. My karma would never be that good." She sighed and balled up her sandwich wrapper. Instead of reading about the exaggerated exploits of a group of people she'd once loathed and no longer cared about, she should be using her time to put her classroom in order. "I'm so not an e-mail loop person."

"Truer words," Jana agreed, having been the first one to point that out a week earlier, when Lucy had signed up on a whim after receiving the invite. Thankfully she didn't rub it in. But then, the look on her face precluded that necessity. "But you're a first-class lurker, I'll give you that. Most entertaining lunch breaks I've had in years. Beats the hell out of listening to that insufferable asshole Winston belch out his latest know-it-all opinions on the Redskins, the Wizards, the Capitals, the effect of the Cold War on American sports, the dawn of the solar system—"

"You're just pissed because he got picked up for syndication."

"Damn straight I am. His columns are pompous and arrogant, not to mention uninformed. And I don't care if his father once played for the Senators. It's not like he's a fucking sports guru just because his dad had a three forty-one career batting average and came within one season of tying DiMaggio's record." She lobbed her wadded-up trash at the small wastebasket beside Lucy's desk, sinking the shot as smoothly as if she'd been standing right over it instead of halfway across the classroom.

"Yeah," Lucy said, "but can he sink a three-pointer with his fanny wedged in a second-grade desk? I think not."

Jana sighed and tipped back in the chair. "True, so true."

Smiling, Lucy went back to unpacking. One thing she loved about her best friend. Jana might be quick to boil—a much-hated redhead cliché that she nevertheless owned up to—but she simmered down just as fast. "I agree with you, if it makes any difference," Lucy offered. "I like your columns. You're not condescending, and you have the kind of style and energy in your writing that can make even a totally uncoordinated loser like me read the sports page. Well, a column of it anyway." She glanced over her shoulder at Jana, who'd turned back to the computer terminal in the rear of the classroom. "Of course, you're no Sally Jenkins, but—"

"I have deadly aim," Jana reminded Lucy, never looking away from the screen as she casually clicked through posts. "And a whole box of Crayolas within easy reach."

Lucy grinned and went back to stocking the tempera paint and brushes in the locking overhead cabinet, well away from the ever-questing fingers of her next batch of heathens. She'd given up on the honor system last year after coming back from a quick hallway consultation with the principal to find Billy Cantrell drinking Sunshine Yellow, straight up, no twist. Fellow classmate Doug "The Pusher" Blackwell had convinced him it would make him fly. Of course, Doug was her prime candidate for being the first student ever busted in Meadow Lane Elementary for selling a controlled substance. Billy would probably be his first customer.

"So, should we unsubscribe?" Jana's finger hovered over the delete button.

"No!" Lucy almost dumped a whole carton of Sky Blue and Clifford Red in her efforts to get to Jana before she could act.

"Whoa, whoa," Jana said, laughing. "What's up with this? Did we not just agree that reestablishing any kind of umbilical relationship with these people is detrimental to our psychological health? Not to mention our hard-won self-esteem?"

Lucy skidded to a stop and vainly attempted to reclaim what was left of her dignity. "That's no reason not to enjoy ourselves at their expense, right? I mean, they did that to us for years. What's a few more weeks?"

Jana's gaze narrowed. "You are *not* still considering actually going to the dance, are you?"

Lucy swallowed.

Jana swore beneath her breath. "Didn't we take enough abuse from the hands of these people once before? Are we such gluttons for punishment that ten years later we want to give them another shot? Why would you even consider putting yourself in that position?"

"What, are you writing an article or something?" Lucy asked. As a defense, it was weak at best; but then, it was the only one she had at the moment, since she had no idea why she was considering this either. Well, she did, but she hadn't admitted that to herself yet, much less Jana. "Class reunions are making the sports pages now, are they?"

Jana tapped a finger to her chin. "Hmm, maybe they should: *Gearing Up for Your High School Reunion: A Full-Contact Psychological Sport, Not for the Timid.*"

Lucy took the seat next to Jana. Which, considering her frame, was easier said than done. "So you're saying I should have my head examined for even considering this? Maybe the whole point of going back is to prove we've progressed beyond allowing others to define ourselves." There, that sounded much better. She almost believed it herself.

"I'm saying there is nothing wrong with enjoying mocking our pretentious, overzealous, label-conscious classmates in the sanctity of your empty classroom. With complete anonymity. Considering it's like a million degrees outside, this is the best lunchtime sport going. But why ruin the fun by giving them a chance to reciprocate?" Jana clicked through the messages posted since their last lunch get-together several days before, skimming for something juicy they could pounce on. "You know, I thought we were on the same team here. Unified in our conviction to let the overbearing assholes inflict themselves on one another while we go out and do something less painful, like getting matching root canals. Why the sudden change of heart?" Then her fingers paused on the keys before quickly clicking back to the previous message. "What in the . . ." Jana pushed her glasses up and leaned closer to the screen.

Then she turned an accusing glare at Lucy, who suddenly pretended a great interest in the last dregs of her diet soda. Dammit, why hadn't she just let Jana unsubscribe when she had the chance?

Redheads, as it happened, made the best glarers. They'd known each other over twenty years, and Lucy was still not immune.

She fidgeted, which was hard to do, wedged as she now was in the tiny desk/chair combo. "What?" she finally asked, feigning complete innocence even though she knew she was already busted. She set her empty can on the desk. Where was a good stiff belt of Sunshine Yellow when you needed it?

"Riley Prescott is what. And you damn well know it. Did you think I wouldn't find out? My God, I'm surprised every other freaking post isn't already about the golden boy coming home. Fatted calves are probably being slaughtered as we speak."

"It's been ten years. I'm pretty sure the golden-boy statute runs out somewhere by sophomore year of college."

"Maybe for mere mortals."

"My wanting to go has nothing to do with Riley Prescott. Not specifically anyway."

"Ah-hah!"

"Don't *ah-hah* me." She fished the rolled-up magazine from her shoulder bag and smoothed it open. "If blame must be placed, focus your derision and scorn here."

Jana adjusted her glasses and picked up the magazine, folding it back. She read silently. Well, mostly silently. There was the occasional snort, punctuated by the occasional eye roll and sigh of disgust. Finally she dropped it back on the computer station like a piece of contaminated sewage, then lowered her glasses and looked at Lucy over the wire rims. Another thing redheads were good at. "So, you're honestly considering going to Beauty Queen Boot Camp? Have you completely lost your mind?"

Lucy snatched the magazine back and stuffed it in her purse. "I knew you'd be judgmental."

Jana just laughed. "Oh yeah. And with good reason. Ten years of maintaining absolute distance from your past, a decade of proving to yourself that you're everything they claimed you'd never be." She ticked them off on her fingers. "Successful. Happy."

"Alone." She hadn't meant to say that out loud, but it had just popped out.

Jana goggled. "And?" She waved Lucy silent. "First off, you're single. Hardly alone. And hardly a curse, I might add."

"Says the happily married woman who found someone who adores her." Lucy's tone turned dust dry. "Frizzy hair, obnoxious attitude, and all."

"Yeah. A guy who gets hit in the head with flying pucks for a living. Obviously he's an anomaly of the species." But she had that smile. That smile she always got when the subject of Dave came up. Jana might be all harsh talk and frizzy edges, but mention her husband, and something in her softened in a way Lucy had never seen before.

Was it so wrong that she envied her best friend at that telltale softening moment?

"But being single has nothing to do with this," Lucy said, determined to get control of this conversation. She just wished she'd thought out her defense a little better before revealing her decision. "I'm not going to the reunion to meet men."

"Maybe not men, plural. But are you telling me that finding out Prescott is single and RSVP'd for one didn't set this whole thing in motion?" She waved her nail-bitten hand in Lucy's face. "Hello? I was at that homecoming dance, remember? And I was also by your side for the remainder of that year, listening to you moon and moan over that asshole."

"He's not—"

Jana flipped her hand up. "Unh- unh. Not a word."

"Fine," Lucy said with a huff. "But he's not the reason. I was already considering going to Glass Slipper before I found out Riley was coming back." She studied her own short, chipped nails. "But you're right. Reading that post did cement the decision." She looked up at Jana, serious now. "Is it really so awful that I want to get back some of what they took from me?"

Jana sighed now, and reached for Lucy's hands, folding them in her strong-fingered grip. "Oh, sweetie. How can you let them matter to you again? It's been ten years." She squeezed Lucy's hands. "You're a fabulous person. And the very last group of people you need to validate that fact is those idiots. You do this and it's all but shouting at them that they've won."

"I don't remember anyone declaring war. The battle ended the day we picked up our diplomas."

"And yet you're sending our troops right back in there." She shook her head. "Enough with the combat metaphors, no matter how appropriate. It's just that to me, it feels like you're selling out."

Lucy tugged her hands free. "I don't want to argue about this, okay? If any two people have hashed and rehashed why appearances aren't everything, it's you and me. And it's not like I'm the walking wounded, ten years later." Her gaze flickered to the computer screen, then back to Jana's raised eyebrows. "Okay, yes, reading these posts did dredge up a few unpleasant emotions that I thought were long since gone. I'm not proud that I let them get to me." She fingered the corners of the magazine. "But I can't deny that when I saw the cover story about their two-week intensive makeover program I wasn't at least a little tempted. It's like beating them at their own game. You know, Julia Roberts rubbing it in the face of those snotty bitches in *Pretty Woman*. Everyone cheered her, everyone got that moment of triumph."

"Lucy—"

"No, let me finish. Is it really so bad to want that moment? I know it's a hollow victory, that these people mean nothing to me in my life today. Their opinion has nothing to do with me anymore. But . . ." She shrugged. "I don't know. Maybe I have to prove something to myself."

"Then prove it by going back the way you are right now and being fine in your own skin."

Lucy shook her head. "I've already signed up." She forced a smile in the face of Jana's sincere concern. "If nothing else, it will make for a great how-I-spent-my-summer-vacation story, right?"

"I wish you didn't feel you needed this."

"It's not like they're hurling me into the lion pit." Lucy stood up, decision made. "I mean, really, what's the worst that can happen?"